BLACK OPAL

Steven Helsel

BLACK OPAL

DOUBLE DRAGON

Chapter 1 - Angel

The sweet smell of burning oil filled the room, the lamps illuminated one side of the basement leaving the other half pitched in darkness. A pouch full of coins had recently been paid to have this lower level dug, twelve feet floor to ceiling. The construction was devoid of worked stone. The floor was dirt, with thick wooden beams supporting the ceiling. An ecosystem of worms and roots grew out of the walls lending to an already damp, earthy smell. Mirrors of different sizes and shapes hung from long iron nails driven into the walls. There were racks holding mundane weapons of wood and steel and special ones forged with blades of silver, gold, iron and bronze. The ground had been swept clear of loose debris leaving tiny long legged spiders to creep across it. On the center of the floor at the apex of light and darkness was a three-foot diameter circle drawn with silver dust and filled with a complicated series of arcane symbols scribed with bone powder. An earthen staircase was the only exit.

Garthadon's team of undead hunters waited quietly upstairs. An archer, a ranger and a priest sat in quiet readiness. They waited, occasionally getting up to pace, as they listened for any indication of something gone awry below. They knew what the mage attempted and were careful not to disturb him. The trio had complete confidence in their leader, nevertheless nerves and boredom tested their patience.

Garthadon put his face to the ground and checked to be sure that there were no breaks in the circle and that the thickness of the silver powder was consistent along its circumference. All the sigils and diagrams were prepared. He began his casting making slight movements with his wrists, arms, and hands. He softly chanted incantations. The wizard's brown eyes narrowed and a ray of red light streamed from his hand. The magic circle held the light causing the silver dust to glow with a soft red hue. Then he increased the rhythm of his archaic chant. He continued for nine minutes, thrice repeating a lengthy chorus as wisps of prismatic light fell off him. Garthadon's focus was intent, outwardly he would have seemed a man possessed. He sped up, his voice beckoning with an authority that was not his own, "*Megeara!*"

An outline of crackling red energy began to take shape within the circle, vaguely human, with large wings protruding from its back. Inside the outline the emerging features of the summoned creature swept aside the darkness. Skin moved over emptiness, arms and legs took shape. The great wings became pure white as they stretched slowly to a magnificent wingspan of fourteen feet, exceeding the boundary of the silver ash, taking on the substance of a beautiful feathered bird. Garthadon ceased his casting, and beheld his summoned creature with awe. His knees were somewhat bent, his head somewhat lowered, his eyes stared up.

The Angel stood before him, encircled by the silver powder that still glowed with colored light. The energy that formed her, or rather transported her, was now gone. Burning red irises quickly faded, leaving her with kind violet eyes set in a face that was perfectly serene. Her skin was flawless with a golden tone to it, accentuated by long golden blond hair. She wore a two-piece suit of exceptional steel armor. The top piece was a shapely metal plate that fit seamless around her breasts and shoulders. The lower half was a scalemail skirt that seemed to hang on her hips, with a silver encrusted scabbard and gold hilted longsword attached to her wide, tough belt. Slung over her back she carried a quiver and a mighty composite longbow. She folded her wings down, without a thought, and tilted her head in discernment. A long moment passed as the mage stared at his summoned creature. At first struck with awe, Garthadon's attention fixed on the angel's lips as she spoke to him in a voice every bit as beautiful as she. Beguiled, his mind filled with carnal fantasy until the room was forgotten, and he wanted desperately to touch her. He could hear the melody of her voice but not decipher the words. It took all of Garthadon's concentration to bring his eyes above her neck. His imagination soon went wild and he was unable to make eye contact. He let his gaze fall, his eyes drinking her figure greedily.

"How did you discover my true name?" Her voice finally pierced him, driving the wizard out of his lustful imaginations.

"Huh?" He turned flush, ashamed of his lewd daydreaming about a holy being in her very presence. The mage was astonished with the momentary perversity of his mind. He normally regarded himself, as one that did not dwell on base passions.

She smiled at him with a sympathetic look which further embarrassed him and caused him to wonder if she had been privy to his thoughts. "You used my true name in summoning me. I will know how you came about this knowledge; It is quite forbidden," she said.

"Yes. Please forgive me calling upon you, holy daughter of the heavens." He faltered for the right wording, and smoothed his faded blue cloak with a tug as he sought in his character to have strength in dealing with a creature that impressed him as she did. "I will tell all you ask of me, but first I must tell you why I have called upon you, and if you can forgive my boldness, perhaps we can make a pact."

"My attention is committed." She replied.

"I am a vampire hunter. One of no little accomplishment I might add, though I do not mean to be boastful. There is a particular member of the in-denial-dead I have sought for quite some time. Most of my exploits of the past few years have been leading up to this." The old mage took a breath as he reached for confidence then exhaled. "That is where you come in. I stumbled upon the secret of your name, and the spell for summoning you when my company and I made our last kill. I have finally been able to pinpoint the location of the master vampire I seek."

"What deal do you propose?" The celestial asked, with a voice of consideration.

"The pact is this." He went over the wording in his head. Garthadon knew he should choose his words carefully when making pacts with extra-planer beings. However, this was a creature of law, summoned from the fabric of goodness, and carrying with her the very spirit of honesty. He had assurance that she would not search the terms for a loophole and he did not wish to insult her with undo caution. "You will accompany me to a village called Willowview. There we will confront the master vampire together. You are free to return to the heavens upon his second death, the moment his empty corpse no longer walks in this world. In return for your assistance, I will give you this locket upon which I discovered your identity, and I will not share your name with anyone." He looked at her, waiting for her answer.

"I will accept your terms with the addition of but one clause," She said. The angel let her words hang as she looked over the summoner, increasing his nervousness before returning her gaze to his face and locking her eyes with his. "I shall be obeyed without question."

Her demand startled him. "I don't think so. I would have to discuss that with my fellow hunters"

"You are their leader, and now you must prove it by making a hard decision. I am the only one worthy to lead as my very body is a holy symbol and I have the most at stake," she said, absent a trace of vice in her voice, drawing attention to her form with a gesture of her hands and a deep breath.

His eyes followed her motion and glanced up at her chest as she respired but he caught himself and looked quickly away revolted of his own irreverence. Garthadon lowered his eyes to her feet clad in black leather sandals, interlacing around her calves, to just below her knees. He began to question in himself if he was not in fact unworthy. Looking to the side unwilling to make eye contact he tried again to assert himself. "I know your true name I can compel you to…"

"Careful mortal!" Her voice crackled as she interrupted him with new sternness, spreading her wings to their full glory. The sudden extension of her wings caused him to recoil. "Do not threaten one from the host of heaven."

Her wings slowly receded. "Make your choice without reluctance, for I will consider you equally bound." Her temperament lightened and she spoke softly to him. "I want to help you, dear Garthadon. I would help without condition, just for the sake of righteousness, except that I have so much at stake, and you have driven a hard bargain."

It startled him somewhat that she knew his name, though it shouldn't have been much of a surprise. He stared at her, taking in the compassionate look she wore on her face, all the sensuality gone, just kind violet eyes mixed with supreme beauty. He resolved to trust her.

She could read in his demeanor the choice he had made. "You may call me Imarra, do not use my true name again."

He marveled at her a moment longer his gaze coming to rest on her eyes. "The deal is sealed according to both of our terms." He said a few words in the language of magic and with a wave of his hand, dismissed the pale light that encircled his new leader.

Imarra stepped towards him, the ring of silver powder gone, consumed by the magic that summoned her. She held out a slender hand, "The locket please." He hesitated before pulling it out of his blue robe, and grasped it in one hand, as it remained fastened around his neck. She moved slowly toward him, reaching her strong slender arms around his neck, bringing her face close to his. "We will find this evil that torments you so, dear mage," she whispered. Her breath smelled of lilacs. The old mage bowed his head as she removed the locket and chain, the smooth skin of her arms warm against his neck, and fastened it around her own.

Chapter 2 - King

"Your Majesty, ever since you granted oversight of the Crown Guard to my son, the commander has demonstrated an unwillingness to cooperate with him. It seems that he misses his autonomy and begrudges Agonius the directorship," Chamberlain Viscus said.

The King looked around his tower war room. The heavy double-doors of oak and iron were shut and locked from within. Several arched openings in the stone walls provided fresh air in mild gusts. The King looked across the large stone table at his brother the Chamberlain then at his nephew Agon. "There is no need for formal pretensions; it is just the three of us. Please speak plainly and tell me what it is that you would have me do."

"Very well Eratide. Agon wishes to replace the commander. He has grown too accustomed to his position and defends it with an assiduity that should be reserved for his chief responsibility," Viscus said.

The King responded by staring at the chamberlain with a blank expression.

"Protecting us Eratide, that is the chief responsibility of the Crown Guard."

"I know that Vis. Who would you replace him with? Who is there that we could trust more than the commander? I appointed him when I was a mere twenty circles old. You advocated his appointment yourself, and my dear wife thought him a true, though single minded man" The King stared again with a blank look that became a gradual smile as he remembered a past conversation with his late Queen. Oh, how these issues of state now wearied him.

The youth stepped closer to the table, it was covered in detailed maps of the city. The king snapped out of his daydream, knowing that these two never missed anything, he hoped they would not mention his wandering mind this time. He then marveled a moment at his nephew's eyes. The Queen also had eyes like Agon's. When she passed away, his nephew's eyes turned silver. He could never get used to looking into them. It was like looking into two coins with their centers bore out, leaving black holes ringed with silver.

Agon was dour as usual. "Uncle, my father pleads my case as your chamberlain and not as my sire. The man in question needs to accept the honors due to him and pass the reigns of the commandership to the next appointee, lest the man and I render each other inept by vice of competing influence."

The King sighed "Who do you propose to replace him with?"

Agon paused for a moment. He usually wore a black cloak with a deep hood that covered his face in shadow, but the king did not like for Agon to keep his face hidden before him so his short light brown hair was uncovered. His skin was well polished and fair. He was thin but not frail. "I believe Alturek would make for a suitable replacement, uncle."

"Corrine's personal bodyguard! Does he even wish the post?" The King walked over to one of the arched windows looking out of the tower. He could see a large portion of Nobleside and knew that beyond this ward of the city was his beloved daughter. She was probably arriving at the festival in Black Square even as he conducted this meeting. Alturek was undoubtedly with her and that was perhaps the greatest reason he had not to fear for her safety. "He has been my daughter's protector since she was born. What would she say? Who would we replace *him* with?"

"Please Uncle." Agon said. "This matter does not require undo urgency, but your thoughtful attention. All I am asking, is permission to place potential candidates before you. If they will not do, then keep Alturek, no harm done. If I do however find a man worthy to be her royal highness's protector, then release Alturek from his current duty so that I may promote him."

"Very well, Agon," the king said, turning toward his nephew. "I will consider who you put before me albeit with a very critical eye and I am doubtful that I will ever agree to release Alturek. Have you advised him of your intentions?"

"Of course not, uncle. I am sure he will claim that his is the greatest responsibility already. He may even consider his elevation a demotion. He is a modest man without any ambition above his sworn duty. It is for this very reason that he is a better choice than any other to be the commander of the Crown Guard. Furthermore, Corrine shall be Queen someday and whom do you want then to head the Crown Guard, who would be more appropriate than her most faithful protector?"

The King sighed.

"Well," said Viscus, "It seems my role here is

finished and I have a festival to get to, as do you two. If you don't mind, I shall take my leave now."

"Goodbye little brother," the king said. "Agon and I shall be right behind you."

"Don't forget your lines. The rabble looks forward to your vision to guide the course of the city. You must prepare them for the possibility of war from below." The Chamberlain gestured with his hands a somatic recitation for the spell of teleportation as he muttered unintelligible words, then vanished without a trace.

"Uncle," Agon said, "Do you think war will come from the Denizens below? It has been many centuries since they last attempted an assault upon the city. Some have relegated their potential as a threat to the annals of history."

"I don't know Agon. They stir beneath us and I fear their threat is in fact quite real. You must appreciate the great amount of trust being placed in you. No one is better placed to threaten my daughter's throne if something were to happen to me."

Agon was taken aback by his unexpected words. "I do appreciate it and I have no desire to be. . .King. Mine is the path of the arcane, ruler-ship would probably be intolerably boring and grievous." Agon moved to look out the window. "Also, I love and admire my cousin. I would never attempt to raise myself above her as I shall gain more satisfaction elevating her. As a matter of fact, I doubt any, in your absence would protect her with greater dedication then me, my father and Alturek. If ever I give you cause to doubt this, I will step down from my positions and seal myself in my

15

tower. It would be a great disappointment but I would go without wrath."

"I do trust you completely, Agon. I held you as a babe and gave to you everything that would have been my own sons if Crotear had ever seen fit to grant me one. What is an uncle if not a second father, not a usurper of the natural father but an extension of him? I had to speak to you about it because your prominence in stately matters has been greater than Corrine's. This has certainly been noticed by the council. I hope I haven't insulted you Agon."

"A little uncle, but I will get over it. I suppose we should get to the festival. Is it true that you will be sitting in a dunking tank?"

"It's true," The king answered with disconcertion evident in the wrinkling of his forehead. "Corrine wished for me to take a more festive role in the celebrations this year."

"Ha, how did she get you to agree to that? Was it blackmail uncle?"

The King laughed. "Agon, if you had a daughter you would not even wonder about it. That girl can get me to do nearly anything with nothing more than the expression she wears on her face."

"Then it is true, the princess is the power behind the throne already."

"She is." The king answered with a grin. "Come let us be off." The king unlocked the door with his golden scepter, by waving it before the entry.

"Where are you going?" Agon asked. "I can get us there much quicker. I know you hate to travel this way but considering you're already late...

"A king is never late Agon," They exchanged a

16

smirk. "Go ahead teleport us. Just hold on to me in case I faint from it."

"The whole city is early uncle?

"Not the whole city just a few thousand"

"Very well," Agon grabbed King Eratide's shoulders. "Look at me your majesty, stare into my eyes."

"Ok, I'm staring, let's go." The King stared as Agon's pupils turned to blood and began to trickle slightly over his lower eye lid.

"We are already there, uncle. I prepared the spell ahead of time." The sounds of celebration followed the Mage's voice. "Do not get disjointed, slowly look away from me."

Eratide pulled himself back, slowly taking in the world around him. His breath shortened for a moment and his heart beat fast then he felt fine. He was surrounded by his elite guard. He turned around to see his daughter awaiting his arrival. Alturek stood below her ever vigilant. Princess Corrine catching site of her father stood up and waved excitedly at him. Eratide returned the wave then looked over at the dunking tank.

"I can't believe I am going to sit in that cage like some damn fool," the King grumbled to himself, "This is beneath me."

Agon stood next to the king looking him up and down. "Are you going to wear that your majesty, what happens when you get dunked?"

"Are you mad, Agon?" The King removed his heavy robe of white and gold. "I am King Eratide Amorgoden of the Armor-Goden-Deznirian linage, nobody would dare dunk me." The king handed his robe to his nephew then entered the dunking booth's cage and sat on the stool.

He couldn't help but notice how uncomfortable the simple stool was compared to the cushions that he was used to. As the event opened and people lined up, King Eratide began hurtling insults into the crowd. "Do any of you lanky armed, halfwit fools have the skill to hit the target?"

The contestants would throw a large onion from twenty feet away attempting to hit a lever that would open a trapdoor below his majesty, dropping him into a vault of cold water. Princess Corrine's blond curls and blue eyes were seventeen circles old. She sat on a purple cushion with gold fringe, in her box-seat a few feet above the crowd. She watched her father's antics with amusement, accompanied by her two attendant ladies who were seated in the box upon their own extravagant cushions alongside her.

Chapter 3 - Slum

In the nation-city of Blakoepal, from the first crack of sunrise until the setting of dawn, the day of merriment was in full rage. All over the city was revelry with the festival as its epicenter. The festival was a grand convergence in the city's center of such enormity it was known to the citizens of Blakoepal, simply as The Festival. Here venders sold their wares, foodstuffs, jewelry, toys and knickknacks. Dancers danced and jesters jested. Buffoons engaged in buffoonery while mimes silently made their way around the festival entertaining all who stopped to see. Children had their faces painted in an array of colors and others in gray. Urchins and other waifs roamed boisterously on the outskirts of the fairground; while spoiled brats and homeless bastards alike role-played the historic battles against the denizens with wooden swords and wands. It was this historic war that the Day of Merriment commemorated. Tents lined the park, holding card games, dice games, wine and ale. Bards told stories, read poetry and sang with tantalizing magical aid, allowing the audience to see the stories and even feel and smell the elements described in the songs. The Crown Guard and many Council Inquisitors drove out beggars, common prostitutes, and other riffraff. Anyone you did not know could potentially be a Guardsmen or an Inquisitor. Most of the Inquisitors wore uniforms, except the judges, who always acted anonymously. By the tournament site was a cage for prisoners, allowing the jailed to view the fighting and subsequent executions of condemned men and women. Stockades dotted the park waiting to receive the newly arrested. The churches and knightly orders all had huge closed tents where their members congregated and leaders ministered. Members fought duels and hazed younger initiates. There were dogfights, cockfights, fistfights, and sword fights. There was laughter, crying, cheating and lying. There were all you can eat and drink contests. Young lovers had their first kiss, estranged couples their last argument. Those destined to be drunkards enjoyed the smooth sapidity of their first drink, while veteran drunkards choked on their last. In the midst of it all, in a daisy-encircled pavilion was the Black Opal, the city's namesake. Here was the site of the main event. Every year on the last evening of the festival, the ruler of the city-state of Blakoepal would look into the magnificent gem and see a glimpse of the city's year ahead, or so the people believed.

"The Blood Stones are brutal, greedy cunts." Jynx said to Enigma, his fellow rogue and friend. Jynx and Enigma walked the fairground with Enigma's twin sister, Whisper. The three of them were inseparable. They grew up together in Slumside, the gutter of Blakoepal, where the stair to the Under City was located.

"If not them, who are we to work for," Enigma asked, "Perhaps the Black Spiders or maybe even the Agenda?" He said this last one with a smirk as the three of them walked past the throng of vendors at the festival site in Black Square.

"The Black Spiders aren't half bad but they are too damn big already," Jynx responded.

"What of the Agenda?" Enigma pressed.

"Did your bottle pop its cork? They have been trying forever to steal the opal. Why in Gehenna do they want the Opal, what good would it do if all of Sophia knew about our humble city state?"

"Maybe, they think the city would be better off if it were opened for trade, instead of completely isolated."

"Whisper, what the first hell is wrong with your brother? Did he drop his coppers?"

She looked at Jynx, nearly laughing. "Deep down inside he wants to steal the opal, just because it's impossible."

"Well impossible is the fat word, followed closely by words such as stupid, stupid."

"Ha, I believe you said stupid twice." Enigma said.

"I know I did. I thought you were too short on coppers to catch it the first time. Besides, could you imagine trying to fence the city's namesake?"

"I'm sure the Agenda would buy it."

The three of them walked past a pair of Council Inquisitors. They wore grey uniforms. On their tunics was the emblem of their authority, a sword pointing up before the scales of justice. The Slumsiders stopped talking and stared at the ground as they walked past. "I hate Inquisitor cunts." Jynx said in a low voice as they moved beyond earshot of them.

"Calm down," Whisper said, "It is too early to get kicked out of the square."

"Hey." Enigma said, looking back discreetly. "Do you see that pouch hanging off of that cunt Inquisitor's belt?"

"Don't even think about it Enigma." Whisper

said.

"Come on. Are we here for work or fun?" he asked.

"Fun," Jynx answered at once.

"This could be both profitable and fun," Enigma pleaded. "Come on, cast that spell of silence on me, Whisper"

"Fine," Whisper said, then made the utterance that would manifest one of her few spells.

Enigma attempted to yell at the top of his lungs but he was unable to emit any sound. He started jumping up and down while screaming, further testing the spell. Not a sound was produced. Enigma used his Shadow Walk ability; stepping into Jynx's shadow. Enigma vanished and reemerged behind the Inquisitors, stepping out of their shadows.

Jynx and Whisper watched as Enigma appeared behind the two inquisitors. "Your brother is a showoff, Whisper. Next time he is testing the silence, you should dismiss the spell."

Whisper laughed, "I did, three days ago."

"It never gets stale, trust me."

They watched as he approached the guards from behind. First, he took the coin pouch then he kneeled down as if to adjust his boots. "Jynx what is he doing with their boots. Tell me that he is not tying their boots together."

"I believe he is."

"There are people everywhere, how is nobody noticing this?" Whisper asked in a hushed voice.

When Enigma was done, he walked back over to them. He tried to speak but was unable to make a sound. "I think I prefer him this way, Jynx." Whisper quipped.

"As do I."

Enigma folded his hands together as he made all the gestures of begging. Whisper shook her head. "Very well I will give you your sound back. Even though I do enjoy making you grovel, I truly can't stand the site of it." She uttered a single word unknown to the other two and Enigma regained his ability to speak.

"Thanks. You know what to do." Enigma said.

"Yeah, yeah" Whisper directed her familiar, a crow that was empathetically connected to her, to fly down and perch itself on a tent several yards off to the side of the Inquisitors.

"Thief, thief" The bird squawked with Whisper's voice. The Inquisitors immediately went to move when the thin leather cord connecting their boots went taut and they fell one on top of the other. Jynx, Enigma and Whisper laughed hysterically with all the people in the vicinity of the two inquisitors.

They fell again as they tried to pull themselves up. "Get moving or I'll see you all in the stocks, or the gods be damned dungeon!" One of them shouted while the other one struggled to free his boot. "Just cut it you damn fool!" The guard shot dirty glances at all who laughed.

The other inquisitor drew a knife from his boot and cut the string. "Them, it was them!" He yelled as he spotted the three rogues stationary, embroiled in a fit of unrestrained hilarity.

"It's time to go." Whisper said but her companions were too involved in their merriment to respond. "Guys, it's time to go!" Whisper yelled as the two guards stood.

"You three, don't move! You are under arrest!" The Inquisitor yelled.

Jynx and Enigma halted their jollity. They stared at the inquisitors and the inquisitors stared back at them. After a fleeting moment the two Inquisitors drew their short swords. This spurred the three rogues to do what they usually did when pissed off Inquisitors drew on them…

"Run!" Whisper yelled. Enigma vanished suddenly from view using his shadow walk. Whisper and Jynx split up. The leader of the two guards chased Jynx, the other chased Whisper but not for long. She ran straight for a tent, casting a spell as she went. She moved through the tent magically passing through to the inside. In the tent was an old woman reading a man's fortune with cards spread on a table between them. They both jumped up at the intrusion.

"Sorry," Whisper said as she jumped on the table and continued running, exiting through the entrance of the tent. The guard that chased her slammed into the wall of the tent and was thrown in a dramatic backward tumble, inspiring laughter and sarcasm from a new gaggle of witnesses.

Jynx dashed into a dense crowd, crouching he searched for a way out of it, and then he ran into a red tent where he startled a rich couple standing, engaged in an embrace. "How much did she pay you to discover us here," the man demanded.

"Oh, my gods, I am ruined." The woman cried out in embarrassment. She buried her face into her lover's hairy chest, wanting to hide her shame."

Jynx was caught totally off guard by this. He was speechless, for a pause. "Fifty crown pieces."

he improvised.

"Fifty, is that all." The man complained. "Is that all I am worth to her."

"I understand you're disappointed" Jynx said. He couldn't believe the conversation he was having even as he spoke. "She did hire me at discount but the good news for you is that it will be cheap to keep me quiet, I'd say, emm, double what she paid."

"Now I am being blackmailed? I will never pay. My pride hails from a lofty height, on my honor as a gentleman I shall never relinquish it." He stood firm, holding his mistress as he comforted her. She cried with annoyingly excessive flair"

"Are you serious?" Jynx asked "You are cheating on your wife. Never mind, suit yourself. I will give your wife my report then." Jynx replied acting as though he would turn and leave.

"No, wait. Here take my cufflinks they are easily worth thrice what she paid you." The rich man removed the jewelry from his sleeves and handed it to Jynx.

"Pleasure doing business with you," Jynx said. He walked past the couple as they stared at him. Jynx drew a dagger from his sleeve causing the couple to gasp in unison. The rogue gave a wry smile then made a long cut in the back of the tent. "Don't worry; your secret is safe with me." Jynx stepped out of the tear he made in the canvas.

"Just get out of here," The man commanded as Jynx disappeared from view.

A moment later Jynx stuck his head back through the cut, startling them anew. "You didn't see me." he told the couple.

"Just go!" The man again ordered him.

"Good luck on your affair!" Jynx yelled as he ran away from the red tent.

A few breaths later the Inquisitor ran into the tent startling the couple a third time. "Did you see an obnoxious rogue by chance?"

"Yes, he went that way," The man pointed at the cut in the tent. "He stole my cufflinks!" He yelled as the guard disappeared through the new opening.

Enigma waited at the big well where the three of them had agreed to rendezvous in the event that they were separated. Whisper approached. "That was your fault Enigma." She scolded her twin.

"Nobody made you cast that silence on me."

"I thought you were going to steal a treat, not tie their boots together."

"I did grab the treat. I don't recall saying 'Whisper cast the silence on me I am only going to lift their pouch.'"

"Urgg," she growled. "You're lucky Jynx got away. Here he comes.

"Lucky?"

"Yes, you would be breaking him out of the stockades yourself if he had been caught." She said.

"Then who would break me out if I got caught?" He asked.

"They would probably just execute you on the spot." She insisted sardonically.

"I'm wounded," Enigma said. "I never doubted him for a moment."

"Are you ok Jynx?" Whisper asked.

"Save your sisterly concern for that dirt collecting dunce." Jynx said indicating who he spoke of by giving Enigma a shove. The three rogues began walking together. "I am glad that he can teleport from shadows and you can walk through walls," Jynx said. "I had the strangest encounter in some random tent."

"So did I," Whisper said.

"I don't teleport," Enigma corrected. "I move through the Shadowland, teleportation is instantaneous."

"We know!" Jynx and Whisper said at the same time as they had a hundred times before.

Jynx stopped suddenly. "Hey look, they are trying to dunk the King."

Enigma grunted and made a ridiculous expression. "If you think I am falling for that then it is you who are a dunce." Enigma noticed surprise on his sister's face, as she looked in the same direction as Jynx. She was probably playing him, but he could not resist. In spite of himself, he peeked in the direction his companions stared. The three young rogues could not believe their eyes. "Wow, they really are. Look, those people stink. They couldn't hit the target if they had a Rime-Giant's snowball." Enigma said.

"I wonder who the king lost a bet with," Whisper considered aloud.

"Jynx, the sign says, 'sink the king and keep your money, one crown piece.' I bet you could do better than those uncoordinated saps." Enigma encouraged, instigating his friend's ego.

"I'm doing it." Jynx proudly declared. "This is a once in a lifetime opportunity, there is no way I am passing it up."

The two young men walked voraciously toward the booth. Whisper hurried to catch up to them as she protested their intentions. She was on occasion the voice of good sense among the three of them.

Chapter 4 - Prey

The archer paced in the kitchen stopping only to pet Elanor's war dog. "I'm getting worried. Garth should be done by now." He said to his fellow hunters.

Adriel was an expert shot with a bow. He tried his hand at a lot of vocations but archery was the only thing he did well. Twelve summers ago, when he was but fifteen circles old, the mage downstairs found him lost and alone. Garthadon took him under his wing. He was probably the only man Adriel genuinely admired. The marksman was a quick-tempered man, with a chip on his shoulder, and a point to prove.

"Garth told us it could take this long," Elanor said. "Still, I didn't agree with this in the first place."

Elanor Ashtop waited on a stool, her large Wolfhound lying at her feet. A warrior and woods expert, she was the groups ranger. She also held the distinction of being the only female member and newest to the party of hunters. She joined the group two winters back when they were hunting the very same vampire she sought. For her it had been personal, the vampire killed her family in front of her when she was a child. It had spared her only so she could relate the horror of what she witnessed to her village. She could still hear her mother's dying words when the blood sucker emptied her life-force. Gods save sweet Elanor. Mother had tried to scream but it had been only a feeble whisper. Elanor spent all of her life in service to the vow she had made once she regained the courage to speak. She got along well with her new family. Their common desire for vengeance bound her to them even after her vow had been fulfilled. All of them had a personal tragedy involving vampires, except perhaps Garth. No one knew why he formed the group or why he hunted, his disincentive was a mystery to them but they loved him unanimously. Elanor thought him to be the nicest man she had ever met. He was the father of her new family. A family brought up to destroy the undead.

Mandathar, a cleric of Crotear, stroked his reddish-brown beard, looking back and forth between his two allies as he sat waiting for Garthadon to finish his work in the basement. He could not see a reason to add his opinion. They both knew his viewpoint before the start of this. The master vampire would be too formidable for them to deal with alone. What more could they ask for than the assistance of a divine being? No doubt, Crotear had designed for them to find that locket and given Garthadon the ability to fill in the missing parts of its inscription.

"This is boring," Adriel complained. "I could be at a tavern well into my cups impressing some young wench with my trick shot and tickling her with my fletching."

"Ugh" Elanor groaned.

"As long as I have this," Adriel raised his composite long bow with one hand, "and this," he raised his middle finger on his other hand "I will remain in high demand."

"What are you talking about Adriel?" Elanor asked. "You delude yourself. You always start off the night harassing the sultriest dame in the taproom and end up drooling and spilling your ale over the homeliest frump left standing at the wee hours of dawn."

"I am an archer Elanor. If I have learned anything from my trade it is that sometimes you must aim high to hit your mark."

Mandathar let out several puffs of smoke as he lit his clay pipe. If Garthadon was the father of this small, surrogate family of hunters then Mandathar was its uncle. "He is indecorous and yet a proverb stumbles out of his mouth."

Elanor laughed despite herself.

"If I find out that was an insult Mandathar I will cut off your beard while you sleep."

Mandathar answered him by directing a large puff of tobacco smoke toward him.

Adriel began coughing. "One day that stinking pipe smoke is going to kill you Mandathar."

"The summoning is complete!" The mage yelled out from below. Startled, the three became alert. Adriel led the way with an arrow ready. The ranger cocked her crossbow and followed him downstairs, her wolfhound right beside her. Mandathar followed last, not one to get into a rush.

Garthadon turned to greet them as they moved, sidestepping down the stairs. "This is Imarra, the angel that will aid us in our quest, put away your weapons." They made their way down, Adriel and Elanor put away their weapons slowly. Wonder showed on all three of their faces. They could barely contain themselves as they marveled at the beautiful winged woman. Adriel observed the angel's quiver filled with an assortment of multicolored fletching though most were red or black. As he moved down the stairs he smelt sulfur but as he approached nearer to the celestial woman a flowery fragrance he was unfamiliar with filled his nose. The hunters stood shoulder to shoulder before the angel with Garthadon between.

They stared unabashedly. "Imarra, this is Elanor." Elanor bowed modestly keeping her eyes on the summoned creature. "She is a lover of Sylvia and all the life and wonders contained therein. She is our ranger and the bravest woodland warrior I have ever known. Beside her is her companion hound, Onyx, her nose is second to none at sniffing out the unnatural" Onyx whinnied sitting down next to Elanor and nestled her hand with her head.

The old mage motioned to the archer, "This sturdy young man is Adriel." Adriel, was middle-aged but Garthadon still considered him to be youthful. The archer acknowledged the mage with a nod. "He is a superb shot with a longbow and pretty decent with a sword, wooden or otherwise. He has saved untold lives by destroying countless undead monstrosities up close and many more from a distance. He is a little rough around the edges but his service to humanity greatly outweighs his shortcomings. All men drink from the same pool of proclivity and so we forgive him where he is weak and celebrate him where he is strong."

Garthadon walked over to Mandathar and placed a hand on the cleric's shoulder. "This is my longtime companion Mandathar. He is a priest of the benevolent god Crotear, a champion of right cause. He was humble enough to remain a village priest for the rest of his life, until he was forced to deal with a child that had gone missing in the woods but returned with that hideous affliction we all work to eradicate. It so affected him that he dedicated his life to the obliteration of these murderous creatures in honor of that poor lost little boy. It is Mandathar that is our moral compass." Garthadon took his hand from Mandathar's shoulder.

The priest walked up to Imarra and stooped to one knee on the dirt floor before her. He bowed deeply, "Please allow me to serve you." Mandathar supplicated.

"She will lead us to victory. I have given whatever authority I might have over to her. Please do as she bids you to." Garthadon smiled at his beloved team.

Elanor was disturbed by the sexual appeal this angel possessed. How could a being of purity be endowed with the seductive essence of a temptress? After a long moment, she shook away her reservations, attributing them to her own perverted, mortal nature, the very weakness of humanity. She bowed her head in guilt-ridden servility.

Adriel, however, spoke up, blurting out his trepidation. The lust that had formed in his heart was a feeling he was familiar with, though never so potent. That was not his greatest bother. Adriel did not trust anyone completely but the mage and himself. Now he was supposed to be led by someone he just met, someone not even of this world. "Why would you let her control the team Garth?"

"Because this is the best way," Garthadon answered. "She is incomparable to the rest of us. She has probably spent centuries working against

33

the forces of evil. We will one day be shepherded to our eternal reward by a creature such as this. It is our only hope. This once Adriel, we must trust in something more than my magic, your bow, Mandathar's divine favor and Elanor's swords."

"You still should have consulted us, Garth."

"For what?" Garthadon asked. "We have no time for that. What objections could you possibly raise? Raise them now.

"I don't have any objections. I just wanted to be absolutely sure before we follow someone, something."

Imarra ignored him and walked toward the priest. Squatting down in front of him she placed her soft hands on his bearded cheeks, and gently guided his head from its bowed position so he would look up at her as she spoke. "I am a messenger of love and life," she said in her kind, enchanting voice, "Called upon by you to destroy a monster of hatred, who loves death but will not abide by it." She looked squarely into Mandathar's eyes. "Where is the nearest high priest of our faith, devoted slave of Crotear?"

"He is two days from here, in the Cathedral of Pathos." The priest answered quickly, enraptured in the violet hues of inexpressible gentleness that were her eyes.

"Go to him, tell him of my arrival, and let him know of this good omen Garthadon has brought upon the faithful. Take one of these warriors for your protection. We shall depart when you return."

Mandathar rose to his feet with the gentle urging of Imarra's hands, as she herself stood. "Elanor, we must go prepare for our journey," the priest said.

The ranger looked at Garthadon with a questioning face. He responded with a nod and said gently, "go." The ranger did as she was bid, Onyx followed. Trailing behind the Cleric as he took the stairs, she stole a final glance. She could see that Garthadon's attention was fixed on Imarra. She thought to herself, if he trusts the angel then so must I. Mandathar looked only forward, filled with encouragement and his determination to serve. The two of them left to ready their horses and collect their gear. It could be a dangerous journey through the autumn woodland.

Chapter 5 - Dunk

The king beheld the commoner before him. An assortment of dark patches covered his faded blue cloak. His short dark hair was uncombed. He had a barely developed moustache on his upper lip, a late arrival given the man's twenty-three circles. Determined brown eyes visualized the path the onion would take to its target. This was the contestant's first close-up of the king in all his life. The smirk he wore as he received a large onion from a helper, revealed boldness. *If this peasant misses, it is not going to be on purpose*, the king thought. "You could have at least wiped the filth from your upper lip before appearing in front of your king." King Eratide taunted. "A puny boy like you should eat that onion, not throw it away!"

"This is for the liquor tax!" Jynx yelled, drawing the crowd's eyes to him. He pitched, releasing the vegetable missile. It hit the target dead on. There was the sudden clang of the trap doors falling open, hitting the sides of the cage, followed by an immediate splash. All who were witness, besides Jynx and Enigma, gasped loudly in unison, fearful of the sight. The king had seemed suspended in midair for a split second, with an incredibly dumb look upon his face, then the big splash.

Enigma and Jynx entered a hysterical cachinnation and gave each other a high five in the midst of it then grabbed each other's forearms and danced in a circle. They didn't quite notice the horror worn on the faces around them. The king's upper body emerged from the water, standing soaked to the bone and shaking from the cold. His usually bushy goatee, now matted to his face, stood straight up at the end. His majesty showed flush with indignation and the onlookers fell completely silent, Enigma and Jynx being the last to catch on. King Eratide's eyes shifted to his daughter Corrine, as she watched. He noted her blond curls and bright eyes. The serious look on her face, betrayed a smile starting to give way. Her dimples began to show as she fought emerging laughter. The king's rage waned swiftly as his heart replaced rage with mirthful adoration. Father and daughter erupted into laughter, much to the relief of all, Jynx and the twins especially. Slowly the crowd joined the mirth as it grew to abounding.

Feyless Dargon, Margravine of the sixth noble house inserted herself to the front of the line, onion in hand. She wore a lavender dress with a silver necklace, rings, bracelets and a sterling headband with a sapphire in the front. The forty-one winters she had witnessed were gentle to her. The noble woman's youthful charm had not faded, but rather matured, her face was brightened by wisdom. The spectacle's attendants reset the trapdoor after the King climbed up the side of the cage out of the water. "No magic tricks here witch," The king called out to his noble challenger as he reclaimed his seat.

"In that case I guess I won't levitate you out of your public bath." She retorted. The king began a response, but was stopped short and splashed again into the pool. The crowd, no longer tense cheered and people began to line up for their chance to dunk the king. Nobility, the common folk and even guardsmen joined in. Princess Corrine and her two Chosen Ladies giggled and clapped every time someone hit their mark and dropped the king into the tank.

Margravine Dargon approached Jynx as he enjoyed the spectacle. "Thank you for your courage in saving this event. Do you have a name sir?"

"Yes," Jynx bowed excessively. Jynx is the name my unlucky mother granted me, well-met" Jynx held out his arm, prepared to greet in the customary manner of grabbing each other's wrists and squeezing. The noble lady was either unfamiliar with the custom or found it unfavorable. Whatever the reason, she gawked at his arm with wide eyes. It seemed clear to Jynx that she was rejecting his courtesy so he put his arm down. "What can I do for you milady? Judging by the sapphire you wear combined with the fact that you are a lady must mean that a Margravine stands before me."

"Why yes," the Margravine answered. "I am impressed that you knew that."

"Sometimes I impress myself with my lack of ignorance. Although I have had more access to books than your average Slumsider, I am typical of my sector in every other respect. I am not wanting in poverty, and my name is slang to you.

"I meant no insult. I forgot that the people of the slums were often not given proper names. What are the names of your companions?" Margravine Dargon asked.

"Of course. You probably don't make it to Slumside very often." Jynx said. "This is my friend, improperly named Whisper." Whisper responded by kicking Jynx discreetly in the ankle.

"And I am improperly Enigma, at your service milady." Enigma said smiling.

The Margravine laughed. "Your point is well taken gentlemen. For changing the tone of this event and in apology for my insult, I would like you three to be my personal guests at the kings table. I will inform the commander of the crown guard. The guards will scrutinize you and then let you through. I am certain the princess is even more grateful then I am." She looked them over one last time. They were speechless. "The feast is at dusk. I will take my leave now, be blessed of Crotear." She left, leaving them to ponder.

They remained quiet for a change, until Enigma could not stand it and broke the silence. "She confused your audacity with courage, Jynx."

Jynx pushed him. "You're just jealous that she was all over me and not you."

Whisper rolled her eyes. "She is nearly twice your age, Jynx, she could be your mother"

"Not so, I have seen his mother and she don't look anything like that," Enigma said.

They continued in silence a while longer, until again Enigma could not bear to be quiet. "You sure took a pretty big chance risking a crown piece for nothing. I didn't think you had that much on you."

"I don't," Jynx said.

Whisper's coffee colored eyes got big and she punched Jynx in the back. "And you called my brother a dunce." She hit him again, this time he felt it. "Do you know what would have happened if you had missed with that onion and didn't have the crown piece to pay?"

He dodged out of range, avoiding her third

strike. "I don't like thinking about it. The point is we are going to get a free meal at the most prestigious table in the city. Plenty of people would pay money to lie on the floor beneath it and eat the scraps like a dog. Look at you, all you can think about is the, what ifs, bringing your stormy clouds to my sunny day"

"You two knock it off," Enigma interrupted. "I have to find some place to stash my finger blades, caltrops, and this coin pouch I lifted while you dazzled the crowd with your onion throwing skills."

Whisper looked over at him. "How much did you get?"

"Don't ask. You know I do not count my treats until the day's end. It is bad luck."

Whisper sighed and shook her head, "How the hells did I end up with you two?"

Chapter 6 - Night

The borderlands were home to many ruined castles and other structures. It was known that an ancient kingdom thrived there two thousand years ago, keeping the land tame. The Histories of Sophia states that the nobles abandoned their lands and retreated into the capital city to escape a terror of dragons and plague. They filled the city with people from every corner of the kingdom, as many as the city could hold took refuge within before some great sorcery hid the city. The borderlands fell into chaos as monsters infested the region. It is taught to all the human inhabitants that the day will come when the ancient kingdom of Deznire shall return to reclaim their holds and bring order to this savage corner of Sophia.

The hunter's temporary abode sat at the outskirts of a quiet village along Frontiers Road. Garthadon had purchased the cabin from a trapper that tired of the hazards of the borderlands. The villagers were eager to welcome a group of capable combatants into their frontier community. The further one traveled north from the village of Echo, the greater the peril. Two week's journey to the north was the haven of Smallfort. Beyond that point, the monster nuisance grew into an infestation. Garthadon sat at a table in his laboratory across from Imarra. She had the power to alter herself which she used to make her wings disappear. Only her great pulchritude would cast suspicion upon her human guise. Adriel's snoring could be heard from the bedroom where he slept broken up by the occasional dry cough. He talked a bit in his sleep even saying the angel's name several times. Imarra seemed to ignore him as she spoke to Garthadon, looking at him intently through a break in the mystical clutter that covered the table. "Tell me Garthadon, what do you have planned, who is this master vampire?"

"Drusus Lexore is the monster's name." Garth answered. "He...It, abides in the town of Willowview, a week's ride to the north. I have not shared these details with my fellow hunters yet. I was going to tell everyone at once but now I shall tell Mandathar and Elanor when they return. Don't say anything to Adriel, please. He will be angry if he finds out that I told you before him. I will inform him myself in the morning."

"I will not say a word to him about it, it is not my place."

"Thank you," The old mage said. "Drusus is an extremely powerful foe. Even with your help this may be a suicide mission for the rest of us." Garthadon paused a moment as he reflected briefly upon his life. "The others do not know this either but this shall be my last journey with them rather we fail or succeed. When Drusus is destroyed, if I yet live, I am going to take a modest portion of the wealth we recover and retire to a life of quiet in this very village. I want to be a part of creating something for once in my life. I have spent my adult years destroying evil; I would like to spend my final years building and adding in whatever small way I can to the good of others.

"You deserve to spend some time in the light after all your hard years of sacrifice in the darkness.

Do not be troubled kind mage, they will understand. You are not abandoning them. You guided them and nurtured them and now you are setting them free to plot their own course. Your wisdom and council will continue to help them as they hear your voice in moments of trial."

"Thank you," the old mage said plainly, with sincerity. His eyes sparkled as they accumulated with the water of sentiment, which Garth wiped away with a threadbare sleeve. "Willowview is not a large town but it is larger than any other community that far north. I do not know how many vampires we will face there. The town is filled with living people who do not know the true nature of Drusus. We will also have to contend with his chosen one. She is his bodyguard and concubine. Her name is Ashenath. She is a foul tempered creature, cruel, calculating and above all jealous. She has destroyed many of Drusus's vampires herself. Next to Drusus, she is the most dangerous vampire I know of. If he is slain before she is destroyed, she will become a free willed vampire. If she were freed she would undoubtedly become a master vampire herself. It is imperative that we kill her. Ashenath's potential for evil is boundless." Garthadon yawned.

"Go to sleep dear hunter, I will carry you to this Drusus when it is time to confront him."

"One of us stands guard when we sleep at night. If the vampire's suspect us they will become the hunters and we will be the hunted," Garthadon said.

The angel got up and walked over to the old wizard. She held out her hand, helping him to his feet. "I shall bear that responsibility from hence forth. I do not require sleep."

Garthadon walked toward the shared bedroom where four mattresses of straw covered with animal hide lay for the use of the team. "I hope it is you that escorts me to eternity" Garth said to Imarra as he laid down on one of the mattresses and closed his eyes.

"It will be, good mage." Imarra said to him before kissing him on the forehead as he drifted off to sleep. Garthadon slept more peacefully for a few minutes than he had in decades.

Imarra stood in silence listening to Adriel and Garthadon's breathing. She remained still as she watched their chests raise and drop. Thunder bellowed outside, then a downpour followed, an ominous announcement. Imarra considered thoughtfully as she waited for Garth's sleep to deepen, for his eyes to move spontaneously below their lids, which of these two men were more dangerous. When she was certain that Garth had entered a dream, she decided he posed the greater threat.

She stood between their two beds and drew her gold hilted longsword. Looking over Garthadon, she raised the sword high, and quickly brought it down in a slashing movement, loping off his head and granting permanency to his slumber. Then she spun around, pulling her weapon up and then down, driving it into Adriel's chest barely missing his heart. He woke instantly, paralyzed with pain and horror as he beheld the angel looking down upon him. Her beautiful white wings tore forth from her back to the extent of their span. He watched as the white feathers of her wings became black and streaked with stains of blood, two small, boney horns grew from her head.

Imarra smiled. "Oh, I had no idea you were going to die slowly," She said in the kindest voice she possessed, pulling her sword slowly out of him. It was a level of cruelty, he only seen once, when a blood sucker executed his brother in midst of a gleeful fit. "Were you dreaming about me?" She asked sadistically, sitting down next to Garthadon's corpse, and crossing her legs, in a pointedly teasing fashion. "What sort of dirty things did you have me doing in your dreams?" She uncrossed her legs and slipped her hand into her mailed skirt flitting with her fingers, her moans a mocking exaggeration, her lips moist from her tongue as it glided across her lips.

The archer struggled to sit up. "You...you bitch!" Adriel choked out, before coughing out a profusion of blood. He hated her. "Why!" He cried out, tears salting his cheeks in great streams.

Imarra paused, smiled, gave the facial expression of one who was well pleased. "Thank you for the crying, it is the perfect seasoning to my ecstasy. I must say I have painted a little masterpiece here," she said before her hand moved again, her fingers dancing under her shiny steel skirt, her eyes filled with lascivious hunger. He sobbed uncontrollably, fluids pouring out of him, as he vomited blood, cried and pissed himself. "The single most common question asked by you weak little mortals is 'why?' She took heavier breaths, her words broken by exasperated whines. "The reason is quite simple...actually." "I am an angel, as you thought; just a darker breed than poor Garthadon

45

realized. Mmmm, how his misplaced trust damned your whole party." She mused, letting out a squeak. "I am as stunned as you are." She climaxed then removed her hand, panting. "One moment I am feasting on the soul of a dead coward in hell and the next I am standing in the realm of mortals, talking to some fool who thinks I am from the seven heavens. Although, I must say, I have no idea where this locket came from. I am going to have to kill who ever made it." Imarra placed her finger upon his lip, "shhh."

His breathing ceased. Adriel's open dead eyes reflected her image of resplendent terror.

She stood up, turning to look at Garthadon's dead face, giddy from the excitement of unleashing herself upon the mortal world. "Now I must see to the terms of that deal, dear Garth. We will confront the master vampire together as I am bound to do. Though I don't believe we agreed on any stipulations that you were to remain alive or that we were to actually kill the vampire," She ran her tongue up the length of her sword tasting the mage's blood. "This is the most open ended contract I have ever had," she said to Garthadon's head as she picked it up to look squarely at his face. "Perhaps this vampire will prove to be an ally, what was his name again Garth? Ah yes... Drusus." Her wings retracted into her back disappearing completely and her horns receded into her head causing her to look indistinguishably human, once again. "If we are going to confront the master vampire together Garth, it will not do to lug your body around with me." With that, she tossed his head into the fireplace. Without a word, she sculpted an urn into

46

existence with her hand. She walked over to the fireplace and set it on the mantel. Imarra then proceeded outside to the pile of wet lumber where she easily freed the axe they used for firewood. Lightning flashed and thunder screamed as she walked forthright and drenched into the cabin. Raising the axe high above her head she set about making the old mage fit better into the fire which kindled, spontaneously, her invocation an afterthought.

Chapter 7 - Charity

The time neared for Evening Feast. Jynx and the twins crossed the festival, sauntering toward the pavilion that held the kings table. They walked past many large tents belonging to the city's noble families. The autumn air was cool and a light wind prevailed. All around the center of the park were the upper-class of Oepal society. The three rogues couldn't help but notice the sideways glances and sometimes outright staring as they moved amongst the gentry. Jynx was surprised not to see more Inquisitors in this part. He resolved that it would be insane to steal from the people on this side of the festival. Though the Inquisitor presence was surprisingly low, each of the nobles had small private armies of house guards in attendance. The majority of knights, clerics and mages hailed from the noble houses. Pick pocketing and other activities of larcenous aggrandizement could be a fatal affair in this part of the festival, despite their extraordinary accomplishment at such professional endeavors. Jynx and his two companions decided to ignore the many stares of the city's upper crust and enjoy their moment of prestige regardless of its brevity. They were out of their traditional element and were somewhat uncomfortable. The three of them walked toward the pavilion in the center of the park amidst the throng of Noblesiders. They stopped short when they encountered a perimeter of Crown Guardsmen many yards before the pavilion that the Kings table occupied. There were several tents between the perimeter and the pavilion so that one could not get a clear view of the royal feast without being allowed to enter by the guard. The guards were mostly men-at-arms carrying heavy crossbows and brandishing long swords. They wore white tabards over chainmail bearing the royal heraldry. There were guards who wore plate armor, carried sword and shield also wearing white tabards bearing the royal emblem: The Black Opal with blue fire in its center, before the breast of a great gold dragon on a white field draped in purple. Whisper's crow perched itself on the roof of the pavilion as the three rogues approached the least intimidating of the guardsmen. "We are here to eat with the King," Jynx declared.

"Is that so?" The guard asked with apparent skepticism.

"I'm sorry," Whisper said. "Forgive my friend. He suffers from a curse where foolishness occasionally burps forth from his food hole. We are actually guests of the fair Margravine, Feyless Dargon."

Two other guardsmen approached. "What is going on here?" One of them asked.

"They say they are guests of Margravine Dargon, I will see." The guardsmen left to consult with his sergeant. He returned after a couple of minutes. "My apologies milady, you and these two gentlemen may pass."

The three, smiled wide as they walked into the throng of the pavilion and were soon approached by a man in a blue tunic, bearing the Dargon insignia: a black gem, blue fire within it and wrapped twice with a silver scarf. He carried two dark-blue tunics. "Please put these on, they will be more suitable for the occasion." He handed the tunics to Jynx and Enigma. "Follow me please."

"Who are you, good sir?" Whisper asked as her brother and their friend removed their cloaks and plain tunics, replacing them with the fine ones as they walked.

"I am the Margravine's chamberlain."

"I thought only the king had a chamberlain." Jynx said as he slid the new tunic on.

"You are speaking of the Royal High Chamberlain. I am a Lord High Chamberlain. Most of the major noble families employ a chamberlain as their head steward."

"What does a head steward do?" Whisper asked as they came to a halt at the entrance of a large night-blue tent. A heavily armored guard wearing a tabard with the Dargon coat of arms stood at the opening.

"We do everything. My voice is the echo of the Margravine's will. This way please." The Margravine's chamberlain stood to face the drape over the tent opening. The sentry pulled the flap open allowing the Slumsiders and their escort to enter. They stepped into the main room of the tent. There were entrances to three more rooms beyond the first that were draped closed. A large chunk of amber in a lantern hanging at the peak of the tent, cast illumination into the room to such magnitude that it seemed to have the full light of the sun, yet was not blinding. You could look upon it and identify it as the source and it would not burn your eyes. Enigma contemplated the worth of such a treasure. The walls of the main room were covered in tapestries of enormous value. A table in the center held numerous fabrics of exquisite quality. A smaller table off to the wall of the spacious tent sat four soldiers who played a game with large cards and laughed quietly amongst each other. "You two will need to wash up." The Chamberlain indicated a tall stand of silver with an affixed sink and silver jugs upside down that fed water to the sink at the turn of a lever in a way that the rogues did not quite understand.

"Forgive me sir, but shouldn't I wash up as well?" Whisper asked.

"Yes dear. We have everything necessary for the preparations of a proper lady in that room. Go ahead, and take your time, we will summon you when ready."

Jynx and Enigma laughed. "She is both proper and a lady to be sure," Enigma said.

"Yes," Jynx added, "But never both at the same time." He smirked with self-approval as he elicited laughter from Enigma and the guards at the card table.

Whisper answered them with a cutting glance and a wry smile. It was the smile that stopped their laughter short and brought them into line. The smile they both knew meant that she had thought of some clever and fitting form of revenge. Their only hope was that she would forget, a dim hope indeed. Whisper entered into the room shutting the curtain behind her.

Jynx and Enigma played cards and exchanged jokes and tales with the guards, while they waited for Whisper to emerge from the room. Every now and then a female attendant would move from one of the rooms that were closed off to the other that

Whisper occupied. After an hour, Whisper stepped out of the room. Jynx looked up and then back to the table before he realized that something had caught his eye causing him to look up again. He stared at Whisper, as she stood nervously waiting to be bombarded with jokes from Jynx and her brother. Enigma noticed Jynx and the guardsmen staring and looked up himself. Whisper's black hair was arranged in a milkmaid braid and she was adorned with earrings and a necklace of cut lapis lazuli. She wore a dress of simple dark blue that left her shoulders bare and pronounced her hips and breasts unlike anything she had ever worn. She was both uncomfortable in it and in love with it. She felt naked, as parts of her body were exposed that she had always kept covered but she also for the first time in her life felt truly pretty and couldn't help but give an uncharacteristic, girlish giggle as all the men in the tent stared. Horrified she attempted to restrain her smile, but the more she attempted to resist the more her smile grew, the white gleam of which was the final adornment needed to make her glamor complete.

"Priceless" was all Jynx could manage as he stared at her as if this were the first time he had ever saw her. He realized at once the word he chose was a fumble, Whisper thought it was her arraignment he admired but she was mistaken as it was her sudden and unexpected beauty that froze him in place, allowing only one foolishly chosen word to fall from his lips.

Chapter 8 - Journey

"It looks as though a storm will soon join us," Elanor said. "We will have to set up camp soon." The two hunters sat on the saddled backs of their horses alongside of each other. The road they traveled was etched through the forest. It twisted and turned, rolling up and down the hills of the woodland. The air was comfortable, the wind was slight and their noses inhaled the fresh scent of an ineluctable rain soon to arrive. Yellow and orange leaves danced across the road in a wispy, gentle ballad.

"There," Mandathar said, pointing ahead. "Do you see that thin pillar of smoke? There must be a camp up ahead."

"It seems as though they are of like mind. No doubt they wanted to make shelter before the rain arrived," Elanor said.

"That or they are highway men seeking to waylay travelers from Echo."

"It could be, but either way we need to reach the camp before it rains."

"Agreed," Mandathar said. "It is most difficult to smoke my pipe in the rain."

The pair of vampire hunters galloped forward on their horses until they were near enough to the roadside camp to discern some details of it. The two remained alongside of each other as they reduced speed to an amble.

"I see a child." Elanor said.

"Well if that is not a sure sign of a safe camp then I don't know what is. Even vampires for all their craftiness and cunning have never figured out how to make horrified children play. Only the most despicable highwayman would put his own child as bait."

As the two travelers arrived at the perimeter of the camp a large man carrying an equally large sword upon his back stood before them with his arms crossed while several of his men aimed crossbows from various vantage points. This was not surprising to Mandathar and Elanor as they did not hide their approach. It was so common to greet travelers on the road this way that it could be considered a custom. Mandathar and Elanor both assessed the camp. Elanor's wolfhound sat watching and waiting. There were four covered wagons and roughly twenty armed men protecting them.

"What are you riders about?" The large man lent a course tone.

"We are part of a group of adventurers. My name is Mandathar and I am a cleric of Crotear. My companion Elanor is a ranger. We seek to share your camp for the night, as it appears inclement weather is soon to be upon us." Mandathar noticed a little boy less than ten winters old hiding underneath the foremost wagon. Mandathar's features lightened and he gave a big hearty smile and a little wave to the young onlooker.

The child sank back beneath the wagon alarmed by the cleric's notice of him. The lead man cast a sideways glance and spotted the child as he moved beyond view. "Get my boy into shelter." The large man barked at one of his men.

The guard walked up to the large man and nervously held out his crossbow to him, "Its loaded sir".

"Give me that," The leader grabbed the crossbow. "Get about your task." The lead caravan guard turned his attention back to the travelers as his subordinate hurried off. "My name is Rondo. I am the personal bodyguard of the Vandersen merchant family. If you don't mind, I will be requiring some proof that you are not scoundrels." Rondo wore a chest-plate leaving his arms and massive shoulders bear.

"Of course, Mandathar said. I am a priest of competent powers. If any of your camp requires healing I would be happy to provide what I can in exchange for a dry place to smoke my pipe and for me and my companion to rest our heads."

"Actually," Rondo said. "My employer's daughter was taken ill shortly after the onset of our journey. It appears to be the poxes and all in this camp are distressed because of it. If you can help her or ease her suffering in any way it would be worth a lot more than a place at our camp."

The guards relaxed a bit lowering their crossbows as Rondo brought the two hunters to the wagon in the center of the convoy. "Mr. Vandersen," Rondo called out from the back of the wagon. Thunder clapped loudly as the sky darkened above.

A well dressed, lanky man climbed out of the wagon. "Is everything well Rondo?" Mr. Vandersen asked.

"Yes sir, it is going to rain any moment now and the two travelers appear to be harmless adventurers. This one," Rondo motioned toward Mandathar, "is a priest and may be able to help

Kalexis."

"Oh I hope so, this is a good turn of events," Mr. Vandersen said. He looked at Mandathar. "If you help my daughter I will reward you greatly."

"Let me see her sir, I shall do whatever Crotear's providence will grant me the power to do. There is no need of reward, for if she is healed it will be the will of the merciful one."

Mr. Vandersen, Elanor and Mandathar climbed into the covered wagon. A young lady about twelve circles old lay covered in furs with an opulently dressed woman sitting near the girls head holding a candle. Distress was evident on the woman's face. Mandathar supposed her to be the sick girl's mother.

"Who are these strangers, Judian?" The woman asked.

"They may be of some help my dear."

"I certainly hope so," Mrs. Vandersen said bluntly. "The bearded fellow reeks of tobacco."

Mandathar looked at her. "I am sorry Mrs. Vandersen." Mandathar walked hunched over and kneeled down next to the sleeping girl, his knees ached from his weight driving them into the planks of the wagon. He pulled the furs on the girl down to her waist. She wore a splendid night gown light-blue in color. Mandathar could see in the flickering light that her face and her arms were covered in circular lesions, her skin was a sickly white and the pink of her lips was faded. The sound of a downpour came suddenly causing the girl to stir. The stirring gave way to coughing and Mandathar's patient grabbed her shoulders trying to relieve the pain in her chest with pressure. "The bad news," Mandathar said in his gruff, bellowing voice, "Is that you may not have made it to a priest if you had turned around in the morning."

"That was our very plan. We are only one day out from Pathos." Mr. Vandersen said. "Is there good news I pray?"

"Yes, there is. Not having time to reach a priest, Crotear has sent me to you, he shall heal her." Mandathar began the invoking of divine power. He spoke the words of an incantation that had the sound of a sermon. He raised his arms up to the heavens and he demanded that for his sake and the sake of the humble child, that Crotear remove this fatal disease from one of his children with the ease in which a father wipes the tears from his daughter's cheek. Golden light emanated from Mandathar's hands and welled up in his eyes like pools of electricity. He grabbed Kalexis, startling her parents. The divine energy of golden light proceeded out of his hands as it drained from his eyes, the girl was covered in this radiance and then it vanished.

For a moment, all were still and then Kalexis opened her eyes. A long moment seemed to pass. Judian and his wife were frozen with anxious anticipation. Finally, she spoke, her voice small but unbroken. "Is it supper time Mommy? I feel like I haven't ate since last moon." The Vandersen's grabbed their daughter crying tears of relief. Mr. Vandersen looked to Rondo, "Order the servants to get her something to eat and arrange a place for this cleric and his companion they are my honored guest at this campsite."

Mandathar and Elanor climbed out of the wagon to find the guards had finished setting up the camp. Two wagons on one side of the road and two on the other with a fire set in the middle. Several large canvases were secured over top of the camp area, excepting for a circular opening in the center of the canopy allowing the smoke from the campfire to escape. It was a large tent-like set up that incorporated the covered wagons allowing one to walk from one side to the other and remain mostly dry when the rain poured down. Wolves could be heard in the woods howling in a wild chorus of thunder, rain, and canine. Mandathar, Elanor, Rondo and a couple of the guards sat in a circle upon large logs watching as the campfire was extinguished by the rainfall. Mandathar smoked his pipe. Elanor retrieved a blanket from one of the saddlebags on her horse then stretched out on the ground using Onyx as a pillow.

Mr. Vandersen eventually came to sit at the circle along with Kalexis. "She wanted to see you." Mr. Vandersen said to Mandathar.

Kalexis was slender with long light brown hair and wore an expensive yellow cloak. "Thank you." She said to Mandathar. Suddenly she hugged the smoky man causing him to exhale a large puff of smoke. Elanor and the guards present all laughed as did Mandathar when he recovered from his coughing fit. "Perhaps one day I can be a servant of Crotear."

"Oh, but you already are," Mandathar said. "Here, have a seat. I have something I would like to give to you."

"You have already given plenty," said Mr. Vandersen, "and we are greatly indebted to you.

"Where are you headed?" Mandathar asked the

merchant as Kalexis took a seat next to him.

"We are headed to Willowview," the merchant said. There is noble man there which sought to buy my textile business. I've decided not to sell my whole business to him but I have brought enough fabrics to start a shop in Willowview if he would like to be my partner in this endeavor."

"Huh. And what is this nobleman's name?" Mandathar asked.

"It is Drusus Lexore."

"Well," Mandathar said, "The north lands are fraught with peril," he pulled a necklace of woven hemp from around his neck. It carried a white stone. He handed it to Kalexis "This necklace is divinely powered to save your life. Let us hope you never need it. You must keep it around your neck at all times."

"Thank you so much Father Mandathar," Kalexis said. She put the necklace around her neck.

"That is a gift of enormous value to contain such an enchantment." Mr. Vandersen said. "If you will accept no recompense than I shall at least pay for the erection of a shrine in your honor good cleric.

Onyx came to her feet causing Elanor's head to hit the dirt road. The wolfhound first sniffed the air then began barking and growling at something unseen in the woods. Elanor stood up. "What's the matter girl?" Elanor asked the dog, stroking her black fur in an effort to calm her. Onyx would not be calmed and became angrier, snarling and howling. "We've got company!" Elanor shouted as she grabbed her crossbow up and loaded a bolt.

"Run to cover!" Mandathar ordered the

Vandersen's as he stood up brandishing his heavy mace.

"We are under attack!" One of the guards outside the canopy yelled.

The sounds of combat could be heard outside of the camp. All the guards not beyond the canopy on watch, armed themselves and made their way to the center. Many crossbow bolts tore into the camp from the trees, through the openings between the covered wagons. Mandathar raised his shield in time to hear a couple of quarrels shatter against it. Elanor cried out as one lodged itself in her arm. Judian and his daughter fell to the ground.

"Get her out of here!" Mandathar screamed.

Judian and Kalexis sprang to their feet and ran to their wagon hand in hand as large wolves charged into the camp from the forest. Judian hurriedly lifted his daughter into the wagon, throwing her in with the strength of terror aiding him. He followed her in at once. Rondo's young son was in the back of the wagon holding a wooden sword in a defensive posture.

The wolves' masters entered the camp. Orc's, tall humanoids with large muscles, skin ranging from mottled gray to dark green, covered with warts and blemishes and an oily secretion that smelt like offal. The heads of the creatures resembled a wart hog more than it did a human's. An orc's temper was an inferno of wrath and hate. Man, orc and wolf converged in the center of camp in a chaotic melee. The orcs came in from in between the wagons and from the trees above tearing the canvas down as they entered, tangling and covering many of the caravan guards.

Mandathar wielded his heavy mace with ferocious retribution. The heavy spiked ball of the weapon fractured the skull of a charging wolf causing its brains to fall out of its head like a cracked egg. An orc charged him with a curved sword. There was a clang as the chain on Mandathar's mace struck the orc's scimitar. The ball wrapped around the sword and Mandathar yanked the weapon from the monster's grasp. The orc drew a long knife as Mandathar swung his mace in the air with great vorticity and brought it down on the orcs head with a violent crack. He followed with his shield, slamming into the creature throwing his foe to the ground.

Elanor dropped her crossbow. The bolt lodged in her arm caused blood to spray her face as she pulled her two swords from the scabbards on her back.

Onyx was wrapped in the jaws of two wolves. The three canines rolled and spun about in lurid clash of tooth and claw. The beasts slammed into the back of a guard's legs causing him to fall. A nearby orc, marked by the savagery and lack of honor of his kind, seized the opportunity, slashing the man wide open with his scimitar, he rolled dumping his entrails on the ground.

Elanor having witnessed the grizzly act charged the orc. He noticed her and raised his curved blade above his head. She was faster, and deadlier. Before he could bring the sword down she drove one of her blades through the pit of his arm and the other through his throat. Elanor kicked him hard in the abdomen using the force of the falling monster to unsheathe her swords from his body. Turning about she dispatched one of the wolves fighting Onyx but missed with her other blade as her injured arm grew heavy and struck Onyx by mistake.

The thunder continued to roar. The warriors were drenched from the rain and visibility was greatly impaired. The canvas hung down in some places and was torn down in others. Mandathar swung his mace breaking an orc's piggish snout, then struck him again and again hammering the orc in the face as the beastly humanoid refused to fall even after it had died. He hit the orc many times before finally it fell, it's face completely destroyed. The priest felt the jaws of a wolf clamp down on his calf. It felt as if his leg was in a vice and the bone might be crushed. He tried to hit the beast with his mace but it was to close and he couldn't get enough momentum to hurt the creature. Feeling the beginnings of panic rising within, he dropped down to one knee. Letting go of his mace and shield, he took his thick hands and grabbed the creature's snout on the top and the bottom. He pulled as hard as he could and broke the creatures jaw with a snap.

Through the rain the priest could make out the dark, shadowy form of an orc charging at him. Mandathar grabbed his weapon in one hand and his shield in the other. Sliding his arm through the brace on the back of the shield he stood raising the shield fast and hard. The top of the shield connected with the bottom of the orcs large jaw. Mandathar was almost knocked over as the creature's body flailed against the shield before landing on its back. Mandathar whipped his mace through the air spinning it a full revolution before bringing it down on the monster's head pulverizing part of the skull to powder. Then he found a moment free from combat. Thanking Crotear for the blessing he looked around as the rain lightened from a torrent to a drizzle. At least a dozen guards plus himself and Elanor remained alive each fighting one or more opponents. The priest took note of his companion's wound and exhaustion, seeing her struggle against a particularly large orc. Mandathar raised his mace high in the air and called upon Crotear in the old tongue. His eyes flashed with electricity as a bolt of lightning came down out of the storm incinerating the large orc that Elanor was fighting and spider webbing out of his burning body. Five bolts shot out of this orc striking five more targets and shifting the momentum to the caravan's advantage.

Elanor commanded Onyx to protect a wagon. Onyx ran to the center wagon and jumped into it then stood with her head sticking out of the opening. A gash by her ear streamed with blood. Kalexis, her family and Rondo's son, gasped fearfully at Onyx before they realized she was not one of the wolves.

Mandathar threw his head back and roared with divine power. Any who did not see him do this would have thought a bear was near. This spell rejuvenated the stamina of many of the warriors as they persisted to fight for their lives past the point of exhaustion. Mandathar moved across the battlefield looking for fallen warriors. The dead ones he passed over until he found a guardswoman that was dying. He put away his mace. One hand crackling with divine energy he laid it upon the dying guard. Her cracked skull and broken hand healed under the energy. The woman stood up having regained full utility of her body.

"Go finish the fight," Mandathar commanded. The guard armed herself and sought an enemy to kill. Mandathar set about finding more warriors to heal as the fighting winded down.

Soon there was a cheer as the remaining orcs broke rank and fled leaving the bodies of the wolves and their fallen brethren behind.

"Do not give chase." Rondo yelled after lopping an orc's arm off, who then fled leaving the limb behind.

Mandathar continued healing all the injured including Elanor, from the most heavily wounded to those who were less so, until he depleted his healing magic for the day.

Elanor and Mandathar stayed with the company helping to set up the camp and bury fallen warriors. Mr. Vandersen approached the two hunters with Kalexis and his wife Sema at his side. "Is there anything we can do to convince you to complete the journey with us?"

Elanor looked at Mandathar. He knew she would take whatever course he decided.

"I am sorry. I very much wish to see your family carried safely to your destination but our business is of critical importance. The charm that I have given this young girl and my prayers will have to suffice"

"I am sorry to hear that," Judian Vandersen said. "But my gratitude is in no way diminished. I hope that you will pay a stop by our home or one of our shops when your path brings you near to us again."

Chapter 9 - Vision

Jynx, Enigma and Whisper stood next to their seats as did all the other guests at the king's table. A Herald announced King Eratide, who approached the table from the royal tent. A servant pulled his large chair out, then he pushed the seat gently into the back of the king's legs. The king recognized the cue and took his seat at the head of the royal table. It was uncomfortable and King Eratide readjusted his sitting as much as he could short of standing up and doing the whole ordeal over without help. Then the Dinner Herald announced the princess. She approached observing every punctilio of decorum to an extent that only a teacher of etiquette could fully appreciate her discipline. Corrine bowed modestly toward her sire. "May I join you father?" She asked, as was the protocol. Her blue eyes sparkled, her smile was sincere and her voice was sweet.

"It would be my honor." His majesty said. Then the King stood up and in a blatant violation of protocol he pulled out his daughter's chair. Most of the nobles gasped but some thought it refreshing and smiled. "Are you comfortable?" He asked as she took her place.

"Thank you, father, I am most comfortable," Corrine said with a smile.

Jynx having no training in protocol, noticed that all were staring directly at the princess. In an effort to imitate those around him he stared as well but he still managed to embarrass himself staring directly into her eyes. She locked gazes with him for a moment, amused. He immediately lost all confidence and looked down. The eyes of nearly every guest turned scandalously toward him causing perspiration to accumulate on his brow. He thought of the consequences of turning around and running back to Slumside but knew it to be a rash idea. He stood embarrassed in a moment that seemed to occupy more than its fair share of time. The Herald then announced the Royal High Chamberlain, followed by Prince Orginus Dreadhawk the seventh, son of Grand Duke Orginus Dreadhawk the sixth. Then came Margravine Feyless Dargon, each in turn requested the permission of the King to sit and was aided in doing so by their attendant servant, always the most beautiful and youthful one employed by their house. It was a sort of competition among the city's elite, seeing who had procured the most beautiful servants. The King granted their requests as it was a formality. They were at his table because they were invited to be months in advance. The herald proceeded to announce the common nobility that had managed to win a seat at his table. This went on for quite a few minutes so that the king contemplated the political consequences of sitting at a shorter table next year as he nodded and waved permission to each individual to sit. Finally, when only three remained the herald pronounced, "Honored guests of Margravine, Feyless Dargon of the Sixth Noble house, Jynx."

"Uh... may I, um, thank you, please." Jynx said confusing himself more with every rambling word that fell out of his mouth. His face turned red and the King stared at him blankly. Murmuring began in hushed tones.

This young man looked familiar to the King but he could not place where. Then it dawned on him. He shot a glance at Lady Dargon who wore an exaggerated, guilty look on her face. The princess who was ahead of her father in ascertaining what was going on let out a laugh, covering it with her hand. Jynx thought the princess laughed at him and he could hear the murmuring from the gentry. He was more embarrassed than ever in his life. Just when he thought he could not take it anymore he felt Whispers hand upon his. She gave his hand a squeeze, to let him know that he had a friend and that she seen what he was going through. The red in his face went away. As she gripped his hand his embarrassment diminished.

The King noticed the anguish he was putting him through. "Have a seat young man," King Eratide said. "You are welcome at my table and so are your companions. They may take a seat as well." The three sat closer to the king then most of the nobility. As guests of the Margravine, Jynx had only her and the royal chamberlain between him and the King to his left.

The meal and the entertainment was the best the three ever had. Waiters served them six courses beginning with roast pig, then pickled beef, a variety of breads, vegetable stews, and fish from the river, quail, potato soup and a host of bakery delicacies. They experimented freely with rare spices such as pepper. They tried many different types of liquors, from a rum known as Illusion to a sweet red wine called Dark Dog, along with expensive Elvin mead given as a gift by the nobles of Greenside. The rogues ate and drank in silence.

Their mouths were perpetually filled with some exquisite victual or choice vintage. In between bites they gave hearty laughs at the jesters, jugglers, and mimes. Bards performed and a rogue demonstrated sleight of hand unaided by magic, even Enigma was impressed.

The upper caste carried on about trivial nonsense. Jynx was surprised. He had imagined that the rich always discussed politics and the business of the state. To his surprise, they gossiped about each other more than anything else and kept up whatever facade they had built for themselves. Occasionally they would ridicule the lazy inferior masses. Jynx overheard this and thought it to be a great hypocrisy. Highborn men and woman spent inordinate amounts of time sculpting their hair and receiving manicures not even laboring to provide their own seat. Some even had their own cup bearer, a boy or girl whose only function was to stand ready for their master with a cup full of their favorite spirit, and others could not be bothered to wipe their own mouths. When Jynx first noticed, a noble having the side of his mouth wiped by a servant, he held his breath. He could not, however fight the image in his mind of an infant being so cared for by its mother. He quickly turned his attention to the entertainment, to mask the cause of his ensuing burst of laughter. His timing was not good and he laughed hysterically at just the moment everyone else's laughter had stopped.

The princess was not an aggressive socialite. She politely spoke when spoken to, but otherwise was not very engaging. Jynx was shoveling a piece of bread with stew dripping off of it, into his mouth, when he glanced over at the princess, catching her staring at him. She smiled, this time it was her that was embarrassed so that she quickly looked away. The King noticed. "So tell us about yourselves. Jynx is it? Odd name," The king said.

"Not much to say, this is my friend Enigma and next to me is his twin sister Whisper. All three of us hail from Slumside." The other guests at the table exchanged looks of haughty disbelief at the mention of the city's most chaotic district, and a sigh could be heard down the table as the news traveled.

"That's good." King Eratide said. "Last time I checked, I was king over Slumside." The king made an effort to silence the prejudice of the snobbish gentry dining with them. "What do you do for a living?"

Jynx thought for a moment. "Well I clean homes and businesses. My friend Enigma is a locksmith, but we are both freelance, so sometimes we help each other.

"I see" the King said, "And what of your woman?"

"Oh, Whisper? She mostly cooks for us and tends to our apartment. Ouch" Whisper kicked his leg under the table and then quickly smiled at the king.

"Are you ok?" the king asked.

"No, I mean yes, just burnt my lip. This is excellent stew."

A young man in an expensive black cloak, with silver eyes approached the king and spoke discreetly into his ear, secretly passing him something. The king whispered back to him. Enigma strained to hear what they said, as he stole the gold-plated spoon that he had eaten with. The cloaked man looked over at Enigma, with eyes like silver coins, catching him in the theft. Then he turned and left without a word, leaving Enigma unsettled.

The festivities of the day of Merriment started to wind down, thousands gathered around the pavilion in the center of the city. The King walked up the steps of the stone edifice. The rogues at his table had a backstage view as he looked to the masses with his back to the pavilion. The King peered into the large Black Opal, energy crackled on its surface, with blue fire in its heart as the light broke up within it. Thousands looked on with eager anticipation. He always saw nothing. The opal never granted more than one vision per human life. Unbeknownst to the population, the king was not exempt from this rule. Thus, the night before, he had fabricated a vision to share with his people. It was a long-standing family secret and tradition, both of which there were many. He had received his vision from the Opal as a young man. It made known to him how to win the heart of the woman he loved, the one who became his queen. The opal alone decided what to reveal and when. It could be of the past, or of the future. You could look into it every day and never see anything. It could show you a vision after many attempts, or just one, but never did it give more than one, never...before this day.

The image forming around the king distressed him. He felt as though he was physically in the opal, watching a scene play out before him but powerless to intervene. He glimpsed the future and did not like what he saw. *How can this be?* He thought to

70

himself. *Please, let it not be true, I want this to stop*, "Noooo!" He was back in the pavilion. Only a second had passed and he had screamed before all the spectators who were waiting in eagerness for his revelation.

He was dumbfounded as he looked around, thousands staring intently at him, surprise and anticipation worn on their faces. "Uh...I was just joking people." He faked a laugh, trying to cover up his mistaken outburst and push the images out of his mind in earnest. He imagined that his brother was burying his face in his hands while shaking his head. "Wow," He paused. "A very interesting year lies before us." He could not remember the lie he had prepared and was definitely not sharing what he had just seen with the public. "There will be plenty of food and even some intrigue among the nobles..." He struggled with what to say. Then a thought came from earlier. "No more liquor tax!" He declared for the masses. "The Black Opal showed me we should do away with the liquor tax, an unfair burden for patron and barkeep alike." The gathered citizenry began to cheer. He looked around. With the back of his hand, he wiped perspiration from his forehead.

The king stepped down from the pavilion, guards following, and joined his brother the Chamberlain.

They walked toward the long tables stretched out on the grass near the pavilion. "No liquor tax eh? I had no idea you were going to have such an extreme vision." The king's brother said sarcastically. "Do you have any idea how much lost revenue this will mean, or the amount of papers I will need to have drawn up? Not to mention all the new taverns that will open up, and the drunkards that will be…"

"Ok! I get it." The king interjected. "I forgot my script and the liquor thing just came to me. That damn boy from earlier, that damn Jynx, what a fitting name for him."

The chamberlain sighed as they approached the royal table and retook their places.

"Couldn't you have had a construction idea just come to you." Viscus said as they were seated.

Chapter 10 - Princess

Princess Corrine looked up, visualizing the words before she spoke. "The Black Opal was infused with magic by a forgotten power in a time long past. Some say it was Crotear, others say it was the One Above the Watchers that did it, but then much is attributed to the True God because of broken history. Some say the two are one and the same. All that is known is that it was one of the great gems used as a source of magic for the ancient City of Man, before its cataclysm. The orb rests in its place at the center of our city sustaining the veil that keeps Blakoepal and her people hidden from the world. Orthe is fraught with peril, its top a frozen darkness, its bottom a burning wasteland. Below the darkness is the ring of Fall, above the burning wasteland is the ring of Summer. The equator hosts every season in its turn. Dragons and the children of the Watchers roam all the great lands of Orthe including Sophia, where Blakoepal, our beloved home is hidden. The Black Opal must never be removed lest all we hold near to our hearts be exposed to the hateful inhabitants of Orthe." The Princess winced at the thought. She had recited those words many times to her tutor throughout the years.

Princess Corrine looked over to her tutor and reflected upon how the old maid had taught her mother as well guiding her as a young noble and watching her flourish as an admired Queen, until her majesty left the city, that is to say she died.

Princess Corrine found comfort in her teacher

being the one who had instructed her mother. Ruth was like a grandmother to her. Warm, with raven black hair, a loving smile and well-earned wrinkles that alluded to untold wisdom. She was capable of displaying both deliberate coldness and calming kindness. She did not give her correction lightly, nor did one receive it lightly. Her advice was a charity of truth and insight. Corrine looked forward to these lessons on the east balcony, which provided her favorite view.

"Now state the oath of the royal house, Amorgoden," bid the aged instructor.

Corrine walked across the wide terrace that hung out from the palace. Crossing her arms against her chest, she leaned on the banister, resting against the edge. She took a moment to appreciate the scene stretched before her, the autumn colored orchard below and Cranberry Road lying quietly some distance away. "The Amorgoden house is sworn to protect the city state of Blakoepal. Its laws are our laws, its people are our people and the Black Opal is our charge. The blood of the crown, the Council of the Twelve Noble Houses and our people are to be preserved and defended at all costs, for without, there is no crown."

The princess paused as she searched for the correct wording. "I am Amorgoden. I shall judge fairly, without partiality to moralistic perceptions when interpreting the law or interceding between nobles. I shall wage war against Blakoepal's enemies within and if necessary, even beyond her mists. I shall show kindness and favor to those who sow peace."

"Dear child, you will make as fine a Queen as

your mother did." Ruth declared as her highness watched a flock of sparrows' glide below her sixth story height. Corrine smiled. Her heart would skip a beat whenever Ruth compared her to her mother. At first, she would smile but then she would quietly despair. She was remembering being on this very balcony with her mom when she was little, it had been her mother's favorite place, first. Corrine's attention diverted toward the inner room at the arrival of a guest. Royal High Chamberlain Viscus Amorgoden passed through the sheer drapery that served as barrier between the inner room and the balcony.

Her uncle the chamberlain, was the king's top adviser and closest confident. He ran his fingers down his long, dark goatee bringing the hair to a point. Adorned in stately robes of red with the golden Amorgoden dragon embroidered on the garment, the Chamberlain-prince was a stately man. Corrine's bodyguard, Alturek, escorted the Royal High Chamberlain onto the balcony. Corrine smiled as she thought about how different they were. Alturek wore leather armor, stained black and overlaid with steel studs. He was a rough but handsome man with dark hair and eyes. A thick scar ran from his left temple to the high part of his cheek and lent to his dangerous look. He was quite the contrast of the regal Chamberlain. Alturek carried an enchanted crossbow and a longsword. Chamberlain Viscus had no need of such armaments, relying instead on an arsenal of deadly spells.

The young princess considered the oddity of such an intrusion as the two approached a respectful distance. Never in her seventeen circles had one of her lessons been interrupted by her uncle the chamberlain. He bowed deeply as was the custom when greeting one of higher station. As he slid back into an upright posture, he spoke sorrowfully to her. "It is with great dispiritedness that I must inform her highness, that his majesty the king has fallen gravely ill."

Ruth barley managed a gasp when Corrine startled them by breaking between the two men, racing through the drapery into the inner room and up to the door. She slammed it open as she moved through, flying past all manner of rooms and people, directly toward her father's bedchamber. Alturek took off instinctively behind her. She could vaguely make out the clang of servants dropping held objects as she took them by surprise and they frantically sought to bow. She seemed to move within an enveloping wind of fearful anguish, the hall and the people she passed, all a shiny blur. She approached the double doors to the king's room without a thought to the speed at which she moved. Stationed outside his door were heavily armored sentries. Surprised by her flight they hurriedly moved out of her way, some falling clumsily into others. Her thoughts were racing. Everyone becomes ill at times but it never before was cause to interrupt her lessons and it certainly never required her uncle to decree it unto her.

The princess threw open the doors. There laid the king in his bed appearing pale, heavy and still. She fell at his side clutching his hand, the skin seemed loose and hung off him. How could she be too late? Bemoaning his death, she cried fervently.

She wanted to scream, *Not you to!* and *Watchers be damned!* but she could emit only the smallest shriek from her throat, though her mouth was open wide enough to roar.

A thin man stepped out of the corner from the far side of the room. Of average height, he was neither frail nor large. Light brown hair dangled precariously above the intense silver eyes that peered out of his boyish face. His garb consisted of a soft, black cloak that hung open revealing dark trousers and a black sleeveless vest in accordance with the current style of a young mage. A silver medallion embellished his neck. Agon was seven circles the Princess's elder and favorite of her cousins. He positioned himself across the bed from her, noting Alturek's arrival with a nod. "Do not mourn dear cousin, as of yet he is merely sleeping."

She looked up at him, sobbing. Her face was awash in sadness. Sparkling blue eyes filled to the brim with tears. She turned away, burying her face in the bed. Agon approached quietly behind her and stretched forth his hand, placing it on her shoulder. The kneeling heir found some small comfort in Agon's presence, she reached out for her father's hand and squeezed it with all she had, then cried that he had not awoken. She was grateful that Agon was there, anyone else would have been too afraid to touch the royal princess.

Chapter 11 - Deal

The Restful Chalice was the only establishment of any quality in the little village of Willowview. Downstairs in the modest taproom, there were never anymore then forty patrons. Two stories of rooms to rent and a basement pantry made this building the second largest in town, second only to Lexore mansion.

In the Chalice's most comfortable suite, on the second floor, Judian Vandersen and his wife Sema said goodnight to their daughter, Kalexis. They came to this town to do business with the local lord, Drusus Lexore. Judian owned a textiles company and had made himself a name with his choice line of vintage clothing. Tonight he was to meet with Drusus, who had sent word he wished to purchase the company for a generous amount of metals and jewels.

Judian's wife retreated to the front room leaving the merchant alone with his daughter as she slept. How fast she had grown, he thought to himself, she was nearly a woman. Though he lamented the nearing of the day that she would be another man's responsibility, he could not help feeling proud of how beautifully she had grown in both intelligence and compassion. He appreciated moments such as these more than ever before, unsure how much longer she would be his little girl. Judian bent over and kissed his daughter gently on her forehead. She stirred, briefly smiling in her sleep. Judian felt weepy but managed to hold back all but one of the tears. The one that made it through he wiped away with his finger, smiled at his sleeping treasure and then turned to join his wife in the den.

The merchant opened a bottle of Sambrien wine, pouring a modest glass for his wife and a less modest one for himself. There was a soft couch, with a short table in front of it and two comfortable chairs on the other side, all of it arranged on a red rug. Across the room was a window looking out into the forest and a small table with a single wooden chair in front of it. The small table by the window had a quill, inkwell and some papers resting on it. Judian thought about how he used to give the full glass to his wife, seeking to ease her nerves, hoping she might lavish him with sensual affection. He had long ago abandoned such nonsense and now gave himself the fuller glass to cope with his wife's rejection of him. He looked over at her and she gave him her ever rare smile. Rare only for him that was. For all that visited his shop adored her and her false smile. There was a time that he would have believed the promise of her smile but now it just caused him to picture in his mind one of their brief sexual encounters of which there weren't too many. He would have to ask, she always made him ask, then she would pull her dress up and bend over. If he took too long she would scold him. In and out in awkward silence, then he would retrieve his pants as she left the room, taking a piece of his soul with her when she went. Judian shook his head in disgust, it had been a while since he had resorted to that. There was much more dignity in employing a whore, he thought as he took a long drink.

Judian had built his business, from his mother's humble seamstress shop, selling and trading tailored goods. He became successful while still young and married the girl he always adored. Twelve years ago, at the age of twenty-three, his wife gave birth to their only child. After the birth of Kalexis, Sema grew distant from him. He responded by throwing himself into his daughter and his business.

On the second floor of the Chalice, a woman made her way down the hall to the window at its end. She unlatched and opened it. Night had just arrived, stars blanketed the sky and Lumina glowed brightly with soft light. The candles in the hallway flickered as something moved quickly through the window. The woman saw the flapping silhouette of a bat, casting its shadow on the wall. When she turned to see it, the bat flew up to her face and shrieked. She was unafraid and watched as it transformed into a man, nose to nose with her. She wore a busty dress of exquisite couture that matched her master's black and yellow garb in a style that fell out of favor centuries ago. "Lord Drusus," she curtsied playfully. He issued a sly smile then straightened his Vandersen suit. "You look as dead as ever," She said, looking him up and down before giving him an ice-cold kiss upon his cheek.

Drusus knocked on the door to Judian Vandersen's room. The merchant opened it, inviting the man and his female companion inside.

They were greeted by the merchant's wife as they entered. "You may sit where you prefer, as I am certain you are already familiar with the accommodations of this establishment." Sema said, giving them a convincing smile and motioning toward the furniture. Drusus and Ashenath made themselves at home sitting on the cushy sofa. Ashenath crossed her legs and leaned on her escort with her hands gripping his arm. Sema and Judian both found seats in the comfortable chairs across from them. They exchanged pleasantries and engaged in small talk.

After socializing, and laughing a bit with dry humor, Judian abruptly moved the conversation, straight to the point. "I have decided that I will not sell my business to you or to anyone for that matter. It represents my life's achievement and I wish for my daughter to inherit it."

Drusus grinned, "Well I figured you would probably try to screw with me, Mr. Vandersen, sir." Ashenath giggled as she watched the wife's reaction to Lord Lexore's surprising rudeness. Sema sat back, mouth agape, unaccustomed to such a deliberate and insulting assertion. She looked over at Ashenath, who just shrugged with an inappropriate smile.

"I am sorry you feel that way, Lord Drusus. It is just... I built this business with my own hands."

"No worry sir. My foresight holds no value."

"I'm sorry?" Judian asked, most perplexed.

"You see, I never intended to purchase it from you," Drusus answered, furthering the man's confusion.

"Then what is the meaning of bringing me here and what of this meeting?" Judian raised his voice and stood up. "Sema, go and fetch Rondo!" Sema stood fast, poised to go get their bodyguard from downstairs.

"Wait, Sema." Drusus ordered the man's wife.

She turned to look at him, making eye contact. She tried to resist him, but Drusus mastered her will, as he stared into her eyes. Judian was dizzy with confusion. "Sema go, I told you to go!"

"Come to me Sema," Drusus commanded.

Sema licked her lips, this was the kinda man she had always wanted. The tips of her breasts hardened, she took a step forward, she could see herself in his arms. It was as if their souls were connected, she could sense his will, and she would obey whatever he demanded of her. To Judian's disbelief she walked over to Drusus, embracing the lord, and kissing his neck. Drusus looked up at Judian revealing long pointed fangs. Terror reached into the merchant and caused him to fall backwards into his chair nearly fainting.

"No! The business is yours, you can have it, please don't hurt my family!" The merchant cried desperately, pleading with the vampire.

Ashenath reached under the bed, retrieving a chest she had stashed there prior to the Vandersen's renting the room. Pulling a small key from her bosom, she unlocked it and tossed the key aside. The chest contained only a noose and a pair of manacles, which she removed then approached the weeping man.

Ashenath looked him in the eye, asserting sharp fangs and then stepped onto the chair with cold-blooded indifference. She stepped up onto the chair the merchant sat in, as he continued to beg for his family's life. He watched painfully as his wife and Drusus exchanged kisses and caresses. The master vampire reveled in mentally and emotionally, torturing the merchant. Ashenath fastened the noose to a metal ring attached to the ceiling. Normally a lantern, affixed to a short chain, hung there to give light to the whole room but she had taken it down days earlier and placed it in one of the suite's armoires. She grabbed the merchant's arms and started lifting him up, he could feel how much stronger she was. "You are going to die," She spoke directly to his hopelessness. "You can save your wife by doing as you are commanded." She wrapped the noose around his neck, and tightened it. He did not resist. Helplessness paralyzed him. Judian began to accept his life as being over and held onto a spark of hope that they would not kill his wife or discover his daughter.

Drusus laid Sema onto the couch then produced a parchment scroll. He unrolled it and walked to the table by the windows. He picked up the quill, dipped it in the ink then brought it over to the condemned man. "Sign away your life's accomplishment at the X." Drusus ordered.

Judian did as commanded.

"It is a pleasure doing business with you, sir." Lord Drusus said before bringing his attention back to the wife.

Ashenath imprisoned the merchant's hands behind his back with the manacles and then turned to her master. "May I feed on the daughter now, master?" She asked.

"Of course, just make sure you leave enough blood for her to bleed to death," He answered her, looking up at the pitiful man.

Ashenath went to the daughter's room.

"She said you wouldn't harm my family! Please, please do not hurt them! Stop it, stop it, stop it!" He cried to the point of convulsion.

"A woman's word is worthy, only of a fools trust." Drusus said mockingly before ravishing the merchant's wife in front of him. He let her out of the trance and covered her mouth as he moved up and down entering and leaving her harder and harder so that she cried and moaned as Judian listened to her muffled screams. Judian, could bear no more. He gave up completely and kicked the chair out from underneath himself, strangling to death while he listened to the screams of his wife, as she die.

Ashenath returned to her master. She licked the girl's blood from her lips and waited for him to finish feeding on the wife. When he was done, he stood and looked at her, favorite amongst his corruptions. Ecstasy was in his eyes; his mouth was full of blood. He moaned from the pleasure of feeding, warmth covering his body.

"You got him to kill himself, master." Ashenath said to Lord Drusus. He kissed her on the mouth, letting blood run from his mouth into hers, sharing his last drink of the woman's life force with her. She made a pleasurable noise as she drank the blood from his mouth and licked it from his chin.

"It looks natural," She said looking at Judian's hanging body, wiping her face with a clean portion of the wife's torn garment.

"No." Drusus corrected. "It is natural."

He pulled a knife and its sheath from his belt. He tied the sheath around the dead man's leg, under his breeches. Then, holding the knife, he walked over to his female victim. With it, he stabbed her in the neck and chest. Wherever there were bite marks, he covered them with stab wounds.

Ashenath removed the man's manacles and wiped blood on his hands and shirt. She restored the manacles to the chest and walked over to the window, opened it, then dropped the chest down. Drusus handed her the knife. "Do the same to your dinner, then go back downstairs." He left the room, transforming into a bat as he flew out the window. Ashenath went into the daughter's room and set upon her with the knife. She dropped the knife by the body of the daughter then proceeded out of the suite.

She paused to adjust her dress making it snug around the curves of her attractive figure. Her walk echoed her attitude as she approached the hall window. She stared outside then closed her eyes. The wind blew gently in short gusts. For a moment, she missed the sensitivity her skin possessed when she was living. The thoughts of the vampiress shifted to her master. Ashenath smiled devilishly then placed a kiss on her fingertips and blew it to the wind. She closed the window and made her way downstairs.

Chapter 12 - Confront

Under Ashenath's management, the quality of The Chalice had steadily improved. Her father was the actual proprietor, but it had been many circles since anyone seen or heard from him. She held a particular hatred for her dad and kept him at home, drained of almost all his blood. She was careful not to kill him, although she would inherit The Chalice if she did. The point was moot since she ran the place and took all of its profit for herself. When she became angry, she found solace in torturing him and left him alive solely for the purpose of dragging out his death. The village folk believed him to be indefinitely afflicted and were ignorantly correct.

Ashenath stood on the landing of the stairs overlooking the taproom of The Chalice, examining the makeup of the room. Two of her wenches were working the tables. The third, she assumed was in one of the rooms with a guest, giving him a good reason to return to Willowview. Her barmaids served her, with the promise of one day receiving the dark blessing of undeath. Their charge was to compel rich new arrivals to return, preferably in larger wealthier company. The girls would feign genuine interest in their patrons, lavishing great affection on those few, well-to-do visitors, that passed through Willowview. Judian had been one such visitor, a season earlier.

A bell chimed at the front of door of the establishment and Ashenath noticed as a lone maiden entered her father's tavern, wearing a black cloak with a hood covering her head. She wore a long bow and a full quiver on her back. The damsel scanned the room, and paused intently on the vampiress watching her. The stranger smiled warmly as she pushed her hood back revealing impossible beauty. She shook her golden hair out then looked back up at Ashenath. She ran her fingers through her hair, situating it, now that it was free from the confines of her hood. Renewing her warm expression, she turned away and sought a seat at the bar. Ashenath was excited as she descended the stairs. Drusus would be quite pleased with a gift such as the maiden would make. The vampire's thoughts stopped her suddenly on the steps. What would happen if he chose to share his immortality with this stranger or even worse, what if he came to favor her? Ashenath had never seen such beauty and Drusus's callous heart was fickle. Still he always brought his favor home to her, so far anyways.

"I'll, take care of her." Ashenath said, dismissing her barmaid as she approached the woman from the business side of the bar.

"Yes mistress," the youngest of the barmaids bowed and then left to go wait on a table full of locals.

"May I help you?" Ashenath asked of the woman in her kindest voice, catching the gaze of her soft violet eyes.

"I wish to see your master," The beauty answered, her voice very light.

At first Ashenath was startled. Then gazing at her features, she relaxed. "I am the master of this establishment. May I serve you something to drink?"

"Yes, you may. I'll have some blood please."

The maiden answered her and looked up at her quite harmlessly.

Ashenath nearly came unhinged. Then she realized the lady must be speaking of Berry Blood, a wine of high quality she rarely served. It was not a popular request due to its cost but she did have a few bottles of the spirit. She relaxed again. The negative energy that allowed her to move in spite of her death quieted in her nerves. "Berry Blood, of course. Yes, I will be happy to serve you some." Ashenath retrieved a bottle and a tall thin glass a little way down the bar. She uncorked it and poured the wine in front of the stranger, setting the bottle next to her glass.

"There you are. How else may I serve you?" The tavern's mistress asked.

"Allow me to clarify something miss." The woman spoke with a warm tone. "Pay attention to my words. I always mean exactly what I say and I don't much care to repeat myself. I said blood, not wine. I said your master, meaning Drusus." Ashenath's eyes narrowed as she listened in disbelief. "I am usually patient and I would love to play tiger and mouse with you but I consider this matter urgent. Now go get Drusus before I rip your fangs out and ask someone else where he is."

Ashenath was shocked. She considered attacking the woman right there, but knew she should not. "I will see if he is interested, though I doubt he will forgive you your boldness. I definitely will not."

"I am not interested in his playthings threats. Now be a good slave and do as I told you. Tell him I bring a gift." Ashenath was insulted to the near

88

breaking point, her dinner rushed to her face, making her pale skin blotchy.

"Who are you?" The vampire asked.

"Your greatest fear, if you do not as I command." The stranger said in her sweet voice, smiling once again, this time showing her own fangs. "Tell him, I am his Angel." She kept eye contact with the vampire, savoring the confused hatred boiling to the brim within her. "Tell him my name is Imarra and I carry the old mage Garthadon with me." She retrieved an urn from her cloak and set it on the bar. "Tell him, I am an envoy."

"An envoy, from where?" Ashenath asked.

"From Hel."

Chapter 13 - Curse

When they had discovered Adriel dead and their leader Garthadon missing, they both believed they knew what had happened and consequently they knew what had to be done. The master vampire must have struck first, killing Adriel when he seen that the group had divided. They must have destroyed the angel and carried Garthadon off, surely, he was dead or even undead by now, they hoped for the former. How long had the master vampire been watching them they wondered? Poor old mage put too much faith in that angel he summoned. "Summoned creatures," Garthadon had told them, "leave no remains when they are vanquished."

Now Mandathar and Elanor were three, days ride from Willowview. They took a noon break to give their horses a much-needed rest after pushing double-time from Echo. The horses napped while Elanor and Mandathar ate some of their meager rations they bought in Echo. "Do you hear that Mandathar?" Elanor stood, "It sounds like horsemen are approaching from around the curve up ahead."

"How many, can you tell?" The priest asked taking a large bite of his cured beef.

"It's hard to say. Less than twenty I'm sure." Onyx was on her feet with her ears sticking straight up and began sniffing the air.

"Well," Mandathar said as he rose to his feet, still chewing. "I suppose we should get ready for battle."

The riders came to a halt. Eleven armed

horsemen positioned themselves in a defensive posture around a small-framed central rider and a young boy. The central rider wore an expensive red and gold cloak with a deep hood. It was too large for the person who wore it. Possibly another child Mandathar thought. Two of the horsemen rode up to Mandathar and Elanor. As they approached both groups recognized each other. "Rondo!" Mandathar exclaimed. "How in the heavens are you? Where is your charge?"

Rondo and his subordinate stopped a few feet from them and dismounted. "Hail." Rondo said. The two vampire hunters noted the somber look on his face as he waved the rest of his companions over. "We are in distress. It's a blessing, coming across you two again."

"Whatever is the problem friend? I would be happy to render any healing your company might need. Well, speak up."

"Perhaps it is best if I show you." Rondo motioned the cloaked rider over. "I must warn you that if you attack we will have to do battle."

Elanor placed her hands on her waist readying herself to draw her swords. Mandathar's concern increased. Rondo nodded at the cloaked rider, who pulled her hood back.

"Kalexis," Mandathar said in recognition, "Why would I attack you sweet child?"

Kalexis sat upon her horse. Downcast and straight faced she stared at the priest. Rondo grabbed the reins of her horse. "Show them," He commanded. Kalexis smiled awkwardly revealing two short fangs. Elanor drew her weapons with startling speed. Mandathar instinctively reached for his mace. All of the horsemen drew their crossbows or swords. Onyx growled, ready to pounce. The midday sun beat down upon them as they all stood as if frozen, ready for the slightest flinch.

"Wait!" Mandathar yelled, cutting through the tension. "The sun, Elanor, put away your weapons!"

"She is a vampire!" Elanor yelled.

"No she is not!" Mandathar yelled back throwing his mace to the ground. "She would be dust if she were Elanor! The sun is shining directly on her. She is not a vampire! Put away your damned swords and trust me, please.

Elanor sheathed her weapons with reluctance. "You better be right Mandathar." All of Rondo's company reciprocated the move putting away their weapons. Onyx sat down with a whiney and licked her chops.

"How did this come to be Kalexis?" The priest asked.

"She has not spoken since her parents were murdered." Rondo answered for her.

"Has she attempted to harm anyone?"

"No."

"What happened?"

Rondo addressed his men. "We will camp early. Get everything set up, starting with Miss Vandersen's tent." One of his men helped Kalexis dismount and escorted her away as the others began setting up camp alongside the narrow road. Rondo started to walk, speaking to Mandathar as he went. The two hunters fell into step with him. "We arrived in town for the Vandersen's meeting with Lord Lexore. Everything seemed fine. Lord Lexore was set to meet with Mr. Vandersen in his room at the local tavern there. We never saw Lord Lexore arrive though. After a while I went up to the Vandersen's room. I always check on them right before I retire for the night. When they didn't answer the door, I forced it open." Rondo stopped and stared for a moment still experiencing disbelief. "I found Mr. Vandersen hanging in the main room and Sema was lying on the bed with Kalexis holding on to her. It looked as though Mr. Vandersen had attempted to kill his family and then himself. Sema was stabbed to death and Kalexis had several stab marks on her neck as well. Mr. Vandersen's body held the knife's sheath. I know Mr. Vandersen well enough to know that he would never harm those girls for anything in the world. I figure that whoever wanted it to look like a murder and a suicide must have thought that Kalexis was dead. I draped a sheet over Mr. and Mrs. Vandersen and over Kalexis to. My men went to put them in one of the wagons but when we approached the wagons, Drusus Lexore and the town militia said we couldn't because they were now owned by Drusus. I was madder than hel but being that we were outnumbered by two to one we couldn't do anything about it. So we had to wait until the next day when the general store opened to buy a cart. The whole while, Kalexis was playing possum under a sheet next to her parents stinking corpses. The next morning, we bought a cart and put 'em on it. Then we got the hel out of there. As soon as we got a good distance from Willowview we gave the Mr. and Mrs. a proper burial. I would have taken them out of there that night but the wolves were howling and would have been attracted by the scent of the dead."

"What happened to the rest of your men?" Mandathar asked.

"Well, after we got some ways away some of the men started to notice that the girl was different. Her skin is pale but more polished. Her hair seems to shine. Her eyes are mesmerizing and the fangs... It was the fangs that got everyone. It started with one person. He called her a devil and tried to persuade the rest of us to kill her. He approached her carrying a knife. Before I could get to him she ripped out his throat with her bare hands then licked the blood from the flesh she held, bearing those fangs and all. I got to say it frightened me. Before I knew it over half the company was in mutiny. We had to battle them. What you see here are the ones that were left standing on both sides.

"That poor girl." Elanor felt remorse for her earlier hastiness. "If she is not a vampire then what is she Mandathar? She certainly has a lust for blood."

"A lust yess but not an overpowering one," Mandathar said. "She can control it. The undead have almost no control and kill to satiate themselves. Kalexis can live her life and get by eating red meat and drinking animal blood."

"So, she is alive then?" Elanor asked.

"Very much so. Garthadon once told me about how he encountered a very similar case. He referred to it as half-cursed."

"Half-cursed?" Rondo asked.

"Yes, half-cursed." Mandathar cleared his throat before continuing in his deep tone. "What I believe happened is that the vampires drank them almost dry, then covered the bite marks with knife wounds. Kalexis died. The vampire set up the scene as you described then left, probably out the window. A few moments later the charm I gave to that poor girl activated and resurrected her. Because she was slain by a vampire there was a chance that she would return as one. So when she was resurrected she came back to life but attained some of the attributes of the vampire."

"Grizzly shit," was all Elanor could manage.

"Vampires?" Rondo asked.

"Yes. We are hunters and slayers of the dead which refuse to die. We are actually on our way to kill the very vampire which has plagued you.

Rondo grimaced in anger. "If you knew of this vampire why didn't you warn us when we let you know of our destination?"

"Relax," Elanor said. "We didn't know. When we returned to Echo we discovered the remains of one of our companions. Our leader Garthadon, was missing and all of his personal effects were left behind. We went through his writings and determined that the master vampire resides in Willowview. That must be this Drusus you speak of."

"I am sorry. I just don't know what to do." Rondo said.

"Go back to Pathos," Mandathar told him. "Take care of the girl and keep her condition a secret. If Elanor or I live we will come back for her. Kalexis is very strong now. She will be disgusted with garlic. Her reflection will seem faded and may flicker. She will eat primarily bloody meats. In time she will learn to retract her fangs. She will age until she reaches the prime of her life, probably around twenty circles give or take. From then on, she will be ageless. She will not grow any older and she will only die if beheaded in direct sunlight or staked through the heart."

"Will she fear holy things?" Rondo asked. "No. If anything, her fascination for the divine will grow. Also, when she learns how, she will be able to charm you with only a glance, beware of this. Most importantly though Rondo, she still possesses free agency."

"What do you mean?"

"Good and evil is still her choice, the corruption did not transform her heart as it does with full vampires."

"Well that's a good thing, right?"

"Yes, but she could still choose evil."

96

Chapter 14 - Take

Ashenath lay awake in her coffin, frustrated as she traced her fingertips across her sleek nightgown. She wanted desperately to feel the material under her hand as she did when she was mortal. To her touch, it felt artificial, as all things now did. She could distinguish only the slightest differences with her dulled tactile sense. It was in this difference that she anguished. Sometimes she thought she felt the smooth fabric, but her wanting deceived her. Like all of her kind, she possessed a special form of vision. It allowed her sight to penetrate total darkness, though making use of this boon left color a mystery. The vampiress stared blankly, in black and white, at the designs engraved on the inside of her resting place. She laid there thinking, in reminiscence of the recent.

She could not sleep, not that she required it, but it made passing through the hunger of the daytime, bearable. The more blood she consumed during the night the better she would slumber during the day. The sleepless vampire lamented mentally her master's recent shift in affections. Ashenath never expected to be more than her master's favorite plaything. Yet, she had been his most exalted servant. The newcomer was definitely more beautiful than any she had ever seen. Even Ashenath admitted in her thoughts, the woman had a charmingly veiled, sadistic manner to her. This acknowledgement only increased her jealousy and improved her hatred accordingly, the stranger seemed human enough. She appeared to breathe and

Ashenath hoped, would bleed like any other human. If Drusus was so fond of her, he could just make her his slave, what stopped him? Why leave her among the living, if she is only some insanely bold, mortal woman. She must be a powerful cleric or wizard, Ashenath decided, either way her time would come.

Whatever her story the vampiress hated her. She knew nothing about her, except that she called herself by the name Imarra, which was probably not her real name. I should have killed her when she first entered The Chalice, Ashenath kept repeating in her mind, alongside fantasies of torturing the seductress. In Ashenath's eyes, the woman was trespassing in a cold, black heart that she had no place in. Her hatred for Imarra had been so great that she finished off her father, hoping that Drusus, who knew her most intimately, would see how upset she was and return her to his esteem. Instead he only cackled.

Ashenath in a fit ended her father's misery by increasing it. She destroyed him with a hundred old hooks, two inches of rusted metal each fastened with fishing line. She pierced the hooks through his body and face and fastened the fishing line to spools all over the walls, ceiling, and floor of his empty bloodstained bed chamber. She fastened hooks to his most sensitive skin. The dull metal pulled his flabby skin in all directions. When he leaned one way to relieve the resistance of some lines, it increased the tension of the others, ripping him viciously. He had muttered something at that point in his slaughter. The only word she had been able to make out was, "*daughter*."

"I am no man's daughter," she had responded

in anger. She grabbed a twelve-inch double bladed knife with a straight blade on one side, the other featuring a hook pointing back to the handle, perfect for gutting. She drove it halfway into his stomach. With vengeance in her smile, and a glare in her eye, she slowly pushed her instrument in further, moving it side-to-side, careful not to puncture his back, then slowly ripping it back out of his abdomen, bringing some of his insides with it. This caused the wretched man so much pain, that he could not help but squirm. The movement tore large portions of meat and skin from his face and body, dislodging many hooks. Yet from all of this he still had not died. She wrapped and bound the wound from the knife, afraid he would bleed to death too soon. She then repeated the process with the knife once more without haste, driving it deep enough that it tore slightly through his back. He squealed like a pig being slaughtered, shrieking with a shivering pitch.

Finally, he had fallen to the floor, so many hooks tearing free he was no longer recognizable as a man. His bowels released while he screamed as loudly as his torn throat could manage, trying desperately to drown out his pain with the noise. It did not work. Ashenath spit on her sire, driving the blade quickly through his side. She left it there. Denying herself even a drop of blood, she turned away from her patricide and exited the room.

When Ashenath came to tell Druses what she had done, he and Imarra were bathing in a wide tub in the basement of Lexore Mansion. The tub, ornately cut from the floor, occupied the center of a large room with many pillars. Marble covered the surface of everything in the room from the ceiling

99

down to the floor. Blood filled the tub nearly to the brim, leaving the couple's top quarter exposed and dripping with the dark red fluid. Their hair was wet and matted down. Young servile women infatuated with the master, poured blood over the two of them with small basins, rubbing it on their skin with their hands while the two mingled playfully together.

Bathing in blood was one of the vampire's favorite leisure activities. Submersion in water would destroy a vampire but submersion in blood was fine and devil forbid if someone came and blessed the blood it would not burn him like holy water, which was as fire to a vampire. Perhaps most importantly though, blood was a thick liquid and Drusus could actually feel it on his skin, it was soothing and gave him a feeling of ecstasy as he drank, bathed and enjoyed the company of his companion. While a vampire drank of the blood their ability to feel physical sensation would return, arousing their sexual desire and bringing to them euphoria.

Ashenath watched with depredation burning in her bosom and rage encroaching upon her reason. "I have been idle as of late and I finished off my father," she had said, expecting that Drusus would show at least temporary pause, since he knew on a personal level how mammoth an ordeal this was to her.

"Pity, a father is irreplaceable." was all he cared to say.

Imarra made it a point to let out a giggle, covering her mouth in mock shame, as if her laugh had been an accidental outburst. Druses contributed further to the humor by adding to it a tenor pitched

100

laugh. This kindled in Ashenath grinding hatred for her master. If she had a living heart, it would have been broken. She felt like crying uncontrollably but tears are for the living and she could not produce moisture enough to express her pain. Her heart had died with the rest of her and her tear ducts had dried up. Those sensations manifested themselves as malice and fury. However, she was his creature and could not act against him. Should the opportunity not to act present itself, she thought to herself, then that would be an entirely different matter. *Hel could not produce such fury as Ashenath, once scorned.*

She sensed daytime was ending. By now, her coffin, with her awake inside of it, was far toward the darkness. Imarra had made some sort of deal with Druses. He had told Ashenath that they must travel with Imarra to the hunting territory of a slain vampire once known as Obtuse the calm. He had been with Drusus since his very beginning. Obtuse had sired one whom he never knew, that grew to be an old mage named Garthadon, who would be the very one that destroyed him with the help of a rag-tag group of sob stories.

Ashenath was still in disbelief that Drusus was willing to trust Imarra in traveling this way. They had two wagons and a carriage, each driven by a hired hand. They had an escort of a dozen armed men. All were instructed not to look at the cargo in the two wagons, on pain of not receiving their lucrative commissions. Drusus felt that a man's greed was at least as reliable as a locked vault. If however, curiosity overwhelmed good judgment, Drusus had confidence that Imarra could defeat the entire company if necessary. Ashenath did not understand her master's faith in the woman.

The wagons had been still for hours when nightfall arrived. Ashenath opened her coffin the only way it would open, from the inside. She sat up and climbed out of it, shutting it forcefully. She could hear the sounds of their escorts dying outside. Drusus and Imarra had begun the massacre without her.

Some tried to fight, most tried to run, but it was useless. Imarra stood in her carriage next to its dead driver firing at the fleeing men with her mighty bow. Drusus endeavored to create as much suffering in as short a time possible. He lashed out with his fangs, tearing through their heads, arms, and neck, whatever portion was expedient, drinking a little blood here and there as he went.

Ashenath transformed into a wolf as she jumped from the back of her wagon, her gown tearing and barely hanging on to her. Most of the men were alive but immobile. Some had arrows protruding through their legs. Many were weak from loss of blood. She spotted a fresh one, and took off after him. The poor man ran strenuously to preserve his life. Weighed down a bit by his chain shirt and weapons, he provided no sport for the wolf. Ashenath could hear his heart beating dangerously hard. The blood would shoot down her throat. She loved fresh blood flavored with a terrified man's adrenaline. It was the salt of an already delicious meat.

She gave chase and tackled him easily. He turned over on his back in the dirt, pushing himself away desperately with his palms and heels. She snarled in his face with the largest fanged snout he had ever seen. She was larger than a normal wolf though not quite as large as a dire wolf. Then, before his terrified eyes, she transformed into her natural form. Her front paws became small hands, holding his shoulders. Her hind legs gave way to smooth bare thighs that straddled her trembling prey. Even her green eyes changed to a human fitting size, and shape. Fear mixed with confusion as he stared wide-eyed at his assailant. She was a creature of surpassing beauty coupled with unnatural strength and agility wearing only her torn silken nightwear; only barely covering her, and leaving much exposed. With a straight-lipped expression, she regarded her victim, as she was oft to do before she stole from them their next day.

Surprised by the sudden emergence of an arrow in her arm, Ashenath recoiled. It did not hurt but it did serve to anger her, not to mention distract her from breakfast. She stood straight, turning to look back at Imarra, bearing her fangs.

"I missed." Imarra called to her.

"These arrows are wooden, what if you had hit my heart?" Ashenath yelled, rage coursing through her empty veins.

"I missed." Imarra reiterated, notching another arrow. She aimed in the vampire's direction and then fired. The shaft whizzed past the vampiress, causing her to flinch as it dropped the man who again ran for his life. Imarra smiled at her then jumped down from the carriage to join Drusus as he fed.

"I hate her more than Hel hates angels." Ashenath said to herself as she ripped the arrow straight out of her arm, her skin closing over the wound. Now in the peak of her hunger, she set about finding survivors lying half-dead upon which to feed.

When breakfast was over, and their escorts were dead, the three of them ventured the final hour to their destination, driving the wagons and carriage themselves. They arrived at Small Fort tavern, which was more a fortified keep than anything else. Surrounded by a wall twenty feet high, with one gate, the place boasted a full stable and court. Several artisans and farmers from the surrounding thorpes and hamlets would set up booths in the court, during the day. Smallfort had three stories of rooms above a large taproom on the ground level and dining room on the second level. The place doubled as a bunker for the citizens in the regions tiny scattered communities. Two towers flanked the gate. Each of the walls four corners comprised of a tower, with one more in the center of the back wall. The towers were usually unmanned, except when the many dangerous humanoid tribes in the region swept through the area. Then the militia, made up of volunteers from the participating communities and homesteads would ban together and man the fort.

The lone watchman cried out, as the three murderous creatures approached. "Who goes there?"

"It is I Imarra," the devil answered in a broken tone. "I am a merchant's daughter from the direction of the fire. My father's caravan was attacked by orcs and wolves...he did not make it." Imarra began to sob, speaking in hollowed tones, strengthening her lie with a spring of sorrow buried deep within. "Only my fiancé and I survived and my poor sister who has been deaf and dumb since childhood. Please kind watchmen, spare us further travail and raise the portcullis." Drusus tried to suppress his laughter, while Ashenath mumbled obscenities.

"How many were the orcs dear maid? And how far away were you attacked?"

"There were about a dozen, sir, toward the fire, several miles. If you send a scout, he will surely discover the carnage." Imarra trembled, pretending to be fearful. Drusus put a comforting arm around her. They both acted the part of people shaken from a horrible experience of near death. Ashenath just followed along, seething. The man raised the portcullis letting them in with their vehicles and horses. The watchmen took notice of Ashenath still mumbling a plethora of colorful language.

"See what I mean." Imarra said to the night man as Drusus stabled the horses.

"Yes, I do." The watchmen said looking with pity at the vampiress before addressing her in a slow and choppy manner in case she could not understand normal speech. "If- their- is- anything- I- can- do- for you, just let me know."

When he started to stare at her, Imarra thanked him then directed him back to his job. The three monsters walked up the steps of the tavern and across the wide porch. Drusus opened the door for his companions, bowing and motioning them in. "This way ladies." Dedicated to the taproom inside were two levels of tables with two bars. The second of the two, the balcony level, was a dining area. You could look over the short railing down into the first level where the larger bar and an assortment of games resided. The ceiling was high with three more levels of rooms above. There was only one man working, a scrawny fellow, with bucked teeth and a receding hairline. "Hello, wow you sure do keep pretty company sir. What can I get for you?"

"You're biggest, most luxurious suite and the keys." Drusus commanded

"Yhu... yes sir. I think you'll will be like'n it here. My uncle owns the place, and he sure makes us work hard to keep our guests happy."

Those were the last of his ramblings before joining the living dead. When Drusus finished feeding on the man, he looked to his female companions. "There are three levels of rooms. I will take the first, Imarra the second and Ashes the third. " Lock a few up in the pantry and drain the rest into wine bottles. First though, help me clean the tap room." Drusus looked over at the few patrons and the servers that were making use of the taproom. All were staring over at the vampires. The three heralds of death lunged at those in the room, breaking their stare and causing a panic as the killing began.

Chapter 15 - Knight

Archduke Treant Cavalaries was considered noble in the finest sense of the word. When the occasional somewhat debauched idea began to surface in his mind, he quickly stifled it and set out to perform a good deed or penance. He was fond of showing kindness, he gave generously to the Temple of Crotear which sponsored charities to the poor, the feeble and the lonely. Be it coins, or benevolent doings, the Bishop of Crotear knew the Temple had a champion in Treant. He fought valiantly against the denizens of the under-city and stood with resolve in his opposition to the evil organizations that operated legally within Blakoepal. For all this, Treant could hold his head high, and he did.

Archduke Cavalaries, lord of the first noble house of the council, stood in his castle armory with arms outstretched, his shoulder length, blond hair tied in the back while the elder of his two pages helped him don his suit of glistening black platemail. "I feel great pity for her highness the princess," The knight spoke to his errant. "I know the grief she most certainly is feeling. I lost my parents and had the lordship of the first noble house thrust upon me while I was still a boy."

Coran locked the breastplate in place. "Milord I prey to Crotear for the king's swift recovery, a month is a long time for the king to slumber."

Stavid the House Steward appeared at the doorway. With exception for the latrines and the entrances to the castle, there were no closed doors in castle Cavalaries. It was Treant's reasoning that there were no secrets within his walls. That is not to say however that there was no privacy. A servant would stand in a doorway with their head respectfully bowed until acknowledged.

"Do come in and speak with freedom Stavid," Treant directed without granting more than a slight glance.

"My liege, the noble baroness and squire, Lady Ringheart awaits you in the front hall." Treant's squire was always ready and waiting for him an hour after sunrise. She loved him like a big brother or perhaps a young uncle. Baroness Avriel Ringheart, was overdue for initiation into the Black Knights of Opal some time ago. Her lordship had been procrastinating on submitting her to the commander of the Black Knights, Prince Orginus Dreadhawk. Sir Dreadhawk was Treant's superior in the brotherhood, yet Orginus was the son of the second lord of the council, Grand Duke Dreadhawk, which meant Treant was actually of higher rank in the whole of Oepalian society. The situation would have been disagreeable was it not that the two were friends of a sort with an amiable rivalry between them. The situation was quite a feat of history considering that centuries past Dreadhawk was first among the council and the Cavalaries' family once worshiped at the temple of Asmodeus. even now, a disinherited cousin of Treant's was a priest of status in Asmodeus's clergy.

"Today I shall grant Lady Ringheart, knighthood, with her holy vows being held as soon as the matter of his majesties health is decided. I will seek agreement from Prince Orginus after the

108

meeting of the council," Treant announced to his first page and his House Steward. Coran grinned approvingly having love and admiration for the virtuous dame, Lady Avriel. Occurring second and deepening his smile was the fact that he was the obvious choice for Treant's new squire.

Baroness Avriel stood in the hall near the main entrance, wearing the same style of polished black armor as her liege, surrounded by many armored manikins and banners. Emblazoned on the floor was the Cavalaries crest, a golden lance crossing a gold armored horse all inside of a Black Opal with the family creed below. *City, Crown and Family, To This End We Wage War, In This Order Will the Cavalaries Defend*. She did not suspect he was going to grant knighthood upon her and was not in any hurry. Being the Archduke's errant was a great honor that brought her contentment and served the debt she felt she owed him. Feeling at home she paced slightly by the entrance. The gallant lady was the only survivor of her house, formerly ninth on the council. When war was announced between the Ringhearts and the house of Bindingfire's she was handed over to the crown for protection. Such hostilities were permissible by the law if both warring families turn one of their children over to the royal palace to prevent the extinction of a noble line. As it was in her case, the youngest most often received this protection.

Avriel grew up in the palace learning and playing with the princess, who was five circles her younger and other protected nobles, most notably Caedis Bindingfire. That is, until his family was victorious over hers and all her relatives were dead.

Caedis went home. She had to stay. The Bindingfires took the twelfth seat on the council. They did not originally have a place and so Avriel did not inherit a position amongst those of the twelve. The Bindingfires were affiliated with White Thorn, a knightly order opposed and despised by the Black Knights of Opal for their allegiance to the temple of Asmodeus. Sworn to uphold the rule of the crown, they operated legally, much to the annoyance of the favored Black Knights.

So, it happened by chance, at the tournament of honor, that Treant had dueled the young Bindingfire's father and killed him ten feet from the Black Opal in Black Square in the center of the city. It being illegal to initiate war with a lower house, Treant demonstrated his disdain for the Bindingfire's by taking Avriel, who was already well acquainted with the sword, under his wing as squire. Sometime later, Caedis, who by then had a younger brother, took the mantle of Viscount and lord of the twelfth upon the day of his mother's suicide.

"Hail dear squire, today is a fated day," Treant greeted his errant.

Her red hair fell forward to veil her face, as she bowed courteously. "I observe this day not to be ill-fated, given the merriness of your approach Lord Knight." She responded while raising her head and meeting his expression with a smile of her own. "I have taken the liberty to order your page, Vektor, to ready our horses. We are to pick up your gift of condolence, from the jeweler in the Eastward.

Outside at his stable, Treant, along with Coran and Avriel found their horses tied to a tree, with no sign of Vektor. "Vektor where are you? Come forth boy!" Treant called out by the stable doors. His tolerance for the younger of his two pages was short, tested on a seemingly daily basis.

Vek woke up lying in the straw of the stable floor. He hurried outside to where his lord was beckoning. "I am here milord" Vektor exclaimed with childish panic as he ran then stopped quickly before his liege, almost falling forward. Treant looked the boy up and down, his head was bowed, straw intermingled with his hair, dirt was on his clothes and the unmistakable odor of horse emerged from him, meeting Treant's nose.

"Are you alright? Did you get into a fight with one of my chargers," Treant asked facetiously?

The boy looked up, guilt shown on his face. "I was wide awake milord, ready to fight the forces of Asmodeus when an enchantment fell upon me, I slumbered for only a moment,"

Lady Avriel turned to hide her amusement as Treant replaced his stupefied look with one of sternness. Treant's blue eyes locked with Vektor's "Have no fear Vektor, there is a cure for such enchantments as the one that overtook you."

"There is?" The boy of twelve circles asked uncertain he wanted to hear the answer.

"Indeed, there is," Treant affirmed with a menacing tone. "You should see about this remedy with haste."

"What is it, milord?" The young page dared to ask, now certain he did not want to know.

"Chores, you will assist my servants in the kitchen and do whatever tasks they can muster for you until I return tonight, late tonight. I am certain

111

they have some jobs too troublesome or disgusting that they have been putting off in anticipation of your next reprimand." Treant issued the punishment then dismissed the delinquent page with a wave. Vektor ran off with tears in his eyes but he wiped them away before reporting to the kitchen.

The Knight, his squire and his first page mounted their horses and left, leaving Vektor's steed tied to the tree. They traveled on horseback past the mansions and the forts of other prominent nobles all the way through Nobleside to Eastward. A wall and large tower manned by the Crown Swords, Oepal's Army, guarded the passage between these two sectors. The trip through Eastward, an area peopled by the city's average peasantry and shopkeepers, went mostly uneventful. A group of children in the street waved to them, a retired soldier of the Crown Swords saluted and Asmodian artisans and peasants stared scornfully at them as they made their way to the jeweler. Overall, they had a pleasant journey.

Treant and his company arrived at the jewelers. It was a storefront on the first level, a home on the second and an apartment on the third. On the third level a barbaric man from Slumside resided who protected the shop in place of paying rent. A sign in the window read- OPEN, a word even the illiterate of the Oepal could read. They entered through the front door sounding a little bell connected by a string to the door, leaving Coran outside with the horses.

Inside were modest furnishings, a comfortable couch, a faded red and green rug and a door on the wall opposite the entrance. A long glass case served as a counter top in addition to housing beautiful and expensive adornments. The case was kept secure with an exceptional lock that was, undoubtedly imbued with magic. Next to the case stood a hulking monster of a man, six feet, six inches tall and probably almost three hundred and fifty stone of massive muscle. A great sword hung sheathed over his back. Lengthy brown hair covered many scars and imperfections.

The shopkeeper, an older woman with slightly cuspidate ears, giving away her partial elven heritage, walked through the inner door. She had copper colored hair, with dull green eyes. The dullness and her thin but not extremely so, frame, testified to her human parentage. In her hand was a gold trimmed box made of cherry wood. She opened it showing its contents to Lord Cavalaries. The box was inlaid with purple velvet. He pulled the jewelry out. A wide and elegant gold bracelet with white rose blooms living in the metal. They were enspelled not to wither and if plucked would immediately grow back. The fragrance of the roses would not perish and the bracelet granted protection from evil on the wearer. If the wearer held hands with one she loved the roses would change to yellow or red depending on if she loved them as a friend or as more.

Treant handed the craftswoman a small bag, inside of which was a valuable tip. He had paid for the enchanted jewelry already upon having it commissioned. He thanked her politely while placing the box in a sack and handing it to his lady squire. He bid the jeweler farewell and the knightly pair took their leave.

They rode their mounts through the Eastward at a relaxed pace, side by side. The trio turned the corner on to Coin Street, a road flanked mostly by residence. The area was inactive. Most people were at their shops or plowing fields within the Ulterior Farms. The princess was due to speak before the council shortly. Treant was looking forward to seeing her and offering his gift as well as his obedience. He was certain that his gift was the most thoughtful and the most expensive.

None of them had a worry in the world, until a large stray dog emerged out of an alley charging toward them. Treant pulled his horse's reins bringing it to its rear legs, trying to avoid trampling the poor mutt. The sounds of galloping and screams brought confusion as Treant's horse returned to all fours crushing the canine's ribs and twisting his warhorse's leg. He skillfully guided his horse's fall, allowing him to remain standing. Then he turned to his left to see a mounted knight with glistening steel armor wearing a close faced helm with a white plume atop, barreling into him with a lance. Archduke Cavalaries fell prone his chest horribly wounded and the wind knocked out of him. He hurried back to his feet, struggling to draw his sword and accessing the situation while he strained to cope with his pain. The white knight was turning around to make another pass, joined in this assault by two of the same order, the Black Knight's hated foe, White Thorn.

Avriel chased one of the three rival equestrians into the dog's alley. She raced after him through the tight path with only half a foot of clearance on either side. She followed as the rider before her passed an intersecting alley. Then she heard a clanging sound, felt her steed charging forward without her and a sensation as if she were floating for a moment before she hit the ground hard on her back. She never saw the chain that dropped in her path. Her head pounded and her nose bled as she lay there drawing her sword and grasping for her wind.

Coran was losing a mounted melee trying desperately to hit his enemy with his long sword. The murderous villain raised his single black gauntlet, the only contrast to his white décor. Swinging down with the morningstar held in his black clad hand, he knocked Coran's sword to the ground. Coran raised his hands in desperate guard, yelling fearfully as the morningstar crashed through his raised arms striking his head, and joining the sounds of combat with the shattering of a boy's bones.

Treant stood in defensive posture while the white knight galloped full speed, and directly at him. The black duke moved his body in such a way as to avoid the attack and then thrust with his long sword, piercing the aggressor's leg and wounding the white adorned horse. A feint light of silver-white from the sword burned the man. The white knight's stallion kicked its front hooves up, mirroring in contrast Treant's steed earlier, except the rider fell back, rolling off the rear of the horse. The pull of the earth and heavy steel armor welcomed him to the ground with a temper.

The air was pierced by a girl's scream. It froze the black knight in place. Horror filled him as he realized to whom the scream belonged. He ran toward Coran pausing at the opening of the ally,

115

where he looked to see a black knight lying on the ground fighting on with her sword, while a white fringed warrior standing above her hammered at her defenses with a Morningstar.

Then he turned back to Coran who sat slouching lifelessly over on his horse. He watched the black hand of a white knight wield once more its wicked tool. He swung out at the helpless young page crushing his skull, continuing to bludgeon him even after his soul had fled his body, seeming to glory in the marriage of blood and steel. Coran slid off his mount falling like a branch to the earth and assuring his killer a place in Hel upon his own death. For this day however, he lived on and rode off.

Archduke Treant felt powerless to stop the carnage and was overcome with hatred. Heavy, worn, and injured he charged, not for his dead page, nor for his squire who still battled on for her life. Instead, he turned back toward the knight that led the charge, who was struggling to get back on his feet. Treant attacked him and fought with ferocious anger, knocking the warrior back down before he could recover. His aggressiveness or was it eagerness, filled his enemy's heart with fear, fear the black knight could taste. The white one pleaded with Treant for a parlay. Treant disarmed him with a turn of his sword. The white knight kneeled before the black lord begging for mercy. "You are a Black Knight it is against your code to kill me when I have surrendered and am unarmed."

"Remove your helmet" Treant ordered. The white knight took off his helmet casting it aside as he persisted to plead for mercy. Treant looked

116

directly into the man's eyes, recognizing him as a lesser noble prominent in White Thorn. The black knight's mind filled with the grisly murder of his page. The sound of steel on steel echoed from the alley, drowning below Avriel's final scream. Hatred owned him. By impulse, he drove his sword into the kneeling knight, sinking it to the hilt then slowly removed it, smiling at the joy of a new pleasure. For a moment, it felt as though his hands were holding the warrior's soul. Then it was gone, the white knight before him fell forward mingling dirt, blood, and steel.

Treant progressed slowly to the alley looking sideways at his page's corpse until disgust and guilt repelled his eyes. He seemed to stager as he dragged the point of his sword in the dirt beside him, blood still sliding slowly down the blades thin channels. The despondent noble removed his helmet as he approached his squire's body, terrified that it was too late, at the same time grimly aware in his heart that it was. He fell by her head caressing her face, having no fight in him to prevent the deluge of sadness from flowing down his cheeks. The tears dripped off of his chin onto her bloodied skin. Trying to stave off dizziness, Treant placed his hands on her face and called silently for his divine power to heal. When the healing glow of golden light did not appear under his hands, he knew her to be dead. He lay there for some time, and wept.

After a while Treant remembered the council meeting and stood up determined not to fail in all his duties this day. Though wracked with grief, duty was all he now possessed. With a heavy heart and wounded pride, he walked to his horse. He could sense that Striker was irritated. Lord Treant guided his steed to its feet. The warhorse lifted its injured hoof and immediately started its difficult walk home, limping as it went. "Halt Striker, let me heal you first" Striker ignored his master and walked off with difficulty snorting and showed his teeth. Striker was no ordinary horse. He was a magical creature, spiritually connected to his owner. The mount had never resisted him before. This angered and confused the horse's noble master. "Striker, how can you forsake me? Now of all times?" Treant pled as his mount made his way off showing only its rear. Treant decided to take a different way home not having the patience to deal with his temperamental horse. Striker would most certainly return to his stable and wait for healing.

Two hours later the wounded knight arrived at his castle. He stumbled up to the entrance where one of his guards saw him and opened the massive doors to the front hall. The dutiful sentinel announced his masters return to the estate. As news of his injuries spread throughout the castle, his servants flocked out to the main hall to welcome him and discover what had happened. Treant sat down on the floor trying in vain to remove his heavy armor. Vektor ran in. "Milord what happened? Are you hurt? Where are my brother and sister in arms? Milord you will be late for the council."

"The council, I must go." Treant interrupted the boy, his voice strained. "I am grieved to say to you...all of you, that Avriel our lady squire and Coran our poor page are..." He choked and coughed his throat felt as though he swallowed a rock. "Dead," he finally managed to force out. He spoke with his words broken, at an almost whisper. "We were beset by White Thorn while in the Eastward."

The boy's eyes were glossy, yet he somehow suppressed his urge to fall apart. Others in the room were not so strong and there was much weeping in the hall. "We will have vengeance," The boy shouted then removed the apron he had been wearing while scrubbing pots and pans.

"Vengeance is evil," Treant, blurted. Then he took a moment to settle down. "It is evil" he explained, more calmly. His head was foggy, and he had a large gash in his chest. Purple and blue bruises surrounded his wound, swollen and bleeding. It was a fleshly volcano at the end of its eruption. Stavid offered him a bucket of water and a towel, which he accepted and put to use. Stavid's daughter, Valley, brought him a fresh black tunic and breeches of black color, and noble quality. She stared at his wounds as he changed there in the hall. He began yelling curses for those who had brought upon him this misery. "Vek, fetch your fallen compatriots then seek the high priest of Ethad's temple in Deadside. Turn their remains over to him, and await my arrival. Oh, and Vek, we shall see about justice shortly."

Vektor left upon this order, taking some of the staff with, leaving behind him the lamentations of a house in mourning. Before the page was only grief and rain. The noise of a newly arrived storm bellowed throughout the city, pulling at the groaning in his breast. The two sounds touching with each thundering.

119

Chapter 16 - Work

Do you think we will be accused of having something to do with the king falling ill?" Whisper asked Jynx, as they sat alone on the porch of the Coin Street Tavern. They were casing the weapon shop across the street.

"No way in the hells are they going to pin that on us." Jynx declared, alarmed at the very suggestion.

"We were amongst the last to see him at the festival. I am surprised the Crown Guard hasn't questioned us," she said. "They've had a month."

"Ha. They probably can't find us," Jynx said. "No doubt that makes us seem even more suspicious."

The rogues were quiet for a time. Jynx watched people coming and going across the street. Whisper, stared blankly at their target, her mind was somewhere else.

"Snap out of it, I need you to pay attention. You always notice the details that I miss," Jynx said, catching her daydreaming.

Whisper's attention returned to the job at hand in response to her comrades goading. She kept her medium length black hair tied up, so as not to fall in her face at an inconvenient time. She was little over five feet tall, and seemed to be light as a feather. Her brown eyes were so dark, anyone who had not studied them carefully presumed them to be black. Today her cloak was dull green, an unremarkable shade and perfect for not drawing attention to herself. Known only to a few, Whisper had a gift for wielding magic. She rarely used her sorcery and her identity together in public, preferring that only the three of them knew of this gift.

Whisper's crow familiar was only a magical incarnation of a bird, empathetically connected to her. It possessed the appearance and all of the characteristics of a real crow except that it had no need of sustenance though it could feed. While they watched the shop, the familiar perched itself on the object of their surveillance. If inquisitors approached, the bird would squawk then fly away in the direction of her master's best chance of escape.

"Sorry Jynx. I was just thinking about something that I saw when I was over here earlier. Anyways, it is not important. How long do you think Enigma will be?"

"I don't know, but I am kind of worried about him. He keeps making jokes about joining different guilds of scum. I am starting to think he is seriously considering it."

Whisper sighed as her thoughts drifted to her twin. "Jynx, you know Enigma is a good person, one of the best. He is just tired of losing contracts to rogues with half his skill, only because they belong to something. If anything, he just wants to play them, for more challenging jobs."

"He already belongs to something. For me thievery is just about survival and balancing the unfairness of our low births but for Enigma, it is an art form in its own right. That said, he doesn't need to be a member of any guild, we can step things up a bit on our own."

"Look." Whisper interrupted, directing Jynx's attention, with her eyes. "Do you see that man there?"

"Do you mean the one discreetly picking his nose?" Jynx asked.

She looked over to see whom Jynx was referring to and laughed. "No, you dummy, the man walking out of the shop, wearing a long sword. His sword is magic."

"Well, since I can't see magic aura's when I feel like it, I'll just take your word for it, but why do we care? Lots of people own enhanced weapons, ourselves included."

"That man goes their every day, and never makes more than a small purchase," Whisper explained.

Jynx was not surprised he never noticed him before. "We need to determine who he is before we act. He's probably just some stupid guard."

"Or he could be an Inquisitor, baiting us." Whisper offered.

"You are as obsessed with Inquisitors as your brother is with thieves' guilds. Though I must admit, the man could also be part of a guild protection racquet. In that case, we would have to pass on this job."

Chapter 17 - Black

Enigma finished touching up the tar on the blade of his short sword. He slid the weapon into the dark wooden scabbard fastened securely to his back. He straightened out his night-suit, making sure that it was tight, but not restrictive. Then he gathered three small pieces of metal. One was buried in the dirt of a houseplant that rested in the window. The second was in the seam of a cloak, hanging on a hook. The third was in his straw mattress. He fit the three pieces together and turned them opposite each other. When he finished, he held a key, with which he unlocked a chest, sitting next to a removed floorboard. Enigma bypassed the poisonous gas trap designed to prevent others from liberating his belongings.

Inside he retrieved his enchanted, soft-soled boots. Slipping them on, they became snug, fitting his feet perfectly. With these, he could walk on sheer surfaces, the same way a spider would. He reached back into the chest retrieving his other gear. He removed steel bracers for his wrists, a gold chain with a dark red amulet. He put on these magic items hiding the amulet under his tight shirt. Next, he took a pair of gloves from the chest and slid them on. These special gloves aided the wearer with pick pocketing and sleight of hand. Finally, he equipped himself with a short metal tube. When tapped against a lock or a secured door it could magically disengage locks and open closed doors.

At last he opened the trunk's false bottom, where resided, his most prized property. He kept his records of past larcenies on sheets of paper. Enigma painstakingly kept detailed notes on profits reaped each day, where the treasure came from and the averages he maintained. His sister and Jynx thought it crazy for him to keep account. For him, this was the one thing where pride preceded caution, so they didn't press. Besides, the notes had come in handy a few times.

Enigma put the false bottom back, leaving his records there. He picked up a small black sack. It was a special sort of sack. The inside was larger than the out so that it could contain the contents of an entire room. Inside his bag were his more mundane tools, a few potions and some magic dust. Enigma put on a black cloak, then threw a green and a brown one into his bag. He turned, walking out of his personal room, through an open door and into the living area that he shared with his friend and his sister.

Halfway in, he decided something was not right. The sun illuminated the room in declining light through the window as the day began to perish. Enigma stood in the center of the room, listening sharply and quickly scanning the room with his eyes. The room's furnishings were quaint but comfortable. Pictures of Nobleside adorned the walls. Something, his intuition told him, was definitely amiss but what? Then he heard movement outside the entry door. He spun quickly on his feet nearly slamming into a man he did not know was standing behind him.

The man was short, hooded, with two eyes staring out, from a black painted face. In his hand was a scimitar coated in the very same tar as

Enigma's blade. Enigma stepped back drawing his sword, as the entrance door opened behind him, and armed men filed in. Two warriors, another rogue and a black robed wizard, none of whom Enigma recognized, stood between him and the door. The warriors held battle axes, the mage a wand, and the rogue several darts with glistening points.

Enigma stood in the middle looking back and forth between the man on one side and the group on the other. He held his sword straight up in the air with his right hand and then addressed the intruders hoping to stall and perhaps gain some information, while he plotted out the final touches of his escape. "What do you want from me?" Enigma asked, in no particular direction.

The rogue that stood alone spoke up, reinforcing Enigma's suspicion that he was leader of the perpetrators. His voice was course. "Enigma, you have heard of the Agenda of the empty hand, have you not?"

"Did you corner me up here to ask rhetorical questions?" Enigma responded without pause. Having decided what his move would be, he hoped to learn as much as possible.

"Enigma, we want you to join the Agenda. You have been invited before, why haven't you joined us."

"Actually," Enigma mused. "I was considering it. I just can't seem to get past the fact, that you people are a few picks short of a locksmith."

"What!"

"You heard me. I think you are lunatics. I don't want to destroy the city, or take it over. I just wish to perfect my art, line my pockets, and keep my conscience clear."

"Good." The lead intruder said his face relaxing some.

Enigma jumped suddenly for the nearest wall, vanishing into the shadow. The five perpetrators converged on the wall as Enigma stepped out of a shadow near the door. He smiled as he watched them from behind their position. They stood in puzzlement, looking for any trace of him against the wall.

Then the rogue with the darts in hand, noticed him. "There!" He yelled, throwing two darts.

Enigma slipped through the doorway, darts sticking harmlessly into the open door.

In the hall, that separated the rogue's apartment from another's, there were stairs at one end, and an open window at the other. Enigma dashed for the window. Diving through it, he grabbed the wall, and clung to it. I love these shoes, he thought to himself, as he climbed up the wall and around the window like a four-legged arachnid. He positioned himself above the window, in time to see one of the warriors stick their head out and look down.

"I don't know how he wasn't killed but he has disappeared." The warrior yelled, "Quick, take the stairs!"

Enigma grabbed the top of the windowsill from above then released himself from the wall. He held on as he flipped over, slipping back into the window, feet first. He landed silently, onto the hall floor, and turned to watch as the intruders raced to the stairs. He wiped his brow sarcastically. "Whew." Then he strolled back to the apartment. Now that their safe-house was compromised, the rogue would have to gather his companion's belongings. "I cannot believe the Agenda tried to force me to join them." Enigma said to himself. "Well...I said it before, they are madmen" He walked through the door. He tried to move out of the way, but for once his reflexes were not fast enough. The net unfolded in the air, wrapping around him as he attempted to evade it. Enigma fell to the floor, caught like a dumb animal unable to avoid the net. The more he struggled, the tighter it became. It was clearly an enchanted net.

The first of the intruders stood above him. "I knew you would return when you thought you gave us the slip, though I admit, I didn't think it would be so soon."

"So now what?" Enigma asked angrily.

"Well now that I have caught you, I will reveal the true nature of my visit." The man said openly.

"You call this a visit." Enigma quipped, lying on his chest. "Well you are definitely not welcome back."

"That's enough with the sarcasm thief. I am not really with the Agenda, I am an Inquisitor and you and your two roommates are in trouble." The man looked down upon him as he spoke. "Do you know what for?"

"There are so many different things that might have caught your attention, forgive me if I don't commit to one."

"We believe that the king may have been poisoned. Would you like to guess who we think is responsible?"

Enigma looked at him through the netting a deep feeling of foreboding began to settle upon him,

"Us?"

"No," The inquisitor laughed, "The Agenda. However, you three are obvious suspects and will be taking the fall for this, unless..." He let the word hang deliberately.

"Unless what?" Enigma asked certain the answer would be unpleasant.

The Inquisitor cracked his neck before he spoke. "Unless you infiltrate the Agenda and report back to the Council Inquisitors."

"You're mad!" Enigma exclaimed in disbelief.

Just then, the inquisitor's comrades returned. "You're a slippery bastard, aren't you?" One of the warriors said to the netted rogue.

The leader looked at his fellow inquisitors. "You guys are on time for the best part. You see Enigma, you stole your place setting at the kings table. Do you want to guess what the penalty for stealing from the royal family is?"

"I repay the king, say sorry, and everything is better." Enigma answered with mock hopefulness.

"You are pretty stupid, smarting off to an Inquisitor when your life and the lives of those you care about are on the line."

"Perhaps then, Inquisitor, you should spare me the stupid questions and get to the point."

The man scoffed, looked over at his comrades then back to Enigma, still helpless in the net with one of his arms folded under him. "Go get the judge." He ordered one of his men, still keeping his eyes trained on the captured thief. "Death...Enigma, for your friend and for your sister, but for you...you will spend your life in the dungeon. The church of Asmodeus will carry out the executions. Who can imagine how long they will suffer? You broke the law, and the law is beyond reproach, it is the only good. Was it worth it, I must know?"

Enigma said nothing but stared at him, visualizing the lawman's death, seething with hatred.

The judge arrived. He, or perhaps she, wore black head to heel. A silk mask covered his face permitting the judge to see out but allowing none to see the high inquisitor's face. "Has he decided yet?" The judge asked in a nondescript voice, the result of obvious magic, still not betraying any distinguishing characteristics. Only the judge's height and size were discernible and even that was probably an illusion. Fair or unfair, good or evil, one knew nothing about a judge, except the Supreme Inquisitor who answered only to the council. When the Judges were not in their official garments, they blended in with society. Shop keepers, beggars, anyone could be a judge waiting to accuse those that have broken the law. "I have their death sentences here; they lack only my seal." The judge said, holding three rolled up sheets of parchment in gloved hands.

Enigma felt helpless and hopeless, rage began to surface like a fever warming his skin, but he suppressed it because he knew it could not help at the moment. "How will it work?" He asked without bothering to disguise the scorn in his voice.

The man that netted him spoke up. "There is a woman named Davania, she walks past the Slumside Tavern, to that sectors main well on the third day of the week at midnight. She sits in Jirtle Park on the seventh day of each week at noon.

Report to her at least once a month and give her all the information you have. Sometimes she will have a message for you. Do whatever she tells you without question. If you provide good and reliable information, these sentences will be destroyed." The Inquisitor paused for a moment thoughtfully. "Another thing, don't give her any lip, she does not know anything about your situation. She just moves information and she never forgets a detail."

"I will do it, what choice do I have?" Enigma agreed reluctantly.

With his business concluded the judge vanished.

Enigma's captor spoke as his fellows released the shadow walker from the net, and forcefully stood him up. "You can tell no one who you really work for, not even your sister, or you're so called friend. If you do we will know."

Enigma stood before him, free of his bondage. "If you harm them, you will die." Enigma threatened, more serious than ever.

The inquisitor looked him in the eye, and smirked. "Good, very good," he said, nodding with approval. "One more thing Enigma, your alias is Gold Spoon. It seems quite appropriate, doesn't it? When dealing with inquisitors, use that name and keep your face hidden." The men left, leaving Enigma there alone. His companions expected him to be on Coin Street in Eastward with them and no doubt were wondering about his absence. Enigma sat to think. After some time, he pulled out a sheet of parchment and began writing.

Chapter 18 - Council

Ten noble lords sat at a long, curved table of dark, oak in the meeting hall of the council's small keep. The walls to the sides held six banners apiece, each representing one of the twelve high families. The first six were called upper houses the next six, lower and the rest were lesser. The stone rectangle that passed for a hall was damp and cool, illuminated by torches that appeared to burn with a flickering spectrum of colored light. The light was existent enough to see by, but the burning was a mere illusion. Here at the approach of the cold season heat would surely have been welcomed, whatever its source, by the humans in this chilled council. Any warmth felt from these torches was a figment, for they had no warmth to give. To look upon them as you shivered, was as looking into a mirror, you see the person before you and yet you cannot draw your fingers across the lines on their face. The table was shaped like a horseshoe, in the center of the open-ended, semi-circle was a dais, two feet high. On the dais sat a white block cut from a single stone draped in blue and purple velvet, with a gold crown of thirteen points resting upon it. There was a large peak in the center of the crown bearing a red ruby and surrounded by twelve lesser peaks, ten of which bore varies precious stones and two of which sat unadorned. Next to the crown was a rod of Ivory set with a large pearl.

Princess Corrine stood in the center of the room on the dais, with the stone block behind her. Her eyes were bright blue, and the source of daily compliments. Her hair was light blond, silk in texture with natural curls and fixed in stylized braids that seemed to be weaved around the base of her gold crown. In her petite, hands she grasped the royal scepter. It was set with garnets evenly down its length of four feet and topped with a cut ruby. The scepter she had always thought looked small in her father's grip now looked disproportionately large in her own. Her crown was affixed with four diamonds, like compass points. Each possessed a dim blue light and one of them had the property of keeping her highness at peace from the cold. No doubt one of the prettiest and most eloquent girls of any age in all Blakoepal, she stood before the nobles dressed in a stately gown of white and gold. This day her usually fair skin had a hint of paleness and her steps seemed somewhat forced despite the effort she made to appear sturdy and of sound health. Darkness rimmed around her eyes slightly, betraying late nights filled with distress. She hardly concealed it, wearing only minimal eye makeup, the color drawn from the red mulberries that grew on the palace grounds. "Where are Archduke Cavalaries and Viscount Bindingfire? It is nearly half the hour past, is this conduct becoming of what my father expects from this illustrious body?" The princess startled those in attendance with her unexpected forthrightness and her obvious agitation. "She knew none would keep her father waiting and wished to prevent any disrespect for the crown.

"I heard that his grace was at a revel last night, as for Viscount Bindingfire, I will not venture a guess as to what is keeping him." Margrave Delzoun Lighthammer, lord of the fifth remarked.

"Why would I take the word of one who so openly loathes the first lord?" She said castigating him and glaring scornfully at the man's dark eyes and grey beard. Her forcefulness made him nervous, but the princess perceived that she had the love of the people, who would dare challenge her?

"Only repeating what I heard your royal highness." Delzoun said.

Their conversation halted with the entrance of Caedis Bindingfire's herald, who stepped off to the side of the double door entrance, wearing a uniform of orange and black design on a white field. Standing at attention the servant loudly announced Lord Bindingfires arrival.

Caedis, youngest of the council and lord of the twelfth, entered the hall in good spirits. His long black hair hung in his face, down to his chin. He swept it out of his way with one hand as he made his pomp through the hall. He had dark brown eyes and wore a white hooded cloak with matching tunic and breeches. His fingers carried many gold rings set with dark gemstones. An orange metallic brooch kept his white cloak fastened. On his upper lip was a thin scar of unknown origin, unknown to the masses that is. It provided rumor mongers of the lower classes fodder for gossip and Caedis did not seem to mind the attention most of these stories paid to his popularity.

"My most solemn apologies to her royal highness," Lord Bindingfire said meeting the young eyes of the princess as he pulled his chair out from the table with his black gloved hand. "Likewise, to my fellow nobles of the council," He spoke to all, putting his white gloved hand upon his chest in feigned sincerity. He noted Treant's absence with a knowing smile, as he continued his ostentation. "I have no excuse to offer and hope I have not kept our dear princess waiting. I love her as both my princess and even as if I were her older brother. I wish to make known my deepest condolence to her, in her time of grievous uncertainties. I was actually just in deep contemplation about our current state of affairs, wondering in what ways I could be a more dutiful member of this body, and a better servant to you," His eyes returned to her. "There is no other I extol more then you, my future queen."

"Except you're self, that is." Treant interjected from the entrance of the short hall. He appeared unannounced in time to provide an end to Caedis's speech.

"You shock me with your boorishness Archduke." The princess scolded. "How dare you take a complement offered to pay me kindness and twist it like a knave, especially on the heels of your failure to begin this assembly on time? Need I remind you Archduke Cavalaries that Viscount Bindingfire spent some time in the palace with me when he was a boy? His love and his respect are both genuine and mutual."

Treant became flush. He had never been late for anything before. His burden was already full and now one whom he cared for profoundly corrected him in favor of one he despised. "Forgive my impropriety dearest lady, I forget myself. There has been a tragedy in my house. I am not myself. I will make it known after your highness addresses the council." Treant limped over to his chair and sat as a dark stain formed in his tunic barely discernible under the colored lights.

"You are injured. Are you not a paladin? Why haven't you healed yourself?" Princess Corrine inquired eagerly and with compassion.

"A Black Knight never uses his powers to heal himself, unless he is near death." Treant reminded her. There was an awkward moment of silence as Treant along with the rest of the assembly realized how condescendingly he had just spoke to the king's daughter in front of the entirety of the council and at her first formal address no less. After carelessly embarrassing the loved heiress, Archduke Cavalaries sank in his chair dejected and stared blankly, the blood in his cheeks warming him to the point of discomfort, his heart beating forcefully and his wound throbbing.

Duke Sunwater of the third stood up. Blakoepal had a large minority of elves and a smaller inhabitancy of half elves. They were the city's only other racial groups, besides the human majority. Gravius Sunwater was the Oepal's prominent elf. He was one of three elves sitting on the council and a powerful mystic that commanded magic, both Arcane and Divine. His medium length hair was copper and his eyes were an intense green. Garbed in white, with gold and green regalia, he walked quietly over to the black knight reciting a prayer and clutching the gold disk that hung around his neck, stamped with a child's silver footprint. He approached Treant placing his slender hands on the injured knight's shoulders. A golden radiance appeared from under the third lord's hands permeating Treant's skin, and healing his physical wounds.

"Thank you." Treant said simply. His emotional pain came upon him as a flood at the moment of his release from physical pain. He struggled not to come apart as his wounds were all that provided enough distraction to keep him rigid.

Gravius accepted his thanks with a nod, and a gentle, "Your welcome, brother." Then he returned to his seat.

Caedis stood momentarily and spoke to the council, disregarding Treant and Gravius "I have something that I wish to share with the council as well. It is not a tragedy, in fact quite the contrary. I will wait however, until after the princess speaks."

A council attendant approached the late arrivals expectantly, holding a gold saucer inlaid with a purple velvet bottom. The two tardy nobles in turn, each placed a small steel tube onto the velvet. He walked to another servant beside the stone, who handled the crown of the council. With some ceremony, the second attendant removed a gemstone from each of the two cylinders. Treant's was a Black Spinel and Lord Bindingfire's was a Topaz. Both were added to the crown on the stone. Then all the servants walked out of the room and closed the doors behind them, leaving, the twelve, Chamberlain Viscus, Princess Amorgoden, and her steadfast personal guard Alturek.

"This meeting is now in session." Princess Corrine Amorgoden spoke with a crisp voice to the waiting ears of nobles, doing her best not to let a hint of sadness into her words. "His majesty the king remains alive in his coma. It is as though he were sleeping, and that is how we will continue to operate. As when he lays down for the night, he is still our king, so it is that he is still our king now. I will not be foolish however, until the day his respite ends I shall administer all matters of the royal court, personally or by proxy at my discretion. I will decide matters of high justice once a week." Sighs issued from amongst the attendant nobles. Some thought she was too gentle and would consequently be too soft, others contended she would be careless, perhaps even reckless.

"I am aware of my age and my sex. I am also receptive of the concerns of you who fear I do not have the experience to handle matters of state. It is true that I have spent only a minimal amount of time watching my father make decisions in the royal court. Only recently have I been briefed on threats against our city. I will however remind the council that in our history, the royal scepter has been borne by some even younger than I and by ladies as well. In addition, I remind you that I have arguably the finest education in the Oepal. Royal High Chamberlain Viscus Amorgoden was his majesty, my father's, closest confidant. I will pay special attention to his advice and direction. I will delegate a great deal of responsibility to my uncle the chamberlain. I will watch and learn from him who has spoken on behalf of my father before. I will not however hold my tongue where my decision is required. It is my right and indeed my duty to handle the current crises the way in which I have just decreed. The law has spoken and it is final."

Princess Corrine moved to the side of the stone table. The king's brother stepped on to the dais and stood in front of the white table, before the council nobles. He spoke with a heavy voice. "Men and women of the council, human and elf, I would like to thank you all for your patience as we sorted out this situation and decided how best to deal with the kings unfortunate and quite unexpected condition. I, as my niece's chamberlain and the kings before her, speak with the authority of the royal crown and scepter."

"I wish to warn the council, as you probably already know, the denizens of the dark are gathering in greater numbers below us. Rumors persist that they will invade our city in such numbers as has not been seen since their origin, when the fiend Asfixius led them against our people. It could be that our information is exaggerated, let's hope it is. Still we must take the threat seriously. We will be sending scouting forays into the Undercity and ask that each knightly order spend some time patrolling the many passageways beneath us and the great star as well."

"In an unrelated matter, our diviners report that a disease of some sort is spreading in the villages outside our beloved city state. According to the crown guard, the people are overcome with a bloodlust when bitten by one infected. Those sick from this affliction become what the villagers call vampires, a type of living dead, similar in some ways to the stories of the Tyrant of the damned, below Deadside. The church of Ethad at my request is compiling information on these so-called vampires. Something may need to be done about this. If the disease takes over the villages we may lose our link to information in the outside world. We may need to purge the villages first. I once again thank the council and now yield the platform to His Most Gracious Archduke Treant Cavalaries,

138

Sire of the First Noble House of the Opal."

Lord Treant Cavalaries approached the table slowly and regarded the crown of thirteen stones that rested on the table. Each piece had a dormant power that only functioned in conjunction with two other pieces and a greater power that could only work with all thirteen pieces affixed. The Black Opal granted the magic of both the crown of thirteen stones, and the rod. Treant picked up the council scepter. He stood before the council, weary and worn. His light blond hair combed back with oil, his skin and black garments were clean, except for the fresh bloodstain on his tunic. His eyes, a swirl of blue and grey were an open window into a soul newly at war with itself. "Your majesty, those of the royal court and friends present in the council," Treant began. "First I would like to say that the Council Inquisition has confirmed most of what the chamberlain has shared with us this afternoon. I recommend unison…" Treant paused distracted by memories of the day's earlier carnage. "…uh, I'm sorry…Treant's mouth was dry and he cleared his throat louder than he intended. I think the Council Inquisition and the Crown Guard would do well to share all information about these vampires, as they are so called and work together if it becomes necessary to perform a raid on the outside villages.

Someone in the counsel gasped. Protests and arguing prevailed in the counsel. Such a thing was unheard of.

"The villages do not even realize Blakoepal exists!" One of the Noblemen yelled.

Treant put up a hand. "Order," he commanded

the council. A white light on the scepter began to glow, warning the members of the council that if they were not silent the staff would snuff sound from the chamber. Treant waited as everyone quickly came to order. "Now to share what has befallen me. Knights of White Thorn ambushed me earlier while I was in the company of my first page Coran and the popular Lady Ringheart, my beloved squire. It pains me greatly to report that only I survived." Treant's throat felt raw, as he turned low eyes to his princess, whose mouth was hanging slightly open in disbelief. "I am sorry your highness; I know that she was one of your close friends. I am sorry." Remorsefully he continued, "Their bodies were turned over to the temple of Ethad in preparation for their funeral. I will request their bodies be brought to the Sanctuary of the Shining Sun on the morning of their funeral, two days hence." He seized up for a moment unable to continue, fighting off tears proved harder than battling evil. "I now yield the platform to Illustrious, Viscount Bindingfire."

Caedis took the rod sharply out of Treant's hands, and stood to face the council, looking over to the princess and back toward the nobles as he spoke. "I am grieved to hear this news of our lady Baroness Ringheart. Though our families warred and mine prevailed, having spent two years with her in the palace, she and I had no grudge. In fact, dare I say we were friends. It was not White Thorn that killed her but the constant fighting of the knightly orders. My heart again goes out to the princess for the loss of our childhood friend, our sister, Lady Avriel Ringheart. I only wish she would have taken a different route to knighthood then the one she did." Treant did all he could to control his seething rage as Caedis continued. "I am reluctant to make my announcement with such a shadow looming over the council." He looked dead at the princess who had fresh tears streaming down her cheeks. "I will go forward with my announcement though, knowing in my heart of hearts that the dutiful Lady Ringheart would want me to. I was to be inducted into White Thorn in two weeks, although now I think I will hasten it. In two days hence, I will receive my honors so that I may dedicate it to her worthy memory."

Treant bit his lip until the taste of blood was in his mouth. His head became foggy as his mind spun with racing thoughts. *How can this snake of a man fool the princess or anyone else with his lies about love and friendship? He is going to honor her, his supposed friend, by being ordained into the very order that killed her and on the day that her funeral is to occur. I am going to kill that man.*

"The council is adjourned." Treant heard someone say to him. He walked quickly out to the road, mumbling all the way to the Golden Gauntlet tavern, stopping only to wave his fist, threatening a man who bumped into him. Perhaps struggling so hard to compose himself caused him to unravel further. Truths and lies would spread like wildfire in a city of talkers, about this display and the more colorful moments of the council meeting. Two men followed him separately. One a smiling inconspicuously dressed knight of White Thorn, who enjoyed being witness to the madness descending on the Black Knight. The other a black robed young man with a blank expression and two peering, silver eyes.

Chapter 19 - Sanctuary

The Sanctuary of the Shinning Sun stood high and glorious. It was a vast fortress situated at the peak of a huge mound, surrounded by a deep moat and high walls. The fortified cathedral of the god Crotear was replete with stained glass windows which colored the light that shined through the vaulted ceilings of the inner sanctum, the most beautiful place in this magnificent fortress-church. It was constructed to be both inspiring and defensible. Gold and rosy colored glass gave way to impressive stone walls covered in elaborate mosaics that displayed the sun, numerous achievements of the church and other articles of faith.

There were many pillars lending their strength to the ceiling, adorned with detailed bas-reliefs. Looming arches and expertly worked sculptures dominated an onlooker's view. The art depicted modestly dressed men and woman of both common and noble birth, brave warriors in the peak of their youthful courage, and innocent children and infants displayed in laughter and solemnity. Old knights were shown renewed and vibrant. Hosts of celestial beings were portrayed with white feathered wings, others with bestial heads and sublime countenance. Decorated gold disks, symbolizing the light bearing sun completed the aesthetic arrangements of the inner sanctuary.

A somber crowd filled the worship chambers. The high priest stood by the altar of Crotear in the inner sanctum on a dais, consoling the assembly of mourners before him. Holy Father Egry Plinth was

143

an ordinary merchant class man who had married up. His wife was a member of the Columnfrost house. Egry was a man of stature that commanded a powerful voice and dwarfed most people in both size and kindness. Bishop Plinth was a living pillar of the faith.

Treant stood on the polished black floors listening to Bishop Egry deliver Lady Avriel Ringheart's Eulogy. The high priest had tears in his eyes as he spoke with a particular zeal. Treant recalled the many times the saintly man had described the late paladin to him. Egry had carried great hope for her, describing her as the churches most cherished maiden, second only to the princess. She had overcome so much bitterness and anger, only to die a pointless and violent death. The bishop spoke of the tribulations she had endured as a child and how overcoming these trials were a spiritual victory for Crotear. Treant was not comforted and found himself thinking, rubbish, this is vanity, in the end we all just lay down and die.

Treant chastised himself mentally for denying the words of the high priest. He could not forgive himself the loss of his squire and page, so he mixed guilt over his sacrilegious thoughts into his already convoluted conscience. Staring at the sheen of the black coffin behind the priest, the Black Knight switched back and forth between reminiscent daydreams and listening to the temple elder share his own memories of Lady Ringheart.

Earlier Sir Orginus Dreadhawk knighted Lady Ringheart, posthumously inducting her into the Black Knights officially. Treant only cursed himself for not acting sooner to bestow that deserved commission upon her. The knight's heart was adrift, like a flutter of snow his mind went from pondering to pondering. He looked up at the princess who sat above the congregation in her father's throne dressed in red and black, the colors of the fallen lady's now extinct house. All attendants wore at least a handkerchief of the intertwined Ringheart colors though most completely arrayed themselves in red and black. Lord Cavalaries had a seat of prestige up near the princess but he chose to stand with his fellow knights along the walls flanking the assembly. The balcony had thirteen sections set in a great half-circle, one segment for the royal family, with the stations for the twelve noble houses making up the rest. Followers of other gods could not enter in this holy place by cause of an ancient edict. Many of the seats of honor sat empty, reminding the faithful of the spiritual warfare in which they all perpetually engaged.

When the service was completed, Treant followed Orginus out to the staging area where pages and squires readied horses. The rest of the Black Knights followed suit. The upcoming procession was going to be led by the Black Knights with Treant at the forefront. The march would proceed to Eastward, to the place Avriel died and then turn toward the center of the city, finally coalescing in front of Ringheart Mausoleum on Deadside.

The Archduke stopped suddenly. Standing before the other knights, he stared into the staging area at his page, and steed.

"Are you ok Treant, you look like you've seen a ghost?" Sir Dreadhawk asked.

Treant walked purposefully to where his page stood. "Vektor, how could you bring me the wrong horse? I never ride Redemption. Surly by now you know that Striker is my personal steed. How could you fail in this, they're two different colors and Striker is far more majestic?"

"Ye…Yes milord, But I have not seen Striker in three days," Vektor explained.

"What do you mean you have not seen him in three days? You waited until now to tell me?" Treant's face tinged with wrath.

"Please pardon me, my liege," the boy pled. "You have not been sober."

Treant reached up and then brought the back of his gauntlet down on the side of his page's forehead splitting the boy's brow. The servant boy fell hard to the ground with indiscriminate force cracking a respectable gash into the rear of his head. Vektor grabbed his forehead as blood drained out from under his hand. His lord had never struck him before. He was hurt. Physical pain contested sadness for prominence in the young man's attention.

"Whoa! What are you doing Treant?" Orginus asked interceding.

"He brought the wrong horse and a smart mouth. It is a shame my page Coran has fallen and now I am stuck with this imbecile," Treant answered oblivious to Vektor wincing at his cutting words.

Orginus noticed the other knights and their servitors, staring. "Get into form, and show the Archduke some respect!" He yelled, reminding the men that Treant was their superior in more ways

146

than one. "I ask you brother to understand that Vektor's burden is heavy too and pray you allow me to heal him. His injuries are perhaps more severe than you intended."

"I have no cause to oppose you Orginus." Treant said firmly, his color returning to normal as he tried to reign in his feelings. Treant again found himself embarrassed and did not need to look upon his fellow knights to know the expressions they all wore on their faces.

Orginus removed a gauntlet, and reached out a hand to the boy. Vektor had tears in his eyes. Despite an effort to keep them in, some made their way down his cheeks. He reached cautiously for Sir Dreadhawk's hand not knowing what to expect. There was a glow of gold light crackling with positive energy between their hands, as Orginus pulled him to his feet. The boy's brow healed as if nothing had ever happened to it. The jarring in his head likewise went away. What was more, he felt cleaner somehow, as if he bore not so much as a single sin in his soul. It was the first time a holy knight laid hands on him, healing him. "Why are we not having a big funeral for Coran, he was killed to?" The boy page asked.

Orginus looked the boy in the eye, "Lady Ringheart was the head of a noble house and the last of her line. Coran was the son of a common soldier who had earned favor somehow. Most people do not care about an up jumped peasant boy turned page, except you and the boy's family. They will have a private funeral but *your* duty is to your liege. I am sorry for your loss, both Lady Ringheart and Coran."

Lord Treant Cavalaries mounted Redemption. Orginus echoed his move with his own horse then called out to his brother and sister knights. "Mount up for Lady Avriel Ringheart, a shining example of chivalry!" There was a cheer as Black Knights mounted in unison followed by the thundering of dozens of mounted Knights galloping to take their place in the procession.

Chapter 20 - Run

Jynx and Whisper sat on the porch of the Coin Street tavern. They were continuing their surveillance of the weapon shop down the road, on the other side, but they were idle and unable to find their resolve. The two of them sat in silence for several hours, only halfway watching. They were short on enthusiasm and had no new plans for the heist. Since Enigma left, their spirits were low and their words had been few.

A commotion began on the street as trumpets sounded in the distance. At first, neither of them paid it any attention but as it persisted and drew nearer, they perked up with curiosity. A large but scattered group of common people, mostly tradesmen and farmers, began to converge on the locale. People came from inside their houses to stand on the side of the road. Others made their way up to the rooftops. Jynx and Whisper were no longer alone on the porch as the taverns inhabitants pressed out to determine the cause of the trumpeting.

Seven horses bearing youthful riders galloped into the neighborhood stopping in front of the tavern. They wore the standard of house Amorgoden and six of them carried long trumpets, which they sounded with vigor. The boy in the middle yelled out to all onlookers. "Make way for her most gracious majesty, daughter of King Eratide, acting regent of our nation city of Blakoepal, benevolent ruler of both great and small, her royal highness Princess Corrine Amorgoden!"

They waited awhile after heralding her highness's arrival before riding off to issue the same declaration again further along the route.

The people were soon abuzz, chatting voraciously with each other as rumor smiths crafted fantastic gossip. Prominent amongst these stories was that the king had finally died. Everyone cheered when the head of the procession appeared and the glistening suits of the Black Knights followed in the distance, shining brightly in the sun. All the citizens that were present strained themselves for a view of the princess during her first tour through the Eastward neighborhood.

Jynx leaned, practically bent in half over the railing of the now crowded porch. Whisper laughed at how ridiculous he looked trying to see someone who no doubt had already forgotten he existed. He looked over to Whisper, catching her smiling. He smiled back then turned to search the approaching parade for the princess. He did not notice the smile fade on Whispers face, given over with hurt as she realized that she had just felt happy for the first time in three days.

The Black Knights went by, Lady Avriel's coffin in their midst being towed by her horse Jet. Garland and roses of white and red covered her coffin. Several knights proudly carried her banner.

Whisper recognized the fallen nobles crest. She pulled out a handkerchief she had found, bearing the same insignia. Whisper hastily looked at it. She knew the lady that was to be buried. "Jynx there is something I need to talk to you about." She said to him loud enough that he could hear over the people between them.

"Not now," he said, his eyes never leaving the road. Princess Corrine's carriage now rolled past, along with her entourage of guardsmen, followed by White Thorn. Jynx could not help but place his greatest hope in her, and her upcoming reign. Life was going to change for him and he could feel it. If Enigma wanted to go his own way so badly, then fine. Jynx would determine his own path as well. Still, for Whisper's sake he wished he could bring Enigma back. Many more carriages, knights and nobles went by, followed by a mob of ordinary folks. It was in this mob that Jynx spotted Enigma. There he was discreetly working his way through the people, as if Jynx's own thoughts had conjured him. "Enigma!" Jynx yelled out. "Whisper, I just spotted Enigma!" Jynx yelled at her and pointed to where he had just seen her twin.

She tried but could not see him. "Wait!" She yelled to her friend. Right then the rail he pressed up against broke. Jynx fell forward landing on his fore arms. Whisper hurried after him, wading through the people on the steps of the patio. She got to where he had landed in time to see him disappear into the crowd.

Jynx looked frantically for Enigma at first. Noticing a figure wearing a black cloak, he grabbed the person's shoulder. "How dear you evade me like I was an Inquisitor," Jynx said spinning the person around to face him. It was a lady with a large nose. His mistake caught her on guard and she kicked him sharply in the shin as he stood dumbfounded. Stunned he limped away from her and reached down to rub his shin. When he lifted his head back up, he seen Enigma standing there several feet

151

away, facing him. Jynx began to approach. At this, Enigma sidestepped into one of the many shadows provided by the people walking, then he vanished in plain view. Jynx had seen this trick of the shadow walker before, so he turned quickly around and then in each direction searched with his eyes while the crowd walked by. Usually Enigma liked to emerge from a shadow right behind the person, but not this time. "I think your name has gone to your head you bastard!" Jynx yelled out to him with no thought to where he was. Then he looked at the faces of passersby and realized that he appeared crazed. He decided to lower his profile and join the crowd.

After a slow march through Eastward, then Westward the parade finally came to a stop in Deadside. A detachment of crown guards had taken control of the gates into this walled sector. Other than the royal entourage, only nobles and knights gained entrance without hassle. Those of low birth needed to present a religious token provided by father Egry to gain admittance.

"I know he is in there," Jynx thought aloud. He walked some ways along the walls perimeter until he came to a tree, across from one of the walls small towers. Word in Slumside was that these towers were usually vacant. The walls were only fifteen feet high, no battlements. Unfortunately, the top of the wall tapered to a peak and was difficult to surmount. Jynx climbed the tree skillfully then hand after hand began to work his way down a branch. When he was above the tower, his branch broke. He hit the cone shaped roof then rolled off, landing with a pang on the grass. Jynx was pleased to see rows of headstones, and burial tombs, indicating to him that he rolled off on the right side. He lay for a long moment catching his breath. "Halt perpetrator." A voice ordered from above and behind him.

Jynx hurried to his feet and drew his sword as the guard climbed down the ladder with due urgency. Jynx slowed the man's determination with the tip of his sword, pushing the point of it up against the back of the man's neck, at the base of his skull.

"I look forward to death," the sentry said as he stood, stuck in mid climb a few steps from the ground, his back to the intruder. Jynx discerned from the badge on the man's uniform that he was a guard for the church of Ethad. Ethad was the god of the dead, neither good nor evil. He had followers that were righteous and those that were despicable in equal measure. Though truth be told, most fell somewhere in between, neither hot nor cold. The church of the dead had, like every other powerful entity in the city, its own military wing, complete with a knightly order, the Death Guard. The church as a whole executed the law without prejudice. To them the law decided what was good and what was evil. Death was the ultimate law.

"Well that is inconvenient, though death you shall be given if you press," Jynx said.

"I pray for my life to end, but Ethad does not permit us to commit suicide," spoke the sentry.

"That is too bad. What a demanding religion, not allowing suicide." The rogue mocked him trying to determine a course of action. He had not planned for this little encounter. In fact, he never really planned for anything. "Strip out of that uniform, starting with your belt." The guard unfastened his sword, dropping it to the ground then proceeded to remove his black and yellow uniform.

Jynx ordered the servant of Ethad down and to his knees. "I will be vindicated in the afterlife," The sentry said.

"Well, not today you mad-dog." Jynx bound and gagged the soldier then left him. He looked in the distance spotting the mausoleum where the highborn gathered.

Jynx was making his way through the vast cemeteries when a crow flew before him, nearly missing him. He recognized the bird to be Whisper's familiar. Jynx kept his eye on it as it led his vision to a mausoleum rooftop several hundred yards over from the one where the people were gathered. Four men in dark cloaks crouched on the roof with large, crossbows. Assassins, Jynx realized as one jumped from a roof and made his way to the crowd blending in with ease. Jynx looked over to see the princess walking up to a podium, apparently to deliver some final words on her deceased friend.

It dawned on Jynx that the rogues on the rooftop were here to kill the princess. Urgency washed over Jynx, he broke into a dash, running hard trying to reach her highness. He slammed into the crowd pushing men and women of the gentry down, forcing his way to the podium.

Chapter 21 - Guard

Surrounded by warriors, Princess Corrine searched for the courage she felt that she lacked, *I am the opposite of these brave men and women around me*, she thought. On her flanks stood the two most distinguished competing orders of knights. The Crown Guard stood between herself and the knights. All around were the carriages of prominent and not so prominent nobles. Avriel's coffin lay on a table in a raised pavilion, in front of her family's tomb. Corrine could see many familiar faces in proximity to her. She was not sure what she would say, and was quite nervous speaking to such a populated crowd. Avriel had been her friend. She wished to honor her with fine words but did not think any speech worthy. Then she saw Agon, who nodded at her, bolstering her confidence. She looked away from him and back at the place of her pending speech with a raised spirit. She started to walk up to the pavilion and transverse the fifteen feet of steps to the top.

Alturek looked everywhere for trouble. When he looked to the next tomb, the sun blared in his eyes causing him a moment of blindness. He ordered a uniformed guardsman to take a squad to secure the area where the sun eliminated his view. Rubbing his eyes, he turned to look back at the Ringheart tomb just past the pavilion. Crouched down was a dark-haired girl working her hands in the arcane somatics of a mage preparing to cast a spell. She looked over at him the instant he noticed her. He read terror on her face. Alturek raised his light crossbow letting fly its poisoned ammunition. The bolt struck her in her abdomen and she let out a whiney and ran, hunched over, around the Ringheart mausoleum. Alturek chased after her.

Corrine was horrified. Alturek, it seemed to her, took off for no apparent reason as a loud commotion was occurring in the audience. Just then, a series of arrows rained in, hitting a couple of guards. The guardsmen and many of the knights took defensive posture. Other knights mounted and charged toward the missiles origins. Two men broke through the crowd, and passed the surprised guards, who quickly gathered their bearings and gave chase. The first attacker moved unnaturally fast, hastened by magic. The second one's sword was ablaze with an enchanted red flame. Then a third, who had been hiding in the rafters of the pavilion, jumped down inches away from the princess. He landed softly, bending at the knees to absorb the shock. He came to a stand as he drew his short sword before the defenseless girl.

A ray of blue light came into existence between Agon's hand and the man at the head of the charge, as he reached the top of the steps. The ray vanished as quickly as it appeared reducing the would-be assassin to dust, dispersed soon after by a light breeze before it could settle on the steps. The runner with the flaming sword arrived at the top of the steps in time to have dust blown into his face.

The princess whirled around taking in bits and pieces, not certain how they all fit. When the killer's blade flashed before her, she knew she was dead and closed her eyes. Her only thought was that she did not want to die. To her astonishment, she detected a flash of light and felt heat. Corrine opened her eyes. The man with the burning sword was cutting the assassin down. Then it went dark again, only this time because knights and guards covered her, pressing their bodies around her as one last hail of arrows dropped two of them.

The princess cried out for her bodyguard and for her cousin. She could feel herself floating, hulled away by many warriors, as if she were an object that could not move by her own will. They inserted her into her carriage. The sheer congestion of her protectors prevented her having any view of what lay beyond. She could make out only Lord Cavalaries and Alturek, the latter who slipped into the carriage with her. He shut the door, aiming his crossbow at it and inquired anxiously if she was hurt. She caught him off guard when she embraced him suddenly. He sat their stiff and uncomfortable, holding the princess. After some thought, he resigned to put his arm around his liege, deciding that comforting her was the appropriate response.

Chapter 22 - Suspect

"We've captured the swordsman, he is here Prince Agonius," a guard captain said, beckoning the king's nephew. "He is a man-at-arms, belonging to the Lifeless Order."

The man who had wielded the flaming sword in defense of the princess hung his head when Agon approached. "Show yourself hero." The mage extended a hand to the man's chin, directing him to look up then withdrawing his hand and considering the fellow before him.

The rogue stared curiously into the silver eyes of royalty and arcane power as the wizard spoke. "I remember this man from the Day of Merriment. This is the commoner who sat at the kings table when he ate his last meal, shortly before he fell into his current state. He is no member of the Lifeless Order. Lock him up in the palace dungeon. I am charging you with his safety. It is important that nothing happen to him before I see him."

"Yes, your eminence," the Captain took command of his soldiers and manacled the rogue.

Jynx felt as though a great weight was upon his shoulders pressing him into the ground. He realized the magnitude of such a coincidence. His timing with the day of merriment and the assassination attempt on the princess was incomprehensible. He would be fortunate to win a quick execution. His thoughts were racing, Enigma, Whisper, the Princess... Thank Crotear she was not killed.

Chapter 23 - Raid

Scholars and seers often speculate at the ultimate source of Evil. Some of the more informed believe it was the bottomless pit of the Abyss, which came first. According to the annals of ancient speculation, eight powerful entities united under the leadership of one superlatively powerful being who dominated the six hundred and sixty sixth layer of the pit, bringing law and order of the most perverted sort. This layer, known as Hel, became so vast and different that it broke off from the others.

Hel divided into nine distinct layers or circles, each was infinite in magnitude. It kept the descending form of a great pit, ending in the ninth and deepest layer. The souls of Hel's nine layers, which formerly spawned the demonic, gave birth to a new breed of demon, one that shunned the chaotic nature of the other demons. This was the rise of the devils.

The layer that formerly existed just above Hel in the bottomless pit of the Abyss broke off as well and split into different planes. They were caught between the influence of Hel and the remainder of the Abyss. Gehenna became a neutral middle ground, a plane contested by the devils and other demon lords. Neither perpetually lawful, nor chaotic, Gehenna was no less evil. In time, it twisted the fiends there into a new faction of demon. The demons that rose from the evil intrinsically woven into the fabric of this plane began calling themselves Daimons. These creatures of unadulterated evil did not accept the order imposed by the devils, nor did they completely disdain it. Instead, they chose to take the middle road, creating yet a third paradigm of Evil.

The fiends of Hel thought to subjugate the demons of the Abyss, who in turn wasted no time in rebelling against Hellish rule. The independent demons considered themselves as evil in its original and natural state, well, those that contemplated it. On the other side, were the devils, who believed that their Hel had formed the bottom and oldest circles of the abyss. When Hel and Gehenna broke from the Abyss, the six hundred and sixty-four layers of primitive evil supported by it no longer held up. The abyss then wormed its way through infinity becoming bottomless. This belief has caused the Devils to view their kind as the primal evil, evolved. While the devils and demons warred with each other, the Daimons exploited the struggle, not allowing either side to triumph. So, the war continues infinitely, the War of the Darkness.

Arguably, more intriguing than the origin of Hel is the mystery surrounding the one that first ruled there. The legend, as the Archangels of the heavenly planes tell it, is that before the fracturing of evil into three primeval factions there was one utterly powerful Archfiend. This fiend, so the story goes, was originally a celestial power of the highest caliber. His exalted place in the multiverse caused him to contemplate his own nature, filling himself with vain ideas of omnipotence. Seeing himself as a creator but unable to create anything, he perverted the natural state of all things. Love he twisted into lust, passion into wrath and from truth he spawned lies and so on with all the good works of creation.

Believing that he should rule everything he rebelled against his own enigmatic creator, The One Above the Watchers.

Of this creator, only one thing is known. He rarely exercised raw power, choosing ultimate restraint and allowing the faithful of his creatures to fight on his behalf knowing that they who remained pure and uncorrupted by the perversion would have the ultimate victory. These creatures fought with the father of evil and his minions who had joined him in the betrayal. Ultimate evil was eventually defeated, cast out of the heavens and thrown into the pit. There it festered for ages.

With the creation of mortal races, the source of all evil and his minions stirred. The heavens, closed to them for a length of time incomprehensible to man, prevented them from waging war with the celestial host. Now through these younger creations they saw a new path to victory. The father of lies adopted his strategies accordingly. Through the introduction of the concept of the exaltation of the creature above the creator, they began corrupting mortals, so they would be unworthy and thereby unable to enter the high planes, known as the Heavens. It is through this venue that the Inventor of Evil was to pursue his objective of conquering the multiverse. Through conquest of souls his influence would spread until the lights of the heavens grew smaller and dimmer eventually blinking out, leaving only the darkness.

To achieve the purpose of his vile design, the Lord of the pit caused himself to fracture into three competing parts, a despicable sort of trinity, at war with itself for one aligned purpose. Of this triad of overlords the most well-known is Asmodeus, lord of the ninth and deepest layer of Hel. Less well known is Apollyon, buried deep in the Abyss, a mighty angel who rules only in the respect that no creature of the Abyss would dare oppose him. The third ruler, master of the Daimons, is much more mysterious. Who knows where this third overlord's home is? Does he possess a name? Does he even continue to exist?

Next was the emergence of super powerful beings, driven and seemingly comprised of conceptualizations of good, evil, order, and anarchy. These beings lived and breathed lofty, balanced or contemptible concepts and were the collectors in the war over the souls of mortals. They were the Watchers, called Gods by some, and their power and survival depended on the devotion of mortals. Why the author of life and original creator of all things allowed this division of his creations is a great mystery tied to the meaning of life.

Between the forces of good and the forces of evil, there was a great gulf, larger than the two sides, from it arrived a middle path with its own gods and planes which were viewed by the others as neither hot nor cold, but tepid and afraid to take sides. These neutral gods, however, see the great divisions as the intention of the creator, pointing to the natural state of the mortal worlds as proof. These adherents of neutrality consider the present state of the multiverse as in harmony and seek to preserve this harmony, seeing themselves as "keepers of balance." Therefore, when the balance leans toward incessantly evil dominion they support good who then views them as on the path to uprightness. When the balance tips with overpowering righteousness, good perceives them as another face of evil that requires sanctification or destruction. The forces of good have faith that they will prevail by winning-over the souls of the neutral. Where good has faith and hope, evil has hate and fear. In its fullest form, evil deigns to corrupt all who are corruptible and none are more corruptible then those who cannot choose between light and dark. Both sides contend that the world of living mortals is neutral so that their life is one long choice that earns them absolution or damnation upon death... the departure from the neutral world.

The balance has tipped slightly at different times. Once, when the balance moved into evil's favor, Hel increased herself. Since growing beyond nine layers would go against the order of the lawful plane, the ninth pit of Hel split in half, maintaining the order of nine hells and creating a new plane altogether. This new plane carried a host of evil gods with it. Acheron was the name of this hellish place.

Megeara was one of Asmodeus's devils. She was only one among many but answered directly to a Pitt Devil. Pitt Devils were amongst the truly powerful of Hel. This particular Pitt Devil was a king, a favored servitor of Asmodeus. Megeara had no memory of her mortal life. Hel fire burned the memories out of her as she took her new form, reborn into a devil. She was a certain species of devil known as a Dirae, resembling an angel but with a special aptitude for tempting mortals. She thrived on the lust of humans, using it to cause lasting torment of the kind that leads to a life of sin, which she hoped would culminate in infinite damnation. Her memory went back hundreds of years to her birth into a Dirae. She had spent much more time as a Dirae than anything else. As most fiends, she was descended from a mortal but she considered her life as such, insignificant. Whatever brought them to Hel in the first place did not matter anymore. Now she found herself in the mortal realm, lover to an undead noble, hunting the source of some foolish mage's mysterious locket.

Megeara, using the name Imarra, had become Drusus's lover. She recognized how powerful the master vampire was. When she met the vampire, he had no god and if destroyed would have been tortured in Hades forever. She made a pact with Drusus that if he turned over the rest of his unlife to Asmodeus, she would see him descend into Hel much as he was. Imarra knew her god's heart. She knew he approved her offering him eternal life in the service of Hel. Drusus was very powerful already and had the sadistic ambition Asmodeus prized so much. In return for this favor, he swore to help her uncover the origins of the locket Garthadon used to summon her. Drusus made a deal with her, thinking it better to have power in Hel then to be a slave in Hades.

Another reason the devil chose to be the vampire's companion was Imarra's love of torturing Ashenath. The passion of Drusus's chosen servant was extraordinary, her malicious envy unrivaled. Imarra thanked Asmodeus for the ecstasy derived from tormenting her. Imarrra so enjoyed Ashenath's suffering that she would lavish Drusus with pleasure and affection whenever Ashenath was nearby. He

164

played along, knowing that every pain Ashenath experienced was a precursor to his own delight.

Imarra was attracted to the master vampire. Though this to her was the least of her reasons for an affair with him. Only his cruelty out-matched his power. If ever she had seen one with the potential to be a great tyrant it was he. She entertained thoughts of conquering the surrounding land together and bringing all around under their iron fist. Imarra knew he was infatuated with her. As an additional benefit, they could torment Ashenath with the sounds and sight of their love forever and she could not die from it because she was already dead.

Imarra lay on the bed in the best room at Smallfort. She chose when to sleep and when to wake. She did not need to sleep but she enjoyed it. Drusus visited her frequently here. In this spacious room, she dreamt Drusus and her, were hand in hand, lords of an immense land. She dreamt also of manipulating Ashenath into destroying herself in an unprecedented post death suicide, unable to cope with the pain of losing her masters affection to another and having it flaunted before her. Then, like every other time she slept since arriving into the realm of mortals, her dreams shifted away from her selfish pleasure to a majestic city with a black gemstone in its center, a castle with a black knight, his shield emblazoned with the star of the dark god, Asmodeus. The strange words that echoed in her head, a man's hushed voice, "Come home Megeara, Megeara, come home Megeara."

She awoke abruptly, the sound of combat in the taproom below. Naked and unarmed she jumped out of bed. Nearby were her chest plate, scalemail skirt and longsword. She struggled to don her chest plate, which had four latches in the back making it suitable for one with wings. She slid her scalemail skirt on, attached her sword belt and scabbard. Imarra armed herself with her quiver and bow as she took off, barefoot, down the hall. She silently commanded her wings out. They grew from her back as she ran. She did not bother with the illusion that would make them appear white. Her wings were as a Malebolge black-bird has, prevalent black with crimson tips and streaks resembling blood splatter. She descended three levels of stairs, running full force with her wings folded behind her.

Imarra emerged on the balcony level above the taproom, she could tell the fighting was fierce. She ran notching an arrow then stepped onto a chair, up to a table and leapt to the banister, her wings spreading to their span and catching the air so she could balance herself on it as she began firing down into the lower taproom.

Looking down into the bar-room below Imarra seen several armored men firing wooden quarrels from crossbows on one side of the taproom. A few of their locally created vampires lay with stakes in their hearts, on fire. Knights wearing black plate armor charged from the backs of armored horses through the Smallfort taproom, bashing their way through table and chairs, armed with magic lances, some aflame others coated with ice or dripping with acid.

There were seven mounted warriors but two looked vague to Imarra, like specters. She recognized that they were invisible to her companions. Her devil eyes could see through almost any illusion, including invisibility. Imarra shot one of them. The arrow went into his shoulder, causing the steel-clad man to become visible to all, and knocking him off of his invisible steed.

Imarra watched with delight as Ashenath forcibly dismounted a knight and ripped his throat out with her bare hands. The vampiress had a large wound where her heart should be. She looked up at Imarra with intense green eyes, a mouth bearing fangs and stained in blood, holding a handful of bloody human pulp. Imarra paused, now seeing what Drusus had seen in her. Ashenath was more than just a beautiful killer, Imarra smiled at her. Perhaps it was how much she relished death and bloodshed that made her so attractive. Their eyes locked together. Ashenath stared at Imarra's wings finally aware that Imarra wasn't human. Another bolt pierced through Ashenath's back and through her chest, reopening a closing wound. She should have been destroyed then, Imarra thought, instead the vampire ripped it out of her chest and charged after its owner. The crossbowman broke rank and ran until she caught him and killed him.

Drusus raised his gloved hand as if he were holding a sword in it. Imarra aimed at the invisible rider who charged in front of a visible, fellow knight toward Drusus with his ice-coated lance. Imarra struck the horse in the breast with an arrow, felling the beast forward, causing the rider to flip over its head still gripping the reins in his off hand and cancelling his invisibility. The other knight skillfully veered around the fallen horse and rider, closing in for the kill.

A bastard sword appeared in the vampire's

raised, gloved hand. It was a very large weapon, requiring two hands for the strongest of warriors to use. On the pommel of the sword was a pulsating red stone. Drusus gripped the hilt with both of his hands, driving it through the chest of the fallen knight. The red stone beat quicker and got darker. Drusus let one hand off of the sword as he swung it out in an arc at the next charging warrior, cutting the head of the horse clean off at the neck while it was in a full gallop. The legs of the horse tripped over the head, throwing the black knight forward with the force of the charge. He had nothing to grab a hold of and flew past the master vampire who made short order of separating his upper half from his lower with Transfusion, his sword. One of the knights spotted this and chose Drusus as his adversary.

Imarra took aim at a knight that was hacking his way through vampire spawn. She fired repeatedly but he always seemed to block the arrows with his shield. Finally, she dropped her bow, drew her sword and jumped from the rail letting her wings carry her down to the floor. He decapitated another spawn of Drusus then shifted his focus to her. She had not noticed prior but there was a kid in a leather jerkin crawling on the floor, stuffing holy wafers into the mouths of the destroyed spawn and pouring what must have been holy water into their eyes. Imarra and the Knight battled with longswords clanging back and forth for a few moments until the knight knocked the sword from the devil's hand. She let out a damsel's cry and caused her wings to retract, pretending to be helpless. The Black Knight threw her down on the table and held his sword to her neck.

"I am not one of them." He heard her melodious plea in his mind, as clear as if she had said it with her mouth.

The knight took off his helmet and stared at her. "Do I know you?" he asked.

Shock betrayed her face for a moment as she stared at him. This was the knight from her dreams. He looked her up and down. The knight never knew such lust and felt shameful for looking at her. She to, felt strange which only served to entice her more, so she leaned forward to kiss him. He jerked away from her, remembering the battle from which he was briefly unengaged. "Orginus!" Treant yelled, looking away from Imarra. He quickly spotted Prince Orginus on the ground struggling to fight off Drusus. Treant charged toward his fellow noblemen and brother-in-arms. He parried the vampire's sword with his shield forcing himself between Drusus and his friend. Treant fought viciously, Drusus was intrigued by the knight's skill and determination, but remained resolute. Sir Orginus was astonished by Treant's malevolent passion and at the same time hopeful that the Duke would slay this manifestation of murder.

"You are quite good," Drusus said smugly.

"Go to Hel, devil," Treant screamed back enraged.

"Most certainly young man, just not today." Drusus tore through Treant's defenses, disarming him and pushing him against the wall at sword point. "Now, what was that you were saying about me going to Hel?" He pulled the sword back some, with a sneer on his face, in preparation for a final, deadly thrust.

Imarra did not understand what was going on, but no one else was going to die until she figured it out. She vanished, reappearing in between the black knight and the vampire's sword.

"You have more surprises then a woman drunk and infatuated," Drusus said, barely flinching at her sudden arrival, pressing the tip of his large sword up to her throat and dragging the point down her breasts, then to her heart.

"Drusus," she said telepathically so only he could hear, "do not kill this man. I believe he has something to do with the locket." She squirmed a little and bit her lower lip.

Treant watched as the vampire stared at her, a smirk forming upon his face. The Black Knight knew she was talking to the vampire, probably pleading for his life, though he could not fathom why. She pressed her backside against him. He held his arm around her small waist, so that if the vampire lunged, he would be prepared to pull her out of the way. The Black Knight noticed her perfume, the aroma was sweet and he imagined he could taste it like a candy in his mouth. Her hair was incredibly soft and silky against his face. The knight only ever felt uncontrollable desire once before. His wanting was on par with his killing of the White Thorn knight the day Avriel and Coran died. Except this time, he was more fully aware of his vice and thought it better to crave her now and repent later. His stomach was a knot, his heart ached and his body trembled but no matter how guilty he felt, Treant wanted to yield to his desire.

Imarra wiggled a little as if to get more

170

comfortable and nestled her head into his neck, which sent chills throughout his body like a pleasurable sort of electricity "Tell me your name before I have him let you go," She said to him telepathically.

"My name is Archduke, Treant Cavalaries, first Lord of the Council," he said in his mind, "I will say no more."

"That is very well Duke, I am Imarra. When can we see each other again?"

"Never, I am sworn to a dire oath, release me now or kill me." The harder he spoke, in his thoughts, the greater his fortitude became.

Drusus removed the sword, at the devil's quiet bidding and Imarra stepped out of the way. Drusus watched him waiting for the slightest provocation. "Remove your dead and wounded boy, and don't come back or I'll grant you a lifetime of slavery."

"Moralis," Treant yelled out the name of Prince Dreadhawk's page. He looked past Drusus and Imarra at a maiden vampire with, dark brown hair and intense green eyes, holding the boy Moralis by the back of his collar. The page's head slumped forward, his body hanging under her grip like a doll. Prince Dreadhawk stood, looking at his dead page in horror.

Ashenath wiped some of the blood from her face with her free arm, smearing it rather than removing it. She revealed her dripping fangs and quivered from satiation. "Be sure to take him with you," she said sharply and then threw his lifeless body forward knocking over an already damaged table.

This display by the maiden vampire infuriated

Imarra. Ashenath was trying to provoke the knights. Sir Orginus drew his sword and peered at Ashenath as she transformed into a wolf. The body of the beast seemed to grow around the fangs. Drusus chose the form of a bat and flew up and over the banister. Orginus and Treant looked over at the seductive fiend who shrugged and smiled then waved goodbye to them before teleporting away.

"Mi Lord," Vektor exclaimed pulling himself free of the deceased. He gazed at the bodies of the undead still burning, the smoke rushing to the front door. The remains of five fallen knights littered the floor accompanied by the corpses of six squires formerly armed with crossbows. Only one of the seven pages present remained alive.

"Vektor, go retrieve the wagon and the priest," Treant ordered his page.

"Yes sir," the boy hardened his face, a deliberate effort not to show weakness as he took in the surrounding carnage. He ran outside and signaled the priest.

172

Chapter 24 - Detention

The cell, if one could call it that, was a place reserved for noble prisoners and consisted of a lavish bedchamber, day room and latrine. They were finer accommodations than Jynx enjoyed when he was free. A nobleman's arrest was very rare, leaving most of the cells on this uppermost level of the royal dungeon vacant. High inquisitors could investigate nobility, but only the crown guard could arrest them. The bedchamber was furnished with a large soft mattress and feathered pillows on a comfortable wood framed bed, decked with a silk canopy. A cast-iron bathing tub sat on an expensive blue runner, embroidered with silver snowflakes. Tapestries displayed scenic beauty from the great city of Blakoepal. A reading table set with plenty of parchment, quills and a slow burning oil lamp were among the furnishings of the room.

Servants brought fresh sheets, toiletries and any other requested articles on a weekly schedule. The dungeon staff treated inmates here with obedient respect, offering all the customary dignities due to one of higher station. Each prisoner in the noble level had assigned to them at least one private servant and some had many more. Jynx's personal servant was a quiet old man who said the least amount of words necessary, even when pressed. The dayroom consisted of a cushy sofa, three soft chairs, a cedar table with four matching chairs, a small library, a full bar and a small pool. There were decorative tapestries and candles that filled the room with a sweet aroma.

The latrine, assessable through a door in the corner of the day room had a stack of animal skins and a toilet. The toilet was nothing more than a stone block with a seat chiseled into it and a hole in the center. Waste would travel through the hole, down a long pipe, deep into the lowest level of the dungeon where those convicted of the worst crimes against the crown lived and died. One could occasionally hear the tortured sounds of the damned coming up from deep below. Those cries served as a warning to imprisoned nobles who might one day commit a crime so insidious as to endanger themselves of having their nobility striped then castaway into the dungeon's deepest reaches.

Most stunning to Jynx was the fact that the door to his cell locked from the inside. Granted the guards had keys to these so-called cells, but inmates could go into the corridor, walk the cellblock and visit other inmates at their own discretion. Many of them had their spouse imprisoned with them and some even had their children and family pet.

Jynx could not stand most of the other prisoners, seeing them as shallow hearted materialists devoid of both passion and honor. They likewise scorned him for a peasant. He did make three exceptions, however.

The first to befriend him was a young man of the gentry, cousin to the Helsoul family, a certain Acmus Coralforge. He previously squired to Hesan Helsoul of the Black Knights when he voluntarily had himself incarcerated. He was guilty of lying to his liege about his whereabouts on the Day of Merriment. Acmus, when pressed on his absence that day offered the lie he had been with a beautiful wench and accepted his punishment. In fact, he had been with a comely wench of ill report. After a week of an increasingly guilty conscience, Acmus confessed to his liege, offering his decommission. Sir Helsoul, out of benevolence for his cousin-squire showed him mercy and arranged for him to spend a month in the dungeon and keep his commission. Jynx found the squire's bravado to be both sincere and amusing.

The second day of Jynx's incarceration, Acmus introduced the warrior-rogue to a witch named Coppernia an older lady who wouldn't speak about why she was imprisoned. She, to Jynx's astonishment, was able to command some magic. Though only the most minor of her powers worked due to an enchanted, chain-linked choker locked around her neck. Still, she could heal minor wounds, mend broken objects and speak with the occasional rodent. She appeared to be a vibrant maiden at the pinnacle of her beauty, though she was admittedly an old woman. She was inquisitive of the goings on within the city, having not seen it for many years.

After a week, Coppernia and Acmus introduced Jynx to an old man whom they referred to affectionately as just that, the old man. He was a nearly blind, lunatic who could hardly see his hand in front of his face yet he did not require any aid due to familiarity with the dungeon's noble level. The old man claimed to be the only surviving defender that helped banish Asfixius centuries ago. According to the old man's imaginations, he cannot die until the fiend's return. Though he did have the look of a living relic, Jynx figured, being in here for too long had shaken up the old man's marbles. Aside from being entertainingly imaginative, the old man had other qualities, such as the ability to make a mean batch of some sort of dark, bitter brew that complimented brown-leaf smoke perfectly and could wake a dead man in the morning.

Jynx was grateful to have made friends for the first time since he met Whisper and Enigma as a child. Officials repeatedly questioned him about the attempt on the princess's life and the twins' whereabouts. Several Priests of Crotear had been present during the first interview. The Chamberlain and his son, both known to be powerful mages, were present as well. They definitely knew he was being honest with them, for if he tried to lie their magic would prevent it. He knew it would be futile to try to deceive them and he figured that if he did try his hand at deception it would mean almost certain death for him and his friends, so he gave up Whisper's location and told them truthfully that he did not know where Enigma was. Jynx hoped they would get Whisper, bring her in for questioning then release them both, being that he saved the princess's life. The rogue even had entertained fantasies of a reward, though he endeavored to dispel such fanciful notions at their emergence. He felt surprised and troubled when they told him that they could not find Whisper. After days of wracking his brain, the only solution that he kept coming back to was an impossible one. She must have disappeared with Enigma. The two abandoned him for whatever reason, how could he guess otherwise? He strained himself trying to understand how they could betray someone so close but conceded to the fact that if Enigma could abruptly walk out of his life then certainly his twin sister could as well. Jynx eventually decided that the old maxim was true, *blood is thicker than water*. He chastised himself for not foreseeing Whisper's inevitable betrayal. He buried his bitterness and indignation deep, suffering quietly at night and pretending not to care by day.

Chapter 25 - Retreat

Vektor ran through the gate of Smallfort where the Black Knights had a covered wagon and a large cart pulled by draft horses. Father Dregor waited with his young assistant healer, an acolyte named Ilsea. Besides the old man and the girl of thirteen circles was a wizard of the tower who's name the young page did not know. Vek remembered that the wizard had insisted on accompanying the Black Knights on the raid of Smallfort but Orginus had ordered him to remain behind the gate. Vektor didn't really trust those who could command the arcane energy of Orthe but now, after what he saw, he wished for a dozen wizards. "Come help!" The page cried out to the three that stood in front of the wagon. "Commander Dreadhawk and my liege, the Archduke command you bring the cart to collect the dead, many of our number have fallen!"

"Which sons and daughters of the Opal have fallen?" The aged priest asked.

"It will be more expedient to name the living," Vek said as he approached father Dregor. "I and the two I have named are the only survivors."

Ilsea and father Dregor gasped in unison.

"Hel be damned," the wizard exclaimed. "I should have been there."

"We have no time for this; the enemy is granting us a short truce to collect our dead."

"They are granting us truce?" Father Dregor repeated in disbelief. "By Crotear we must hurry."

The four proceeded through the gate, leading the horse drawn cart. Terror gripped them as they moved through the dark gate, listening to the song of the cicadas accompanied with the fresh scent of the surrounding forest, all except Vek who was too anxious and duty bound to be afraid at this moment. The other three were on the brink of panic and confusion. The Black Knights defeated by a terrible undead enemy they have never seen before caused their imaginations to run wild showing them potential death in every lurking shadow. The horse whinnied and its hair stood on end. As the group approached the Smallfort Tavern, they noticed a wolf stalking alongside of them. Ilsea nearly jumped out of her skin when she seen it. A large beast, vicious beast, warned them with a low growl. The horse was on edge, even a single howl would no doubt send it flying from them. Ilsea said some soft words and stroked the mare's neck, using her small amount of divine power to calm the animal. Treant and Orginus exited the tavern carrying one of their fallen brethren between them, a lady knight, one of the few dames in their order. They rested her body with two others several feet from the tavern. Ilsea guided the horse and cart up to the bodies while father Dregor placed holy wafers in their mouths and Vektor and the mage lifted the bodies unceremoniously onto the cart.

"Shouldn't we cut off their heads?" Vektor asked, causing the priests to grimace in disgust and eliciting a blank stare from the mage. They all stood looking at each other for a moment then father Dregor answered, "No. They are not vampires; the wafers keep them from turning.

Treant and Orginus arrived with the last body and plopped it on the cart themselves. Father

Dregor, approached this last body with increased temperance unconsciously dropping the holy wafer he held. He removed the knight's damaged helm revealing a horrible sword injury on his head. "Sir Vanmoor," he said as he caressed the man's face.

"Were you close to him?" Ilsea asked.

"I am," Father Dregor said with dew in his eye. I have ministered to his grandfather and all his descendants. They are a good family and he was the baby, this was his first quest as a sworn knight. I shall have to deliver his body to his mother and father, myself." The wolf, ever watching, growled again from their periphery.

"We must go father, give him the wafer. I am sorry for your loss." Vek left the rear of the cart.

"You do not appear to be bitten. Goodbye, little Kip Vanmoor."

Once the Black Knight's company was a quarter mile away they could hear the wolves howling in the distance all around. When they reached the field of fog, the wizard cast invisibility upon them all. High above them flew Imarra, who stopped in disbelief as they vanished from her view. Imarra possessed the infernal ability to see that which is invisible, yet somehow this group disappeared entirely.

Chapter 26 - Test

Jynx and Acmus sparred with wooden training swords while Coppernia watched and the old man, unable to watch, just listened. Jynx was easily the better fighter though he was impressed with the squire's skill and determination. No wonder the city's knights were so exalted, Jynx thought to himself, if the rest had half this man's drive, it would easily justify the fear and awe interwoven with their renown.

"Coppernia, who is winning my dear?" The old man asked, straining to make sense of the two quickly moving figures in the middle of Jynx's day room.

"Jynx is," Coppernia answered, shifting the old man slightly so that he looked in Jynx's direction.

"Oh yes, now I see." The old man armed himself with an imaginary sword and began thrusting and parrying the empty space to his front. Coppernia laughed as did Jynx who was paying almost as much attention to them as he was to Acmus. The lesser swordsman took advantage of the rogue's distraction, slamming his sword into Jynx's weapon forcing him to drop it then pushing the wooden tip against the fighter-thief's chest.

"Ha, I have finally won," Acmus declared proudly.

Jynx was surprised by the turn of events. After a moment of disbelief, he accepted his loss to one of inferior skill, but no less worthy an opponent. Jynx chuckled and pushed the tip of Acmus's sword aside with his hand. "Yes, you did win, and you have clearly demonstrated what I sought to teach you about exploiting distraction." The rogue, glancing past Coppernia and the old man, realized they were not alone. His three fellow inmates turned around and looked at the newcomers. There stood the silver-eyed nephew of the king, alongside the princess's fierce protector, Alturek, and a woman who had met and spoke with him every few days since his detention. She had introduced herself on their first acquaintance as Davania, an important person that he should cooperate with. She was not specific about why she was important or who she was. Her presence in royal company and her obvious authority to question him was evidence to Jynx that she was both truthful about her importance and someone he should cooperate with. Eventually, after he had cooperated with her for some time she mentioned that she was an inquisitor.

Davania was soft spoken and pointed. She never wavered nor showed surprise. She would step from question to question never lingering to long on any detail and never trying to steer him. She inquired mostly of personal matters about his life and history. She asked what he believed on many subjects. Many of them were topics he had never allowed himself to consider for too long. What mystified him most were the answers he had given her, beliefs he never realized he held. He found himself looking forward to her interrogations. Now she appeared as usual in a blue dress that fit close to her body but was stately and modest. Silver hoop earrings and a ring with the symbol of the inquisitors on it was her only noticeable jewelry. The inquisitor wore her long, brown hair down, letting it rest on her shoulders. She was unlike any inquisitor Jynx ever had the displeasure of facing. Indeed, she was just the opposite. Her grey eyes seemed somehow bright and disarming, she was direct but her voice was gentle.

"Your love of jest is your most persistent bane, Slumsider," Alturek said, speaking apparently of how Jynx lost the sparring match. "Sometimes it is his greatest compliment." Davania countered.

"It was only a play fight, nothing serious. Besides it was good for him, winning fans the fires of confidence." Jynx said.

"On the contrary, losing separates those with the courage to become, from them content just to live in mediocrity." Alturek drew his black hilted sword and looked at Agon.

The mage reached into his grey cloak and drew a silver hilted sword of excellent craftsmanship. Agon held the hilt flat in his palm with the blade stretching out toward Jynx. The weight of the blade, strangely did not cause the sword to fall from his hand, it seemed impossibly balanced. Jynx rightly assumed the weapon was enchanted to be light or magically manipulated by the mage.

"Neat trick," The warrior-rogue said to Agon with a cocky, unimpressed attitude.

The silver mage brought his flat opened hand up, causing the hilt to flip off of his palm. The sword spun completely around plus one hundred and eighty degrees ending with Jynx catching it in his right hand.

The rogue began to experiment with the blade, first holding it horizontal with only the hilt resting on his palm then he picked it up out of his right hand by placing his left index finger under the middle of the blade. Jynx balanced the sword on his fingertip, raising it above his head. *Now* he was impressed as he viewed it. "No matter how you hold it, the sword remains balanced."

Alturek lunged at Jynx. Jynx pulled his left arm from under the sword and caught it with his other hand as it dropped. The fight ensued at incredible speed. The two danced and tumbled like acrobatic showman while they fought vigorously. The spectators backed away from them. Coppernia and Acmus watched anxiously, hoping that their new friend could prevail. Coppernia explained what was happening to the old man who then starred at the two blurs with his ear bent toward them. At one point Alturek slapped Jynx in the left cheek with the flat of his blade then seconds later in the other cheek. Jynx turned flush from the loss of pride and became careless.

Alturek then broke from him. "Surrender the sword peasant, I am your master, you will obey me!" Alturek ordered Jynx who was confused and hesitated. Jynx dropped the weapon to the floor and held his arms partially up, palms out. Alturek smiled a coy smile then swung widely at Jynx aiming for his neck. Jynx kicked the sword up to his hand catching it and fixing his feet into a firm stance. Jynx, who held his sword tight with both hands blocked Alturek's blade. The two stood there with their swords in contact, neither man moving. "Why didn't you surrender your sword, my station is above yours, I am an agent of the crown guard and answer only to her majesty Princess Corrine Amorgoden?"

"You were still armed." Jynx responded simply.

"Very well, you have passed your test we shall put away our swords together."

"What test do you speak of?" Jynx asked.

"You will know soon enough," Alturek said as they both gradually relaxed, reducing the tension on their swords. Alturek slid his sword into its scabbard. Jynx considered throwing the sword back to Agon the way he received it, but decided better, instead he handed it to the mage pommel first.

"Coppernia, Old man and Acmus leave us," Davania ordered.

Jynx was flabbergasted as his two friends left his cell. "Does no one know the old man's name? Perhaps he has been forgotten here for decades."

"That is not why we are here," Agon scolded. Jynx quieted at the sound of the royal's voice and bowed his head.

Alturek spoke up in his usual course voice and direct manner. "Now that her highness is the reigning monarch and due to a void at the top of the crown guard's command structure, I have been asked to step forward as commander of the crown guard. I have reluctantly accepted under but one condition; I must approve of my successor." Alturek paused to let Jynx digest what he was saying then he continued. "You have been chosen...and I approve."

"Are you mad? I am a criminal, a thief, a peasant, a Slumside sewer rat." Jynx went silent, cut off in his rant by Alturek.

"I hate to hear what your enemies say about you. You are a hero, not without honor, who put his liege before his own life, nearly disintegrated by Agon"

"Sorry about that by the way." Agon interjected.

"But I acted on impulse not courage, if I had thought about it I do not know if I would do it again. Besides I am not as skilled as you in either stealth or swordsmanship." Jynx continued to protest.

Alturek looked at him intently. "Exactly, we need someone who can react with speed, who isn't impressed with nobility, who won't bow down to everyone of higher station, but someone who is a survivor, who knows how to fight *and* how to hide, someone who knows the tricks of the criminal trade and can intuit a man's motives. You are braver than you give yourself credit for, if I didn't believe that whole heartily, I would not have tested you."

The latter part of what the high guardsmen said must be true, Jynx admitted to himself, but how could it be? "I couldn't even intuit my best friend's motives and what of my skill? How am I qualified to protect the most important person in our world, ruler of Blakoepal?"

"It is far more difficult to see a friend's betrayal coming because you want to believe they are like you. This is why we have chosen one who does not have many friends and will put the princess first at all times as you did at Deadside. As for your skills, they are comparable to mine when I first became her highness's protector the day she was born. You are as qualified as one can be. I am answering the call to commander only because I have confidence in you to replace me."

"What of Whisper have you found her yet," Jynx asked.

Davania stepped forward. "Jynx I am sorry to tell you that she has completely eluded us. There is only one explanation that we can conceive, for even if she were dead we could find her. One of the city's dark guilds must be hiding her. She would have to be important to them or considered a high-level resource for them to take such measures. We suspect that she has joined back up with her brother and abandoned you for membership in the Agenda. I know they often require an act of betrayal as part of their rites of initiation." She paused as he looked down. "I am sorry for your loss."

Jynx refused to display his sorrow. "I will forget them as I have been forgotten."

Agon responded in a somber tone. "You must not be of a divided heart. Such a man is unstable in everything he does. The decision must be absolute. Doubt, must be utterly defeated with your answer."

Jynx looked from Agon, to Davania, to Alturek and regarded each one before he answered. "I will serve unto my last exhale; not for you or even me but for her, and to serve a cause that is above my prior useless life."

Agon nodded at him. "You have crossed destiny's bridge." With undecipherable words and a few peculiar motions made with his hands, Agon the silver mage teleported his group away, along with Jynx.

The four of them arrived in the barracks of the guard complex on the grounds of the city's palace, home to the royal Amorgoden line since the city's founding ages past, prior to the city's disappearance. An entourage of servants was waiting for them, holding in their hands fabrics, armor, Jynx's sword and scabbard, wine, cheeses and chocolates. Agon and the other two left Jynx to the mercy of the servants, who set upon Jynx with scissors, combs and perfumes. He was helpless as they made him over into a man suitably groomed and equipped to be seen in the royal house and protect its lady. They placed on him a suit of black leather armor, studded with small spikes, in the style of Alturek, topped with a jet-black cloak they said would make him more difficult to spot in the shadows. *That will be my life, a shadow, the shadow of a young and beautiful princess, but her shadow will be fierce and deadly.*

When the servants were done having their way with him, several led him through an arch and down a labyrinth of corridors that ended at a set of double doors emblazoned with a solid gold crest, displaying a gold dragon and a red embossed dragon. Large golden pull rings provided a way to open the great doors. Jynx could hear much fanfare on the other side of the giant entrance. Someone was being announced, someone by the name of Justice. One of the male servants stood with his back to the door holding the pull rings. "Walk out there lowly, kneel before the throne and do not speak until spoken to," the servant instructed Jynx and pulled open the doors. He quickly moved out of sight behind one door while another servant caught the other and held it. The servants were careful that no one in the grand hall seen them.

Jynx stood in the door, his heart beating hard as he looked across the great hall. Everywhere were courtesans, nobles and knights bowing deeply, ladies curtsying with graceful dexterity and guardsmen standing at attention. The rogue looked to his right and seen her majesty Corrine Amorgoden standing before her throne on a two-tiered dais, beauty and glory intertwined. Jynx felt lightheaded and his mind went blank. What was he supposed to do, he felt lost? Then he heard the servant in a whispery yell, "Walk lowly!"

Jynx hunched down and walked toward the throne. He looked to the ground with blurry eyes as he went. The rogue felt awkward, nearly tripping over his own feet as he dipped lower and lower unsure of by what degree etiquette demanded he lower himself. After what seemed to take forever, he arrived before the throne. He stooped down on a knee the way he had glanced others doing.

After a moment, Princess Corrine sat down on her throne, cushioned with silk, feather pillows and backed with gold and gem encrusted framework. Jynx could see out of the corner of his eye the nobles standing up in a great wave from before the throne to the other end of the hall, but he kept his head bowed.

"Stand tall," the princess spoke. Jynx stood cautiously, careful not to look up. "You may be at ease," she said gently but loud enough to be heard by those in the front rows.

Jynx looked up hesitantly at the princess. Her throne, rested on a dais with a white and gold embroidered covering, six feet high with steps leading up to the throne. To her right were three lesser thrones on a lower tier three foot from the ground. The Chamberlain and Agon occupied two

189

of them, the last of which stood empty. To her left was a throne that was larger than hers though no more majestic. This is where the king sits, Jynx thought to himself, he made note of Alturek standing to her right on the same level.

Princess Corrine spoke in a voice audible to the entire hall, magically amplified by her royal seat. Her tone was commanding and the only sound in attendance as she spoke. "Do you accept the commission of Royal Guardsmen, Protector of her Highness Princess Corrine Amorgoden?"

Jynx's heart pounded ceaselessly. He started to respond but his throat interfered. He tried to clear it quietly but unfortunately, his throaty response magically carried across the hall. He turned a deeper shade of red as giggling could be heard throughout the hall. The princess smiled in relaxed amusement but then read the embarrassment worn on the rogue's face. She returned to a serious demeanor and raised her left hand, holding it in front of her for a moment. The hall fell silent again and she made eye contact with Jynx.

"I do accept this commission your highness, with all my heart I will serve you." Giggling echoed throughout the hall but quickly ceased at the raising of her majesty's hand.

"From this day forward you shall be known as Justice Throneshadow a name well suited to you. Return to your knee and humble yourself before the throne of Blakoepal." Justice obeyed and stooped down to his left knee. He heard the distinct clamor of a sword being drawn. He lifted his eyes to see. The princess met him with a disarming smile holding a simple, though powerful long sword high

190

in her right hand. When he looked back down she disappeared from the throne and reappeared on the floor in front of Justice. From the front of the hall to the rear like a wave rolling across the magnificent room, every head lowered except the guards. She placed the blade gently on one of his shoulders and then the other. "I dub thee Sir Justice Throneshadow Knight Protector of the Lady, High servant of the Crown of Blakoepal and of the Amorgoden blood, Captain of the Crown Guard and a knight of the realm. Rise Sir Justice Throneshadow, Knight Protector of the lady." Justice stood up. In his suit of black spiked leather armor and cloak, bearing a new name Justice stood with confidence and for the first time in his life, he felt filled with honor.

Chapter 27 - Denizen

"Humanity, at its inception into the world, possessed only one power from its creator, the power of choice, creation or destruction. Humans could continue the grand work of creation through the birth of new life, growing in love and accomplishment, mastering the physical elements to advance humankind and infinitely working against the entropy of the material universe. So it was that the first man and woman took their vows to continue creation, they called their vows marriage. They had many children and grew in happiness fulfilling their destinies as they lived.

Their first son however, had a contemptible spirit and though he appeared to want what his parents lived for, deep down in the recesses of his soul he envied the creator and was not satisfied with his place in life. Those around him thought that his peculiarities were just a hallmark of his individual personality but the force of creation, a discerner of all creatures' hearts, knew better. When this first son of the world's first matrimony did not feel the closeness of the creating principle that those before him and many after him felt, he began to despise the celestial host and those high servants of creation known as watchers. Vorden, the first man who hated, grew up in resentment and festering rage until evil had its work complete in him. Vorden murdered the youngest of his many brothers in a fit of jealousy then fled his homeland. His selfish act wounded the first people, increasing their struggle over morality, making it much more difficult. Many of his family began to hate for the first time, hate Vorden that is, who they were determined to hunt and kill. Most of his kin never found him but those that did were brutally slain, dismembered and eventually even cannibalized.

The grace of creation drained from Vorden causing his skin to become a sickly white. He wandered the land aimlessly until a comforting male voice beckoned to him one night. Vorden followed this voice until it led him to the mouth of a great cave. "Come forth into the cave son, here no watcher's face will look upon you and your enemies will not follow."

"Who are you?" Vorden demanded.

"I am a kindred spirit, follow me and have your revenge on the watchers and men who have all forsaken you. I have no name. The powerful archfiend led him deep into the underworld where he nurtured his new follower. The fiend taught him pure evil, the kind that strode the middle road between law and anarchy, laying claim to all the darkness. True evil was to be the way of this corrupted man. Vorden was left alone with his odious heart for years.

The voice then came to Vorden one day. "It is time for you to create progeny, for you will be the father of outcast nations."

"But where will I find a woman to breed with?" Vorden asked.

The fiendish voice said to him, "One of the daughters of mankind has wandered too far into the wilderness. Seek her out at the mouth of the cave that leads to your home, and take her. She will be the mother of all kinds of evil. Your descendants

193

will be a race separate from humankind known as the Vorden after its father, until the end of time. I will be traveling back to my realm in Geheena to remain among my own kind, the Daimons. I will however return at different points to lead our empire to new levels of strife. You shall join me when you die but the Vorden will endure. Spread your seed and send half of your children out to subdue the different regions of the world, but you yourself remain in this unholy place. Never kill your own carelessly. Lesser and weaker forms of evil destroy themselves like rocks colliding but not you, you must persevere and become a persistent and patient evil. I shall send you the fiend Asfixius. He is my proxy and speaks with my voice."

Corrine looked up from her book. The story of the denizens and the war against them and their archfiend leader was one every man and woman could recall hearing as a youth. The princess sat in a chair beside the unresponsive king, reading out of the storybook that she found resting on the table next to his bed. Corrine did not know if he could hear her words but to believe he could, comforted her on an instinctive level. She thought it odd that he would be reading a book of legends. She remembered the story fondly. It was pleasant to hear the story through older ears and refresh her memory of the denizens, who reports confirmed were stirring beneath their feet.

"I love you father, I know you wish to be with mom again but I still need you here in the city." Corrine said to the unresponsive king. She stared at her sire longing for him to wake up. After a while she turned the page of the thick book and began reading again. "When the first people arrived in the place that would become the glorious city of Blakoepal they were surprised to find a people dwelling underground. The pale-skinned people all had eyes like black pearls, black hair and were quite secretive. Our people called them the denizens though they were known to themselves as the Vorden . . .

Chapter 28 - Balance

Mandathar and Elanor walked down a narrow dirt road to Smallfort, a countryside tavern and marketplace on the midpoint between civilization and wilderness. Their only companion beside each other was Elanor's large and fierce wolfhound Onyx. They were tracking the Master Vampire Drusus and his spawn. Mandathar had prayed daily to Crotear for protection from marauding bands of orcs and it seemed to Elanor to have worked, even though it was a simple prayer and not an invocation of divine energy. Now that they were close to Smallfort they were confident they would find no orcs, for even those monstrosities feared the walking dead. Mandathar and the ranger hadn't spoken much since Willowview, rarely any more than a grunt of affirmation with a head tilt and the occasional uh-huh, was exchanged between them.

They walked down the road that cut through the Black Wood. The morning dew glistened as the sun beat down through slivers in the canopy. Shortly after crossing a river Elanor noticed some wreckage jutting out of the woods. "Mandathar, look," She said pointing in the direction of the wagon. They crossed to the other side of the road and moved into the woods to investigate. It was a wagon. She examined the scene as she moved further into the forest. Toward the back of the wagon they both noticed several skeletons picked clean by scavengers. Onyx sniffed around the area. "There was a battle on the road at this spot." Elanor continued to examine the scene. "It involved a fairly large number of people. It was a pitched battle culminating with the victors chasing down and killing the losers. It is doubtful that any got away.

"Was it our prey? Mandathar asked.

"I cannot tell, the scene is old, but it does fit the time frame.

"Very well," Mandathar responded, "We must expect that it was Drusus but be open to the possibility of other threats in the area."

Elanor nodded in agreement. Then, as if in answer to him, Onyx started barking. Reacting to the surprise Mandathar lifted up his large mace ready to bring it down in a crushing blow as he turned toward the direction Onyx's pointed in as she growled and barked savagely, her short black fur standing straight up. Elanor squatted down on the ground loading her crossbow and taking aim at the subject of the alarm. A brown bear on all fours emerged from the brush, roared at them then stood up on its rear legs.

"Lower your weapon some Mandathar, and try not to upset it." Elanor's words were punctuated by another yell from the hulking animal.

"I think it's already pretty upset El"

"Here girl, we mean you no harm," Elanor said as she moved closer to the beast, crouching with one hand stretched toward it and the other hand setting down the crossbow. As she moved past Onyx, the dog ceased barking but persisted with a grumble.

When Elanor was near enough to almost touch the beast, its fur began to shift across its body. The creature began to shrink and its features started to appear almost humanoid until the transformation was complete. Elanor stepped back, arming herself again with her crossbow. Mandathar took no action except to gasp in astonishment. There stood a human woman of a peculiar earthy beauty. She wore a dark green top that covered only her small breasts and a corresponding loin cloth that hung down to a point above her knees. Her face, midriff and legs were camouflaged with mud based paint. Twigs were woven into her auburn hair with little green leaves hanging off. A thin vine served her for a belt which held a couple leather pouches and a sheath containing a sickle. Strapped to her thigh was a sheathed knife. She looked as though she was a part of nature another plant or rare bush given limbs to move, weapons to fight and a mouth to speak.

Mandathar and Elanor stood ready to fight while Onyx inched closer snarling as viciously as before. The lady of the wood approached Onyx gently. As she took each barefooted step the brush would move to make way for her then return to its original position behind her. Elanor realized that she did not so much as harm a blade of grass as she walked. Her dull green eyes kept the two hunters abreast in her view as her hand glided forward to pet the angry dog without caution. The animal became affable on contact with the lady's hand. Onyx turned her head and sought more attention from her new friend, licking her and chasing her own tail playfully.

"What have you done to my dog?" Elanor demanded.

"She is a good girl and knows that I am harmless to her," The lady of the forest said.

"Harmless to her but what about us," Mandathar chimed in, "Are you a demon or a lycanthrope or something?

"Neither," she responded, "I am a druid and the guardian of the east part of the Black Wood. "You seem to mean no harm to the forest and so are free to go on your way at any time."

Mandathar lowered his weapon and loosened his grip. "Then why appear to us at all?"

"I have observed you for several days, to be sure that you were not a threat to the forest or its creatures. I figured out pretty quickly that you were not, being that she is a ranger," she nodded toward Elanor. "Seeing that you come to destroy the unnatural blight that has taken refuge in Smallfort I wish to join up with you."

"Why should you care?" Elanor asked. "Druids don't care about the struggle between good and evil and vampires drink blood not tree sap.

"You are wrong because your viewpoint faces obstructions that prevent you from seeing the whole canvas. I believe that what is natural and simple is good and that which lays waste and is complicated is evil. Therefore, I strive to be good. The undead however, are an abomination. The natural cycle begins with new life and when it waxes old it dies and a life that is unique and untried begins out of the dust of the first. Unlife is the dust refusing to be dispersed continuing in existence and blocking new life."

Mandathar was perplexed, "Your world view is a mess but I think we are on the same side currently.

"Ha," she laughed "There is also the matter of Smallfort itself. Prior to the takeover of the small community, the orc population and the lesser human population kept each other in check, five orcs for every human. If people do not return to Smallfort the population will swell to over twenty to one and that kind of orc population will result in destruction for much of the Black Wood and its inhabitants. Not to mention the fact that a horde will inevitably emerge out of such a huge population of orcs, and you know what that means."

Mandathar's stomach knotted up. "Every village and hamlet for at least a hundred miles would be decimated, perhaps more.

"Then it is decided," Elanor approached her arm outstretched in greeting. The druid reciprocated the gesture grabbing Elanor's forearms in the customary greeting. "What shall we call you?"

"You may call me Delasy."

"Well met then, Delasy," Mandathar said as he exchanged the same greeting with her.

Together the three of them with Onyx travelled the rest of the way to Smallfort. When they were within view of the place Mandathar cast a spell on the three of them. The spell he said would make them invisible to undead but once they attacked the spell would vanish. Delasy transformed into a small green snake of the garden variety and slithered up to the fort. She slid through the cracks in the wall. Once inside she took her true, human form and unbarred the gate. She walked to the front of the fort. Delasy motioned for the other two to join her. "Stay here," Elanor said to Onyx, petting the wolfhounds head before going. Onyx sat with a protesting whiney. The three pushed open the gate the druid had unlocked for them and then barred it back. They crept around investigating the place and searched every room in the tavern. Eventually it became clear that most of the undead slept beneath the floorboards in the common room. Drusus would most certainly not be there so they decided to save the killing for the next morning and just observe the vampires for the night. As terrifying and dangerous of an idea that was, Drusus had managed to always remain a few moves ahead of them. Now was there opportunity to get ahead of him and they knew if they acted rash, mistakes would be made and another chance such as this might never present itself again. They stood against the wall and waited for nightfall.

Chapter 29 - Enigma

"You have proven yourself... somewhat," the barber said to the skinny rogue as he clipped away at his dark hair with a pair of sharp hand shears. "Evading capture on that botched assassination and managing to save the life of one of your fellows impressed the inner circle. You may choose your reward. Do you want knowledge or riches?"

Enigma regarded the balding old man through the mirror in front of him as he sat on the barber chair wearing an apron that would keep his clothing untouched by the falling hairs. He was getting use to these sorts of choices. Ever since he first sought membership in the Agenda, they presented him with choices that always led to another set of more choices. They were clearly judging him by the decisions he made. He supposed that if he chose wrong they would eventually have him killed but he knew it was useless trying to read the old man's expressions. Most likely, the old barber did not have any clue what he was talking about and probably didn't care what Enigma chose, he was just a go between, nothing more, nothing less. "To increase knowledge is to increase sorrow and though I have sorrows abundant, I desire knowledge because it is the purest gold," Enigma said quoting something he had once read.

"Very well," the barber said, setting down his hand shears and picking up a brush. The old barber began brushing Enigma off. "When you walk out of here tell the dog sitting on the porch that I do good work, then give him a pat on the head and go your way. He is a good boy but he'll probably give off a little growl, you just put your hand out to pet him and he won't bite. You might even need to nudge him a bit to wake him up. That ol' boy is lazy but he's a damn fine mutt."

The strange order, which was just another thing he had grown accustomed to since joining the Agenda, did not surprise him. "Very well, I shall take my leave now," Enigma said as he stood up and donned his cloak. He regarded himself in the mirror for a moment, "Well it is true anyways, you do fine work sir."

Enigma flipped the barber a silver council-piece to determine the quality of the man's reflex. The barber moved to catch it but failed and had to retrieve the coin from the floor. The way Enigma flung the gold piece a frail old woman could have caught it. The barber it seemed feigned rigidity. "My apologies sir, I guess I assumed you to be limber like myself," Enigma lied.

"No-no, I'm just an old barber that makes a few extra coins repeating what I'm told. The little agility I possessed crept away as my age approached me." The old man began to sweep up the hair on the ground, "Good day to you sir."

"And you as well sir," Enigma turned and left the shop. Enigma was sure that the man was telling the truth about his function but he suspected him to be deadlier than he pretended.

Enigma opened the door into the early morning sunlight and walked across the wooden porch to the short steps. The barber's dog was white with black and brown spots and lay at the top of the steps sleeping with a short leather leash attached to the

203

open handrail. Enigma cleared his throat loudly, trying to wake the animal. The dog continued to slumber peacefully. After clearing his throat a second time and not succeeding to wake the dog, he kicked it lightly in its rear end. He paused for a moment then when the pooch failed to respond again, he kicked the dog with a moderate degree of force. Surely, he thought to himself any animal would snap alert by now. When this failed to wake the mutt, Enigma got to thinking that the dog might be dead so he brought his foot back and aimed, getting ready for a big kick in its rump. The rogue let fly his leg but the dog woke up in mid kick and turned to look at him. The poor unsuspecting animal caught it square in the head and flew off the porch. His leash caught on a nearby bench and tightened suddenly. Enigma, who watched horrified, heard a distinct snap from where the mutt went sailing off the porch. After pausing shortly in disbelief, Enigma ran down the brief steps to the site of the dangling dog. The pooch hung dead, the tip of his tail touching the ground. Enigma looked around frantically, people walked by but no one took notice or bothered to get involved. He tried to act nonchalant and stood in front of the hanging dog. He acted so nonchalant that it was downright conspicuous. He thought about what to do. The old man seemed quite attached to this animal. Still, he had to give the signal the barber told him to give and could not risk having a confrontation with the old fellow. Therefore, Enigma took the only course he could think of. "That owner of yours gives a fine hair cut poochy," Enigma said before patting the dead dog on the head then walking off a little quicker than he would have normally.

Enigma tied a black cloth over his face to obscure his sense of smell. He went to the great stair in Slumside. As he traversed the great stair and the bridge community it housed he watched the city deteriorate along the route from the dangerous Slumside to the gutter of the great stair. Two rows of hovelled dwellings, tents and the occasional rundown bar or seedy business stained the sides of this stair as his path took him from a place that was treacherous to one that was nearly unlivable. It smelled like burning excrement everywhere. Large lamps filled with glowing moss cast its purple illumination in some places. In other parts, torches burned brightly, tainting the smell of offal. The inhabitants emptied their chamber pots into large barrels about as often as they emptied them directly onto the stair. Workers emptied the barrels at a dumping site at the end of a path cut out of the wall of the great stair. Often these workers would just dump them on the stair in an accidental spill. The further he went the worse it got. Fortunately, he did not have to go beyond the first landing. The landings were places where the great stair would turn to the opposite direction before continuing to descend further. They were places of concentrated businesses. Like little town squares they were arranged around a single well.

At the top people could be seen everywhere. They were short, skinny and pale from generations of malnutrition and abuse, a shadow of their own humanity. The further down one descended the more subhuman these people seemed to become, more and more denizens could be seen walking about freely most of them a sickly bunch as well.

The half-breeds with their pale skin, dark hair and large black eyes could easily be mistaken for either man or denizen. They usually gravitated to the middle of the stair on the center landing where there was a temple to their furious god. A god of rejects and rebellion who did not accept the other gods, Ssyba god of chaos was the demonic patron deity of the half-men. Ssyba, they say is a servant or perhaps even the bastard son of Apollyon. People say his worshipers could rule this stair if they would organize and make laws. The worshipers of Ssyba claim that they do rule. The absence of legal devices and structure are the very proof of their rule. "Look around," they say, "we keep it like this, the stair is favorable to our god, no creature can tame this place and that is the sign of our dominion. Lawlessness is the order of the day on the great stair."

Looking over his shoulder periodically, Enigma kept his attention on his surroundings as he crept to his apartment at the tavern. The tavern's name was reminiscent of the language in the city above. The Downside tavern was not an upscale place by a normal man's standards. The roof of the great stair was the tavern's roof; the floor of the great stair was its floor. Short steps led directly to the door of this literal hole in the wall. Enigma entered the Downside tavern, shutting the door behind him and removing his scarf. Inside the smell was of scented oil burning in several lamps. Enigma took a breath. The smells were rather heavy yet far preferable to the stench of burnt refuse outside. Men and woman occupied almost every square foot in the Down Side tavern. By far the best place on the first stretch of the stair, it easily rivaled the Slumside Tavern for depravity. Any disgusting fetish was available for purchase here. Murderers waited for hire, both professional and the opportunistic type. Vaguely attractive prostitutes, some quite scrawny and pale were drawn to the bar room of the tavern like moths led by a flame. The prostitutes dressed in scant costumes meant to entice and designed for convenient accessibility often leaving their breasts exposed. The cloths they wore virtually fell off of them as they begged and flirted with the patrons, performing cheap under the table favors and trafficking in sordid rumors. Their lack of modesty was appalling by any standard of decency but the men they serviced were downright barbaric. A small group of bards, possessing mediocre talent at best, played fast-paced music for the men to yell over as they boasted of themselves and the women danced around and up against them. Everyone seemed to be addicted to some powdery concoction that made them edgy and hostile. Jynx's mother was no exception.

The mother of Enigma's former best friend approached Enigma requesting to do business with him and tugging at his cloths and body. Enigma pulled away as uncomfortable as he had ever been. The mother of Jynx was a haggard version of a once attractive woman. She called herself Rag, an appropriate name for one with no self-worth. Her makeup smeared on her face, most of it rubbed off. Her long blond hair knotted, tangled and matted in some places. Rag's breath reeked of cheap alcohol. Her teeth were in fair condition but she had many scars and wore the evidence of many beatings at the hands of brutal men. Yet despite all of this, to look at her, you could tell she once had been pretty in what she remembered as a former life. Enigma felt great pity for her. He ran into her by chance, looking for residence below the city. After encountering Jynx's mother, whom he just barely recognized, at the Downside he decided to get a room their so he could keep an eye on her. Jynx had thought her gone forever.

Enigma handed her a council piece. The silver coin was enough to content her and get her to stop her advances on him but not enough for her to kill herself, which she would undoubtedly do if she had more money, drinking and drugging herself to death. She grabbed him in a big hug around his chest and kissed his shirt. "Thank you. You are my son's best friend, watch over him and never let him see me this way. You are too virtuous for this neighborhood Enigma go back home to slumside."

Again, Enigma felt uncomfortable. He awkwardly rubbed her head as he was filled with an earnest longing for her vindication and peace. He felt her pain as if it was his own and oh, how he missed his sister and his friend. All his feelings rushed over him, he held her head close and for a moment it was as if she was *his* lost mother.

Enigma put his hands on her shoulders and moved her back. They regarded each other's faces as water began to well up in Rag's eyes. She wiped her eyes smearing her makeup further and smiled. Enigma knew her smile to be a thing developed for hiding pain. He decided in his heart to help her get away from addiction, monstrous men and the depravation of the great stair with its evil, insane god. The Inquisitors had not banned him from communicating with Jynx's mother, only Jynx and Whisper. "I have to go now," Enigma, told her, "I will be back." Enigma walked away slipping through the crowd until he got to the stairway leading up. On the second level, he found his room. Enigma could tell someone had entered his room while he was gone. He supposed it was probably the Agenda. He decided that if he was wrong and someone was in there waiting to kill him he would just act surprised.

Enigma entered his apartment taking in the once white wall with pink flowers now a yellow wall with pink blotches. He had two small rooms, a surprising luxury for the Down Side. "Good day, sir." Enigma said acknowledging the presence of an unannounced guest in his apartment and lighting an oil lamp with a large match next to it.

"Enigma…" the man concluded with a hideous laugh before starting again with a high pitched and vile voice. "Being a pupil of the art of shadow is all practice and play." A man wearing a black body suit with a black scarf and hooded cloak walked into the room with Enigma. "When you play, you are practicing and when you practice you are just playing. Isn't it so Enigma?"

All Enigma could think about was, what is wrong with this guy's voice? Did he spend years training himself to sound sinister? His voice was raspy, he was skinny and he paced around creating an air that was disturbing. Still Enigma could not resist. "It is so," Enigma spoke in the same creepy manner as the intruder. "The city is the game board and I play chess with its people."

The man turned his head sharply at Enigma's rendition of his voice. He considered that Enigma was serious but when he seen Enigma's smirk he felt foolish. "I will give you your knowledge or rather your path to it since that was your choice. The princess has a new bodyguard. Alturek was promoted to commander of the crown guard since someone poisoned the previous commander," he said with his shrill voice.

"I wonder who did that." Enigma said sarcastically playing along with this demented man. That of course caused said man to burst forth into a disturbing cacophony of cackling laughter.

"It is your time Enigma. If we need to kill this fool replacing Alturek," his voice deepened with dramatic flair, "It will fall on you to execute him."

"What's this walking corpse's name?" Enigma asked halfhearted.

He let out his hideous laugh again. "His name is Justice! What a name!" He screeched.

"Well say the word when you want him dead and I will make it happen or die trying." Enigma lied. If he had to kill to complete his mission he would, though he would prefer that no one without blame got hurt. Besides, it was not as if the guards were innocent, they chose to set themselves against others.

"Now for your assignment," he said.

"I thought that was my assignment?"

"No, that is your path to knowledge. Your assignment is to infiltrate the Black Spiders and find out what they know about what we know." The intruder began rubbing his slender, gloved hands together, hissing out a new laugh that sounded like he had just lost his voice.

Enigma was shocked. *I was right all along, these people are lunatics,* he thought to himself.

"One more thing Enigma," The intruder asked. "Why did you kill your contacts dog? If you wanted a new contact, we could have set you up with one."

"I didn't mean to." The rogue said somewhat embarrassed.

"Well either way we will have to get you a new contact seeing how your old one wants you dead." The Hidden Hand, as agents of the Agenda were wont to call themselves, departed the room into the darkness of the hallway.

Enigma spent an hour in retrospective contemplation pretending to be asleep, killing time just in case someone he could not detect was spying upon him. Then Enigma donned his disguise, a dangerous veteran of the crown sword, old, with white hair, a loud boisterous temperament and a passion for brandy. Denert, Enigma's alias, went to one of the walls in the mostly empty apartment and pulled away a dresser. As he pulled it away, a space revealed where he had cut through the wall and placed furniture on both sides of the opening. He had fastened a handle on the back of both dressers so that he could recover them to their original positions. Enigma playing the role of Denert entered the other room through the hole. The other room he had rented in his guise as Denert and it was full of furniture and decorations in the appropriate style for an old military veteran.

Denert walked to the door, picked up his old sergeant's hat and went down to the bar below. He mingled with everyone he came across and had a glass of brandy of which he spilt liberally on his clothes. Denert yelled, laughed, and smoked. "I don't care for quiet types," he declared hitting some young drinking buddy on the back. Then he started dancing in a most ridiculous manner as if he were roaring drunk. The patrons laughed and cheered. He bent one of the prostitutes backward giving her a great big kiss then popping back up from it he said farewell to his friends and staggered out of the Down Side tavern and up the Great Stair.

Denert stumbled up the stair with leather nose plugs sticking out of his nostrils. He made it to the top of the great stair and continued down the streets of Slumside, occasionally petitioning passers-by for a drink. Such pedestrians would avoid an old military man that was slurring his words. To approach a drunken warrior was to guarantee a fight. When Denert arrived at Jirtle Park, there was a modest amount of people there. The parks were largely left alone by adult criminals though younger ones would congregate there, selling their poisons, vandalizing, recruiting and moving information. Younger children still frequented the park, hanging near their parents or an older sibling. On a bench facing a swing set, a fair, hooded maiden seemed to relax in her warm cloak as the first snow began to fall gently around her. Denert paused, "There is a picture of beauty that will be frozen in my mind's eye forever." He walked over to her and sat down. "Well to meet, missy."

"And you as well good sir, a fine day for a friendly conversation to be sure."

"Very true indeed," Denert said lowering his voice. Enigma let go of his cover, speaking discreetly in his own voice. "I must gather information on Princess Corrine's new bodyguard. They may require me to assassinate him."

Davania looked at him wide eyed. "You may attack him but you are to lose the battle and barely get away if at all. Under no circumstances are you to kill the guardsmen."

"What do you mean by, 'if at all' this bodyguard is going to know I am coming right?"

"It is important that no one knows. I will provide you with the information you require"

Denert stood up and left without another word. He wandered over to the Slumside Tavern, stumbled in belligerent and seemingly drunk. He spotted a card game at a table where he recognized several members of the Black Spiders by their preference for red and black garments accompanied by Spider tattoos. He insinuated his way into the game by sitting down in the one empty chair at their table.

"How dare you invite yourself to sit here you foolhardy old puke," A brutish thug said as he rose from his seat pointing a hostile figure. He was a muscle-bound man with particularly bold tattoos of black spiders and letters from the ancient alphabet. The ancient characters remained in use by the citizens of Blakoepal but were long forgotten by most that dwelt beyond the city.

Denert right away identified the brutish man as the groups second in charge. He looked at the two who were seated next to him, anticipating one of them to be the leader. "My money is as good as any mans, lad." With that, he threw down a crown piece.

"Sit down," The man to the ruffian's left

ordered him. "He is dangerously foolish but also correct. His gold is as good as anyone's." The man who spoke was a dark featured, thin man who wore a black cloak with a red interior and a large gold and garnet encrusted ring. Then he whispered seemingly to no one, "We need a drink for one more."

A slight wind blew. The bar wench behind him was leaned over pouring a neighboring table ale from a pitcher when she felt the small breeze and stood straight. Her hair danced up on one side as she heard the whisper delivered on the wind. She turned around, "Yes?" The spider mage smiled at her. She then poured a drink for him and provided one for Denert as well.

The individuals of the Black Spider Guild flaunted their membership and status. They enjoyed many benefits for doing so but risked their very lives in the process. This was an organization of boldness and subtlety, where both aspects received their due. Boss was a meaningful rank for the Spiders, it meant he was the leader of a gang. This magic wielding Spider boss could be Enigma's ticket in.

Enigma, in his disguise as Denert played cards until early in the evening when the whole crew was drunk. Many came and went at the Slumside Tavern including many Spiders. Denert noticed that many of them would disappear through a particular door. After a long draw of losing at cards, Denert excused himself for the night. The table burst with laughter as he stumbled into the boss. The rogue emptied two outer pockets and an inner pocket of the mage's cloak into his own hidden pockets while avoiding detection. Then with a small sharp blade affixed to his finger on the inside of his hand he swiped at the mages belt pouch which landed on the floor with a plop. Acting the part of old drunk, Enigma grabbed the mage's shoulders to steady himself. The boss laughed at his new acquaintance's clumsiness.

"Oh, I dropped my damn pouch," Denert said. He quickly retrieved the bag stuffing it into his own bag before standing up and sharing a final laugh with his fellow card players. Denert stumbled away. When no longer being viewed, he quickly moved to the doors he had been watching Spiders disappear through all night. Inside the door was a small meeting room with a round table sitting in the center, paintings on opposite walls and a large tapestry on the back wall. Denert guessed that there was a secret passage behind one of the pictures and predicted that if he chose the wrong one a loud alarm would sound, alerting people whose job it would be to kill him. The large tapestry was of the city, one picture was the gate to the palace and the other was the Black Opal and surrounding park. He decided to wait and see. Enigma hurriedly shed the disguise of Denert placing it into his bag of keeping. He chose a black cloak to wear over his night suit. Then he painted Spiders onto his cheeks and temples with black camouflage using a stencil he had acquired. He didn't have to wait long. He heard the door lever turn. With his boots of the spider walk he jumped on to the table. Then he jumped again, this time as high as he could, kicking up with one of his feet. It landed high on the wall, sticking to it. He brought his other foot up which connected with the ceiling likewise sticking. Then he crouched on the ceiling as Spiders entered through the door.

"That old rascal was alright boss." The brute from earlier said. "He kinda reminded me of my pops, hel I almost felt bad taking his money though I guess I shouldn't since you ended up with it all."

The group's leader pressed the Black Opal on the one picture. A moment later three blocks of stone rose an inch out of the floor work, one in front of each painting and the tapestry. "Yes, he was a real character and a big spender. I hope he comes in again sometime." The Spider boss stepped on the stone in front of the tapestry, which caused all three of them to move back into their recesses and the section of wall holding the picture of the palace gate to open revealing a narrow stair going down. They all entered walking single file. The short stair gave way to an equally narrow corridor. Enigma scurried in above and behind them remaining on the ceiling until the door closed of its own accord. Once the door behind him shut, Enigma dropped to the ground silently. An eerie feeling caught the last man of the group, so he turned around in the pitch-black corridor. He did not detect anything and did not wish to expose himself to the ridicule he would face if he came across as paranoid. So the low rank Spider turned back around reluctantly and followed his betters further down the path.

Eventually the path opened to a five-foot wide tunnel which ended in a small room. Torches in the room reached into the hall with their illumination. Enigma stopped in the corridor just short of the room. He strained to listen as the Spider boss identified himself to someone in the room. It seemed as though there were several men. Peeking

216

inside Enigma could make out an elevator across the room. It had a cord wrapped around a pulley. One operated it by pulling the cord on one side of the pulley up or the one on the other side down with a clamp.

Enigma watched as an agent of the Black Spiders, wearing nothing but a pair of black breeches and a red sash, covered in tattoos boarded the elevator with the boss's group. He began making the elevator descend. Enigma waited for it to disappear from sight then he ran, vanishing into the shadow right before the room's illumination and reemerging in the shadow of the shaft avoiding all the inhabitants of the room. Enigma spider walked down the shaft for an unexpected length of time.

Finally, the elevator stopped in a vault. Enigma was grateful that there was enough room for him to crawl out onto the ceiling.

"Good night to you," the Black Spider boss said to the man who operated the elevator.

"I shall wait for you to exit," he replied.

"Of course." The boss said. He went to reach for something on his belt. Upon discovering that it wasn't there he began patting at his clothing and waist in search of it.

"Problems?" The elevator operator asked sarcastically.

The boss stared ahead as he thought for a moment, mentally walking through the recent past. "That damned foolhardy old puke! He stole my bag!"

"That funny old man from earlier swindled you, boss?" One of his men asked.

"I guess you men are going back up eh?" The

217

operator of the elevator asked.

"Yes, as a matter of fact there is a deceitful old drunk that needs to turn up dead in the alley behind Slumside Tavern."

The gang of Spiders returned to the surface leaving Enigma in the vault. He dropped down to the ground fifteen feet and found himself alone with a door. Going through the Spider boss's bag Enigma found a key. He retrieved a cone shaped device from his bag and placed it over the keyhole. Listening carefully, he could hear quite a commotion from the other side of the door though he could not make out anything specific. He resigned himself to opening the door, another one of life's great gambles he thought. Enigma used the key to unlock the door. He gave it a gentle push and stepped back. The rogue stood there in disbelief. The door had given way to a great cavern filled with hundreds of people with several bars and an arena in the center. Enchanted crystals embedded into the ceiling gave off a light reminiscent of the brightness of a late afternoon. He stood at the entrance to a balcony level thirty feet from the floor of the cavern. There were several balconies; the level on which he stood seemed to be under the control of the Black Spiders.

Enigma could see a seat of stature at the front of the balcony. That must be Silhon Riversnake, lord of the Black Spiders, Enigma thought to himself. He stepped through the door. There were two men, one on either side of the entrance. "Hail, Spider," One of the men said to him. Enigma figured that there was a specific greeting these two men were looking for and he knew he would be unable to foster it, so he ran and shadow jumped in front of the Spider Lord. Enigma drew on the Spider Lord even as his men raised the alarm yelling, "assassin!"

Enigma placed the edge of his sword up against the high Spiders throat, "Stand down," he ordered.

Silhon Riversnake regarded the young rouge thoughtfully. "Do as he says Spiders!" The hostage ordered with unnerving calm.

Enigma smiled as everyone put away their arms. "Now, I need to speak with you in private."

"Certainly, but first put away your sword."

"No. My sword gets put away when I feel safe," answered Enigma.

"Very well," Silhon Riversnake stood half crouched as he was taller than his captor and did not want to inadvertently cut himself. "Crossbowmen and mages in the shadows have you in their aim. So be smart and drop your sword" Silhon turned awkwardly to face the rogue. Enigma was starting to see in his peripheral vision crossbowmen and mages coming out of the shadows. The crowd below was beginning to stare up at him. Silhon faced him, raising his left arm a dagger ejected out of his sleeve into his hand. "I am not Silhon anyway," The imposter Spider lord said, pushing the point of his undoubtedly poisoned tipped dagger up against Enigma's neck. Enigma dropped his sword. Someone approached him with a red handkerchief and blind folded him He didn't even feel the sap hit him on the back of the head before he slid into the thoughtless black of unconsciousness.

When Enigma awoke, he felt throbbing on the

back of his head. He tried to reach for his head when he discovered that he was tied to a chair and still blindfolded. "Who do you work for assassin?" A stern voice inquired.

"I am here to join the Black Spiders," Enigma answered.

"Do you expect me to believe that shadow walker?"

"It is the truth and if you untie me I will be very direct and bold."

Someone cut Enigma's binds. He stood up and grabbed his blindfold pulling it off. Enigma stood facing the man in front of him. He could not believe it as he looked around, whoever this was, he was not afraid to be alone with him. The man was three inches over six feet and built like a gladiator. He wore black pants and a black cloak. His chest was exposed and every part of his body both seen and unseen was covered in geometric tattoos. Enigma could see that a tattoo of a Spider crossed the man's stomach the pincers open where his heart would be. He knew of this tattoo. The rumors he had heard were that Silhon Riversnake had a Spider tattoo on his back with the tail reaching for his heart and that all were forbidden from duplicating this particular tattoo.

"Lord Riversnake, I was forced by the Inquisitors to spy on the Agenda and forced by the Agenda to spy on you. I ask, Spider Lord let me spy on them for you. Let me work for whom I choose against the others. I am through with the Inquisitors blackmailing me and I am tired of working for the insane Agenda. I wish to join the Black Spiders." Enigma looked Silhon in the eye.

"I have been in this business long enough to know when I am being lied to."

Enigma took a heavy breath before Silhon continued. "However, I also know when I hear the truth, welcome Spider boss Enigma. You will maintain your cover by continuing your assignments. I will give you information about us that you can feed to your higher ups in both organizations. Now I have but one question for you?"

"Go ahead my lord." Enigma said curiously.

"Why did you beat that old barber's dog to death earlier today?"

Chapter 30 - Rise

The man opened his mouth wide trying to breath, desperately gasping for air. Terror griped him and he could think of nothing. He did not question who he was or where he was. He did not even know that he was a man. The only thing real for him was the emptiness in his lungs. He had no care for the fact that he was shaking as if in a violent seizure. He pressed his eyes closed, leaving him in pitch-black darkness as his inability to breath completely consumed him.

This went on for some time. Time not measured. He cried out without a thought as to how he could scream and even beg the darkness with no breath. He tried for a moment to be still before quickly throwing himself back into a fit of panic. This went on for a longer time. He would be still then he would flail about screaming with no air to fill his lungs. Finally, he was still and remained that way long enough to contemplate his own existence. Memories started to flood his conscience. He remembered how he was mistreated as a child, ignored by his mother, criticized by his father. He remembered how he fought with his siblings. His training as a knight was fraught with contempt and abuse. He dwelt on every potential love he had known and how they had scorned him until finally he settled for a wife he did not love and who demanded everything from him but offered him nothing in return. He remembered the priest and how he had always sided with his parents. He despised them all. At last he recalled three days ago, when he was finally chosen for an important mission, finally he was given the chance to prove himself but he was killed and the mission was a failure.

He opened his eyes. Seeing only in black, white and shades of grey he discerned the interior of a box. "No!" he yelled, he was inside a coffin. He screamed under the realization that he was dead and buried, kicking and scratching with his long tough nails he began to tear through the top of his resting place. He cried out "Noooooo!" over and over again still acutely discomforted by the absence of breath. "Why?" he yelled, "Gods why!" Then he stopped, looking around his burial box he wondered to himself how he died. "That woman," He said to himself. "This is a gift. She was merciful to me. The only one in my life to ever show me kindness." He started to burn in his chest with a desire to be near her. "She will be my mother, no, my master." Her beauty was burned into his mind all he thought about was serving her, and his thirst. His thirst descended upon him as if every particle of water and blood in his body had dried up. The moisture in his mouth conspicuously missing left it feeling arid. His stomach tightened as he thirsted more and more considering revenge on all the people he had ever known. All people were the same except for her, the one that ended his damned life. "I must find her," he declared overflowing with hatred and thirst. The undead Black Knight realized that he knew her name though he didn't know how, "Ashenath. I am yours to dispose of. Master Ashenath." He began to tear through the inside of the coffin thinking only of her face as the roof of it collapsed and he dug through the dirt tirelessly without pause until his hand broke through the surface. His hand started to burn and recoiled back into the dirt. "Sunlight," he said, "I am destroyed by sunlight." He would have wept if he could. Instead he seethed with vile contemplation and murder.

Chapter 31 - Under

King Napsian waited for weeks to receive the chalice that contained King Eratide's soul. Now the pale-skinned monarch of the Vorden, who occupied the lower city as well as miles of caverns and forts below, traveled to the deep temple. This was the place of their master's imprisonment since the earliest days of the great city.

The Vorden had their own city beneath Blakoepal, complete with buildings and streets, knightly orders and nobles, split into sectors called domains. This second city was deeper than the surface city's graves, sewers and dungeons, yet it was still inside the encompassing shroud of the Black Opal in the center of the city above which prevented their race from leaving the encompassed area. As long as the opal remains in place, their evil is imprisoned within the confines of Blakoepal and the undercity.

A passage in Slumside led down to the city below. It consisted of a wide series of ramps flanked on either end by stairs that descended two miles before converging on an under-city street in a place called the Upper Domain. This ancient passage known as the great stair continued to see use by the commoners of Slumside and the riffraff of the lower city's upper domain. Alongside this great stair was a bridge community, owing fealty to neither the upper city nor the lower. Here lawlessness was the order of the day. Vorden and human intermingled freely, even breeding with each other when the fancy struck. The children of such unions were usually Vorden and in the cases where they seemed human, the Vorden taint was obvious.

Vorden mating ritual was symbolic of their creation myth. A male Vorden would attempt to force himself on the female. A fight would ensue leaving an unsuccessful, injured male or a brutalized female, who would then accept her fate and if not killed by the event, go about raising the child with admiration rather than hostility for the male. Such mating rituals of violent courtship could make life on the chaotic bridge city quite dangerous for human women.

The Warlock-king, Napsian, sat atop his mount staring at the grand Temple of Theories, waiting for his favored mate, the powerful Bealu Belejez.

Napsian rode a type of beast known as a darkbreed. His was of the purple variety, though black, brown and dark green were common of this species. The Vorden were the creators of these creatures. The darkbreed possessed four strong, thick legs that ended in clawed paws, good for climbing and digging. Its head was like a canines but much larger with small sturdy horns protruding out of its forehead, it could attack by ramming with its boney head. It had a short haired coat of fur and large teeth. These creatures could see very far in the darkness.

The Temple of Theories was a place for questioning the cosmos, the meaningless of life and denying the divinity of creation. Here every individual Vorden was a god in their own eyes. Their belief system was faithless, when you die you go to Geheena, when you die again you go nowhere because there is nothing beyond that which is known and since everything in the universe is in a constant state of entropy, everything will eventually waste away leaving nothing. Self-importance was the driving force in this godless, anti-religion. Hatred for all other lesser races was central to their ethos because other races relied on gods as a crutch for personal weakness.

Asfixius, imprisoned in a chamber deep inside the earth, stewed for centuries. Several kings made it their mission to discover the location of his chamber. Once found, a generation was spent excavating it. When this was accomplished the Void Priests built their temple around it. From then on ruler after ruler has tried to free Asfixius in vain. The only comfort for Asfixius was his race of subhuman followers. Asfixius taught a secret form of magic, called Binding, to certain select followers he called Bealu. A Bealu's magic bypassed the gods and most of the Black Opal's influence granting a dark form of arcane magic. To give his Void Priests divine magic he taught them to siphon power from the gods thereby stealing an unholy magic capability.

King Napsian heard the approach of a darkbreed. He did not turn to look expecting it to be Belejez. Even if it was not her approaching, King Napsian had no fear, for Vorden almost never attacked each other, excepting for their violent mating ritual. The thought of someone attacking the chosen of Asfixius was unheard of.

"Your majesty, my quest has been successful." Belejez spoke in an icy tone, riding her darkbreed over to him. He continued to stare at the temple as she approached. A finely polished black obsidian spire loomed before them ten-stories in a gigantic, spacious cavern. Over the chasm was a forbidding stone bridge cut out of the rock, reaching across the hundred-foot chasm dug by his ancestors. A ninety-foot drop onto a spike embedded floor, filled two feet high with acidic sludge awaited those who would fall off the edge of the chasm.

Belejez regarded the temple in the light of hundreds of torches on individual gold stands as she sat upon her mount next to King Napsian. She did not turn her head as she spoke to her king, looking ahead at the path leading to the temple. Chained to the wall flanking the great yellow-stained, double-door was a human man and a woman, unclad with iron collars. Their fate was to starve to death for the pleasure of the Void Priests, who loved to hear them crying and begging as they entered the temple. "I have the chalice on me, why do you stall?"

He waited till until finally he felt moved to speak. "I am the one. After so many worthy predecessors, I am the one. I shall free our master. I am reflecting, not stalling. There is always time for reverential pause before stepping into greatness." Several more minutes passed. "I am ready Belejez, give me the chalice."

She removed the bag from her back, brushing black hair out of her stone-white face. So many years waiting for an item such as this chalice and yet it was her that Napsian had his eyes on, it was her that was most intriguing to him. Part of him wanted to possess her right there and never let her go. She would be a calculating and challenging mate. More and more he was coming to terms with what he was going to have to do. She had killed or maimed many suitors but no other was worthy to be his Queen.

Belejez removed a box from the bag and handed it to the king. The box was plain so as not to appear to hold treasure. He opened the container and removed a chalice of gold, covered in emeralds, rubies, and sapphires and inlaid with platinum. The treasure sparkled, reflecting torch light in all directions, glowing with bejeweled splendor.

King Napsian dismounted his steed, Belejez followed suit. She walked closely behind as he crossed the bridge, taking his time traversing the walkway before finally arriving at the doors. He took in the feeble cries of the humans on either side of him, as if it were a breath of fresh air. Their ribs were clearly visible, their skin was sagging and the woman's hair was starting to fall out. Belejez raised her voice to the doors "Stand aside before the Master of Nobles, his majesty King Napsian Manslayer."

The doors opened in front of him.

"Greetings your Majesty," a hollow voice emerged from the doorway. The two Vorden entered a small foyer that opened into a grand atrium shaped like a hexagram. At the center was a short slab of stone stained with blood, large enough to lay two people on, with copper channels that ran to a drain in the floor. Lying sedated on it was a human woman wearing only a transparent white gown. Six huge pillars held the ceiling up.

The king made his way to the altar. Void Priests, some wearing yellow robes, others wearing purple hued armor stood with their Bealu allies. The assembly of male and female Vorden clergy gathered in the corners of the Atrium. There was no status that could not be held by a female Vorden. The greater the status of the female, the greater prize she was for the male that conquered her. The rare female left unconquered, by a certain age would be off limits and would then seek men to subdue and would often have several servile men though she would never reproduce.

The king and his companion stopped at the altar and waited. Then the High Temple Lord, wearing heavy plate-armor stood before the pillar that was in line with what would be the top point of the hexagram. When he did this, the illusion of the pillar disappeared revealing a spiral staircase leading both up and down. Belejez drew a dagger and slashed the sedated woman's throat without warning then put her dagger away giving the dying woman no more thought. King Napsian and Belejez walked toward the stair. Napsian and the Temple Lord glared at each other with hatred, both jealous of the others power. They would never act against each other though, out of their fear of Asfixius and his command against the spiteful killing of other Vorden. They both knew that the other held value for the Vorden race as a whole. This misanthropy was their transcendental ideal. It allowed them to experience many virtues such as obedience and sacrifice though it be for a vicious end. Those above must wonder, *is virtue for evil still virtue?* What benefited the race, benefited the individual. The ends of their race, of their kind superseded in every respect the ends of the individual. Such was the point of view of the Vorden; in all that they did they sought to serve their race.

The King, Belejez and the Temple Lord descended the stairs. They walked out of the stair into a spacious chamber buried deep within the earth. Shaped like a diamond, the room had four wide pillars, one of which was the staircase. The ceiling was a mere twelve feet high. In the center of the chamber was a circular hole in the floor. All around, treasures abounded, gifts to their master. The king approached the opening in the floor. Hanging out of the ceiling next to it was a thin copper pipe from the altar above. He looked down into the hole, holding the jeweled chalice.

Asfixius looked up from the vault below the hole. The archfiend was the height of a tall man, thin and muscular with dark violet skin, an elongated head featuring horns that seemed to be made from iron. It had a mouth with sharp carnivorous teeth and fangs. Two large round eyes of swirling fire stared at them. Attired in a purple robe and armed with a large, exotic, curved sword. Asfixius reached up catching the chalice as Napsian dropped it through the hole.

There was a field of force wrapped around the vault, nothing living could pass through. Nothing that is, except for the current king or queen of Blakoepal. The barrier of force became visible for a fleeting second as the chalice passed through. The chalice was a phylactery that contained King Eratide's life force.

Asfixius grabbed an ornate bottle of ancient wine from amongst his treasure. He uncorked it with his teeth and poured it into the chalice. Then the fiend tossed the bottle up to king Napsian. Asfixius held the chalice up in the air as if giving a grand toast. King Napsian held the bottle under the copper pipe, which began to flow with the blood of the fresh sacrifice above. This was the catalyst for activating the magic of the chalice. In an unholy transubstantiation, the wine in the chalice turned to blood, the blood of the life force trapped within it. Asfixius drank heartily. Not allowing the overflow to be wasted he wiped his face, licking his hands clean of the blood. He looked up and dropped the chalice, which landed on the floor with a resounding ding. He now had the blood and soul of the King of Blakoepal within him. The Fiend had to act fast because it would only hold for a moment. With all his vigor, he jumped up to the opening in the ceiling, grabbing hold of the edge with his clawed hands and then pulling himself up the rest of the way. Asfixius stood looking first into the chamber then all around him. He let out a great yell that echoed for some time before he finally spoke. "I am free at last. Tremble city above for I am going to visit ruin upon you and remove the cursed Black Opal. Then I shall unleash my people on the whole of Sophia and then all over the Orthe." The Vorden shook with fear and yet were excited. At once falling to the floor they pressed their foreheads to the ground prostrating before their vile master. Asfixius looked over at his worshipers and smiled widely. "My children..."

Chapter 32 - Mourn

". . .Therefore, the circle of archmages banished the cruel fiend Asfixius. They gave up their own lives to fuel the power of the spell. Only one wizard survived, his name was..." As Princess Corrine read her father the story, his body withered and decayed. She looked up just as his bones began to turn to ashes. Corrine let out a gasp and stood so suddenly she did not realize she was standing. Corrine's mouth fell open as her father's form gave way to dust, but not a single sound could come out. It was as if she forgot her language. Corrine felt as though she were going to pass out. Her respect for distance faded and all the objects in the room danced around her. Then almost as suddenly as it began, it stopped. The room came back into focus including the human shaped pile of dust on the bed. Her hand let go of the book, which fell to the floor even as the chalice so far below her fell in that dark chamber of Asfixius.

Treant waited in the hall outside of King Eratide Amorgoden's bedchamber. He was to pay his respects to the king. He was the first to be granted permission to view the king and thereby pay his respects personally. It was a reward for his heroism outside of the city. He stood there in the hall, lined with fifty heavily armed and armored members of the crown guard, waiting patiently for the Princess to call him in. He felt good and was smiling for the first time since the deaths of Avriel and his young page's deaths on Coin Street. He finally had redeemed himself it seemed.

"Hail, Archduke."

Treant turned to look at the speaker. Caedis! "Why are you here, Viscount?" Treant demanded, his smile fading. *Finally, I am going to have a moment of glory and reconciliation with the princess and I should not have to share it with a scoundrel, especially this damn scoundrel.*

"Obviously, the Princess invited me here. I sent her a gift of condolence and she wanted to thank me for it in person. Also, she said something of me and you burying the dagger." Caedis laughed at the thought. Treant felt the ever more familiar feelings of wrath swelling up in him when his anger and Caedis's laugh was cut short by a sharp, high pitched scream from in the king's bedchamber.

The two guards beside the double-doors grabbed the handles of them, pulling them open. Treant and Caedis charged into the room side by side, the crown guard pouring in behind them. Treant looked around frantically, drawing his sword. *Was it another assassin?* The princess fainted. Caedis caught her before she hit the ground and lifted her up. Princess Corrine awoke as suddenly as she had fallen and held her arms around him weeping hysterically. Treant noticed the ashes just as Caedis asked, "Where is the king? Where is the king princess? Where is he?

She pointed at the bed. "He is there!" She yelled, causing her to cough, her tears never ceasing.

Treant took notice of Corrine's bracelet as she pointed. It was gold and had white roses growing out of it, roses that turned yellow as she was in Caedis's grasp. It was the very bracelet Treant had specially made for her. He thought to the last time he seen it. He had given it to Avriel minutes before she died. "Where did you get that bracelet he demanded?"

"She got it from me." Caedis said firmly looking up at him while holding the princess.

"Prepare to die murderer." Treant raised his sword in the direction of Caedis, still holding the princess, who let out a fearful shriek. Treant startled by the terror in Corrine's eyes tried to defuse the situation. "Your majesty, do not be afraid, it is him I am going to smite. He is a traitor, I was going to give you that bracelet but he stole it."

Just then the silver mage, Agon, teleported into the room surprising everyone, including the princess who was not usually startled by his unexpected arrivals.

Justice, her majesty's new bodyguard ordered the soldiers out of his way as he entered the room and coming up to Treant placed the tip of his longsword behind the Archduke's neck. "Drop your sword or lose your life First Lord."

The princess felt rage for the first time in her life. "Treant you have insulted mine and this knight's honor for the last time. You are a vain madman and a liar. My first act as queen will be to remove the Black Knights from their favored status if you remain one of its members!" She pushed Caedis away from her and retrieved the royal scepter, which rested next to the chair she had sat in. "Be gone from my sight you, ignoble bastard!" She waved the scepter which teleported Treant from the palace grounds and deposited him into the street. She turned looking all around her, her vision beginning to blur.

"I have you cousin." Agon grabbed a hold of her, stroking her hair as he tried to comfort her. "Justice, order everyone out."

"You heard the mage, OUT!" All the guards filed out at Justices order, Caedis Stood there. "That means you too, nobleman." Justice snapped.

"You are doing a good job." Caedis remarked as he backed up to the door behind fifty soldiers making their way out. "Thank you by the way for saving the princess. You do deserve to be more than a *common*, Slumside rat."

Jynx glared at him, tightening the grip on his sword and clenching his teeth. "Just get the hel out, nobleman."

When only Agon, Justice and the Princess remained, Agon spoke to the bodyguard once known as Jynx. "Justice, send someone to fetch my father and Alturek, something must be done. I will stay here with the princess."

Chapter 33 - Connoisseur

Drusus and Ashenath entered Smallfort tavern through the front door as their spawn, a mix of former caravan guards and tavern patrons, returned the floorboards of the taproom to their original places. Drusus ordered half of his spawn out into the countryside to hunt for food, the other half he told to man the fort as if nothing had ever happened there. The bumbling moron that was the inn keeper's nephew took up his position behind the bar. Varies tables had vampire spawn sitting at them pretending to be patrons. Each was served a drink. Some were filled, others were only half full of wine or ale so that it would seem that they were actually drinking their spirits. Drusus sat across from Ashenath in silence for a long time before one of his spawn brought in a pitcher. He poured a dark red fluid into his master's wineglass, then followed by pouring Ashenath a glass. The servant vampire spawn left the pitcher on the center of the table and started to walk away when Ashenath stopped him.

"Slave, where did you get this vintage it is rather bitter but very good.

"It was drained from a boy around twelve circles old then mixed with the tears of his weeping sister, Chosen One."

"It is excellent; make sure we have some to keep on stock.

"It is good, but not great," said Drusus, "I prefer the blood of the venerable over that of the young. It has been aged and survived many circles before being uncorked. I prefer the sorrowed tears

237

of the mourning over those cried by the fearful after seeing someone torn apart before them. They have a sincerity and genuine taste that does not need to be bolstered by terror. Though nothing compares to the blood of an elven woman that is with child, there womb is full twice as much and their love for it is twice as strong than a human parent who often cares more for themselves, although I have only had this delicacy once."

Ashenath smiled at her master. "Where is Imarra, master?"

"She has tracked where those Knights came from. It seems there is an enclave hiding about an hour toward the darkness from here, perhaps an entire castle hidden under a shroud of the grey mist. All the land where this enclave sits is a mere illusion covered in thick fog of grey mist."

"I am shocked," Ashenath replied. If this enclave is invisible, then how does she know of it?"

"She observed the three we left alive and some others that were waiting for them cast an invisibility spell on themselves. She can see through magic invisibility so she stalked them then suddenly they vanished completely. We think they entered some sort of area that deepened their magic. Imarra can cause herself to go invisible so she is going to try and enter the place to scout it out and then come back for us."

"You trust her?"

"We have no other choice."

"But Master, you do. I infected one of those knights. I can feel his presence getting closer, he should arrive tonight."

"Ah very good Ashenath and to think I was

toying around with whether to destroy you or not. Perhaps I will free you one day."

"Master, I exist only to continue as your slave." Inside of Ashenath was a burning hatred for Drusus mixed with approbation.

Chapter 34 - Possess

Imarra did not know what she was getting herself into. She paused before using the power that would make her invisible. She theorized that she would be able to enter whatever sort of enclave was hidden. She did not know what to expect and had to be prepared for a hasty retreat. This was the only way she could find out what was going on. She knew the locket that had held her true name was tied to the mystery of this place and she needed answers. She assumed her human form, causing her wings to vanish as she entered the mist. She wore her white cloak with a deep hood that cast her face in shadow. Bow in hand and a full quiver on her back she willed herself invisible.

Instantly the entire visible world changed around her causing her a moment of dizziness as she turned about trying to take in a panoramic view of the newly revealed location. She was in a large park it seemed, in the center of a huge city. People walked about in every direction, entire families, friends, lovers, groups of children playing, every possible combination of human acquaintance. Imarra put her hood back with a sweep of her hand as she took several minutes to absorb the unexpected enormity of her surroundings. "Gods be fooled, what incredible magic it must take to hide such greatness under a rock!" She spoke to herself in a low voice. "How is this possible?"

Imarra looked around the park and seen in the center of a grand pavilion, a single stand resting upon which, was the largest gem her eyes had ever beheld. A man approached the large opal and touched it for a moment and then walked away. Imarra realized that she was drawing unwanted attention from a nearby group of adolescences due to her unearthly beauty and the lost look she wore on her face. She recovered her hood and walked easily toward the pavilion. As she approached there was a child of five or six winters with his parents at the top. She waited at the first step watching intently as the boy touched the gem. The child removed his hand and shook his head. "Maybe next time," said the mother. The boy held his head low as they walked down the stairs paying no attention to Imarra as they left.

She moved slowly up the stairs inexplicably drawn to it. Imarra was greatly intrigued and she wondered if she should hazard to touch it. She stood before it and reached out gradually, her fingertips just a breath away from the mysterious opal, with arcane energy dancing across its circumference. Then as soon as the tips of her fingers made the slightest contact with the orb, the world altered around her again. This time it was like a dream, except that she was totally conscious. The feeling of it was exhilarating. The vision showed her at first, a newborn baby that grew to be a little girl. Imarra felt a familiarity with the girl as she was shown the girls whole life, every important moment, small and great. The girl was sweet and kind but her family was dominated by worship for Imarra's liege Asmodeus, the God of tyranny, master of the ninth circle of Hel. The girl grew up as nobility in the city of Blakoepal. The girls name kept echoing and augmenting vociferously. Megeara, the beginning of

Imarra's true name! Megeara Cavalaries, the girl's heart wanted to do good and be simple but her family tormented her and beat her whenever she was caught showing mercy to anyone. They taught her to hate, to use people, to call an alliance friendship and to call friendship, foolishness. They twisted her and she cried tears of bitterness every night until she grew up into a cold and calculating woman. The Watchers it seemed spared her few mercies. There had been a handsome knight whom she had played with as a child and she desired him as a spouse. Unfortunately, she was not the kindhearted girl he remembered and was prone to fits of jealousy. It seemed to him that she was incapable of genuine love and knew only covetousness, so he married another. Not accepting what he had done, she seduced him and came to be with child but her childbirth was a secret. Her father took the child from her and gave it to her eldest brother whose wife could not produce him an heir. She threw herself into martial and religious study. She married a powerful duke who was also a high priest of Asmodeus. Together with the followers of the righteous god Crotear they defeated and banished the Denizen's fiend Asfixius. Shortly after, Megeara was betrayed by her husband who had become the most powerful priest of Asmodeus. She had never really given herself to him or to the watcher Asmodeus. She was secretly meeting with a priest of Crotear and ready to convert when her husband found her out. He sacrificed Megeara to his god in a ritual to increase his power. She had never been granted a vision from the opal.

The vision ended and Imarra stood before the

opal stunned. So much time had seemed to pass in the vision but only a moment had actually passed in the world around her.

"That was my life," she whispered in a broken voice.

"What did your vision contain?" a voice behind her said.

"What?" She turned to see the youths that had noticed her in the park a short time ago, though for her it had been decades and she was still in shock.

"Your vision, what was it about?" A young man said. "We can tell by the pallor of your face that you received one."

"Imarra stared with a blank expression on her face. "It was lurid," she said before walking off.

"I'm sorry" she heard the boy say as she left, and it caused her to wince.

Megeara Cavalaries had died in a ritual sacrifice and gone to the hellish plane of her watcher Asmodeus where she became a devil going through transformations of which she had no memory until she got to her current form. She had never heard, not even in a myth, of a lost soul recovering the memories of the life that damned them. As far as she knew she was now unique. Her mind was racing. Though a lot had changed she made her way as best she could to Cavalaries Castle, her human home and birthright in a previous existence. In the vision, she had relived her life a second time so that now her human life was closest in her memory giving her a certain measure of humanity that was both disquieting and exhilarating. She could still recall her current existence quite vividly being that she had centuries of time in her present form, although it was a little faded with her human life fresh in her memory. Old passions and old wounds were at the forefront of her consciousness.

Megeara made her way to Cavalaries Castle. *How can it be?* She wondered as she found herself in the very place of her mortal birth. Centuries of torturing and corrupting mortals and immortals alike all began with a lowly human birth in this hidden city. Not only does this defy the diabolical laws of the hellish plane that she possesses a memory of her life but the very fact that she is present here completely perplexed her. It was as if the Opal had called her home.

Megeara approached the gate of Cavalaries Castle. She stared at the place for a long time. Its looming grey walls covered in vines and brush, the spires of the keep rising high above the walls towers. The huge gate was exactly as she remembered it with the Cavalaries standard placed as a great seal on the center of the gate, a golden lance crossing a gold armored horse in the center of a black circle. She placed her hand on the seal and said in a whisper, "Megeara Cavalaries." To her delight the gate unlocked and she was able to enter. *Old magic.* The grounds were filled with trees and she made her way to the back of the estate over by the stables. There she spied a girl of eighteen circles, doing laundry on a washboard in a large basin next to a pond of clear water. The girl was obviously a servant and thought herself alone as she sang a song of romance. She had a natural loveliness with comely garb and raven hair, a simple beauty of the kind only the servant class could produce. *She is perfect*, thought Megeara to herself. The devil stripped, hiding her gear, cloak and clothing behind a bush and waited behind it until the servant girls back was turned then walked boldly out to the pond. She stepped into the water her eyes focused on the servant who carried on singing in an elegant voice and hanging wet clothing on a line. Megeara walked toward the center of the pond lowering more and more of her naked body into the water until she was completely submerged.

The servant turned back toward the pond never doubting that she was completely alone. The servant had a thought come to her in the form of a suggestion that she assumed was her own mind. *I should like to bathe in the pond while the laundry dries*, she decided. Valley, the servant girl, disrobed and entered the edge of the pond. Finding the water warm delightful on her bare feet she entered further, dropping down to her neck. Then she ducked totally under the water and swam to the center of the pond. When her head emerged, she wiped the water from her eyes. Valley felt a tingling sensation in her gut. She began to feel uneasy as if she were not alone. She looked all around in near panic. When she discovered nothing, she laughed at her own paranoia. She had been swimming in this pond her whole life and she knew there were no other servants on this part of the grounds.

She dove forward with a splash trying to swim to the floor of the pond. When she was under the water near the floor of the pond she opened her eyes. Directly in front of her was a woman, naked and seemingly dead. The servant girl let out most of

245

her air and shot straight up to the surface. She started crying. Filled with terror she swam as fast as she could to the edge, swallowing large gulps of water. It felt like something was slowing her down. As if a nightmare had become reality, the harder she tried to swim the slower she seemed to move. She felt dizzy as she flapped desperately in the water crying out for her dad to save her. Then she disappeared into the pond completely. Her mind was being pushed aside by something inside of her. Something was taking over her body and absorbing her memories. She was helpless to stop it but she tried in vain to do so. Everything was still for a moment, and then she felt a hand pull her out of the water. It was a fellow servant, the cook. He was a tall man of large proportions, strong and somewhat fat. He was a hard man but kind to those he felt deserved it and gifted in the kitchen. "Valley! Valley is you ok girl?" The cook asked.

She could see through her eyes and feel the water but she could not open her mouth or move her body. "Yes Chef," she heard her voice say to him, "I don't know what happened." She was crying but she did not have control, something else did.

"Who is in here with me," Valley cried out in her mind.

"You may call me Imarra", a strange voice answered inside of Valley's head so only the two of them could hear the communication. Valley's dad Stavid arrived with two other servants. He rushed to his crying daughter's aid.

Chef, as the cook liked to be called wrapped a rug around her body and picked her up as though he were cradling a baby and carried her to her room in

246

the servants' quarters. A posse of servants fell in step with them as they made their way through the great halls. Word of Valleys near drowning spread through the estate like wildfire through a dry wood. Chef laid the distraught girl on her bed still wrapped in the rug. Her crying gave way to sobbing. The head Matron scurried in as fast as her plump body could manage. She started barking orders to female servants and ordered all the men out. Stavid got up to go when Valley under Megeara's control said, "No daddy, don't go," and grabbed his hand.

"I am not going anywhere honey," he said. Stavid turned around until she was decent with his one arm stretched behind him holding her hand and his other hand wiping fresh tears away. He considered he might have lost his only daughter as he had lost his wife fifteen circles prior. The servant girls dressed Valley in her most comfortable cloths.

"What happened to you dear?" The head Matron asked Valley.

"I don't know," Valley said sobbing less frequently. "I became dizzy and then… It was as if I had no strength… and then I fell under the water…"

"There, there Valley, do not waste one more thought on it. We shall take good care of you dear." Come Stavid, you are the House Steward and there are chores to tend to while I go and inform the master of this little scare we just had. I hate to present him with any bad news given the turmoil of recent times but he must be aware of what goes on in his house."

"No dad, I don't want you to leave, stay with me."

"I wish I could darling but you need to rest

after all that just happened. I was afraid I almost lost you and I am just grateful that I did not. The Matron is right, I have things to do and you need to sleep. You can take the rest of the day off and tomorrow as well. I will have someone else finish your work." Stavid stepped out through the door as his daughter yawned.

In the hall waited Chef. "Is she ok sir?"

"Yes Chef, thank Crotear you got there so soon, I owe you my life."

"Don't be ridiculous sir, we all love that girl and any in the house would have saved her. I was just fortunate to be close enough to hear her scream."

"No, I mean it Chef, I could not live without her."

Valley stared at the door of her room, a helpless automaton unable to do anything but watch, listen and weep internally as Megeara mastered her body. Then a tear fell that was Valley's doing. Her incredible sadness gushed out in a single tear. As she stared at the door the tear travelled down her cheek. "That was me," she said in her mind to the intruder.

"Try if you must but that drop of water is the most you will be able to accomplish without punishment. You are like an insect to me girl and I will destroy every fiber of your being if you cause me any problems. "Your days of servitude to this family are over, your life and even your soul is mine to do as I please with." Then her temper changed and her voice was gentle, "Welcome to submission." Inside of Valley's head there was lamentation.

Chapter 35 - Illuminate

Mandathar stared at the disgusting display of malevolence before him. He and his companions first grew weary of standing, then of sitting in turn until there was a knock at the door, at which time they all stood up in the corner away from Drusus and his spawn. "Enter," Ashenath said, "We have very little night left."

A man walked in wearing fine clothing of an ancient style more antiquated than that which Drusus wore. "Master," he said then moved with the unnatural speed of his new form and fell at Ashenath's feet. "I am yours to dispose of."

"Of course, you are. This is Drusus my master and thereby yours as well. If you ever disobey him you are hereby ordered to destroy yourself immediately, understood?"

"Yes master."

"In addition, you are to refer to me as the Chosen, the Chosen One or as the chosen of Drusus, you get the point right?" Ashenath showed her fangs as she was oft to do when she smiled. She hated telling her spawn that they must serve Drusus. "Now explain where in the nine circles of hel you came from."

"Yes Chosen," he began, "I am from the city-state of Blakoepal, roughly an hour dark of here…

"A city?" Drusus cut him off as he stood. "Are you telling me there is a whole, watchers be damned, city hiding over the hill there and nobody in the Orthe knows it!

"Yes, Master."

"I do not believe it." Drusus said as he sat back down.

"I assure you master, it is true. I was part of the most prestigious knighthood in that city, known as the Black Knights of Opal.

"How big is this city and what's the obsession with opals?" Drusus demanded.

"The city is shrouded and protected by a powerful artifact called the Black Opal that rests in the center of the city for all its citizens to see, it is one of the gems from the ancient city of man. If it is not the biggest city in Sophia it is nearly so, certainly with the Undercity it is."

"The Undercity?" Ashenath asked.

"Yes, beneath the city is a vast underground city that is a dark reflection of the city above."

"Hold on," Drusus interrupted again, quite uncharacteristically. "You mean to tell me that not one but actually two cities are hiding on the other side of that hill, in some *fog*. Don't answer that, I know you cannot lie to Ash. I am truly surprised. When was the last time I was dumbfounded? Ah it was two hundred years ago when I realized my favorite horse was actually a doppelganger come to slay me! Come here," Drusus ordered one of his random spawn from a nearby table to approach him. When the spawn obeyed, Drusus twisted the vampire's head completely around and with his sharp fingernails tore into the creature's neck. Using his great strength, Drusus ripped through his servant's flesh and tore its head off. He threw the head like a ball, far, through the window shattering the glass. A piece of glass hit Mandathar who gasped at the pain unintentionally. He realized his mistake before his next breath.

Every vampire and spawn in the room turned to look in his direction. All they seen was blood dripping from some invisible wound to the floor. Elanor drew her sword and Delasy drew her sickle as they both moved away from Mandathar. Mandathar looked at them and shook his head as if to say no, don't give up your cover.

The vampires approached with Drusus at the lead, slowly walking toward the priest. The master vampire looked with curiosity at the blood dripping. Mandathar grabbed the gold disk with the silver footprint that was around his neck with one hand, and a sharp wooden stake with his other hand. "In the name of Crotear I vanquish you with divine light!" Mandathar ceased to be invisible to the undead as his holy symbol glowed with divine energy and illuminated the whole room for a moment. In that moment half of the vampire spawn in the room were instantly destroyed, in poofs of dust, including the one from Blakoepal. Mandathar raised his mace but never had a chance. Drusus drew his sword Transfusion and severed the man in half before he could bring the weapon to bear. Elanor and Delasy fled yet unknown to the vampires.

Chapter 36 - Lost

"This order has quit me. It has shrunk in the face of our new monarch failing to realize that she is an immature and silly little girl. She lacks the even temperament of her father and is unfit to rule." Treant stared cold and hard at Prince Orginus Dreadhawk, heir of the second noble house and commander of the Black Knights. "I will not succumb to the shameful offer you have made me. Ha! Accept a suspension of duties? That is a semantic dagger you may return to its sheath. I am no longer a Black Knight."

"Do not insult the princess, Treant!" Orginus said in a stern voice before softening his tone. "You are speaking brash and it is this brashness that is causing you to fall. I don't want you to leave the order. I just want you to take some time to get your life together. Treant, you are like a brother to me."

"Don't you dare threaten me brother!" Treant exploded placing his hand on the hilt of his sword. "You just can't resist the opportunity to attempt to exercise authority over me. Can you Orginus? Well I am taking away your power over me. I resign my commission in the Black Knights of Opal but I am still First Lord, Archduke Cavalaries and the princess can say nothing about my rank in this city as you should have no say so in the Order of the Black Knights. I will use my position to oppose her juvenile rule!"

"What of duty Treant, what of your family creed?" Orginus asked.

"What of it? My creed, unlike yours, says the

Cavalaries family is loyal first to the city, not the crown. Seeing how I believe her rule is to the potential detriment of the city, my family vow permits me to oppose her. Nay, it *demands* that I oppose her." Treant turned and started to walk away.

"That means we will be enemies Treant, do you realize that?"

"We already are Prince-Knight," Treant stopped but didn't bother to turn around. "From now on you may address me in the proper manner as is fitting for one that is of superior station." With that the former Black Knight left.

Treant returned to Cavalaries Castle late. He wandered the halls grumbling and wondering which of his suits of armor he would wear to the Tournament of Honor. Treant noticed a light coming from his library, illuminating a small section of hall. Surprised anyone was up so late, he entered through the open archway into the library. There was Valley sitting at a table, old tomes piled up so high that she was nearly hidden behind them. "Valley?" Treant asked.

Valley stood immediately, "Yes, milord."

"Why are you in the library and at this strange hour?" Treant looked at her but tried not to stare. Valley had grown to maturity and he somehow hadn't noticed before this moment. Her black hair draped over her shoulders. She stared up at him, her blue eyes violating etiquette. She wore a red and gold dress replete with black knights riding the length of the thin fabric. The top was teeming and cut low. It was an expensive dress, more appropriate for a noble woman and should have been out of the reach of a mere servant girl. He was baffled by her raiment and yet, he thought it suited her. It was as if this was the first time he looked upon her. She was both alluring and intriguing to him.

"I am sorry milord; I haven't been able to sleep lately." She said in her crisp light voice.

"Of course," He said. "My apologies. How are you? I heard you nearly drowned in the pond."

"I am fine now, milord?" Her eyes flashed momentarily as Imarra controlled her from within, she looked away from him knitting her fingers together, her palms facing to the floor.

"What are you reading about Valley?" Treant asked. He moved around the desk to stand next to her, looking down at the book she had open. He was distracted by the cut of her dress and couldn't help but imagine what she looked like beneath it. He stared down at what he could see of her breasts before turning his gaze to her reading material. Their arms brushed together as they leaned toward the desk reaching for the same book. Treant, ever clothed in black felt her bare arm against his silk sleeve distinctly. They paused momentarily, prolonging their incidental contact. Their mutual consent was manifesting in their inability to retreat from each other. He felt a tingling in his center and his heart beat hard and without warning so that he thought it might pound its way out of his chest. He spurned the fabric of his sleeve an awful barrier between them. Then she pulled away gliding her arm across the length of his, slowly as he reached forward retrieving his book. He glanced first toward the tome and then met her eyes again; her beautiful blue eyes. They left him feeling paralyzed. Treant clutched the book tightly and silently feared his heart would beat so hard as to kill him. "I never knew..." His speech was disrupted as his body sought to supersede his will over it. "...I never knew there was such treasure hidden so near to me," He said, lifting the book up in a vain pretension that it was the book he spoke of. Valley moved as near to him as she could, stopping short of pressing her body up against him. She reached forward to grasp the tome and tug it from his grip.

"It is a book of histories as are the others," Valley said at a virtual whisper looking up at him. She cocked her head, gradually leaning back, guiding him by insinuation to fill the space. He leaned forward and kissed her with gentle passion as he reached around her waist and pulled her near. Their bodies pressed together from head to toe. Valley's arms held the warrior tight; her fingers flitted at his shirt even as his hands searched her body seeking an opening.

The scene played out as an exact picture of Valley's private fantasies. She had a deep infatuation for her lord. As she moved from adolescence to womanhood her crush had only grown. Imarra by her possession of the girl was privy to her most personal thoughts and dreams. She drew from that, this dream come true that she created deliberately. Valley could never have made her fantasy into reality without Imarra's guiding. Imarra went dormant inside Valley. Valley was able to feel and experience the physical movement of her love, yet Imarra ceded complete control to her at the first kiss so that everything beyond that moment was by Valley's own consent. After a few moments

Imarra exercised herself from her host leaving Valley's body and standing over them in her ethereal, spiritual form. She paused for another long moment smiling as the lovers worked to liberate each other from the confines of their clothing. Imarra's body remained at the bottom of the pond in a stasis. She traveled in her spiritual essence out of the library and made her way to Valley's father's room. She whispered in his ear the name of his daughter causing him to awaken. Fearful something was wrong and assuming Imarra's voice came from his own mind as a manifesting of his intuition, he arose to check on her.

Stavid knocked lightly on the door frame of his daughter's room before easing into it. When he seen that her bed was empty his heart became heavy and terror griped him briefly. Stavid ordered his will not to overreact. She was probably up doing chores he told himself. Stavid moved through the labyrinth of hallways when he reached a place where the halls intersected Imarra would whisper to him the direction. This advice he obeyed without consideration. They resembled thoughts and he could not tell they were not his own. Stavid approached the library and as he drew near to it he was surprised to hear the mummers and moaning of love making. How unusual, Stavid thought to himself though somewhat aroused by the sounds. The Archduke is not the type to have a casual affair. He is above the temptations of immediate gratification. In fact, Stavid thought him to be saving himself for matrimony. Stavid proceeded closer, thinking he was going to catch two servants making impermissible use of the Archduke's library,

256

though a part of himself that he despised eagerly sought a glimpse. Stavid loved his late wife but it had been many years since he had enjoyed the pleasure of a physical encounter with a female. Then a thought came to him a thought he would not entertain. He steeled his resolve and his thoughts again came captive to his will. Perhaps after he embarrassed them sufficiently and assigned them extra duties to use all this extra vigor they obviously possessed, he could ask them if they had seen Valley. He moved to stand in the doorway. As he stood there his mouth dropped open of its own accord. He was frozen in stunned in disbelief. Rage and embarrassment swirled around in his heart. Imarra went to stand beside the lovers as they exemplified their passions on the desk. No one could see her. Stavid had murder in his eyes. Valley's moans sharpened with each thrust as Treant went deeper and deeper inside her, breaking through the barrier of her virginity. Stavid grabbed the pull ring of the door slamming it shut before him. Treant and Valley seized their romance suddenly.

Imarra whispered into Valley's ear, "It was nothing." Valley looked into Treant's blue-grey eyes, his pupils were large from the low light. He paused as he noticed his reflection in her eyes.

"It was nothing my love," Valley said to him with a low voice.

Stavid walked down the hall angry tears dropping from his face. "What betrayal! He has betrayed more than me. He has betrayed his own Watcher! He deflowers my daughter on a whim. Who of any worth will want her now? Certainly, the

Archduke will not marry her. Damn him!" He yelled as he entered a lonely section of the castle. "Damn you Treant to the deepest hel."

Chapter 37 - Champion

Caedis Bindingfire stared across the field at his opponent. He was hopeful he would win the event and if not, at least he would give Treant and Orginus some competition this year. There will come a time when I will reach my prime even as Treant waxes old then I, Viscount Caedis Bindingfire will be the greatest knight in the city. But for now, it was only a fantasy. He needed to destroy Treant but for some reason the high Priest of Asmodeus had taken interest in the troubled Archduke and preferred to play games with him. Not that Caedis objected. Treant, once the most esteemed knight in the city for virtue, courage and skill was now broken, angry and lost. Caedis enjoyed tormenting him. He had the upper hand and was going to use it.

Caedis pulled his mind away from thoughts of Treant and fantasies of grandeur and returned to the matter at hand. He sat mounted on his steed, decked in lustrous white plate armor with a black gauntlet on his left hand. One of his pages held his helmet and the other young man, his lance. The noble's mount stirred under the encumbrance of its plate barding. Sir Bindingfire stared down the list at the cavalier he was soon to joust. It was a champion of the Temple of the Unknown God. Caedis was locked between confidence and pride and was certain he would win this bout as he had won so many already today. His opponent wasn't even a knight, just a squire, obviously here hoping to win his commission as a true knight. He couldn't help but take note of the unusual presence of his opponent. His challenger wore black full plate armor, polished to sheen much like the Black Knights wore, except with red cloths tied around the joints, wearing a great helm with a closed face and a large red plume rooted in the top. He bore a large rectangular shield, black with a single red drop emblazoned on the front into the metal. He looked to be a rather thin squire, perhaps just a boy still. Caedis watched as his opponent held out his right gauntlet ready to receive his lance. The White Thorn knight had never known of the Temple to the Unknown God to send a champion to joust. All Caedis knew about them was that they were a bunch of monks that liked to be left alone. They usually sat events like this out. How were they able to provide martial training to anyone when all they are known to do is hide in their sanctuary? Regardless, he thought, this knight hopeful was going down. Caedis donned his helmet and his page armed him with his lance. He took a long hard look at his opponent sitting on a red-haired stallion, fully equipped with black barding, wearing a black covering, a spattering of blood drops embroidered on either side and the bridge of its hood. Several monks dressed in simple brown sack cloth, with hoods stood around the challenger. One of the monks handed him a lance. He was the perfect contrast of Caedis, whose black horse wore a white cover and hood with no symbol. One of his servants equipped him with a large shield bearing his family coat of arms, a burning orange flame. A horn was blown. Caedis closed his visor and charged the other rider leveling his lance as he increased to a full gallop.

As the equestrian warriors charged toward each other the surrounding arena filled with cheers. Flags lined the perimeter of the field. One of the many was the Bindingfire standard. The two raced toward each other with great force. Caedis stared intently at his target, determined to remove the burden from his adversary's war horse. There was the sound of lances shattering against shields. The riders passed each other, neither accomplishing more than the destruction of their disposable lances. They both slowed somewhat as they reached the end of the list then circled around for another charge. The crowd clapped and cheered for more. Caedis and the squire charged immediately, but this time at the apex of the list the monk's champion leaned forward and struck the young nobleman square in the face with a difficult maneuver, causing the White Thorn knight to roll backwards off the rump of his beast. Caedis pulled a muscle in his neck as he flipped off the back of his horse, the weight of his shield kept his arm level as he flew back, bouncing off of the horse's rear and spinning him contrary to his arm which snapped before he hit the ground. He landed hard on his back and began to squirm, forcing a few painful breaths as he hurried to reclaim his air, struggling to remove his helm with his one working hand. The crowd nearly lost control at such an unexpected turn of events. They stomped and shouted.

The princess stood up in her soap box, jerked up by the surprise of the sudden violence. She worried for Caedis, genuinely filled with sympathy for the knight as he lay injured in pride and body.

261

Half the nobles stood up in their boxed seats and the gentry were as jeered as the commoners. Sir Bindingfire's errants ran onto the field to assist their master.

Up in the princess's soapbox stood Agon. She remembered his words to her. A tournament was just the sort of thing the public needed to start the healing of their society, so that it could move forward. He had recommended the event in honor of her ascension to the regency of the city. It was difficult advice to give, he knew it pained her to move the city forward and it would probably be sometime before she joined the city with moving ahead. The princess stood shocked at the dismounting and defeat of Caedis, "Oh Crotear! Agon, I wish he wasn't competing. Everyone dear to me places themselves in danger. He is hurt so bad and I am forbidden by royal etiquette to run to him."

"He is definitely in pain your majesty, but don't be worried, the church of Asmodeus will cast some curative spell on him." Agon replied.

"Why does Caedis follow Asmodeus? He is a harsh god but this is a harsh City. Do you ever think we are wrong by following Crotear?

"Yes and this is a good time for searching out ones soul. Corrine if you never ask these questions you would be doomed to follow Crotear with blind acceptance. Crotear does not want that and neither should you. A little struggle will allow you to serve him because you know it is right and not because others chose him for you.

"How can you say what the mind of Crotear is with such certainty, Agon?"

"Because I have already asked such questions.

It is simple, what sort of subjects do you want? The kind that obey you because of your birthright or the kind that wants to obey you?

"Why would any of them want to obey me, I am just a girl."

"Then it is up to you to earn their respect my cousin, by being more than *just* a girl"

White Thorn removed Caedis from the field. The squire then faced Orginus and bested him by one point. Orginus gracefully conceded victory. There was an intermission of bardic performers, the best singers and dancers in the city. Then Lord Treant ambled out to the list facing his opponent, the monk's champion.

They charged.

"Who is this knight that the monks have entered into the tournament Agon?" Corrine asked.

"I do not know. Strange they chose today to insist on their rights to present a champion."

The two warriors met at the tip of each other's lances. The squire went flying off of his horse landing flat on his back. Treant won as easily as the squire had bested Viscount Bindingfire.

The council herald announced his victory since Treant failed to provide a herald of his own. The many competing knights assembled in front of the royal soap box and bowed their heads. "Archduke Cavalaries you have won the sword and the joust and are this Courts Champion still," The Princess said in a dignified tone. She issued other prizes for other contests until finally she beckoned the Champion of the Unknown God. The Champion stepped forward and bowed his head still wearing his helmet with his visor down. "What do I call you sir knight?"

There was no response for a moment and the princess got a little frustrated. Then a short man, his head covered in stubble, wearing a brown monks garb and a pair of sandals with leather straps, issued forth from behind the row. "Your majesty, I am the voice of this warrior, please suffer me to speak."

"Why does this man have a spokesperson, has he not his own voice?"

"Yes, your grace," The monk bowed his head low. A man of thirty circles, he looked young and chiseled. "We ask you to proclaim this errant warrior the Blood Knight before the assembled crowd in the presence of many witnesses common and noble alike. We also pray that you will not compel this loyal subject of yours to speak nor uncover for both a vow of silence and a vow of modesty are in effect for the temple's champion, your adored majesty."

"Very well then. It is the right of the temple to put forth whatever champion they wish. If this knight has made vows, then I shall respect them. Come hither, squire of the Unknown God."

The red plumed warrior came forth and kneeled before her majesty, Princess Corrine.

"Your sword," the princess commanded.

The humbled equestrian, with head bowed drew forth his sword holding it by the blade, lifting the peaceful end of the weapon toward the princess. Corrine placed her delicate hand on the hilt, seemingly cautious at first then she squeezed the hilt of the sword and raised it sharply above her head with her right hand. She could feel power in the sword as she held it toward the sky. The princess then lowered the sword, taping the blade on each of the new knight's shoulders. "I dub thee, the Blood Knight, a champion of the laws of our nation city, a sword for justice and a vessel of virtue. Stand Blood Knight and take your place among those of your peerage." Princess Corrine handed him back his sword, blade first. The Blood Knight stood and accepted it.

Princess Corrine Amorgoden now reluctantly addressed duke Cavalaries. "Archduke and noble knight Treant Cavalaries, you have won the day. Therefore, I invite you to be the champion of my court. Do you accept the commission Lord Knight?"

Treant removed his helm revealing a head of blond hair, somewhat longer than what he used to keep it. "I must with great disappointment decline the invitation based on a moral prejudice, though I thank her majesty greatly for considering me." Treant looked up at the princess, searching her facade for any hint of despair that he could hold onto to satisfy his vengeance.

At first her majesty was stone faced, she hardened her delicate face, biting down on the insides of her cheeks. She pushed out of her mind any trace of feeling, trying to hide the embarrassment she felt for being rejected before the whole assembly of nobles, church leaders, officials and countless common folk as well. She paused for a long moment, when she thought that she had dismissed her caring and her mind was blank she began to speak. "Does the high Lord think that his princess is immoral?" All the suppressed emotion pressed hard against her voice, even causing it to break at one point before she could subjugate it again.

"Not immoral your greatness," Treant condescended. "It is my belief that you are prudently astute in matters of moral virtue. I believe her majesty to be the most elegant lady of the city and that if I could summon my greatest criticism of you it would be that you who are most chaste and honest among us, are honest to a fault."

"Archduke, I appreciate your flowery compliments. I can only pray that I may possess half of what you ascribe to me but now I must admit that I am baffled. High Lord, did you not just refuse the coveted position of Champion of the Royal Court after fighting hard for it and besting every other knight of note in our city? Then you say to me it is on account of moral law that you refuse the position, only to praise my virtue moments later. I implore you First Lord, please clarify and do not be crass." The high lady of Blakoepal looked down at him anxious to know his mind.

All the attendants of the tournament listened in silence to hear the exchange as it was amplified to the crowd, eagerly anticipating what would occur next. It is not my belief that our Lady, the princess is void of virtue, quite the contrary as I have inadequately enumerated a moment ago. It is my view of the princess, if those with understanding would pardon me, that she is naive and foolish though guided in her foolishness by a moral compass. It would be immoral for me to champion a ruler that I thought lacking in all the vital characteristics of a good ruler save her morality. Such an ill prepared monarch, without the love of her highest caste nor strength in her religion and unequipped with those basic talents of leadership such as was possessed by her predecessor have turned the foolish ruler into a tyrant. I shall oppose both tyranny and foolishness."

Her majesty began to cry, an orphan with no one to hold onto standing before all her people, punctuating the knight's accusations with a demonstration of her inherent weakness and suffering. She remained as composed as she could; standing regal before her people whilst tears dropped to the floor..

The people began to shout and yell as a single crazed mob. Soldiers took up positions all along the stadium. The crown guard took up defensive formation. Justice ran to his liege's side, "Let us retire my princess."

She looked at Justice speaking through gritted teeth, "This is making us look weak which is what he wants."

"We may deal with him later your majesty. The crowd is stirring and might riot. Then you would be in danger." Justice spoke urgently his words ringing in the backdrop of discontent and shouting.

"I shall not fear my people Justice. Now go away from me." Her voice echoed across the tournament site.

"Your Majesty, It is my duty to protect."

"My duty is to the people now get behind me so I may speak and do it now!" She yelled the last part. Justice moved back to his position worried that this might get out of hand, looking every which way. It seemed the guards were regaining control. Corrine moved to the front of her stand, placing her hands on the banister of purple and gold fabric.

As she readied herself to speak, Caedis Bindingfire drew his sword. "Insolent coward!" He yelled at Treant through the visor of his helm and charged the first Lord. Treant drew his sword with lighting speed and easily parried every attempt of Viscount Bindingfire's brash onslaught.

After he exhausted the young knight, gloating and playing to the crowd he disarmed him with a few flicks of his wrist. Treant drove Caedis to the ground. "Remove your helmet foolish enemy." Treant ordered. Caedis complied removing his helmet. He glared at the knight with the hatred his dark god cherished so much.

"Kill me," Caedis yelled.

"Ok." Treant answered taking a step forward.

Corrine looked on in horror. The people began to chant "Mer-cy, mer-cy, mer-cy, mer-cy..." Treant looked every which way, a devilish smile worn on his face, he looked up at the princess with a curse in his gaze. "What say you your majesty?" Treant asked his voice pitched with spite.

"I desire for you to spare him, mercy... Please Lord knight."

His smile widened, "Too bad his life is mine." He brought his sword quickly up and then down. The Blood knight parried the move and kicked Caedis over, perhaps harder than was needed. The Blood Knight quickly disarmed Treant in the split second he was confused. With his sword out of reach, sticking out of the ground, he put his arms out. He moved forward a couple of times to test the knight's reflexes, but his adversary was able to respond with the tip of his sword to every attempt by Treant to maneuver over to his weapon. Treant was a better swordsman but this knight was expert and got him while surprised. The Blood Knight was able to exploit that moment however brief to render him without a weapon and unable to defend. The Blood Knight seemed calm pointing the tip of his sword at Treant.

"This melee is over. The next knight to attack or even speak will be arrested for capital crimes against the crown. I, Princess Corrine Amorgoden heir of the crown of Blakoepal, hereby order a halt to all violence."

The Blood Knight stepped back. Treant leaned in the direction of his sword to get a sense of if it was safe to proceed. The Blood Knight responded by loading his scabbard and walking away. Treant recovered his sword and regained his position in-between Orginus and the Blood Knight, facing the princess.

"If Archduke Cavalaries will refuse my commission," Corrine lent her gaze to the masses and to the knights before her, "Then I shall offer it to the runner up, the one who disarmed him. Blood Knight, come forward."

The Blood Knight stepped forward. He was shorter than Treant and Orginus. The pommel of his sword was as fabric drenched in blood.

"Will you serve as my champion, most capable and deserving knight?"

The Blood-knight bowed his head. The Blood-knight's companion monk walked forward to stand next to him. The monk looked up at the princess, and then bellowed, "The Blood Knight will serve her majesty joyously, with dedication and cheerfully sacrificing her life if necessary!"

The crowd cheered "Blood-knight, Blood-knight, blood-knight!"

Her Majesty raised a hand to signal silence and waited for it to cover the tournament before speaking. "What is your name, monk?"

"My name is Omega."

"Very well, Omega, whatever you say it will be as the very words of the Blood Knight. If he opposes what you have to say or when such a time comes that his vow is satisfied, then let the Blood Knight speak his own words. I also insist that you two take up quarters at the palace that I may call upon my champion when in need. The tournament has ended."

Trumpets punctuated the tournament.

Chapter 38 - Palace

Princess Amorgoden sat in her private dining hall at the head of a long oak table. The table was laid out with a feast worthy of a banquet. Large dishes in the center hosted all manner of meat. Varies types of lettuce and garden greens were available for the creation of a huge diversity of salads. Sixteen steel pots held different soups in each, seventeen loafs of bread, all different but lost among the seemingly endless array of fruits and vegetables. Chocolate butterflies fluttered aimlessly around the room. Confections of every sort imaginable and some quite unimaginable, were spread out on trays in artistic arrangements. Far more than the Princess could hope to eat that month let alone that night as she sat alone meticulously cutting at a poultry that was smothered in some sort of white sauce. The food was beautiful and delicious, created by one of the best chefs in Blakoepal but she was unable to enjoy it. She poked at the plate before her with a golden, double pronged utensil before raising a bite to her mouth and choking down a piece. The food dropped down her throat to her stomach and she felt full, from a single bite. She looked across the table to the main entrance of the hall. Loneliness began to settle upon her. She was much better lately, she didn't cry anymore. Perhaps, she thought, my reservoir is empty and my dry eyes see more clearly now than they ever did. "Justice, come join me." She called across the long table at the open archway. A moment later her trusted bodyguard emerged through the arch.

"How may I serve you, your majesty?" he said. Justice by the nature of his command spent more time with her than any other; as such he had become privy to her majesty's most private and vulnerable moments. He did not wonder at her capability to lead, however. He had never known one whose spirit was so broken yet equally resilient. She could go from a state of devastation and self-pity then shake it off to deal with a forthcoming matter of state, giving not the slightest clue that she had spent any time on her own personal grief. Still he worried about her, how she could continue with so much burden bearing upon her? He would give anything to lighten her load.

"Come here Justice. Please, sit next to me and have dinner."

"As you wish," Justice pulled out a chair and sat comfortably in it.

"Whenever we sit in here together, I wish for you to speak frankly and informally with me." She looked at him with a weak smile.

He smiled back fastidiously and sincerely. "Yes, your majesty."

"Corrine…it is just Corrine when we are here, ok?

"Yes your maj… I mean Corrine."

"How can I be so busy and yet be so bored?"

Justice looked at her blond hair, careful not to stare at its lavish arrangement. Her rubies glimmered from her neck and wrists. Her crown rested gently on her head. She wore a regal dress of white and purple, fitting elegantly over her lithe figure. "Your heart, Corrine…" His eyes looked down and his voice trailed off as he spoke her name.

"Well, finish." She commanded gently. "Don't be afraid, there are few people I trust as I do you. You are a brave man but right now I am not your Princess, I am just a girl seeking your advice and maybe even your friendship. Please be candid with me."

"I am sorry Corrine." He looked up again trying not to stare too long into her blue eyes, somehow, he would get confused and lose track of his thoughts whenever their eyes met. "I just mean that…your heart doesn't seem to be in it. You need to do something... for you."

"I have anything I could desire placed only a few breaths outside of my grasp. There is nothing I need. I have to care for the people."

"If you will forgive me your majesty, sometimes the people are selfish. What good are you to them if you don't take care of you first?"

"My position comes with sacrifice. It is the curse of the crown. I would give every fiber of my body for this people."

"I know you would." Justice narrowed his eyes. "Don't sacrifice yourself needlessly. Your people do not require every fiber of your being right now. You are surrounded by those who selfishly want their own piece of you. Save your sacrifice for when and if it is necessary, only then will it be worthy." There was a momentary silence as his words settled on her mind. "The people need you healthy and vibrant again, eventually they need you to be happy as well.

She bowed her head forward then just as he began to think that he may have been too bold she looked up at him, a timid smile showing on her face. "I like when you speak your mind Justice. Your upbringing has taught you to cut through the pollution of aristocratic niceties and a genteel facade. It is a most desirable manner you speak with and I should hope to hear more of it and not less." Her smile returned somewhat stronger than before. She placed her left hand upon his, guiding it from his lap to rest on the table top where her other hand joined to embrace it. What do you suggest a diffident girl such as me do? She asked pressing his hand with hers to coax him.

Justice felt almost unbearably nervous and sweat began to accumulate on his palms embarrassing him further. "I think you should take a month away from your duties maybe more, whatever you require, to regain your spark for life. Let your Chamberlain deal with all but the most serious of matters."

"The people will see my retreat as incompetence." She said.

"How will they see you when you are completely drained, your Majesty?"

Agon overheard as he approached the open arch to enter and join his cousin for dinner. "He's right, Corrine." Agon said in his always calm and direct manner. Both heads turned to look at him, startled by his interruption. Corrine and Justice both retrieved their hands from each other's grasp. Justice always felt compelled to look Agon in the eye despite how distracting the silver could be and in spite of Agon's habit of always appearing in a cloak with the hood up concealing most of his face.

"Have you arrived to recite one of your poems

274

for us Agon? I can't wait to hear it if you have." She said, her happiness at his arrival obvious to Justice.

"You deserve some time to yourself. My father will make clear to the public that it is their turn to provide some peace of mind to you. Everyone is entitled to some time for bereavement. Your people love you and will understand. As for your enemies in the council, if they feel emboldened they will overplay their hand at any perceived weakness thereby exposing themselves."

"Agon," she exclaimed, "The Crown has no enemies in the Council. The council exists to share the burden of governance and remain as a check against tyranny."

"I am sorry my cousin but the crown's power…your power, is coveted by many on the council. Perhaps more dangerous than your enemies without are those within, who would secretly plot to depose you."

Corrine gasped, she couldn't restrain her disbelief, nor did she ever attempt to hide her true feelings around Agon. There was hardly a person that left her more at ease and freer to be herself than her present company. "My father was never confronted with seditious rogues on the Council as you speak of. What is the purpose of such plotting they could not take away from me my royalty nor confer it upon whom they choose? Only you and I are fit for rulership. All our other cousins are married off or too young or so far removed as to have only the slightest drop of Amorgoden blood in them. Hardly any are the prodigy of our grandfather, King Drezdin the fifth. I cannot conceive of such scheming." She turned her head up in an uncharacteristically snobbish fashion, "humph."

"Corrine," Agon paused, "You are being naive. I know you are not naive so listen closely. There are laws that would allow the Council to abnegate your right to rule, and not just one, there are several such laws. Your father was in fact confronted by the council over a series of affairs that he had. You just can't recall it because it was a long time ago. Once your father had a firm grip on his crown the dissension went away and no one dared to cross him. From that point on all of the court intrigues were designed to curry favor with him instead." Agon continued pretending not to notice his cousin's astonished expression. "Your father became quite a master of court politics, as you surely will. As surely you must."

"What affairs do you speak of Agon? My father had no affairs, he loved my mother."

Agon pushed his hood back, revealing his short hair and pale skin, his eyes a sheen silver. "Of course, he did Corrine," He maneuvered to a chair across from Justice, placing his gloved hands at the back of the chair. He looked at her for an enduring moment. *She is so young, so very elegant and so encumbered*, Agon thought to himself.

"See, you admit it. My father did love my mother."

"Yes, he did. Unfortunately, he also had a lot of power and was tempted often, both by his own appetites and the machinations of others. He was a man after all. He was a man before even he was a king. His affairs were sordid; I could not identify any mistress but I know he finally gained control over his compulsion in time for your birth. For two years they lived, the happiest couple you'd ever seen. When your mother died, your father was ruined for all other women for years."

"What do you mean by, 'for years' Agon? Do not be coy with me."

"My apologies dear cousin, I must be frank with you…"

"You must," she cut him off. "You have been so forthright already why stop now?"

Justice shifted in his seat uncomfortable by the airing out of the royal laundry, taking place before him. He was content to remember the King as a deific ruler who sat on his throne of gold and lived the perfect life never giving in to human carnality.

Agon continued with a gentle tone. "Your father had in recent years begun a secret flirtation which then flowered into a romance over several years. It was a state secret that virtually no one outside of immediate family knew about."

"And it appears even some that are immediate family were not so privy," she chastised. This is a scandalous secret not a state secret. When were you going to tell me this or were you going to wait until one of my enemies whom I did not even know of, determined to rekindle the topic of his adulterous past in his absence."

"Your father was on the verge of letting you in on all the families' secrets. He considered telling you many times and finally had decided to tell you everything, on the very night that he fell asleep. Terrible things are facing us, this very city. If you are going to take time, then do so. We will need you rested and ready soon. Do not dwell on any affairs

277

of state, my father and I will handle everything. If you are to take this time, then use it to full advantage and totally let go. The headship of state is yours to resume on a whim." Agon stood up.

"Thank you Agon," The Princess said as she stood. She put her arms around him and grasped him long and tightly. "I love you so much cousin, please take care of yourself, my life would be void without you."

He held on for an abundant moment then released himself from her embrace as he was certain that her renowned stubbornness would not allow her to be the one to break the bond. "Corrine, the strongest flower I have known, withstanding fire and flood, great gusts of wind blown, I shall lend you my life and my love."

"So you do like poetry." Justice smirked

"It is another family secret," he replied.

"I do not recognize the verse though, who is it?" Corrine asked. "Obviously you changed it to my name, sweet and dear cousin"

"That is an even deeper secret," he said before he kissed her forehead and walked away throwing his hood up as he left.

"I will find it, Agonius Amorgoden," she yelled after him.

"Your cousin, the Royal Mage, is a pretty strange character." Justice offered bringing her attention back to him.

"He is amazingly intelligent and has a peculiar style but he is a good person, and we are loyal to each other completely."

"How can you be so sure your majesty?"

"You struggle with calling me by my name,

don't you?" The princess asked.

"Yes, I do your majesty."

She looked at him laughter sealed up behind her deceptively straight mouth. As a smile started to force itself upon her face, Justice began to smile. "I mean Corrine," he tried, which only caused her to let slip short bursts of muffled laughter as she too lost control of her smile. When she could hold back no more they erupted in laughter together. It was the first time the Princess had genuinely laughed about anything since the night of the festival. Eventually though that realization dawned on her, causing her to feel guilty. Her laughter ceased, her smile faded and she looked down and away as she listened to Justice laugh hysterically as if drunken, never one to catch a hint too soon. When he realized the time for mirth was passed he let out a few last chuckles."

"Corrine, what is wrong? I'm sorry. It's just that you were laughing at first so I..." As her thoughts turned to Justice's lack of social coordination it brought back a smile to her face and soon she was interrupting his plea with laughter again. This time he was afraid to laugh. All he could muster was, "huh?" This confusing display of what he typified as feminine madness reminded him sorely of Whisper, accompanied in memory as reliably as she had been in person, with Enigma.

"Whatever happened to your two friends, from the night of the festival?" She asked as if she had read his mind.

Justice paused for a moment. "Enigma is no longer my friend. He abandoned me and his sister to aid the very devils that made that attempt on your life. That is why I was in Deadside that day. I followed him hoping to confront him. The Crown Guard and the Inquisitors did not tell you all of this?

"No one tells me anything Justice. At least nothing that isn't pertinent to a decision I am being asked to make. That is the summation of my existence to nearly everyone. I make decisions and when I'm not doing that I master rules of etiquette so complex that I can look down on an archmage or priest for taking the easy path with their specializations. It never occurs to anyone that I may be a person and not just a princess. I am a woman of passion, dreams and skills. Come let's walk." Corrine stood first and offered him her hand. Justice stared at it briefly before accepting her dainty, charitable gesture and stood. They walked side by side through the Palace, servants falling to the ground as they passed them in the corridors, at least one, clumsily dropping a half dozen pots and pans. Justice wondered how hard their hearts must be beating as he imagined that he could hear them. He had seen people faint at her presence and he wondered if anyone had ever died. The enormity of the palace kept most servants from ever catching more than a glance of royalty and then usually from afar.

"It seems like important information if you want to make the right decision about allowing me to protect you."

"It was unnecessary. My decision was made the moment Alturek informed me of his promotion. You see Justice, *I* chose you for my bodyguard."

They walked in silence for a while pondering each other's words, until they turned a corner. A maid was walking with a tray of tin cups and a little boy in tow behind her. If she had been walking only slightly faster she would have converged with them at the instant of the turn. Shocked to see the princess and her bodyguard walk so casually around the corner she shrieked. It downright scared the hel out of her as she hurried to prostate herself before her monarch. In her terror, she forgot about her little son, a boy no more than three circles old. He stopped in his tracks and stared at his mother ahead of him on the floor bowing and the Princess with her armored bodyguard, the pair of them now stopped and looking back at him. It was striking to her that this boy paid her no special honor. "Look Justice, to this boy I am just a woman," The Princess remarked. The servant at once realized her mistake and became frantic, struggling to remain bowed and yet bring her son to her side and make him bow. She pleaded incessantly that she be shown mercy and forgiveness.

"That is quite enough, woman," Corrine said. The woman became instantly quiet and returned to her stance of supplication, the boy was confused and decided to imitate his mother by getting onto his knees and bowing before the Princess. "You may come to your feet and stand before your Princess. I desire to speak to you." The woman came to her feet and holding her little sons hand raised him to his feet as well. She stared down at the ground afraid to meet eyes with the majesty of the Opal's lady. The Princess looked ahead and realized that others walking down the hall had caught sight of her and were likewise kneeled with their foreheads pressed to the floor. "You may look upon me as we speak peasant," Corrine told the maid.

Then the princess looked down the hall, "You may all stand up and remain upright. Do not bow before me today in this hall." Corrine looked over at the nervous maid who was trembling. "What is your son's name dear servant?" Corrine asked delicately.

"My great, amazing, wonderful majesty," The woman stumbled terribly with her words not knowing the codes of etiquette one is expected to be guided by when speaking to the crown, "His name is Henta…Sorry…Thank you." The woman looked away in panic.

"He is such a sweetie. Justice I want to hold him," Corrine said to her protector while ogling over the child.

"Your Majesty," Justice started, "I have to caution against physical contact with the boy, he could be an assassin or a vicious beast that has been magically shape shifted into a cute little boy to exploit your feminine instincts and lure you into a false sense of security.

Corrine's mouth dropped open in disbelief. "Or maybe he is just a cute little boy." Corrine gave Justice a friendly, chastising strike to his arm then walked toward the child and his mother. Corrine squatted down in front of the child who was still looking down in imitation of his mother. Corrine reached out to his face and guided his chin up. She noticed immediately how soft the child's skin was and realized that it had been years since she last touched a child.

The boy looked up at her as she stared at him, her heart fluttering joyfully with appreciation for the miracle of children. "Who are you?" The boy asked.

Corrine's smile deepened. She was delighted at

how freely the boy spoke to her without any pretense. It was then that she discovered a profound love for children that felt right, pure and innocent. This was good she thought. There is no grey area when it comes to a child. "I am Princess Corrine. How are you today?"

"Ok but Mama not feels good." The boy answered and took notice of his mother's nervousness.

"Do you know what a Princess is Henta?" Corrine asked.

"Uh huh," the boy said with a nod.

"Well are you going to tell me what it is cutie?"

"It someone im-port-ant, that keep mommy go to work," Henta managed.

Corrine was delighted. "May I pick you up little Henta?" The boy nodded affirmative so Corrine stood then lifted the boy up and rested him on hips that Justice did not know she possessed. "A Princess is someone important and one day I will be important to you but do you know who is more important to you than the Princess?" The boy shook his head no. "It is your mother that is more important than the Princess." Henta looked at his mother as Corrine passed him to her. "I will give you the sign of my favor. All your life you may say that you know me and just once you will be able to request an audience with me." With that, one of the rubies on Corrine's thin platinum crown began to glow. Corrine put her hand on the boys left forearm and kissed him on the cheek. "Now your son possesses the favor of the Royal house and bloodline." Corrine pulled his sleeve up revealing the emblem of the crown and scepter. It seemed to

283

be a tattoo but the rubies on the image of the crown and scepter twinkled."

The mother gasped, "Thank you so much your majesty." The maid kept repeating her thanks.

"Remember," Corrine interrupted, "He will only be able to request an audience with me once, so do not waste it. Bye little Henta," Corrine said as she waved and walked away, Justice at her side.

"Bye, bye," Henta waved as they walked away.

Corrine and Justice made their way down the hall walking past several servants both men and woman who lowered their eyes as she walked by. The men bowed deeply and the women who were not carrying anything curtsied. When they turned again everything went back to normal. Servants would drop down to the ground when she walked past them. "So what happened to the girl you were with on the day of merriment? Were you two engaged in a romance?"

"Whisper? No way, she was like a sister or a cousin or a nagging mother. We could never be romantic; it is a bothersome thing to ponder. She was a great friend though. She would do absolutely anything for you and then never let you forget about it."

"She sounds wonderful, what happened to her?"

I abandoned her. I don't know. I was with her that day on Deadside. I left her so I could chase after her brother. The Crown Guard told me she disappeared, certainly they could have found her if she were hiding. I just don't know.

"We need to find her Justice. She must be somewhere. Where did you say you seen her last?

284

"I left her on Coin Street, at its namesake tavern. Knowing her, she didn't sit around and wait for me."

"No way," The princess grabbed her crown in dramatic gesture.

"What?" Justice asked, stopping in the hall and turning to her.

She lowered her arms and began walking again, he followed suit. "That's the same place that Treant fought a battle with White Thorn. My dear friend Avriel, whose funeral I was at when you saved my life, died in an adjoined alley.

"That is quite a coincidence. Wait. Whisper told me she seen something strange at that same place several days before. Perhaps she witnessed the battle."

"I would definitely like to talk to her then. I have questions. See, now it is to our mutual benefit to find your friend. Crotear must have decreed our friendship. Tomorrow I will take leave of court. I will preside over, only the most pressing matters of state. We will depart at noon, incognito.

"Is there any chance of me convincing you to bring an entourage?" Justice asked as they arrived at the door of her majesty's private chambers. It was flanked by a dozen guards wearing full plate armor and opened face helmets so that they could be both protected and easily recognized. They carried medium sized shields and wore a broad bladed sword on their hips. They were adorned with white uniforms tailored with gold embroidery and had a purple plume affixed to each of their helmets.

"No." She stated explicitly as she turned toward him. "You will protect me."

"What if something happens to me, then where will you be?"

"I have been trained in the arts of music and persuasion. I am something of a bard and I have access to a bit of magic so I am not entirely helpless" She gave him a deliberate smile hoping to lighten his countenance then proceeded through her door and closed it behind her. Justice stood idle for a long moment thinking about everything that she had said. There was no higher priority for Justice, he made certain of her safety first and only then would he dare go to sleep?

Chapter 39 - Disappoint

Valley looked up at her father as he stepped into her room. "Good evening father, it is good to see you. I have been rather busy of late." She said as she sat upon her bed.

"I know," Stavid responded, "The entire staff of the house has noticed."

"What do you mean father?"

He stepped further into the small room. Only a bed, a chest and an old armoire made up the room. "There have been murmurings and rumors abounding about you and the Archduke. You have been spending a great deal of time with him lately. It is not proper."

"I am his to command father. I spend time with him because he desires that I do so. The others are just jealous that the master has come to favor me."

"By Crotear Valley, you are a servant not a slave!" It was the very first time Stavid ever yelled at his daughter. "Perhaps some are jealous but to hel with them. No one who loves you wants to see you earn his favor on your back! You might just be a peasant but you are more than some noble man's whore!"

She was pushed back by the force of his words. She felt worse than if he had physically struck her. "Is that what you think of me father? Is it so impossible that love could transcend station? That I could be good enough to be a nobleman's wife?

"Do you see what happens to those who love him, they find only ruin." Stavid stormed out of the room with fire rising in his chest. He marched down the corridor heading for Cavalaries hall.

Chapter 40 - Bastard

"Ashenath stood in the large sepulcher as she waited for Drusus to join her. The shape of the upper half of the iron and stone sarcophagus was sculpted in a generous likeness of the master vampire. The eyes were two sapphires pressed into the sockets. A life-size replica of his great sword, Transfusion lay upon the sculpture's chest pointing down. As Ashenath stared the sculpted mouth of the sarcophagus sprung open revealing an orifice surrounded by bronze teeth and life like fangs. A green vapor emerged from the mouth of the grim container and began to take on a vaguely human semblance as the gas gradually transformed into Drusus. A mortal would have been terrified by this spectacle but for Ashenath it was a nightly routine and more so, it was a bore. She waited as Drusus finished materializing before her. She stared at him with scorn in her eyes. His usual grimace was replaced today by a sort of stupid grin, she thought. "Master, I have the potions you demanded," she said.

"Oh good, Ashes, are you prepared to take a faithful leap?" Drusus asked his chosen spawn with the accent of an extinct culture.

"Of course, master but I do not understand the risk. It seems to me that it would be so much wiser to send spawn before us.

"You see, my dear? Even undeath is not overly generous to your sex. Let's leave all the machinations to me, alright Ash?" Drusus said in his usual condescending manner.

"Yes Master," she replied. She stood there, taking a moment to imagine him being disintegrated by sunlight. *He is being whimsical,* she thought. It was not much of a shock that Drusus would risk the unlives of his spawn, including Ashenath, but for him to be so careless with his own bothered her. *He is taking risks as if he were some common adventurer. You would think,* she considered to herself, *centuries of existence would have taught him caution but now he is taking his immortality for granted. Perhaps he has finally grown weary of his own long existence or perhaps he has reached a new level of arrogance that blinds him to his own weaknesses. Whatever it is, he is dangerous, more dangerous than ever before, not just to his food but to himself and exceedingly so to me.*

The macabre pair walked for two hours. Drusus wore the cloths of his chosen's spawn, the one that had informed him of Blakoepal. They arrived at the spot, an unremarkable stand of trees in a meadow covered in drifting fog. "This is the place." Drusus pronounced.

"It sure doesn't look very impressive," said Ashenath.

"That is the point dear minion. My potion," he ordered stretching out his arm. Ashenath placed the glass beaker into his grasp, a vapor danced within.

"You first," He said.

"I thought we were going together?" Ashenath asked. "You said…"

"I lied," Drusus retorted. "It is an unnecessary risk, suppose we enter over a body of water or perhaps it is daylight on the other side of the veil. No, my existence is too important and yours is worthless, now go."

"Yes Master." She pulled the other beaker from her cloak. She brought the glass tube to her mouth and paused with the cork near her lips. She did not know what to expect. She pondered what would happen. *Could this all be an elaborate trap of Imarra's design? Am I going to be destroyed if I drink this potion here?* Just then a cool breeze came through the field up to the stand of trees gently lifting her hair, though she could not feel it the way a mortal woman would. She decided then that she did not care what happened to her, it being completely out of her control. She smiled before ripping the cork out with her teeth. She pressed the glass to her cold lips and quaffed the invisible fluid. Clear vapor danced out of the glass and her nostrils as she emptied` the contents into her mouth. The world seemed to spin and she felt weightless as everything around her blurred. She felt as though she had been transformed and she had to suspend disbelief as she realized that she stood in the midst of a great city much larger and more impressive than she had dared to imagine.

She looked around. The vampire stood in a large courtyard surrounded by urban sprawl. The buildings outside the courtyard seemed ancient in their architecture. She looked up at the moon. It seemed to be the same moon and to be in the same spot as when she entered the city. Its fullness cast light upon the park. Was this a different place? Which reality was the illusion? Was it the field with the stand of trees or was this city the lie? The park was mostly empty and quiet. Few people walked around. She could see about fifty yards away; a couple took a moon lit stroll holding hands and chatting freely. *What is the thrill of such fraternizing?* She wondered. *Surely the man just wants the basest satisfaction from his lover and the woman is probably even more pathetic. She,* Ashenath told herself, *wants to feel more important than she actually is, taking a man that is larger and stronger and reduce him to a groveling fool willing to do her bidding. It doesn't matter who is smarter, men have such lack of control over their carnal drives and perverted desires that they and womankind are ultimately more akin to the praying mantis than to any other creature. When they fuck, the female will decapitate the male and cannibalize his head. The male, knows good and well its fate if it pursues the female, but cannot resist what is in his nature. The only difference with humans is, the male lives a long time until it has been totally consumed by the female, who in her turn is destroyed because the body of the male is a poison to her, albeit a poison she cannot resist.*

Ashenath broke from her malice filled thoughts and turned around, her eyes finding the great treasure of the city in a pavilion in which rested a large, black stone with crackling arcane energy circulating on its surface. It looked immediately forbidden, yet she felt drawn to it. She walked toward it, her mind full of questions. *How can such obvious treasure resist the temptations of such a grand city? What power does it hold?* She walked up the pavilion steps and approached the stone as arcane power danced about it. She stared into its sheen blackness of infinite depth. She stretched out her hand slowly, leaning slightly forward until her fingertips barely touched it. Then the world altered, suddenly and completely. Ashenath could feel herself lying on her back. She felt somewhat dizzy from the instantaneous change in orientation. She could barely feel her arms and legs and struggled to open her eyes. There was talking but the voices were deep and she could not make out what they were saying. She forced her eyes open but there was mucus on them which caused her vision to be blurry. She became frustrated but rather than anger she felt something she could only barely recollect. It was before, a cold memory but now it was real and escalating quickly as her body felt warmer. It was helplessness then fear and finally sadness. The profusion of emotions came in a rush like a shattered dam and she burst into tears, crying uncontrollably. She felt so alive and at the same time so sad, she kicked her arms and legs crying desperately. She both wanted it to continue but was afraid it would never end. Then her crying was interrupted by a soothing voice and a firm, but tender, touch. "Oh, poor baby, what's the matter? Are you trying to open your eyes dear?"

Ashenath felt something wet on her eyes wiping the mucus off of them. She looked, now able to see. She was in a basket. A small arm came into view, it was hers. She was an infant. Ashenath struggled to control her arm, holding her tiny hand in front of her. She stopped crying as she stared at it. She heard the voice again, "Oh look she has found her hand, such a joy it is to witness such an important discovery." Ashenath looked in the direction of the voice. It was the face of a kind old maid. The woman smiled at her, causing her fear to be replaced with happiness and warmth. She felt safe and above all, loved. Another face appeared next to the maids, it looked familiar. *My father,* Ashenath recognized. He looked so much younger and he did not repulse her as she remembered him.

"I will miss you little princess," the woman said in a most genuine voice.

"Why do they give her to me?" Ashenath's dad asked.

"Her father cannot acknowledge her. If this child's birth was known, it would be the beginning of his demise. Still though, he loves her and wants to protect her from his enemies. That is why you will raise her. She will never know who she is. You as an agent of the crown guard will keep the royal family abreast of the happenings beyond the city's walls, and more importantly you will protect and raise this child."

"What is her name?" He asked.

The maid looked down at her and said, "Ashenath. You will raise her as your own daughter."

Ashenath's father looked down at her. "No, she *will* be my daughter. Her happiness will be my greatest commission. Long live the King and hail to the great city and its most adorable daughter." He reached down, closing the lid on the basket and picked it up."

All of a sudden, her memories started rushing back to her as she relived one after another, looking through the eyes of a baby, then a little girl and finally a young woman. Her whole life her father had been the kindest and most patient man. Her transformation into a vampire had twisted her memories and filled her with hatred toward her father that he did not deserve. She remembered meeting Drusus, how he manipulated her, how he turned her into a faithless monster bent on murder. Her memories came faster, and faster, causing her to become dizzy as she spun around witnessing one evil deed she had committed after another. Then it just stopped. She stood there staring at the black gem in shock. Overwhelmed, tears started to run down her face. She felt a searing hatred for her master, coupled with guilt and grief. How could it be that she was crying? She felt her teeth. They were still the teeth of a vampire. She was still hungry for blood but now she was hungry for revenge as well. She touched her pale cheeks and felt that they were wet. "I am crying." She sobbed.

"What did you say? Ashenath, what are you doing?" Drusus asked from behind her.

She was startled. Her eyes widened with fear. She hurriedly wiped the tears from her face before turning around. "Master?"

"I cannot feel the link between us? Are you free willed?" He asked as he moved up the steps to meet her.

"I still feel compelled to serve master." She said bowing her head.

"What of this stone?" He asked.

"It is just a large gem, probably worth a great deal but of weak magic."

Drusus raised his arm as quick as lightning strikes and struck her with the back of his hand, causing her to fall backwards to the stone floor. "You lie! You, treacherous bitch! Now whatever power you have acquired from the stone I shall share in it before I destroy you!" Drusus grabbed the Black Opal and felt nothing. Annoyed, he attempted to remove it from its place. The Opal would not be moved even by his strength. He felt a fire within and realized only for a second that he had doomed himself.

Ashenath watched in utter shock as Drusus was reduced to dust right before her. All his centuries of unlife now brought to an end by this powerful artifact, the Black Opal. All his attire and jewelry was destroyed except that which contained magic. She gathered the items that survived, saving the sword for last. Very cautiously she reached for it, knowing it to be an item of great power in its own right. She grasped it, trembling from her newly surfaced human emotions. She hoisted Transfusion up in the air with confidence then slashed out with it as she physically spun around in circles screaming joyfully, "I am master now!"

Chapter 41 - Traitor

"I served under the presupposition that I would one day be a Black Knight, so long as I performed my duties as your page with honor." Vektor spoke nervously to his lord. The page stood in Cavalaries hall. Manikins wearing great and historical suits of armor looking like inanimate guards lined either side of the central approach to the high seat of the Cavalaries family. It was a throne in all but name. Treant occupied this seat now to the discomfort of Vektor, who had never known his lord to give audiences in such pompous fashion. The high noble contrary to Vektor was unarmed and unarmored.

"So," Treant said eyeing his armored page with scorn, and walking down from his seat to stand near to one of his armored manikins next to his page. "You are saying that your loyalty was never to me but rather to a dream." Treant rested his hand on the pommel of one of his ancient kinsmen's swords, its steel housed in the manikin's scabbard.

"No milord, my loyalty is to Crotear who you have abandoned. Now I must take my leave.

Treant gritted his teeth, growling before he screamed, "It was Crotear who abandoned me boy!" Just then a yell came from a side corridor directly behind Treant. The two glanced in the direction of the yell and spotted a man charging through the darkness wielding an axe. Both knight and page drew swords in unison, equally surprised and equally assuming the treachery of the other. But with a sword, in Blakoepal, there were none that were Treant's equal. As Vek's sword drew forward

297

Treant parried it, perfectly anticipating the attack from behind. Vek's sword slid away from its target despite his effort to direct it contrary and pierced into the chest of the assailant, into Stavid the house steward. The three seemed frozen, as the moment pressed for more time. Treant's sword pointed past his servant, his other arm stretched out from the momentum of the maneuver. He stood like a cross between them. Vek gasped, his sword lodged in Stavid's heart. He was in utter disbelief. Vek stared at the servant whom he had known well. He watched as Stavid's head slumped forward and his body became heavy and collapsed to the ground nearly pulling the sword out of Vektor's grasp. Vek yanked his sword from the man's chest and walked backward, his sword arm hanging, his grip on the hilt was sweaty and his arm felt sore.

Treant turned to face him raising up his sword, "You have slain my fiancé's father, prepare to defend yourself villain."

"What?" Vek managed. His mind raced from one confusing thought to another "Valley?" He said as the girl raced barefoot across the stone floor, wearing her new nightgown. She fell at her father's side, cradling his head, weeping.

Treant struck out at his former page swinging hard with his sword as Vek desperately tried to parry but the heaviness of the sword and the power of Treant's swing was too great. He had already lost in his heart as he raised his defenses in panic. Treant the greatest swordsman in the city had taught Vek the use of his weapon as a father would instruct a son. Vek knew confusion, fear and hopelessness as Treat knocked the sword from his pitiful grasp.

Tears escaped Vek's eyes as he seen Treant strike out with the pommel of the sword. He knew that he could not expect mercy and prayed inwardly for a quick death. The blow struck the boy hard, collapsing his brow and driving him to the ground. Treant seemed overcome with blood lust as he feverishly bludgeoned, kicked and stabbed the once hopeful page. He felt vindicated as he mangled the poor boy. Valley's crying an appropriate melody for his bloodletting. Then the crying softened. He stood over Vektor's body, a broken vessel, as he continued somehow to live. Vektor vomited blood with such force that it seemed to jump out of his mouth with bits of teeth even as it poured forth from his numerous lacerations. It seemed Vektor tried to call out "mercy" but it became a gurgled muttering. For the briefest moment Treant felt remorse for the boy and considered helping him.

"Silence the murderer Treant, pleassse!" Valley cried out. With that Treant snapped, returning immediately to his blood thirsty craze. With the turn of his arm he separated Vektor's head from his body.

Valley rushed to her Lord's arms. He grabbed her in a passionate hug, kissing her head as she moistened his chest with grief. They remained like that for some time but he could feel her knees trembling and could sense her becoming weak. Treant lifted the girl and carried her back to his bed chamber, where he laid her down. "We shall give him a King's funeral my love." He said to her as he sat on the bed stroking her hair. It was matted to her face so he freed it with his fingertips and with his hand, wiped her face, as it was wet with perspiration and crying.

"No," she said. He would not have it. We will bury him on your grounds next to my mother." She paused briefly "It is only this house that matters." She buried her face in his pillows.

Treant walked out through the doorway of his room into the torch lit corridor beyond, where several servants awaited orders. They looked fearful as they stared at him. Prepare Valley's father for burial then clean up the mess in my hall. Deliver Vektor to the Black Knights with a note stating that future assassins will not enjoy such a kind death as he was meted out.

"Milord," Valley called out from the room, "Milord, stay with me."

"I am coming, my love." He stopped, taking a moment to consider the terrified faces before him. "Anyone else seeking to be separated from their employment to this house should take their leave before I arise again from my bed chamber. Those who stay shall be rewarded and are to serve Valley as if she were me. She will soon be joined to me in marriage." With that Treant walked back into his bed chamber and did not leave it again until the next afternoon, at which time he had only a dozen left of his nearly two hundred servants.

Chapter 42 - Disguise

The next morning Justice awoke to a knock at his door, Nude except for his loincloth, he scrambled to cover his body. He grabbed his quilted blankets and animal furs and quickly covered himself, revealing only the muscular physique of his upper torso. He drew his sword as it hung encased in its scabbard around the post of his bed. "Who goes there?" he yelled, sitting up in his bed.

"It is I, your liege." The princess announced playfully through the crack in the oak door. "Are you dressed?"

"Only partly dressed your majesty." He said as he struggled to lean to the floor and retrieve his breeches.

"Good enough," she said as she pushed through the door, followed in suit by two of her ladies-in-waiting. Startled by the intrusion, Justice tipped over. He fell to the floor leaving his modesty on the bed and revealing his pride. "Oh my," Corrine exclaimed as she covered her mouth and turned her head away. One of her Ladies giggled and the other threw propriety aside staring directly at the indiscrete state of his loin cloth. Justice stared up at her, expecting her couth would at some point turn her head, instead her eyes widened causing Justice to turn red with embarrassment and scramble to adjust his loin cloth and don his breeches.

With his dignity in order, Princess Corrine and her Lady turned back around, the other lady-in-waiting, continued to stare and failed to hold back her giggling. Justice proceeded to get dressed in front of the three ladies. "Would you mind, my Princess, if I called for my servant to help me with my armor. It is a little more complicated than standard leather. The guard usually sends a young soldier up here to serve me but it seems that I am up a little early today."

"Nonsense, my ladies will attend to you." On her word the two servant girls retrieved his armor from the manikin in his room and started to strap the pieces onto his body.

The two girls worked quickly and efficiently, having him suited up in a matter of minutes.

The indiscreet girl pulled several of the straps and buckles too tight in several places. "Ow...I had no idea that your ladies-in-waiting had such specialized training...ouch. Hey, take it easy there...owe."

"You mean you assumed them to be dumb girls?" Corrine asked conspicuously.

"Well yes...uh, I mean no. Well...I thought they could cook and pour wine and maybe even dance a bit, they are probably good at fashion and fixing your hair, which is very important...to some people..." Justice stumbled about with his words like an uneducated buffoon, incriminating himself further with each utterance.

"That is quite enough. Like I said, you took them for helpless and stupid girls. That may be a popular breed of woman amongst the gentry and among many of the lower classes but it is a state that is intolerable in this house. I hope you did not hold such base assumptions about me?"

"Uh...I thought you were like any young lady in your interests, surely though you were groomed for rulership."

"The ladies of my house are all highly educated, though none seek to be like men, we are all content with our protectors and have no rivalry with them. When I am married, I will not stand in my husband's way as he rules on my behalf because I recognize that a good man's temperament is more suitable to such a burdensome position but I will hardly disappear into an endless monotony of fashion, food and dancing. When he seeks my council and he will often, he will know that he is getting the best informed and most intelligent, and caring advice that he has available to him. Few will the times be when he does not heed my council and on those days I shall not usurp him whether he is right or wrong. For when he is right he will have judged wisely and I will see him as a noble king and when he judges poorly he will see me as his wise and virtuous Queen."

"I am sorry your majesty, I have offended you and your ladies with my rogue prejudice. I hail from Slumside, surely every servant in this house is better educated than I am."

"Nonsense Justice," she responded with a light temperament. "I must admit that I do enjoy being misread. In that way, if no other, we are alike. Remember Justice, I insist that you speak freely with me when we are not in public. I would not like to glut the gossipers of this great city, but I trust you and want you to be free to speak your mind as often as possible."

"Why, your majesty... I mean, Corrine. Why would you want to be underestimated? Does that not invite attack?" Justice asked rather pointedly.

She wandered around his room, taking it in, trying to discern any hints about him that may be revealed in the keeping of his quarters. "When you appear strong, only the strong attack you. When you appear weak, only the weak attack you."

"It is as if each of your years has counted for several in wisdom. Only in beauty and spirit do you seem young."

"That is a very poetic compliment you have paid for one that has sprouted from the gravel. Have you been studying with Agon the poet?"

"Hel no, Agon can have his poems. The only verses I know are the ones my sword speaks as I parry and thrust with her," Justice said seeking to recover his reputation as a crude Slumsider before changing the subject. "Well, if you want to leave by noon then perhaps you should get ready."

"Me and my girls *are* ready?" She said, her confusion apparent on her face.

"Ready?" Justice wore an equally confused look, "You are going out in that?" He looked her over. She wore a burnt orange wool cloak with a large hood, the whole thing fringed in a thick, fluffy, red fabric. He wasn't quite sure he had ever encountered such tailoring before. Her wrists were decked in gold bracelets. Her hair was elaborately configured and ornately adorned with a platinum tiara. Pearls hung from her majesty's earlobes. Silver flecks dusted the tops of her cheeks, her forehead and around her eyes which seemed to be boasting a delicate application of makeup derived from real gold that matched the painting of her fingertips. Underneath her cloak was a dress of white, shimmering with silver and gold specks.

Leather boots stained a light tan clasped tight with gold buckles, completed her dress. "I thought you said incognito?"

"I am," she said seriously, "I did not wear a dress that drags on the ground. I am leaving my entourage at the palace. I'm only bringing my two ladies-in-waiting and I am wearing less than half as much jewelry as normal. I dressed warm because the first snow of the year is upon us and I have never ventured out of the palace grounds without my carriage. I will fit in perfectly with the season. This outfit says late autumn to me. What does it say to you, Justice?"

Justice stared with a blank expression at his liege whom he was realizing was very wise in some things and utterly ignorant in others. "It says...rich person. In fact it is the exact opposite of incognito, Corrine." Justice chose his words carefully, well, carefully for him, "You are very smart about so many things but when it comes to street sense, you have none."

"What do you mean?" she asked.

"There is only one way to put this and I do not wish to hurt your feelings but it takes a lot of love to tell someone the truth. If I were to take you out to Westward as you are, everyone would shortly realize that the princess is running around the city without her guards. The news would spread as quickly as if you announced your presence with a parade. The only difference is you will not have your entourage with all of your guards protecting you. Therefore, you will be in extreme danger from anyone who ever hated the crown and even more from those peasants that love you. As your bodyguard and as someone who cares about you, I can't let you do that."

"I see," the princess swallowed deeply. It had been some time since she was last corrected on anything. She turned away from the three of them and looked at a section of wall on the other side of the room. "You think I am a fool now, don't you?" She said out loud too embarrassed to face him.

Her two attendants rushed over to comfort her. Justice looked over at her thoughtfully. "Your majesty, I know you are not a fool. I'm not in the habit of telling people what they want to hear if what they want to hear is not true. If I thought you were a fool I would be bold and tell you right now. Remember it was me that dunked your father in that water. How could you have any street sense when you have been living in this fantasy for all of your life? That's not saying that everything has been well for you, I know better than that. You have shown me that riches do not provide a rich life but I will say this, you have convinced me of the need for you to get beyond the palace without an entourage. This palace is a prison instead of the home it ought to be for the most important but even more, the kindest Lady in this city." When he finished speaking he realized that the princess and her two servants were staring back at him from the opposite side of the room. Suddenly she rushed him. He would have run but how could he run from the person whom he is sworn to protect? Instead he stood there with a silly expression on his face as the princess hugged him like a little girl. Barely keeping from falling down again, he became nervous about the defenselessness of his position. Then, after a moment, he just let himself appreciate what it was like to be loved. His obedience to his duty transcended obeisance to the crown.

Corrine sent her ladies-in-waiting to retrieve more modest attire from the servant's quarters while she and Justice spoke. She sat at the edge of his bed with her legs crossed in the manner of a lady as he stood facing her. They passed the time away speaking about Corrine's nursemaid and instructor Ruth. When the two girls returned, they brought in three dresses and three cloaks. By no means plain, certainly they were amongst the best garments available to the servants that gave them and palace servants made a decent living. Still they were not lavish and would be perfect for their excursion Justice thought.

"You did not tell the servants whom you got these from that they were for the Princess, did you? Justice asked.

"Most certainly not, Guardsmen," Replied the elder of the two ladies who earlier had stared at his lapse in modesty. The princess took one of the dresses and went behind Justice's changing screen with her two Ladies, who grabbed the remaining outfits.

"Princess, please tell me you are not changing in here." He exclaimed. "I am going to get in trouble, with…someone." Justice turned his back to his changing screen, afraid to see even her face while her body was unclad. He grabbed his head on both sides in helpless protest.

"With whom Justice?" she teased. "I am the most powerful lady in the city. I can pretty much change where I please, seeing how I answer to no one. Besides Justice, there is no way for me to sneak out of here like this from my room. Since when did you become such a prude anyway Justy?" Another round of giggling erupted from behind the screen. Justice's face glowed red with embarrassment.

The Princess and her ladies soon emerged, looking like three very pretty girls from the mercantile class. It was hopeless that they could go totally unnoticed. Their beauty was going to draw some stares. The princess spun about showing off her more modest raiment of white and light blue with a warm blue cloak. "What do you think?" Corrine asked her bodyguard as she drew his attention to what she was wearing.

"I lack words deserving to be found in any description of your beauty Princess," Justice locked eyes with her, and smiles graced their faces.

"And what of my ladies, crude warrior?" She asked with lighthearted humor, "Does your repertoire possess words fitting for a description of their beauty?"

"No, your majesty. Their beauty would be supreme if not sharing the light of yours."

He was answered with a modest smile and uncertain eyes.

The two maidens and the Princess travelled the halls of the palace with Justice testing their disguises. All four wore hooded cloaks. The lady-in-waiting that earlier had teased Justice wore white and red, her fellow lady wore multiple shades of green. Justice's cloak was the usual black with studded leather armor, also stained black. Their disguises worked well, even to the point that they

308

were detained by a pair of Crown Guard officers who thought they were suspicious. "Halt, hooded ones," the senior officer of the pair called out. He was the younger of the two at roughly forty-five full circles but he was the senior in rank. He walked up to the Ladies and their escort, approaching from behind, eyeing the hooded group suspiciously. He and his fellow officer moved to the front of the group and stared directly at them. "Why do you cover your faces in the palace?"

"They are with me," Justice explained to the officers, revealing his signet ring." I took the day off so that I might fraternize with these beautiful damsels." He let out a phony laugh. "They wanted to remain discreet because their company with me is an indiscretion for them."

"Very well," The officer responded. "I would like to see their faces before you pass, I assure you that I will keep their identities in the utmost confidence."

"No," Justice said firmly. I will do no such thing. As the Princesses personal bodyguard, I answer to Alturek and to no one beneath him, such as you and I both are. This was by decree of her majesty. Do you dare set yourself against the will of the crown?"

The guard was a hard veteran with a rough face and over-active perspiration. "Her majesty, though divine in her beauty and knowledge is also a troubled, girl. She is not above making an occasional..." He chose his words carefully, "...miscalculation. Seeing how you are acting suspiciously, I will take my chances with Alturek, whom I am well acquainted with."

Justice became angry and started to respond harshly when the Princess stretched her arm forward revealing a miniature scepter. She spoke a command word and stepped forward. The scepter grew to its normal length of six feet. "I too am well acquainted with Alturek," she said, matter-of-fact as she swept her hood back with her other hand.

The Guard officer and his subordinate began to drop to their knees when she stopped them. "Stand up guardsmen before you give me away, if you haven't already." She shrank her scepter and one of her ladies took that as a queue to pull her majesty's hood up for her. "Well, what have you to say for yourself guardsman?" she asked, sternly tapping her foot, impatient, with arms crossed and looking away from him.

"I am sorry, your highness. I have spoken too carelessly of you. I deserve only your condemnation and eagerly submit to it." He answered.

"How long have you been in the guard, lieutenant?" She asked demonstrating knowledge of military rank.

"Twenty five circles your majesty."

"Have you killed in your service to the crown?"

"Yes, your majesty" He answered, his eyes lowering more as he seemingly reflected upon his long service. "It was hard but I earned my place in the ranks of the officers over a decade past."

"Have you also seen your compatriots slain before you? She pressed.

"Yes, your majesty, I have lost more than a few of my friends in defense of the crown."

"Very well," She said. "You have sacrificed much throughout your service, so I will not deal harshly with you. I realize that though you think I am a foolish girl, you nonetheless serve and protect me. You are forgiven. In the future, you will answer to Justice. You are hereby reassigned to my personal entourage. I understand this is an honor of sorts. Is this pleasing to you Lieutenant?"

"Very much so your highness." He answered trying to hold back his grin.

Corrine looked at the two men. "You two will report to the road in front of the palace, wearing regular garments suitable for the weather. You will seek me there. You have one hour. Do not speak of this to anyone."

Chapter 43 - Betray

The two officers arrived dressed inconspicuously in warm cloaks of dark blue. The lieutenant and his compatriot easily found their charge. The princess regarded the high lieutenant's comrade-in-arms as she greeted them. A mostly bald man with a crescent of prematurely white hair, he also wore a lieutenant's emblem albeit a low Lieutenants. He appeared sturdy enough but did not seem very intimidating. *I'm sure he will hold his own in a fight, if gods forbid there must be one*, she thought.

The group started down the road blending in with the regular traffic. As they escaped the commanding shadow of the palace Corrine's heart began to beat a little harder, excitement moving through her body. She grabbed the blue sleeved arm of her lady-in-waiting. "Samiras, I feel like a bird released from its cage," Corrine said squeezing her maids arm.

Samiras pulled her arm free from Corrine's grasp and placed it around her far shoulder more like a friend or sister would, as they continued to walk. "When is the last time you called me by my name rather than Minty?"

"Why does she call you Minty? Justice asked.

"It is short for Water Mint." Samiras answered.

"Oh. Why does she call you Water Mint?"

Corrine's other lady picked up her step to keep her place on the princess's right side. "When Corrine was but a little girl learning of the different plants she thought it would be fun to name all of us after the royal gardens foliage, to help her remember and as a sort of a private name amongst us when we would play on the palace grounds. The names just happened to stick and when we are in private we refer to each other by our garden names. Mine is Attar of Roses or just plain Attar for short.

Justice roared in laughter at this, catching everyone by surprise. He laughed so hard grabbing his knees that it was necessary to stop until he had finished. The group halted and stared at him while he carried on. The lady's fidgeted, slightly embarrassed both at the fact that he was laughing at them but also at the scene he was making. Corrine stood with a stern look on her face, tapping her foot steadily. "Are you nearly done?" She asked impatiently. "You are being ridiculous and people are staring at you because you look like a fool." This seemed to increase Justice's mirth. "You know sometimes your inappropriate behavior is funny, even charming but right now it is just annoying and what of blending with the common folk? Suit yourself we shall continue without you. Ladies, Lieutenants, let us go and leave him to wallow in his foolishness."

The group moved on. Justice stopped laughing and hurried several steps to walk back amongst them. After another brief fit of laughter, he composed himself enough to speak. "So, your highness…? Justice started still bearing a smirk on his face.

"Choose your words carefully or else I shall rename you after flowery foliage. Sweethearts would be good I think. I love sweethearts there so, so clingy, kind of like you."

This time the officers let a smirk creep across their face, the bald one covered his mouth and the other revealing a toothy grin. "At ease gentlemen, you may laugh freely and you may speak freely, that way our group will look natural and besides I did not leave the palace only to bring its many rules of etiquette with us."

"Yes, your highness," they muttered in unison careful not to be overheard by any passersby.

"I'm not clingy," Justice protested.

"Sure you are, you follow me everywhere I go. Gentlemen, you may refer to me as Meadow Sweet for the duration of this trip." Without looking in her bodyguard's direction she answered the grin that was undoubtedly forming on his face threatening to overcome him with another round of laughter. "Wipe that dumb look off your face... Sweet Hearts." His expression changed immediately to concern. The two lieutenants laughed at him reading the distress on his face. Let us continue commander Sweetheart the senior ranked of the two, jested. At this, Corrine and her two ladies laughed.

"Seriously Corrine, I mean Meadow Sweet, you are not going to let them call me that, right?" Justice plead. There was another round of short laughs and giggles that did not comfort him in any way. "Corrine, I mean Meadow Sweet, I love flowers," he entreated.

Corrine snickered one last time, "Guys, we will let him get away with it this once. Justice has easy feelings and a garden name might negatively affect his prowess with a sword."

"Then again," The balding guard reconsidered, "It might make him meaner."

The group taunted and jested at Justice's expense as they carried on. Eventually they made their way to Coin Street. Justice looked around, there was no difference between it now and how he remembered it, except that he did not recall it being so ran down. All the time he spent in the palace, the height of decadence swirling constantly around him, he had grown accustomed to it, more so than he had realized. Now he understood that he had been changed. He had always found his home in the garbage heap of Slumside. He always looked up at the lives of those in Eastward. Now as he stood there on Coin Street in the near center of Eastward he realized he was looking down upon the lives of this wards people. *Am I better than them? Surely not* he thought to himself. He had risen from beneath their feet, how could he be better? Did all those he had known in the slums possess the same latent potential to rise above their station, did they lack only in opportunity or was their lacking natural?

"Jynx, are you going in? The princess asked using his old name so as to not arouse suspicion from any who might overhear.

The sound of his old name being called out in this place as he stood in reflection of the past rattled him. For a moment, he thought it was Whisper that called upon him.

"Huh? Oh yes. Wait here while I go in." Justice put up his hood, went in and spoke to the bar keep. The bar keep, a fellow of almost forty circles informed Justice that he had not seen Whisper since last, he saw the two of them together. Perhaps Slumside he suggested. Justice thanked the man and

315

exited the tavern. He walked across the porch and stood at the peak of the small stair leading down to the road.

Corrine looked up at him anxiously "Was there any word, Jynx?" she asked. He smiled at her as he realized how much she cared. No one had ever been so selflessly concerned for his happiness?

As he began to answer her he spotted a rogue slip out of the thin pedestrian traffic behind her majesty about fifteen paces. The hooded rogue leveled a loaded crossbow in his and the princess's direction. Horror spread quickly through him, knowing he was out of range to protect his princess. Everything seemed to move in slow motion as he simultaneously drew his sword and yelled, "Look Out!" The distinct sound of the crossbow bolt echoed through his mind as the ladies in waiting scrambled to cover the princess. They drew forth daggers that grew to be full length long swords and their clothing transformed into fine, light weight chainmail of a bluish hue. The lead Lieutenant armed himself scanning passersby for an opponent. Hooded swordsmen charged, already armed, toward the group. The bolt found its target with a thick sound punctuating its firing to Justices left. Justice turned in time to see a rogue armed with a short sword, his hood pinned to his head with a crossbow bolt, falling backwards slowly. The action then became distinctly hyper as another rogue stood behind the first, sword in hand. Justice and the assassin began fighting fiercely. There was something familiar about this assassin's movements that he could not place, not having time for thinking. He was in a soldier's mental zone battling with single minded focus as adrenaline caused his peripheral vision to disappear and heightened his reflexes.

Below the porch, on Coin Street the princess's ladies stood on either side of Corrine with their backs to her. The two of them had already cut down three would be assassins as two more traded steel with them in disbelief of the women's skill. The lead lieutenant fought two warriors, one in front of him and one behind him in a whirling display of swordsmanship.

The princess looked past the fight before her. A monk caught in the fray, stood at the mouth of the alley on the right side of Coin Street. A half dozen more warriors attempted to move into the battle from the alley. As the first of the group tried to run full speed past the monk, paying him no attention, the monk spun one hundred and eighty degrees, extending his arm with a flat hand, striking the potential assassin in the throat hard. The strike destroyed the man's Adams-apple and broke his neck. His feet flew up in the air as his body folded at the neck before landing in a twisted heap next to the monk. Shocked the five remaining warriors stopped in their tracks, staring at the monk with swords drawn. The monk withdrew his cowl with both hands revealing himself to be Omega, companion of the Blood Knight from the tournament a few days earlier. The monk curled his hands into fists challenging the men to attempt passing him. "Kill him," one of the five shouted and they all charged forward to their death as the monk parried their sword strikes with his arms as though they were made of iron, and struck them with his fists and feet. He moved with extraordinary agility and coordination. One by one they fell.

Corrine looked to the other side of the street where six more combatants entered from the alley. The Blood Knight in anticipation of their arrival charged through the chaos on the street. He was mounted on his armored steed, in full knightly adornment, black steel and blood red fabric, lance leveled for the attack. As the knight entered the alley, he drove his lance through the first of the surprised warriors. The blood knight released his grip on the lance as he barreled through the group causing them to throw themselves against the brick buildings on either side of the alley. The Blood knight blew past them thirty feet then turned to face them. They stood shaken with fear as the Blood knight reared his horse onto its hind legs, drawing his steel longsword which glinted with light from the sun as he raised it in the air with his left hand, the gauntlet locking the sword into his grip with a distinct mechanical clang, his large rectangular shield on the right side. The Blood knight charged forward. They wanted to run but knew better than to turn their backs to the mounted warrior. Two of the men threw their swords to the ground and covered their heads desperately afraid, the other three fearfully attempted to defend their selves. The Blood knight's steed made a thunderous fury as it galloped down the alley. The Knight cut down two of the men on his left and smashed one on the forehead with his shield causing the man to fall backwards and crack the back of his head open on the stone wall of a building. Blood flowed from both places, the man dying in the next few moments as he became sufficiently drained. The champion stopped his horse at the opening of the alley onto Coin Street. He turned his warhorse sideways letting it shift a little, due to its excitement and looked down the alley. The two men who threw their swords down leaned on opposite walls quivering their hands still fearfully up. As they lowered their arms with hesitation the men looked distinctly, first at the blood knight, then their dead companions and finally each other. Abruptly in unified spontaneity they dashed down the alley, away from the Blood Knight, running faster than they ever knew they could.

The balding Lieutenant moved to the perimeter of the fight, standing below the porch where Justice dueled above. A large, ugly man with equal measure of fat and muscle approached him bearing a heavy war hammer in his hand. He stood before the Lieutenant, smiling with a disgusting scowl, thinking the Lieutenant too afraid to move as he lifted his great war-hammer with both hands. The barbaric man froze in place, something was wrong. His face admitted his confusion at the Lieutenant whose eye color changed to silver. The barbarian struggled to maintain his stance as he felt his eyes and his mouth dry up, his grip on his hammer wavered and he dropped the weapon behind him. His skin began to shrivel up as all the moisture in his body evaporated mysteriously. He was helpless to stop it and died right there a shriveled prune-like remnant of what had been a terrible man.

As Corrine's compatriots bested their enemies and the battle winded down, Justice continued to battle furiously with his enemy. The assassin wore a black hooded cloak, with his face painted black and the blade of his weapon stained black as well. Justice backed the rogue to the rail of the porch. The black clad assassin jumped up landing on the rail, swinging his sword violently he almost overcame Justice. Justice was surprised by the acrobatic prowess of the rogue but recovered and seeing an apparent opening swung at chest level. The sword hissed through the air as he tried to cut off the man's feet. The rogue took his acrobatics further, evading the blow with a surprising backwards flip, landing him on the ground below the porch. His hood fell off as he landed. Justice used his free hand to brace himself as he leapt over the rail to the ground below. Meeting his opponent eye to eye he knocked his hood back with his free hand.

"Jynx?" The assassin asked in a familiar but troubled voice.

"Enigma? That better not be you." Justice said in total surprise. There were no two people he loved more than Whisper and Corrine but Enigma was a scorn to both. Justice felt rage sweep over him like a fever. He charged the rogue unexpectedly. "Die you, murderous vagabond!"

Corrine, the Blood Knight and the rest of the company began to gather in the street watching the melee ensue. Justice hammered at Enigma's defenses he slashed and thrust with his sword-hand striking Enigma in the mouth with his fist. The metal studs set in a leather band on Justices hand made it all the more devastating. Justice knocked his childhood friend to the ground pummeling him in the face brutally with his metal fist as he straddled him. Blood tossed from multiple cuts on his face as his face seemed to melt with every blow. Justice cocked back his sword for what would have been a killing strike unhesitatingly executed if not for the interruption. "JYNX! NO! A woman's voice tore through the air desperately. It wasn't Corrine's. He looked up. His mind raced, it was the rogue from earlier, the one that saved him by firing a bolt into the head of the first assassin that tried to kill him. Justice thought the rogue meant to hit him but had missed.

Who is she? How does she know me by my old name?

Whisper removed her hood. "Jynx, please... please spare my brother."

Enigma, still grasping his short sword, pressed the tip into Justice pushing him backwards, as he himself stood.

Justice's companions moved to attack the assassin.

Holding the sword tip pressed into Justices chest, Enigma somersaulted away from Justice into the shadow from the porch railing, and vanished into it leaving the sword to fall. Everyone was confused, everyone but Justice and Whisper. They immediately turned around as Enigma, worn and bloodied, dark-red, muddying his black painted face and staining his cloths, stepped from the shadow of another house. "Whisper, I am sorry." He said as they locked eyes, "I never wanted it to be this way." As Whisper began to cry he cast a hateful look over to his onetime friend. "You tried to kill me and for that you are no longer anyone to me. You would be wise to avoid me in combat, sir. Why don't you rescue your poor mother Noblesider? Before she dies of whoredom in a dump called the Downside tavern on the first stretch of the great stair! Or are you too good for even your own mother now?" Enigma stepped back into the shadows and disappeared, this time not reappearing where they could see him, even as his sister began to plead.

Jynx held his sword in the air and yelled back at him, unsure if he could even hear him. "It was you that abandoned us! You to, would be wise to avoid me, especially if your sister is not here to save you, coward!"

Chapter 44 - Company

"Are any of them alive?" Jynx called out, an open invitation for any who would answer.

"All are dead or escaped," the monk answered as he approached. The Princess's company, the Blood Knight, the monk and Whisper began to gather into a circle as they spoke. No one except Jynx had sustained any injuries.

The Blood Knight scanned the assembling crowd until he spotted a boy no more than twelve circles old. He pointed at him.

The boy pointed back to himself as if to ask, *who? Me?*

The Blood Knight motioned him over. The boy complied and walked up, staring at the Blood Knight in awe, he had never seen a real knight this close before. The Blood Knight dismounted and walked toward the front of the war horse. He pet the horse for a moment then handed the reins to the boy. The boy knew what to do, having been a stable boy from time to time amidst an assortment of other temporary jobs. The Blood Knight moved to join the circle as the boy lead his steed down the alley to the small stable behind the Coin Street Tavern.

"Looks like Crown Swords and Inquisitors noticed the commotion." Attar said to the group.

"I hate Inquisitors," Whisper blurted, drawing gazes from everyone else.

"Your Majesty," The bald officer spoke. "If you want to protect your cover go into the tavern with everyone else. Me and the Lieutenant will take command of the Swords and send the Inquisitors on their way."

"Our cover is compromised already. We must get the princess back to the palace before another attempt is made on her life." Jynx said

"It looked like the attempt was on your life, Jynxy" Whisper said with a passive aggressive snootiness'.

"Nonsense," Jynx answered, "They changed their tactics. They figured I was the biggest obstacle to killing the princess, so they thought to neutralize me first. Then nothing would stand between them and the princess. They obviously were not informed about the prowess of her majesty's ladies or aware, as we weren't that the princess's champion also seen through our attempt to be inconspicuous and was following us with his monk friend. They even used the best assassin in the group to keep me busy."

"He is not an assassin, Jynx!"

"How would you know? What are you even doing here, trying to get close so the next attempt succeeds?"

"I saved your life!

"Maybe that was all for show!" Jynx yelled angrily

"Go to Hel, Jynx" Whisper said.

"Everyone inside!" Corrine ordered, raising her voice to what would pass as a yell only for her. "We will have this discussion in the Tavern."

Whisper and Jynx locked eyes for a moment while everyone minus them and the two officers walked toward the tavern door. Then guilt turned Jynx's face away and the two of them proceeded with the others to enter the tavern. Jynx was the last one to enter. He flipped the wooden sign hanging on the door to its opposite. "Your closed," he said to the bar keep as he walked into the tavern.

As the Crown Swords and the Inquisitors approached they met the two officers. The Inquisitors were all hooded and looked like rogues but one of them, the one who came forward.

The highest ranking of the soldiers stepped forward as well, a sergeant. "Well, we have a conundrum here," the Lieutenant said. "It seems that we have Guardsmen, Swords and Inquisitors here. I am going to have to insist that the Crown Guard has jurisdiction at this scene seeing how we were involved in the fray personally and matters of royal security are at stake."

"That's funny," the lead inquisitor said removing her hood revealing her face and long brown hair arranged in a severe chignon. "My name is Captain Davania and I to, am involved in this incident and in point of fact, the Inquisition is working closely with the Crown Guard on this matter, albeit with officers higher up the food chain then a couple of Lieutenants. Now, unless you possess a writ from someone that bleeds purple then I am in charge. Since I am the highest-ranking officer and therefore in charge, I am going to have to insist for starters..." Davania pointed at the sergeant and his men, "...that they take a hike. You two, however..." she turned back toward the Lieutenants, "...can remain for questioning. You will not resist manacles, will you? They are for your safety as well as for ours." She said with sarcasm.

"How could you possibly know about this before us?" The head Lieutenant asked in protest,

"We didn't even know about it until it was happening?"

"Exactly, you are nobody and therefore know nothing. Comply with my orders before you end up unemployed and forgotten in one of the Inquisition's fine dungeons."

"Excuse me," the bald guard interjected.

"What?" Davania asked.

"I don't exactly bleed purple but I do think you meant that figuratively. Still I must insist..." the bald guardsmen's eyes began to turn silver as they had earlier and his voice changed terrifyingly to one of arcane authority, That caused the wind to blow in her face as he spoke, "I must insist that you do not hinder me any further."

"Agon," she gasped in recognition. "I, I did not know you were personally accompanying the princess."

Agon returned completely to his disguise, as the bald Lieutenant. "Now you know. I am glad it is you Davania. I can trust someone as important as you to clean this mess up and make sure that the crowd disperses"

Davania turned flush with embarrassment. "I am not usually that arrogant, I thought I was dealing with a common officer and needed to be pushy to protect my investigation."

"I know. You are a good officer, Davania. If not for you and your agent, the wrong people could have been killed here."

"I am unworthy of such a compliment, Prince Agon, I will work harder to deserve it."

"You are doing a great job, I would like to pull you away from the counsel but I suspect that Lady

Dargon would not let you go easily. Anyway, me and the Lieutenant are needed inside, good morrow to you Captain." The two Lieutenants walked into the Coin Street Tavern. The bald Lieutenant looked around. Inside the group had pulled two tables together.

"Is everything well, Lieutenants?" The princess asked as they entered.

"All is well Meadow Sweet," The first Lieutenant answered.

"We have the bar keep cooking us a meal. We also have pitchers of ale, I am about to have my very first one ever. To celebrate our victory"

The Lieutenants sat at the table. "Where is the Blood Knight?"

"He is in a room upstairs," Whisper answered. "The Blood Knight has committed to other vows beyond silence. One such vow is that he eats alone."

"How do you know so much about the Blood Knight?" Jynx demanded. "And you never answered my question earlier. What are you doing here?"

"Well, since you are so important now I will answer you. I am the Blood Knights scout. I follow the Blood Knight everywhere he goes. In fact, the only person here, who trumps the Blood Knight when it comes to my loyalty is, her majesty Princess Corrine." Whisper looked over to the princess, "It is an honor to meet you again your majesty."

"Please, there is no need for formalities at this moment, such proclivity strains communication and jeopardizes my disguise as a merchant class lady," the princess said.

Whisper looked back to Jynx. "That should

suffice to answer both questions. Now if I might be bold, given all the informality around here, what are all of you doing outside of the palace?"

"Allow me to explain," Corrine said. "My personal bodyguard, your friend, set off to locate you."

"You mean to tell me that this is all because of me? Whisper asked. "You placed your life at risk to help Jynx find insignificant me? Please tell me you jest." Whisper put her forehead in her hands as she contemplated Corrine's words.

Corrine felt pity for her. "In a way, this is all for you but it is also for me. If I am going to rule these people, then I want to know who they are and how they live. I can never know that unless I walk among them. Surely, I cannot meet every individual but I can gain an understanding if I try. This is why we must go to the stair. What better way to learn of my city then on a quest to rescue my brave bodyguard's mother" Every head was already affixed on her, even the barkeep as he laid his very best food out having figured out that royalty was among him. At her mention of the stair everyone became more attentive, their reactions betraying their astonishment. Whisper leaned back, Jynx leaned forward. The monk turned his head. The high Lieutenant spilt his ale, the barkeep spilled a bowl of soup he was serving. The ladies jumped up from the hot soup spilled before them and the bald Lieutenant's eyes narrowed. "We must save Jynx's mother. You all heard Whisper's brother. She is in distress and probably doesn't even know the good fortune of her son. It will give me the perfect opportunity to see the stair."

"That is fucking insane! With all love and respect your majesty, there is no way in Hel that we can do that." Jynx blurted.

"I will do it with or without your help Jynx."

"Why? Why would you risk your life over some prostitute you don't even know? You are going to be queen. The stair is more dangerous than you realize. I have only been their once, very briefly. It's not even considered part of your domain and that's a good thing. Slumside has problems with criminals but the stair is filled with downright reprobates, the worse of the worse. The people that go there are so evil or so desperately hopeless that they might as well be the living dead. I became your bodyguard to keep you safe not get you killed, or worse.

Princess Corrine sat thoughtfully for a few moments, giving Jynx a chance to calm down. No one said a word as they all waited for Corrine to make some sort of comment. When she was satisfied that the tension Jynx created had subsided enough she spoke, carefully in her softest voice. "Jynx I have asked you to speak your mind with me and I am glad that you have. I am disappointed you would use your words so harshly in describing the woman that bore you life. It must have been very hard for her to carry you before you were born and even more so afterwards. She could have momentarily quenched her poverty by being rid of you or selling you to one of the monsters on the stair. If she had loved you less and took the easy way out you would not be sitting here now." She let her words settle for a few breaths before she continued. "I would not be sitting here either, for it

329

was her son that saved my life. If bearing you and protecting you so that one day you could protect me, was the only good she ever did, it would be enough to deserve my favor and a chance at redemption. I believe that one of the greatest things our society should believe in is redemption for those who earn it. You who were once a common thief should believe this as well. As far as I am concerned Jynx, a debt of gratitude is owed to your mother and she does not belong where she is. Also I wish to see the nightmare that is the great stair once before I become Queen. I will not be timid in my rule. There will be monumental changes over circles to come. Our city state is so obsessed with hiding we never ask ourselves if we should be hiding. The world may contain a lot of evil but we possess that quality in no small amount ourselves. Is it possible that perhaps the world is like us in this respect? Perhaps we are missing out on a lot of good for fear of evil? I desire the opinions of all who possess them."

"I am shocked by the revolutionary statements you have made as I am shocked that you wish to travel to the great stair to rescue my mother. I have no more comments to make, whatever you decide is right for me and I will follow you without wavering. I just desire to keep you safe. I exist to protect you"

"You exist for whatever purpose the gods have decided or at least whatever purpose you have decided. It is your occupation to protect me, perhaps it is even your duty Jynx, but it is not the summation of your existence. You possess your own choice as any man does and it is up to you to decide what sort of man you will be." Corrine looked at Whisper anticipating her views on the topic.

"I am not sure of all you were speaking about," Whisper stated honestly. "I assumed you had a council of advisers that you went to with your ideas. I know I speak for the Blood Knight and Omega when I say that we would accompany you to the first layer of Hel and beyond. So, we will no doubt accompany you to the stair and trust in *your* compass to be our guide."

"I wish you wouldn't but since your mind is made up I will have to share in those fancy words given by Miss Whisper." The high lieutenant said.

"You already know our minds Meadow." Minty said on behalf of her and Attar.

"I think it is a great idea," The Bald Lieutenant said to everyone's dismay.

The princess looked at the bar keep as he cleaned up the messes that were made. "What do you think sir?

"Me?"

"Yes barkeep you are present so speak your piece."

The barkeep shifted about in nervousness as he answered. "Uh... I am happy with my lot in life, uh... I am no merchant but this tavern provides me a decent living. Some are, um, not as fortunate as me, um. I think I see how everyone feels. So me thinks it is a good idea, uh, but your safety should be guaranteed as much as possible if you go, um. I would probably not be much, uh, use to you your majesty and I must admit that I am not a terribly brave man, not like one of your, um, knights but I would do whatever you asked and try to keep my wits about me."

Corrine smiled at him. "All I ask of you, good man, is to keep secret who was here today until I am safe in the palace. Then you may tell people that I was here.

"Yes ma'am," the bar-keep answered.

Corrine lifted her mug in salute, the rest of her company did likewise. "To the Coin Street Tavern, where her Royal Highness Princess Corrine Amorgoden, in the company of her brave companions, had her very first swallow of Ale. By royal edict I declare my company, The Coin Street Company, a chartered company of heroes on par with any other order and free to leave the city at will." With this she slugged her ale then slammed her mug down two thirds empty making a throaty noise. "Oh, dear gods, what a vile substance!"

Jynx laughed "It is an acquired taste your majesty." The Company of The Lady's Companions enjoyed a hearty lunch and relaxed for an hour besides. Afterwards they picked themselves up and set off toward Slumside and the great stair.

Chapter 45 - Reflect

Valley slid out of bed, careful not to rouse her sleeping Lord. She panicked momentarily as she realized that her father was dead, but as her eyes were drained the previous evening she hid her face in her hands and could only muster a sob. She turned around and looked at Treant. She couldn't help but smile as she stood idle, thinking. *Should I wake him and make love to him or should I allow him to continue in his peaceful slumber? How, she wondered, could my greatest joy and gravest sorrow join together in a common arrival? Father had been a good man and Treant to, but the same God tasked with protecting Treant was likewise tasked with protecting my father. Both had served Crotear in their own way. Misery was the only reward anyone was granted by this despotic and ungrateful god. To Hel with him, Valley thought. But what do I know of Asmodeus? Is he not malicious and selfish? No, He is not selfish. He just seeks his own glory, the way that Crotear seeks his own.* She heard Imarra's voice in her mind. Sometimes she thought Imarra's musings to be her own as they grew more and more inexorably blended. Even Imarra, who had possessed mortals before, never experienced such connectivity with one. More and more the lines between the two of them became blurred. Valley looked across the room and seen a large drape covering a wall hanging. She walked over, looking at it curiously. Intrigued she pulled down the drape, revealing a huge mirror. It reflected everything in the room accurately. Everything except her. She appeared as she stood, wearing an expensive leather loincloth with a long rectangle covering her between her legs, front and back. The rest of her body was naked except for a necklace of pearls. Her hair showed blond in the mirror rather than brown though otherwise a perfect reflection of its current, messy arrangement. The image in the mirror had violet eyes and was exceedingly attractive, more so than her. The reflection was taller, her skin was flawless, her breasts were fuller, lips thicker, her body was supple and curvier. "The necklace looks better on you then it does on me," she spoke to the image.

"Something unusual is happening," Valley's lips moved as Imarra answered out loud. To Valley it seemed as though the image in the mirror spoke to her. "I feel a change taking place in your body. I am experiencing all of your emotions much more vividly... and personally, then I ever have with anyone before."

"You are losing the power to control me," Valley said. The image of Imarra did not move its lips as it listened to the servant girl. "I am controlling us, you are just along for the ride. Why don't you leave me and go back to your own body? You don't need to control me anymore."

"I am not ready to," Imarra lied.

"You can't," Valley laughed, "Your soul is trapped in my body, isn't it?"

"Chose your words carefully, girl. You think the women on your world of Orthe are vindictive? Hel already knows my fury?"

Valley smiled, prompting Imarra's reflection to smile in kind, "I am sorry, dear Angel. I laugh not at you but at the predicament, it is so unexpected. Besides, I owe you. You gave me courage that I never possessed on my own. You are like a sister to me and I feel your frustration in the same way that you feel my heart."

Imarra smirked. "Remember that, for I do know one way for sure that we may be separated."

Just then Valley noticed Treant standing behind Imarra in the mirror. She was confused for a moment, then as he raised a sword she spun around to look at the nobleman.

"Treant, my love, sheath your weapon. It is I Valley. I am to be your wife."

Treant stared at her and the image in the mirror, in disbelief. The image in the mirror stayed facing him as Valley turned around. Both looked at him seemingly unconnected with each other.

"You," he pointed his sword at the mirror "You are that creature that spared me from those demons."

"Actually," Imarra spoke through Valley's lips in her own voice, though the lips of her image moved as well. It had a disorienting effect on the knight, "I am the devil that saved your life from those vampires."

"Who are you and why are you in my mirror?" Treant asked, emotion apparent in his voice.

"You are the descendent of my brother. I too am a Cavalaries," Valley's voice raised under the control of Imarra. "I was cast into Hel. I believe Asmodeus has sent me to aid you in your awakening. Crotear has reneged on your relationship and has striped you of your holy powers. You lost your supernatural steed, your power to heal, your ability to repel the undead and to smite evil with divine energy. What is more is that he has allowed your enemies to be elevated above you, so that they could fully enjoy your anguish. I entered your lover's body to get close enough to deliver this message. To tell you that those powers can be replaced and you can again be exalted higher than ever before if you agree to call my lord master. By serving Asmodeus you are really serving yourself and he is the Watcher and commander of those who command themselves, those who rule over others with an iron fist. You must go to his most powerful servant and swear obeisance."

"What am I supposed to do?" Treant asked. "I cannot go near the temple of strife, anyone associated with Asmodeus will kill me the moment they get the chance, especially White Thorn and the temple clergy."

"You must ask one who is more favored of Asmodeus then his high priest,"

Treant looked at her image dismayed, "And who might that be, someone beyond the city?"

Imarra smiled. "No, below it. Not as far down as the denizens. The chosen one of Asmodeus, exists below Deadside in the catacombs of an extinct noble house."

"The Tyrant of the Damned? Do you speak of the legend of the lich? He is supposed to have great power over the lost souls of the dead. I did not think he was real. Why would I want to serve Asmodeus?

"He does exist and you already serve Asmodeus foolish man. You have served him every time you have failed to show mercy, every time you have sought revenge, every time you have taken what you have wanted without regard for others." Imarra's eyes shifted looking over at Valley to emphasize her meaning. "It is wrong, that it is wrong, for it should be right to take that which you want. Asmodeus wants for you to have what your heart desires and to have it in abundance."

"I want Valley back." Treant blurted.

"Yes, well that is something else we will seek advice on. It seems that the bond between me and your servant girl is stronger than I anticipated. The two of us are hopelessly linked until I can figure out how to leave her body without killing her. Until then we share this body and every sensation and emotion that comes with it."

The image of Imarra spun around as an accurate reflection of Valley's movements, but otherwise remained Imarra "Treant," Valley called out in a low voice. "I have wrested control from her but you must understand that we are one. I can't tell which thoughts are hers and which are mine. I remember things that I never knew, my recollections stretching back for centuries. My body and soul are the driving force but all these things have been added to me. Every moment I recall a little bit of her life as if it were mine."

Treant yelled at her grabbing her shoulders. "Is it you though? Are you my Valley?"

"Yes," she grabbed his face kissing him passionately. "Yes," her voice elevated with excitement as she continued to kiss him, breaking away every few moments to reassure him that it was her or to declare how much she loved him. She kissed his neck as she pulled his shirt open with no regard for the top two buttons which were cast away to the floor. He could feel her breath hot on his skin as she moistened it with her lips and the tip of her tongue. She began to kiss his chest working her way down when he looked over to the mirror. In the glass, it was Imarra that kissed him, Imarra whose hands searched between his legs. Her eyes looked up at him and she smiled her eyes glazed over with lust.

Chapter 46 - Pity

The Coin Street Company approached one of the large gates that facilitated entrance to Slumside. Throughout the day four arch-shaped gates were open allowing free passage through the thirty-foot-high interior wall. At night and during periods of civil unrest however, the gates were sealed leaving the Slumside ghetto cut off from the rest of the city. Blakoepal was very much segregated. Every sector of the city was segmented by walls, though none as high as the ones around the slums. Only Eastward and Westward had no boundary between the two. This caused distinct cultures to develop in each sector of the city over the centuries. As a result, you could usually determine what sector of the city someone belonged in just by looking at them or even listening to the way they spoke.

Passage from one sector to another had its own hazards. The Inquisitors stationed at the archway invariably would harass interlopers. The only way around this was to pay a generous bribe or to be someone of importance. Corrine and Jynx walked at the head of the company. "Who goes thur?" A large man wearing heavy plates of armor and carrying a bastard sword on his back asked.

"We desire to enter the slums," Jynx answered.

The man leered at Corrine to the great disgust of her companions. Jynx grabbed the hilt of his sword. Corrine anticipated this and touched his sword arm. "Relax dear guard." She said softly. The other Inquisitor sentries stood at the sign of hostility, crossbows at the ready.

The Gate Warden sneered at Jynx. "What is such a good-looking bunch of armed travelers from Westward need to get to Slumside for?"

"Our business is our own, now stand aside miscreant" Jynx snarled.

"What in blazing hades did he call me?" The brutish man asked his fellows with a pretense of indignation.

"I believe he called you a mis-cre-ant Bone." One of his subordinates responded in a raspy voice.

"What in Gehenna is a mis-cre-ant?" The Inquisitor, Bone, asked his men

"I think it means he is smarter than you," one called out.

"I think it is an abyssal fungus," shouted another.

"Hey Bone, me thinks it means that you're the son of a fat Nobleside wench," the third instigator suggested as they all enjoyed a hearty laugh.

"I got this, boys," Bone said as he lifted his large right palm up toward his men. "I am afraid you must pay the gate tax for your company. It is five crowns per person.

"Five crowns per person is outrageous," Jynx said. "Last time I passed through the gate it cost me three crown pieces, my only crown pieces, one for the King, one for the council and one for the hospitality of the gate guards."

Whisper stepped forward angrily, "I remember, it was the day of Lady Ringheart's funeral. I did not have to pay the hospitality tax with gold because I was groped by your scurrilous swine."

"Everyone pays the hospitality tax," Bone laughed. "I guess the King didn't get his that day."

The Blood Knight grabbed the hilt of his sword. The locking mechanism of the gauntlet was audible and drew Bone's gaze past Jynx, Corrine and Whisper.

The high lieutenant decided this was an opportune time to intervene. "Bone, is it?" The Lieutenant stepped forward. He pulled his medallion from his shirt so the Gate Warden could see it. "You sir, are impeding crown business, stand aside and hope we forget about your ribald behavior, miscreant."

Bone's eyes got big when he seen the emblem. "I am sorry. I was just giving you guys a hard time. I've been working long hours and have a terrible tooth ache. I was just doing my job."

"Spare us your excuses," Corrine interrupted. "I will speak with your commander later."

"It is my commander that has tasked me with keeping the scum bottled up in Slumside. What business could the crown guard have in there?"

"That is not your concern little tyrant." The princess said. "I am beginning to understand why the lower classes despise the Inquisitors so much. Let's go Company."

A brief mechanical sound could be heard as the Blood Knight disengaged his locking gauntlet. The companions entered the Slumside ghetto. Whisper, and Omega walked alongside the Blood Knight as he rode his war horse drawing the gaze of many pedestrians. The young boy that had stabled the horse at the Coin Street tavern was with them and led the horse by the bridle. It seemed the Blood Knight had chosen the boy to be a page, or perhaps it was the great, war horse that had chosen. The boy lived with his mother and uncle and would not be missed for a couple days, so Omega figured they could stop by the boy's Uncle's house on the way back to the palace. Corrine, her two ladies, two Lieutenants and Jynx walked ahead. The princess talked about the gate warden, and how she will never tolerate such tyranny. It took them a couple hours to get to the stair. The slums got progressively worse the deeper the companions entered. Tears came to Corrine's eyes as she was witness to large groups of orphans roaming the streets. She saw kids playing in the dirt roads scantily clad and barefoot. The ones with parents were so neglected that they were little better than orphans themselves. There were also groups of elderly people as well. They stood along the road drinking large bottles of cheap wine. Many of the people loitering alongside of the street were disfigured in some way, most of them were simpletons, and nearly all had a great empty space in their minds called- ignorance.

They were so filthy that Corrine gasped more than once, holding her cloak tight around her as if afraid that she too would succumb to the filth the way these wretched people had. Never had she bore witness to such squalor. Corrine felt as though she were walking through some wilderness. These were her subjects. She was their protector. How did it get this bad? Often her and her companions were hailed for a few coppers, a nearly worthless form of currency. Most of the people she seen were very skinny though some were fat from eating large amounts of cheap food. Nobody seemed healthy. Every so often she would hear someone yell or a dog bark. It seemed that every hovel contained a bitch that barked incessantly at passersby. The Blood Knight's page was a pauper but even he was afraid of this section of the city. Corrine began to feel guilty for the opulence and ignorance she lived in. Smoke rose from the small chimneys in the hovels that were the homes of this destitute people. "Are there no options for these people Jynx?" Corrine asked desperately. "I was told that these are people that don't like to work and have sowed their own fate."

Jynx put his arm around her shoulder. He to fought back tears, he knew it was bad in this part of the city, he had lived in this depression all his life. Slumside was painted on to the canopy of his eyes and he had never thought of anything but leaving it. He separated from it gradually, in his mind first, before the Princess plucked him out like a flower that has somehow thrived rather then faded growing on the hard dirt road. Somehow sunshine had singled him out. "Can you imagine what it is like to ask someone for a job when you are but a child, perhaps injured from some assault, dirty, without clothes to change into? As you become older and your childish hopes begin to die your attitude becomes untenable and you possess no skills of any worth. Why then should someone hire you? Some do get one of the scarce jobs that are around here. Their employers always know how desperate they are and as a result they are treated as indentures."

"But they are not slaves Jynx, they have freedom, they do not have to work for anyone they do not wish to." Corrine said, her voice trailing off as she realized that her argument was weak.

"Such assertions are always made by scholars

as they stand in cozy rooms dressed like princes, smoking a pipe filled with the choicest tobacco in between considerations of the subtle differences of expensive wines and chocolates. Never are these arguments made in the slums where parentless children roam free, barefoot and ribs exposed as they beat each other senselessly instead of playing, because selfishness was their mother and violence their father."

They turned a corner and walked past one of the Slumside parks. It was an area of mostly dead grass and a polluted pond. It was filled with adolescents. Most wore a dagger or brandished a club. The boys wore loose fitting tunics and breeches. The girls wore the tightest, most daring scraps of clothing they could find. Both hung on each other. It seemed that the most common activity for this unskilled ignorant lot was laying waste to time. With no hope of ever being something more to society then a Slumside cunt they had to be everything to their small group of dysfunctional friends. Jynx stopped and stared at the children playing, thinking themselves adults. Whisper walked up to him and placed her head against his shoulder. He wrapped his free hand around her.

"Do you know this place Justice?" Corrine asked.

He winced as she broke her own rule and referred to him by his new name in the very habitat of his old one. When had he become two people? He thought that Jynx had died. He actually had been forgetting about his old life. Not even realizing that he was burying who he once was and calling it redemption. After reflecting a moment, he nodded in the direction of three youths. "We used to be here every day. We were quick to laugh, quick to cry and quick to fight. Those three could be me, Whisper and Enigma. The only thing we looked forward to when we were children was being together. That is the only time when our hopes were revived and seemed to have some small amount of substance." Jynx let his arm fall away from Whisper as he and Corrine started to walk.

"They have freedom alright, the freedom to be hungry and miserable. Most employers exploit these people because they are a dime a dozen. You have seen firsthand that the only incarnation of the law these people know are the thugs and cowards who make their living shaking these poor wretches down for whatever taxes they can collect from their vices and violations. The laws themselves are often set up in opposition to them. Even the Crown Swords won't take most of them as they often have established a record of these violations while they are still very young. The one thing that the Council Inquisitors do well is keeping records on everyone and watching. The first time you violate a law or fail to pay a tax you are branded with a number establishing an identity for you, so as to make the duties of the High Inquisitors easier. This new identity takes the place of your reputation." As they were walking a young girl ran up to Jynx and the princess. The companions immediately brandished their weapons. The young girl hugged Jynx with all she had, oblivious to the fuss she created and the clanging of the Blood Knights gauntlet. When the companions seen that there was no harm intended by the little girl they sheathed their weapons. The girl of eleven circles was filthy from playing all day. Approaching the companions was a small posse of children her age. "This is my cousin Brema," Jynx announced to the companions. "How are you Breem?"

"We are great, Papa has been fixing up the shack with the money you sent, oh and we bought a killer dog. Nobody has broke in the shack once, since us gots him. Hey Whisper. Where is Nigma? Where the Hel have you guys been, people are saying you became cunt Inquisitors but I tell them that is horse shit."

"You shouldn't talk like that Brema," Jynx said starting to get a little embarrassed because of the noble company with him.

"When did you start talk'n like a Nobleside dandy. A girl has to be a bitch in this sector, you know. You never cared how I talked before."

"It's not that I didn't care..." Jynx started.

Corrine cut him off sensing his discomfort and wanting to set him at ease. "What's your dog's name Brema?"

"His name is Killer because he is going to kill any son of a whore that steps on our porch uninvited. You're pretty," Brema said changing the subject. "You have nice cloths, you must be rich. Jynxy doesn't usually go for your kind, no offense. He likes Slumside wenches. My mama says only Slumside wenches are real."

"Oh," Corrine said, "Do you hear that Jynx?" Corrine was now uncomfortable as well.

"Well I am happy to see you Brema, but I have to work so that I can buy you something nice. Give my love to your sisters and brothers and your dad.

In a couple of days I am going to come get you and show you my shack." Jynx gave her a big hug and kissed her on top of the head.

The companions started off again. Jynx was roiled from the encounter with his cousin. They turned another corner and walked past a house with the front door wide open. There must have been two dozen Inquisitors armed with crossbows, walking in and out of it and standing guard over a half dozen men and a woman, their forearms manacled. "Well, looks like they're going to be going to the stocks in Westward or Eastward," Jynx commented as they walked by. "Maybe a few of them to the chopping block."

"The slums are truly a horrible place Jynx. Why don't you move your family out of here?" Corrine asked.

"You think I haven't tried." My uncle is deranged; he likes it here. You see how my cousin acts and her brothers and sisters are no better. They would get arrested within one week of moving out of the slums for sure. They don't know how to live anywhere else."

"Then they are hopeless unlike you." Corrine said with disappointment, looking down toward the dirt road.

"I am different." Jynx said. "And I am the same. You know when you close your eyes, when all is black and silent, there is no difference between where you live and where they live. Most people don't imagine anything different when they are older. But when they are children they can be anyone. If there is any hope for Slumside it is in these skinny, dirty, brawling, children."

Corrine let out a giggle, "You forgot cussing."

"Yes," he corrected, "These brawling, cussing children." They both laughed and then he realized that they were alone and she was holding his hand in hers. Startled then nervous, he pulled his hand out of hers and looked back at the group. They had all stopped to stare at them and see how far they would get before they realized they were alone. They laughed at the two, everyone except the Blood Knight who never showed emotion. Everybody was thinking the same thing, except for Jynx and Corrine, well except for Jynx. "The stair is in sight now," Jynx said. "Are you certain you wish to go down there? You have seen enough in this sector alone. The stair is not even considered part of Blakoepal."

"I am determined, Sir." Corrine said. "I feel safe here. When I am with you the danger of this sector doesn't trouble me."

"Very well, but know this, down the stair is a place that even I have sought to avoid all my life."

Chapter 47 - Tomb

Treant and Valley, side by side, rode their horses to Deadside. They arrived as the sun was going down but before the gates were closed. They made their way to the Mausoleum and cemetery of the extinct house of Cadavranos. Treant and his companion rode through the plots outside the grand structure, where many favored servants and distant cousins of house Cadavranos lay buried. They waited for half of an hour at the bottom of the steps for Treant's cousin to arrive. Finally, Dax approached on a dark horse. A companion rode alongside of him wearing dark colors and his face hidden in a hood. "Hail cousin, it pleases me greatly to see you after all of these years." Treant said.

"I would be surprised if that were true, cousin," Answered Dax Cavalaries as he stopped his horse a few feet in front of Treant and Valley. He cast a discerning gaze at the two of them. He sat atop his steed wearing the white clerical vestments of a high priest of Asmodeus as well as the accompanying plate mail armor. In his right hand, which wore a black gauntlet, was a Morning Star. Around his neck was the symbol of his god, a black pentacle. His Bald head was tattooed with the markings of his terrible god.

"It is true. I am sworn not to move against you as you are likewise sworn." I ask you to accompany me into the crypt in search of the legendary Tyrant of the Damned, the most powerful priest to ever call our city-state home.

"You have gone mad, Archduke. Mordon

Cadavranos has long ago left this world."

"You are partially correct Dax. He has left the land of the living and now resides in his crypt, a powerful type of undead master called a lich. I received a sign, your watcher blesses me."

"What of your watcher then?"

Treant looked his kinsmen in the eye and stepped forward, "To hel with my watcher and damn him, he is a hypocrite, his sensitivities make him weak and I am accursed of him. He has removed his self from my being and taken my granted powers. The other high priests of your temple would kill me the moment they discovered this and your temples leader the Tyrant of the Masses has a death warrant on me for all the trouble I have caused him. The Tyrant of the Damned will see my worth and shield me from your temple, I am prepared to offer him my allegiance."

"Very well, I will accompany you to see how this goes. But know cousin, my first loyalty is to my watcher. I am a cleric of Asmodeus. My oath to him supersedes our family creed."

"Understood. Now who is your companion?"

"This is the Black Mage, Tretch," Dax looked over at his companion, "He will be opening the door."

Tretch and Dax dismounted and the company approached the door to the mausoleum. With the wave of his hand and the issuance of a short mumble the Black Mage reached forward and knocked on one of the large double doors. That door, seemingly of its own accord, opened. The mage then made several more mutterings and with an arcane configuration of his hands he cast a spell upon himself. "I now possess the magic vision of dark sight. I shall cast it on each of you so that we are not unnecessarily encumbered by torches."

"Go ahead mage," said Treant.

Tretch cast his spell on the three men. "We are ready, go ahead Lord Cavalaries and lead the way.

Treant looked at the mage scornfully and pointed at Valley, "What of her mage, doesn't she need to see?"

Dax interjected "We did not know you intended to bring her, cousin. Are you certain that this is the sort of quest a servant girl would be likely to survive?"

Treant struggled to keep composed then he turned to his cousin, "Do you see that she is wearing a sword? And under her cloak she wears a suit of chain. She is no servant; she is soon to be my wife. Asmodeus has blessed her with knowledge of swordsmanship and archery that would rival most of the elite soldiers in this city"

"How can this be?" Dax asked. "How did she come upon such skill by Asmodeus?"

"I awoke with it," Valley answered matter-of-fact going to her horse and removing her composite long bow that Treant had given her that day, along with her quiver full of arrows which she slung over her shoulder. Tretch approached her and cast his spell upon her.

With Treant at the lead followed by Dax then the other two, they entered the mausoleum. Inside the air was arid and dusty and smelled stale. The group's throats felt as if the moisture in them had suddenly been extinguished. One dry cough after another ensued as Treant's group worked its way

351

down three levels to what appeared to be the lowest level of the crypt. They all searched this level, opening ancient stone coffins and hacking in the resultant cloud of dust, and investigating the carved niches that riddled the walls where the dead lay undisturbed for hundreds of years. There was no treasure of any kind in this room. The Black Mage cast a spell while the others searched. "I can find nothing master," Valley said.

"I've found something," The mage announced. "There," he pointed at one of the stone ossuaries, "There is an inscription upon it."

Valley wiped the thick layer of dust off the heavy stone lid. "Here."

Dax approached, "It is a riddle. What ascends and descends yet moveth not?

Imarra whispers the answer in Valley's mind.

"I know the answer," Valley tells Treant excitedly. "It is stairs."

As soon as she said the word stairs, the ossuary crumbled to dust and debris leaving a spiral staircase descending further into the crypt. Some of the rocks fell down the stairs. The four explorers entered the stairs and walked down them going deep into the earth at least sixty feet. At the bottom of the stair was a wide room filled with ornate platforms upon which rested ancient corpses covered with silk sheets. All along the perimeter of the room were the skeletal remains of a dozen warriors seemingly standing of their own strength. All four held weapons. Treant's group spread out in the room walking down the rows of dead Cadavranos's. As they slowly walked across the spacious room Treant called out to his comrades. "There is something unnatural about those skeleton warriors so be ready. Valley, stay by the mage and cover us."

Valley notched an arrow with her bow. The bow had a mild enchantment on it as did all the groups weapons which were of the finest quality of craftsmanship and could strike creatures that were supernatural and consequently immune to the mundane.

It happened suddenly. Even though they were half expecting it, it startled all of them at once. The skeleton warriors animated abruptly in unison and started walking surprisingly fast toward the company brandishing broad swords as they advanced. "It's on," Treant called out, as he raised his shield and charged forward to greet the skeletons with his blade.

One of the skeletons struck first, Treant's shield absorbed the blow. Treant thrust with his sword but the blade got caught up between the bones and armor of the skeleton and did no discernible damage to it. Treant retracted the weapon. He blocked an attack on his left front, with his shield and on his right front with his sword. An arrow whizzed past his head and lodged itself in the empty eye socket of the skeleton he was failing to damage. The skeleton persisted seemingly oblivious to the situation of having an arrow protruding out of its eye socket.

The Black Mage, Tretch finished casting and shot a flame the size of a pea toward the rear of the skeletons. The flame reached one of the skeletons and burst into a large radius incinerating five of the skeletons instantly and destroying everything else in the immediate vicinity. Just as quick as it came the fire was completely gone, no smoke or burning artifacts just deep black scorch marks on everything that survived in that quarter of the room. The skeletons that were not destroyed pressed, undaunted by their reduction in numbers.

Treant finally got a clean shot at the skeleton he had been trying to destroy. With the edge of his sword, he caught it in the leg, separating it, causing the skeleton to fall and become more of a nuisance as it struck out at him with its sword. Treant heard Valley let loose another arrow this one striking true and going straight through the skull and draining it of the last little bit of negative energy it possessed. It collapsed the rest of the way as it ceased to be animated. Another skeleton moved in to replace him. They hammered at Treant's defenses.

Dax stepped over a pile of bones he had just been fighting with and struck the next skeleton hard with his Morning Star in an over hand attack. This knocked the undead creature back a couple feet. The skeleton immediately attacked him again. But he was faster striking the skeleton and reducing it to a heap. Dax called out for the power of Asmodeus to bring these unnatural creatures into his subjection. At once the skeletons seized their attack. Treant almost fell over from the sudden halting of aggression. The three remaining skeletons stood like statues.

"What is going on?" Treant demanded

"Asmodeus grants me power over undead so long as they are not more powerful than I am and there is not so many as to be more powerful then I. They are mine, I can command them to do my bidding."

"Very well, put one ahead of me, one at the rear

and have the other one guard your mage friend. Let's get going." Treant began the march anew. At the other end of the room amidst a scorched wall was a door. "Order your skeleton servant to open the door." Treant said to Dax waiting in earnest for something to rush out at him. The Skeleton grabbed the pull ring on the door and as the undead thing opened the door it burst into flames, causing the four adventurers to step back startled. Treant looked in disbelief at the ashes on the ground, "Dax, do send another one of those skeletons over here."

Dax obliged.

They entered the doorway now having to walk single file down a long corridor. Every Twenty feet or so there would be a bricked over doorway on either side with the name of a Lord and/or Lady inscribed above it. Eventually they got to the end where the name of the last duke and duchess of the Cadavranos house was inscribed, Mordon and Megeara Cadavranos.

"That is my burial." Imarra said in Valley's head. I know you already know my true name, Megeara Cavalaries Cadavranos I gave my child to my brother, Treant is mine and my child's descendant.

"We must get to the other side of this doorway!" Valley yelled to Treant.

"Not a problem. I have just the solution." The mage cast another spell causing the brick to become like dirt in its consistency, and split in the middle. Then the brick hardened again leaving an opening for them to squeeze through.

Chapter 48 - Choke

Princess Corrine's company stood at the top of the stairs peering into the subsuming darkness. The ceiling of the stair always had a billowing cloud of smoke rolling out of the opening. Only the impressive size of the stair made travel on it tolerable. The ceiling of the stair was vaulted halfway down each layer, with channels directing the smoke out. It was bearable but still nauseating for newcomers who could expect to be sick after their first ten or twenty trips down until they adjusted to the poor air quality. Most of the pure breed humans who lived on the stair would develop Frog Cough. It was a disease known for creating green and grey blotches on the skin and causing coughing fits where small pieces of lung make their way up with a loud croak. The victim becomes weak and pale and dies in a very long drawn out period of increasingly intense fits.

The great stair was more of a ramp then a stair. Both sides along the wall were ramps twenty feet wide, as was the center ramp. On both sides of the center ramp were steps that were ten feet wide. The companions walked down the center ramp as though it were a steep street, which was the natural tendency of all who came to the stair. As they ventured further down the stair, coughing periodically as they went, the ramps along the sides of the walls began to be cluttered with tents and small makeshift huts. There was violet illumination from lanterns containing a squishy luminescent substance harvested by the denizens at the bottom of the stair. The smell of burning excrement pervaded the noses of the company. The inhabitants here were truly hopeless. Many wore scarfs around their faces, many others no longer bothered, having become adjusted to the smell. They did not see any children, though there must have been some. The company paused for a minute, taking their cue from the inhabitants they began searching for fabric to cover their noses with. Fortunately for them Corrine's Ladies always carried colorful scarfs and veils.

"Will you not cover your nose Omega?" Corrine asked the monk when she noticed that he refused a cover from her ladies.

"I am testing myself Lady," Omega answered in polite refusal.

"Very well," she said, "If you change your mind just say so." As they walked the stair became more densely populated and they over-took a cart being led by a fat, revolting creature. It appeared ferocious except that it seemed to struggle with the yoke and moved very slowly.

"That is a slothing." Corrine exclaimed. I have read of those. They eat bones but only digest the marrow." She was interrupted by the beast's gasses. "The flatulence of these creatures is legendary." She said as she squirmed and hurried to get passed it.

Jynx wanted to laugh but was overwhelmed with disgust. He decided to laugh about it later. "They have no natural predators despite how slow they move."

As they continued down the stair they seen more Slothings, accompanied by sick looking humans. Many of whom painted their faces with an ashen mixture. It was warm on the stair and many of the male inhabitants wore only breeches with females also wearing only a sparse top. The grey and purple ashen paints sufficed for a covering for many. At this level of the stair however there were still a significant amount of people that were in appearance very much like the people of Slumside.

At last they came to the first landing. There were large tents, fixed structures and places where passage or businesses were hewn right out of the stone. The princess wondered what kind of person would go through the trouble and the toil necessary to carve directly into the stone to make these buildings possible. Amongst these pitiful buildings was one that bore a sign, the Downside Tavern, spelled D-o-u-n-s-i-d-e t-a-v-R-U-n.

"I guess this is our place?" Jynx said sarcastically. He was half hoping that he wouldn't find his mother alive. *Perhaps she has found the peace of death*, he thought. He was afraid and couldn't admit to himself that it was fear. Fear that he would find her and that she would be little better than the living dead.

The companions entered the small tavern, all except the blood knight and his stable boy. The place had a modest number of patrons. The bar keep was an obese and hairy man that did not have the decency to wear a tunic. He sat on a couple of crates behind the bar smoking a fat cigar in spite of the lack of ventilation and drinking some of his wares while sweat rolled across his large stomach. "Rag you got more customers," The sickly blob of human waste called to one of his wenches.

Jynx's eyes narrowed when his gaze locked on

the barmaid named Rag. "Mother!" Jynx called out at the very moment she recognized him.

"Jynx?" She said, amazed to see her son. He moved directly to her, knocking a stool out of the way as he went. He embraced her small, frail body, careful not to crush her as she cried.

"I thought you were dead." Jynx said pulling back from her so that he could look her over. She seemed so much older than when he last seen her, as if age had suddenly grabbed her.

"I was dead. If not for your brother Enigma I still would be."

"Brother?" Jynx said.

"Well he is too dear a friend to be anything but a brother." She looked at him and at his companions. "You certainly keep proper company these days."

"Rag, break up the family reunion. If they ain't drink'n they need to get. I have paying customers that are thirsty, and horny." The barkeep said with a laugh. "If he wants a tumble he can pay full price like everyone else."

Jynx turned to the lieutenants. "Would you two mind escorting the ladies out front and guarding them there. I need to tender my mother's resignation, it will only take a moment." At once the lieutenants, led all of the women with them, including Jynx's mother out to the landing and shut the door, leaving only Omega and Jynx in the tavern with the patrons. Immediately everyone that wanted to participate in the fight stood up brandishing weapons, from swords and axes down to broken wine bottles and stools. In all, counting the bar keep, there were fourteen armed men crammed in there. The remainder of the patrons that were paying attention remained in their seats ready to watch the show go down. Also there were a few that were not paying attention but instead were in a euphoric trance.

"Well this isn't very fair." Omega commented.

"You stayed?" Jynx asked, his anger ready to peak at any moment.

"Don't think you can send me away, and have all the fun by yourself." Omega said. "You take those three over there, protecting the bar tending pimp. I will handle these ten."

"Are you sure?"

"Yes. Say go."

"Go." Jynx rushed forward. He struck his first combatant on the point of the chin with the pommel of his sword as he drew it from his scabbard. Then he brought it down stabbing the man in the foot. The man collapsed. The next bruiser, a tall ruffian with a black beard and goatee swung at Jynx with an axe which Jynx easily side stepped. He swung again and this time Jynx parried the blow with his sword, pinning the axe against the bar. Before Jynx could persist in thrashing this man he noticed the man's attention was not on his own fight. Rather he kept glancing over to the other side of the taproom. Jynx followed the man's gaze as they both stared at the monk who already had half of his enemies bested, on the ground bleeding and unconscious. Jynx and his opponent watched, their weapons still locked together in mid struggle as they put their battle on hold to spectate.

Omega punched one of the men directly in the head. His skull fracturing was audible. The monk brought his elbow back breaking the nose of a man behind him. Then he kicked behind him. His foot broke through the man's kneecap before he could even scream about his broken nose. The man was unconscious before he hit the floor.

Jynx and his opponent both said, "Ouch." simultaneously and cringed at each blow the monk landed.

The last three rushed Omega, who responded by jumping in the air kicking the one in front and the one behind simultaneously in the face while twisting his waist in midair and punching the one to his side, square in the face.

The sound of all three noses breaking in unison let off a loud popping sound eliciting a "ugh" from Jynx and his opponent.

Omega smacked his hands together a couple of times as if to knock dirt from them and then looked up at Jynx. "I thought you would be done by now."

The sound of a wine bottle landing on the ground indicated that Jynx's next opponent after the man with the axe had decided to forfeit. Jynx pulled his sword away from the axe, unpinning the weapon.

The axe man looked over at the monk and then offered the axe to Jynx.

Jynx sheathed his sword and accepted the axe and even said "Thanks." Jynx walked up to the slobbering swine of a barkeep and punched him several times in the face. Then he grabbed the man's hand. "Did you touch my mother with this hand?" Jynx yelled.

"She *is* one of my wenches." The man cried desperately. "A lot of men have had her."

361

Jynx's heart filled with rage. "Wrong answer!" Jynx put the man's arm on a crate, brandishing the axe he raised it up and brought it down on the man's wrist, severing the barkeep's hand breaking through the boards in the crate and shattering bottles of wine within. Jynx grabbed the Bar keeps other hand. "Did you touch my mother with this hand?"

"No!" The fat pimp of a barkeep cried, begging and pleading. "I have never touched anybody with that hand!"

"Nor shall you." Jynx placed the Bar Keep's other hand on another crate.

The one-handed pimp made a feeble effort to withdraw his hand but committed most of his effort to begging. "Mercy, please show me mercy. I will never touch her again." He whined.

"Mercy? Mercy! How do you speak words that you do not understand? Have you ever in your wicked life shown mercy? It is too late!" He punctuated his sentence by bringing down the axe and lopping off the man's other hand. The fat man fell back crying. Now I have made certain that you will never handle a woman again."

As they walked from behind the bar, one of the drunks, a veteran soldier from the look of him, stood by the men Omega defeated. The sounds of moaning and crying resounded in the tavern, but not from the man at the veteran's feet. "You killed him." The veteran, who sported a face full of bruises himself, said to Omega.

"He committed suicide," The monk answered simply.

That seemed to satisfy the veteran who stepped over him and walked past Jynx and Omega to go

362

behind the bar. Once there he grabbed a mug and went to one of the Kegs and filled his mug with free ale. "Hey everybody. Drinks are on me." He said rallying the few remaining patrons that had minded their own business. There was a light cheer, amidst the moans of agony. Jynx spit on the floor then turned and exited the establishment with Omega.

Chapter 49 - Imp

Valley pushed past and was the first through the doorway. There were two sarcophagi in the room and a great deal of gold and silver. The two Sarcophagi were of exquisite material and make. Both rested on a granite slab, both constructed in the vague resemblance of how the occupant looked in life, one a man, the other a woman. The men began to work on opening the man's sepulcher. Valley strained to open the female's, whose inscription read Megeara Cavalaries Cadavranos. Both sepulchers were empty. Then a voice called out in a dim and strained voice, "What do you seek? The startled group scrambled to arm themselves and came to stand together searching for the source of the voice. Then they heard it again and were able to pinpoint it. The portrait of Lord Cadavranos seemed to be alive, the face turned toward them, the eyes seemed to look at them, then the mouth spoke, "What is it you seek?" The voice was cryptic and haunting.

"I seek Lord Mordon Cadavranos, Tyrant of the Damned. I am a fallen paladin. I wish to offer my allegiance to the Tyrant seeing how we are kin."

"The Tyrant of the Damned has no kin, why should he listen to another word you say?" The picture responded.

"I am Archduke Treant Cavalaries, of the first noble house. You married a woman of my house." Treant strained his mind for words that would grant him an audience. "I was sent here by a dark angel that serves Asmodeus. A devil named Megeara. I

364

believe you know the rest of that name."

The picture shut its eyes. From the wall beneath it a small humanoid creature with red skin walked out. It looked like a little devil and Treant knew it to be an imp, though he had never seen one in person. "The master has decided to spare your life for a few more hours and grant you an audience. Stay close or it will mean your premature destruction."

"What if we turn back now?" The mage asked.

"We will go," Valley cut him off.

"Very well," The creature hissed, seemingly amused.

The imp walked through the wall, his tail seeming to stick out of it for a pause then vanished all together. Treant attempted to follow. He put his hands up feeling the rock surface with his palms then getting very close to it and trying to push through to no avail. "It is a real wall." He said, turning to look at his companions.

"It is an illusion and can be disbelieved, cousin." The priest stared at it for a moment and then said, "See, for me the wall is gone. I can see the passage beyond. We must go. The imp is not waiting for us." Dax entered.

The other three stood staring at the wall. Then Valley proceeded forward, seeming to the other two to walk into the wall. Treant looked at the mage, "It still looks like a wall to me, it probably did not help that I reinforced my belief in it by touching it and trying to push it."

"That is the problem Archduke," the mage explained. "When you refer to it, you are referring to a wall that doesn't exist and not to the illusion."

"I am trying not to believe but it is hard.

Believing in things I cannot see, seems to come more easily to me than not believing in things that I can see."

"No matter," Tretch said. With the wave of a hand and a few cryptic words, the illusion faded, revealing a dark tunnel. Treant had to rub his eyes. "You first," the mage insisted.

They entered the tunnel moving at a brisk pace leaving their skeleton escort behind. In short time, they caught up with the other two. They all moved purposefully so as to keep up with the imp, unable to be as cautious as they would have certainly preferred. They walked single file through a labyrinth of twists and turns. The walking dead stood aside and permitted them to pass at numerous places. The undead were innumerable down here. Treant and his party were grimly aware that the imp's presence alone was keeping them alive. The tunnels were far vaster and the undead far more numerous than they had imagined. The imp moved ahead of them without looking back seemingly trying to lose them. They were hopelessly lost without the imp. After hours of walking the imp disappeared. The four of them came to a halt in a wide portion of the tunnel. "It seems that our guide has gone on without us." Valley said to the three men as they joined her in the chamber.

"Well," Dax said, "There is only two ways. Behind us and ahead."

Treant walked ahead a few steps. "I will take the lead. There is only one way, ahead." Treant drew his sword. Peering ahead for a moment, he could see the next sixty feet in a spectrum of black and white. The tunnel continued beyond his vision in a blur of gray. As they advanced the walls became smoother, the floor had less rocks and loose dirt until the corridor ended in a solid iron door. The door had once been artistically decorated but now displayed only paint chips and rust. It had a large handle and a keyhole, light was visible through the keyhole. Treant reached for the handle of the door. He griped it tight, pausing for a moment as he half expected to burst into flames. When nothing happened, he pulled the door open. Inside was a hall decorated with a fortune in gold and tapestries. Torchlight flickered from sconces on either side of the wall. Bone pillars in the center of the hall held the ceiling up. The hall was twenty feet wide and a hundred long. At the opposite end were two iron men, nine feet in height.

Dax looked ahead at the statues. "Something tells me those are not just there for decoration."

"I agree," said Treant. "I hope you are ready mage."

"They are constructs and very formidable, I might add." Tretch answered.

"They do look formidable." Valley added. She took up position with her bow behind a pillar.

The black mage stayed to her rear alongside of the wall. Dax stayed ahead of the last pillar and off to the side so as not to be in the line of the other two's fire. Treant approached to several feet in front of the large iron men, who stood in silent guard before a, ten-foot-high door. "I am Archduke Treant Cavalaries, lord of the first noble house of Blakoepal. I request an audience with the one known as the Tyrant of the Damned, his highness Duke Mordon Cadavranos."

The door opened as if it had answered him itself. A huge figure could be seen, burning pools for eyes glowing from the darkness beyond the door. "The Tyrant will see you," The voice appeared inside of their heads. It was deep and commanding. They all found it disconcerting to have their minds so invaded. Especially valley whose mind was crowded as is.

"It is a Skull Devil, the high inquisitors of hel," Imarra told Valley. "This Tyrant is truly powerful."

Valley kept her bow ready with an arrow notched. "Show yourself bone devil!" She yelled. The creature stepped forward. His skeletal body looked vaguely human in shape but with boney horns crowning its head, burning pools inexplicably fixed in deep, otherwise dark sockets. Its skeletal hands bore powerful claws. It stood ten feet tall.

Chapter 50 - War

"What is going on out here?" Jynx asked. There was a large commotion outside. All kinds of people were running up the stairs from below the first landing in sheer panic.

"We don't know," Whisper answered. "I have never heard of anything like this. These people are so scared that I wonder if we should be running as well."

Omega ran fast up to one of the men and forced him to the ground for Jynx to question.

"What is the problem with you man?" Jynx asked

"An army is coming, destroying all within its wake."

Jynx became frustrated. "An army? What Army? From where? The only army is in the city where you people are running to."

"The Denizens." Corrine said. "The Denizens are coming. Dear Crotear, we are at war!"

The company stared at Corrine, watching as horror griped her face.

"The denizens are coming!" The captured man cried out. Jynx released his grip and drew his sword. The man ran away repeating "The Denizens are coming, The Denizens are coming!"

The companions followed Jynx in drawing their weapons, all except the bald lieutenant. Just then a unit of denizen soldiers in advance of the larger army ran on to the landing led by a musclebound denizen on the back of a terrible beast. The soldiers cut people down at a whim with powerful axes, swords and hammers. The leader, seeing the companions tarrying ordered his soldiers to attack then charged from the back of the monster. The Blood Knight mounted his horse, and armed himself with his heavy lance from the side of his mount and charged across the landing. As the mounted warriors raced toward each other the bald lieutenant made a dismissive gesture with his hands, shedding his and the other lieutenant's illusory disguises.

"Agon, Alturek? Corrine said astonished.

Just as the Blood Knight clashed with the mounted denizen, Agon unleashed a pea-sized wad of hot blood that shot out of his hand at the soldiers. It exploded amongst them in an amazing burst of boiling blood fifty feet in diameter, burning to death all of the denizen soldiers in that unit, except the rider who was instantly killed when he connected with the blood knights lance. The rider's beast attacked the Blood knight's horse, knocking it over, and throwing the knight off as it struggled to bite the horse, impeded by its steel plated barding. The Blood Knight got to his feet and charged the monster on foot, drawing his sword as he moved and stabbing it repeatedly as it refused to be dispatched, protesting its looming death with roars then growls, then whining, whimpering and a final weak howl.

"Agon what did you do with the officers?" Corrine demanded with adrenalin induced aggression.

"We are the lieutenants. I and Alturek disguised ourselves so we could help keep you safe." Agon answered.

"Damn you Agon, don't you ever deceive me

again!" Corrine yelled over the commotion of people fleeing the stairs and giving him a punch to the chest.

"You said that last time I deceived you."

"We don't have time for this you two!" Jynx looked at Corrine. "We have to get you out of here and back to the castle!"

"I have a spell that I can use to take Corrine back with me." Agon said.

"Guys there are more coming!" Whisper yelled as she began firing with her crossbow.

"I don't like it." Jynx said. "But I don't have any better ideas."

"No." The princes declared. "I am not going without Jynx's mother."

"What!" Jynx, Agon, Alturek and Jynx's mother, herself both confused and terrified, exclaimed in stupefied unison.

"She is not strong enough to escape. If she stays she will die."

"She is not going to be queen and is not needed to set the cities war machine in motion, only you can do this." Alturek reasoned with her.

"I will not leave her." Corrine answered in stubborn defiance.

"Then I will stay." Agon declared. "I can fight my way out of this. I will send you straight to the throne room. Call upon your generals and nobles at once. Slumside is doomed as is the whole city if we do not meet this force, and stop it." Agon made gestures and spoke commands in the arcane language. Instantly Corrine and Rag were teleported away.

371

Chapter 51 - Damned

"This way," The devil insisted telepathically as it motioned toward the door. In the blink of an eye it vanished. Treant walked through the door first. It was a large chamber. It had the look of a wizards' laboratory, torture chamber and throne room all rolled up into one. There were jars with dismembered human and animal parts. A huge table cluttered with bubbling alchemist substances of every color and texture made up one corner of the room. Beakers, test tubes, ancient tomes left opened or closed and stacked five or six high. Parchments littered the table as well as ink wells and quills plucked from strange creatures. In the center of the table was the remains of a large, almost spherical creature. Large teeth hung threw the place like streamers from one side of the room to another. Leather hides stretched across the walls. The floors were covered in the furs of unknown beasts. Large ovens, as would be suitable for a forge were off to the right of Treant. There was also an archway, with a cart full of books parked next to its opening. To his left were many torture devices, a metallic bull, an Iron Maiden and a stretching device amongst others. All the machinery was stained with blood, with withered pieces of flesh, as was the table. The table was fixed with metal and rope restraints. The walls held restraints as well. Bones were thrown about the floor of the left side of the grim room to such an extent as to potentially hinder movement.

There was a man who still had flesh on him though he made not a sound. He was naked and badly bruised all over the surface of his body, he appeared to have been castrated in addition to having several fingers and one foot amputated. His hair was stiff and caked with grimy blood. He hung there seemingly lifeless. His skin was starting to wither from lack of moisture, looking leathery and exposing his bones in some places. A couple of his ribs jutted out of his skin, obviously broken. The seemingly dead man slowly raised his head to make eye contact with Treant.

"Better you, then me." Treant said coldly to the man. The broken man's head fell, but he did not make a sound.

All across the chamber were metal grates. Rats and bugs fed on the scraps of the dead. Treant stepped further into the dimly lit room as his companions joined him. Suddenly torches flared up on the far side of the room. A throne sat at the top of three levels of granite with a staircase made from the bones of the dead leading up to it.

At the peak, standing to the left of the throne was the Skull devil. The devil spoke, in their heads and out loud simultaneously, "All bow before the Tyrant of the Damned, Regent of the necropolis Cadavranos."

The macabre throne was made entirely from human bone inlaid and adorned with gold and velvet. Upon it sat a skeleton with beady, blue light for eyes wearing faded clothing, tattered but once of regal quality. The skeleton wore a gem encrusted crown of gold and held in his hand a white scepter also of bone. "You, have requested audience with me, young lord?" The tyrant sounded exasperated as it strained its weak vocal cords to speak.

"Yes your eminence. I wish to serve you as a knight. I was a paladin of Crotear but he has rejected me, he has cursed me.

"I have been waiting for you young Lord. Many centuries ago when I sacrificed my own wife upon the alter, I commanded her spirit to return to me with a champion. I placed her true name into a locket that could summon her from the pits of Hel but unfortunately, it could only be activated by a good and powerful wizard, so I gave it to one of my young servants along with the blessing of unlife and sent him out of the city. I never expected her to provide me a champion from one of the noble houses of Blakoepal."

"Drusus knew of the city?" Valley asked anxiously at Imarra's bidding.

"No, Drusus knew nothing of the city, though his father, Obtuse the calm hailed from here. He was the true master vampire and the one I gave the locket to. Seventy circles ago he unknowingly sired a child with a priestess of Crotear and that child was immune to the blessing of vampirism. The mother survived her attack after an ordeal and gave birth to a young man named Garthadon. She moved to a hamlet in the far country where she settled down with a simple and pious woodsman. That is where I came in. I occupied a mysterious tower on the outskirts of town, perfect for drawing in the curiosity of a young boy. I taught him the arcane arts and bred in him a hatred for the undead. Then when he was a man I arranged for him to witness the destruction of his home and the death of his mother, siblings and the man he grew up believing was his father, all at the hands of Obtuse. When he confronted Obtuse and discovered the locket it was inevitable that he should summon my forsaken wife Megeara. The only disappointment for me was that Garthadon proved to be my finest apprentice and it was a shame for his life to be thrown away, I would have liked to have twisted him to the service of Asmodeus after he summoned his angel.

"I will be your apprentice Lord," Tretch blurted.

"Ah, as indeed you shall be," The lich agreed. "First however, since you may be unworthy, you must pass a test to be sure you have what it takes to be my apprentice"

"Of course, I accept." Tretch called out with no thought to the consequence as he craved the lich's power.

"Very well," the Tyrant made some subtle motions with his body and mumbled an incantation. Tretch yelled out in pain. The others watched as Tretch appeared to wither like a prune before him. The spell seemed to drain the fluids from his body. Tretch fell to the ground curling into an almost fetal position, begging for water as his voice became raspy and indecipherable.

"Do you have such a test for me, sire?" Treant asked.

"There is your test," the tyrant's hands emerged from his long sleeves as he pointed a boney figure to the man they had observed suffering earlier, his arms in irons attached to the wall.

Treant looked up at the tyrant and then over to the all but dead man. He approached the man slowly then paused halfway to him.

"You should know," the Tyrant declared louder

than he had seemed capable, his voice echoing across the chamber, "He is a good man, a father of four and the husband of a good wife. He gives a quarter of his wages to the church of Crotear every month."

Treant continued until he approached the man. The Archduke stared at the bruised and bloodied man as he placed his hand upon the hilt of his sword. Then he removed his hand from the hilt and instead grabbed his small canteen, half full of water. He unstopped the canteen and squatted down, helping the man to lift his ragged head and put the canteen to his mouth, helping him to slowly take a drink. He was careful not to pour it too fast down the man's throat. When the man had finished drinking, Treant dropped the canteen on the ground and walked back to his original position. The man thanked him, and blessed him as he walked away.

"Ah good, you have passed," The Tyrant smiled a boney smile.

"I don't understand," Dax said. "He helped the poor fool."

Valley smiled. "Killing the man would have been the merciful thing to do. By giving him just enough water to keep him from dying, he gave the fool a glimmer of false hope that he might get out of this alive. Now his suffering will be prolonged"

"Correct," the lich declared. "You have much to learn priest. You will abandon the temple of Asmodeus in the Oepal. You will be my champion's religious counsel and you will aid in the building of a new, greater temple outside the walls of the city."

"Yes master," was all Dax could manage as he bowed, confused about why it would be desired for him to leave the city and how he could then give Treant spiritual guidance.

"And you servant girl, are the sweetest thing aren't you. You will be snubbed by the women of the other noble houses, who despise your common roots and envy your power as it will be much greater than theirs. I will join you and the young Lord myself into unholy matrimony. I suspect that Megeara is using you as a host and when I speak you both can hear me, is that not true?"

Valley trembled only a little, her nerves steeled by Imarra's presence, "Yes, milord."

"Why is it that she currently possesses you but gives you autonomy and yet does not appear in her own hellish body?" The Tyrant asked with curiosity evident in his cryptic voice.

"I have suppressed her will, it seems that she is trapped inside of me" Valley answered becoming more afraid.

"Interesting." The lich began to float down the stairs to get closer to her. Treant and his companions stood in a line before the throne except Tretch who was curled over on the ground still pleading raspy gibberish. The tyrant rattled off something unintelligible to the group in the infernal language as he came to stand before Valley, who was now shaken with fear. He stared at her placing a skeletal hand on her cheek. Treant tensed as he stood, hoping that another demented test was not about to ensue. The Tyrant looked over at him as he stood looking right at him.

"I am your servant," Treant declared even as he quietly prayed in his head to Asmodeus, that she be not taken from him, that she be his reward from the hellish watcher for his conversion and future exploits of tyranny. Just then tears of fear ran down Valley's cheek and unto the Tyrants boney hand. The Tyrant turned back to her suddenly and extended an overly large, pock covered fleshy tongue. She squirmed in his grip afraid to run and afraid to stay still, her eyes looking back and forth from Treant to his disgusting tongue, issuing more tears as The Tyrant inched closer finally licking the tears off her one cheek. Just then a red, devilish imp, perhaps the one that guided them to here or perhaps another identical one, ran from the archway up to the lich carrying a large book. The lich's tongue retreated suddenly back into his mouth as he released her.

He turned toward his servant and with a twist of his wrist and a single indecipherable word, levitated the book. The Tyrant teleported back to his throne. The book floated up the stairs to hover before him, with the wave of his hand he flipped the pages back and forth for several minutes, pausing every few moments to read a little of the page and then back to flipping through them. Finally, he came to rest on a particular page. After having read it for a few minutes he closed his hand which caused the book to slam shut then he waved it away causing it to vanish followed abruptly by the sound of broken glass over at the laboratory section of the room.

"There are only a few things that can cause a possessing force to become trapped in its host," The Tyrant educated the company. "The only one that fits in this particular set of conditions has several precursors that must be satisfied. I will spare you the whole story but once the baby is delivered you will be separated."

"Baby?" Treant, Dax, Valley and Megeara inside of Valley's head, asked in chorus.

"Yes," The Tyrant said almost amused. "Congratulations Treant you have sired a child to advance the cause of Asmodeus."

"I am to be a mother?" Valley asked.

"Yes, it appears that you and your possessing devil are going to be mothers, I am elated to see how this works." The Tyrant said. Valley's countenance dropped and Treant looked over at her with pity. "In the meantime, to more pressing concerns. We must baptize Treant into Asmodeus and ask the dark god to replace the young lord's status as a holy knight with that of an unholy knight."

"Unholy?" Dax asked.

"Chaos is about to break loose in the city, and it is up to you three to make sure Treant is perceived as the hero." Just then Tretch stood up, his fluids restored but his skin hideously tainted by the ordeal, having the appearance of petrified wood. "My apprentice has survived his test. Now that is what a Black Mage is supposed to look like." The Tyrant made a hideous noise that could only vaguely be considered laughter. Tretch wept loudly.

Chapter 52 - Found

"Slumside is a total loss your highness." Chamberlain Viscus declared as he looked into the pool of water in the center of the room. "Asfixius leads the denizen horde personally. Any moment the wall will be breeched and they will descend on the rest of the city. They should reach the city center by dusk"

"What is their goal Chamberlain? Is it extermination?" The princess asked clutching her scepter and looking over at the twenty Guardsmen standing along the walls of the windowless room.

"No. Their primary goal is the Black Opal. That is what their fiendish lord has always wanted. He would use its power to blight all of the border lands."

"Then it is not just our city that is at stake! The gem shall be protected above all else...even above maintaining the secrecy of the city."

"Your majesty?"

"How do we move the gem, uncle?"

"Your majesty, the gem chooses one person alive who may handle it. When that person dies, it chooses another."

"So, who is chosen of the opal? How do we find him?

"The one that the opal chooses is given a mark. Your mother had the mark last and when she passed away..."

"It is Agon! Agon with his silver eyes! My mother also had those silver eyes." Corrine looked away. "Agon remained on the stair because of me."

"It does not matter. The decision to remove the stone is his. It has never been done before. The fiend Asfixius can also remove it and he will if he gets to it. We must concentrate our forces on the center of the city.

"Your right uncle." Corrine stepped closer to the stone perimeter of the pool. Staring into it she could watch as the defenses at the Slumside gates crumbled. The Denizens employed powerful magic of the arcane and unholy kinds. Their Bealus's grew dragon like wings and claws then descended on the battlements from above. A torrential rain of wooden shafts and steel points from both sides of the wall brought many warriors to their nadir. She watched as the Bealus landed on the other side and opened the gate, even as their wizards destroyed entire sections of wall with powerful spells. Some caused the earth to shake and some created terrifying explosions, still others transmuted the stone to dirt. "Our force is no match for them, is it?"

"The crown swords, our wizard guilds and our knightly orders are going to bear the brunt of this. They will be reinforced by the Elves from Greenside and the household armies of the nobles. With all of this we *may* resist them but not forever. Then there is the matter of the fiend. It will take great cooperative magic just to hurt him with no hope of destroying him. There is a mage of greater power then I in the dungeon. I have sent word to him."

"Why is such a mage in the dungeon?"

"That will have to be explained later. For now, I will assemble the city's most powerful casters around the Black Opal. The priests are already embedded with the crown swords in the center of the city."

"You must take the Crown Guard to protect the circle of casters and serve as a last line of defense."

"Absolutely not!" Viscus said with sternness.

"We have no time for argument uncle. I will keep these twenty guardsmen with me and join you at the rear as soon as the mage from the dungeon reports."

"Your majesty I must..."

"You must nothing!" Corrine cut him off as she looked at him with her own sternness, her voice raised with fervor. "I am the ruling monarch and I will not sit on some cushion in the palace while my people are slaughtered in Slumside. We will have total victory or absolute destruction. Those are our options! Without the Guard our chances are still slim. Send a rider to the Temple of the Unknown God as well. I have seen one of their monk's in battle. Their presence on the field is required."

"I will do all you command dear niece. Before I go, I want you to know that I love you. You and Agon are everything to me."

Corrine hugged her uncle as tight as she could. "I love you as well uncle. I only wish my father were here to lead."

"You have given the very orders that he himself would have issued. Farewell and may we survive this war together."

"Fare thee well dear uncle." She turned back to the pool as he walked out of the chamber. She witnessed one death after another as she watched the pool. She worried about Justice, Agon and the others. The common folk were being decimated. All over the streets and alleys of Slumside, Inquisitors and criminals fought side by side against the horde as it moved throughout the sector.

After a long hour of watching and waiting, the door to the room opened. Corrine looked up from the pool as her protectors drew their swords and took up position in a semicircle before the unknown intruder. The figure in the doorway wore a black cloak with elbow length gloves to match. She had long black hair and green eyes. "Is this how you welcome all of your kin folk princess?" The woman in the doorway asked.

"My kin? I do not know you." Corrine answered.

"I am your kin and you do not know me because our father sent me away and let me die before I ever met you."

"I caution you to choose your words carefully when you speak of my father.

"You mean, our father." The intruder corrected her.

"Who are you and what do you mean when you say that you died?"

"My name is Ashenath, bastard daughter of King Eratide. I was sent to live outside of the city, where I was killed," Ashenath showed her fangs, "by a vampire." The soldiers in the room took a step forward. Corrine stood still, somewhat shaken with fear.

"You lie!" One of the soldiers yelled as he attacked. He charged with his shield and swung with his sword.

Drusus's sword Transfusion appeared in the gloved hand of Ashenath. She swung the great sword with one hand, meeting his blade with her own. His sword was sundered. He held only the hilt and a broken blade as the rest of his steel fell to the stone floor. Transfusion disappeared back into her glove as she grabbed the guard's shield. He yelled out as she ripped it from his grasp and threw it against the wall.

The guard presented his broken sword, ready to continue in defiance of his fear as he stood fast, shaking. Ashenath walked forward grabbing his neck, lifting him enough so that only his toes touched the ground. The guard shoved his broken blade into her side. She offered no resistance and acted like she didn't notice the eight inches of broken steel piercing her.

"Enough!" Corrine commanded.

Ashenath looked at her sister as she held the guardsman in her grip. "The next one will die." Ashenath released the man. He fell to the ground then scurried back to the defensive line of his comrades.

"I know you are not lying, sister. All know it is impossible to lie convincingly to me when I bear the staff" Corrine walked forward at a cautious pace. "But what is it that you want? Is it my throne?

"You can keep your damn chair."

"Is it my life?" Corrine asked.

"You can keep that as well sister." Ashenath and Corrine stood a breath apart, memorizing each other's face. Corrine gave her the same tight hug that she would give to any relative. She squeezed the surprised vampire. Ashenath did not know what to do. Her newfound emotions were coupled with intensifying hunger as she noticed the princesses exposed neck. Ashenath's gums tingled as she lost herself in fantasy. Corrine's skin looked so soft. Her fangs would just slide right through to the vain. Her blood was probably nice and hot...

Chapter 53 - Witch

The druid led Elanor for days through the dense Blackwood. Elanor felt alone. Delasy talked to her but just as frequently she talked to animals they came across. Once in a while she would even speak to the trees. Elanor never understood a word of it, for it was always in the sylvan language of the wood and seemed one-sided as she never heard the creatures or trees speak back. Finally, they reached a trail that led to a small clearing just big enough for the humble dwelling that occupied it. The house was built of timber and brick and looked quaint amidst the Blackwood. "Come, my friend anticipates our arrival with eagerness." Delasy said before increasing to a brisk walk.

"How could that be?" Elanor asked.

"I sent a courier in advance, to let her know we would be arriving soon."

Elanor was perplexed. "But I have been with you the whole time. When could you have done this and where would you...

"I told the squirrels. I sent them ahead to notify my friend we were coming, now come on." The druid started into a jog.

"Of course. She told the squirrels Elanor. How could you be so thick?" Elanor said to herself then started jogging to keep pace with Delasy.

When they arrived, Delasy knocked on the door. "Coppernia! It is I Delasy!"

After a while a woman, seemingly in her early forties answered the door. "Delasy, how are you?"

"I am well. This is Elanor. We have some

questions we hoped you could answer."

"Well, I would invite you in for tea but I have an urgent matter to deal with. What is your question?"

"There are vampires in the Blackwood." Elanor spoke up.

"There are many things in the Blackwood child."

"Yes. But these vampires I hunt spoke of a city hidden in a great field amidst the Blackwood. Do you know anything of this?"

"I am afraid I do."

"Well, these vampires have already entered the so-called city. The inhabitants of that city are in great peril. I am an expert in killing these creatures. I need to get to the city if that is what it is."

"Very well. The city is in greater peril then you might imagine. Even if you were just another blade you could help. I will bring you both and present you to the princess,"

"The princess?" Delasy and Elanor asked in unison.

Coppernia then led the two girls through the front door of the cabin. It was quaint and homey, decorated with all manner of wood carvings and furs. Across the main room was a door. They entered. It led to a large spacious room of stone that's very existence defied Elanor's reasoning. Elanor looked around in amazement. It seemed impossible that such a room could exist inside of such a small cabin.

"It is an extra dimensional space. Kind of like a tree spirit's mansion." Delasy said.

"Actually, you have entered the palace dungeon

of Blakoepal." Coppernia explained. "You have walked through an anomaly where the invisible city touches my cabin on the edge of the wood."

A door opened in the room and an old man walked in. "They are waiting for us Coppernia."

"Yes. You are right old man, let's go." A guard led the group to the dungeon exit and through the palace to the room where Corrine was waiting. Elanor and Delasy stalled, looking around in amazement until finally Coppernia had to urge them along. *"Girls*, there is no time for this."

The old man walked through the open door first. Ashenath and Corrine were embracing each other. Ashenath was fighting the urge to feed on her sister even as she lusted for her blood. She heard the sound of the old man's footsteps. Ashenath spun herself and Corrine around, maintaining the hug, so that she could see who was coming. Ashenath looked over her sister's shoulder, bearing her fangs. Elanor and Delasy walked in and drew their weapons. The old man made a fast-somatic gesture and muttered an incantation. Corrine pulled back as she felt Ashenath go stiff. The vampire was paralyzed by the old man's magic. Before anyone could react, Elanor charged forward with a long wooden knife and plunged it into the chest of Ashenath. Onyx took a defensive position next to her master and growled a warning to any that would move on her.

"No!" Corrine yelled. "Everyone is to stop!"

All in the chamber stood still and looked at the princess, except Elanor who quickly drew the room's attention. "Why are you not destroyed?" Elanor looked the vampire up and down then

388

withdrew her dagger from Ashenath's chest. Elanor peered into the hole she had made then it dawned on her. "Your heart is on the other side of your chest!"

"Stop her!" Corrine commanded. Her soldiers rushed forth but would not have been quick enough.

The old man caused Elanor to be paralyzed as well. Princess Corrine looked over at him. "I am the old man from the dungeon," He said in a carefree manner. "I am supposed to attend a circle of cooperative magic."

Corrine looked over at Coppernia. "And who might you be?"

"I am the witch Coppernia. I believe you know my daughter. Her name is Ruth. She was your mentor and I was hers."

"I am most pleased to meet you Coppernia."

"You have met me before, many times and Ashenath just once. You were both too young to remember. The time for this however is not now." The witch's appearance changed. She appeared much younger and more beautiful. Many eyes widened at the surprise of her sudden alteration. "It is the young that die best and besides I shall be more protective of this body then the one of the middle-aged grandmother." Coppernia said in answer to the questioning looks she received.

Corrine walked over to Elanor's paralyzed body. "All warriors are to join me behind the circle. No one is to make an attempt upon Princess Ashenath's life. She is to harm no one but the enemy. Any who disobey me will be put to death or destroyed, whichever is applicable. Old man, release them both. They are strong warriors and Blackoepal needs them."

Chapter 54 - Begin

The core of the denizen horde slashed and hacked its way down the road toward the center of the city. Detachments from the denizen army moved through the other streets and alleys terrorizing the citizens of Eastward and Westward in an attempt to flank the center of the city. Denizen knights charged forward from the backs of their darkbreeds decimating the front lines of the Crown Swords. When the defense managed to erect a spear wall, the denizens would pull back their knights and attack with warlock's that could blast the defenders with eldritch magic. Asfixius worked his way through Eastward with some shock troops, hacking through the little resistance he encountered with ease.

In the pavilion that housed the Black Opal stood the circle of archmages. Chamberlain Viscus and four others were joined by the old man and Coppernia. Princess Corrine, Ashenath, Elanor, and Delasy guarded the pavilion. Corrine bore the royal scepter and crown and all the magic infused therein. Delasy transformed into a bear. Elanor drew her swords and stood ready with Onyx. The twenty guardsmen joined the rest of the Crown Guard in a defensive posture around the pavilion. Chamberlain Viscus addressed those within proximity to the pavilion with a voice amplified by magic. "We can hold off the front but are going to be attacked on both flanks soon!" Down the street toward Slumside was the sound of explosions and flashes of colored light ranging the whole spectrum as wizards clashed with warlocks and priests with priests from behind the front lines of both forces.

The air was crisp and still. Fear was present in the entire city as everyone stared at the lights blasting forth from the front. Then a large force of denizen soldiers and shock troops, led by Asfixius, entered from the direction of Eastward. The force was twice the size of Princess Corrine's force assembled in Black Square. The circle began the lengthy casting of a powerful spell as the archmages all held hands and spoke in an arcane language not even they understood.

Asfixius was determined to cut a path directly to the pavilion. He severed entire bodies in half two or three at a time with fiendish efficiency and precision. The fighting got close enough that the princess herself summoned a multicolored force field with her staff that surrounded her. She raised the staff and began casting great bolts of lightning. When she struck Asfixius with a bolt, he was not fazed. The bolt reflected back at her, knocking her to the ground despite her magic shield. The bolt entered her. The shock felt like a constriction of all the nerves in her body. It seemed that she was going to die and could think only about the pain then it stopped. The bolt issued out of her striking one of her nearest guardsmen, who screamed and fell.

Corrine's guard was getting thinned out and only three soldiers were left near her, the rest pressing into the enemy with all they had. Ashenath called forth her sword. She cut down anything that came near her with Transfusion. Ashenath then cut a perimeter around the Princess. She fought as though she intended to win the war herself. The sword satiated her blood lust faster than she had every experienced before. This sent her into a frenzy. She gored some with her teeth and dismembered others with Transfusion her ferocious rage noticed and feared by even those who fought on the same side. Dead denizens began to pile up two or three deep in a circle around the princess, Ashenath and her two remaining guards.

Elanor and her companion Onyx worked as a team dropping one enemy after another as the denizens trickled into her area. Soon the trickle turned into a flood and she moved back. Elanor and Onyx jumped over bodies as they entered the circle of Ashenath's fury killing the occasional denizen that slipped through.

Delasy fought with great courage in the form of a bear. When she began to be overwhelmed she transformed into a hawk and flew over the heads of the soldiers in each direction. The battle was scattered all over with every man and woman fighting for their lives. Then she remembered that the Denizens would attack on both flanks yet they only attacked on one. She flew in the direction that the denizen third wave was supposed to come from. The battle seemed hopeless and desperate already, a third wave would be decisive. They must be holding it back for reserve, she thought. They must think their current forces sufficient. She flew in search of the third wave and could not believe what she found. The force of denizens was all but wiped out. A large army of animated corpses and skeletons routed what was left of the Denizen third wave and made their way to the fight in Black Square. The undead army carried in its midst a platform with a throne.

On the throne was the face of death, a skeletal figure with tattered robes that blasted a group of denizens with a spell that caused all of their skin and bones to vanish leaving only blood that for an ephemeral moment resembled their silhouettes before splashing on the ground to the horror of their remaining compatriots. Alongside this throne was a knight in black armor with a red pentagram upon his shield. He rode a black horse with smoke issuing from its nostrils and its feet aflame with fire. Standing on the edge of the platform a beautiful girl with dark hair launched arrows at fleeing denizens. The skeleton on the throne looked up at a hawk overhead and said telepathically, "the Archduke Treant Cavalaries and the Tyrant of the Damned have arrived on the field."

Delasy flew to the pavilion and landed upon it in human form. The archmages were still casting their spell as guardsmen desperately fought their way to the pavilion to protect the casters, knowing the spell was their only hope at defeating Asfixius. An arrow lodged itself in the arm of one of the casters. Then another pierced the head of Coppernia. She fell from the circle rolling off of the pavilion and landing on the ground dead. Her body was trampled by guardsmen trying to close a gap in their defenses as a powerful denizen knight charged for the opening. As it neared the pavilion a heavy lance tore through his darkbreed beast. The lance tore all the way through the creature, causing the denizen knight to fly forward and hit the wall of the pavilion. The Blood Knight drew his sword and galloped to the fallen knight, finishing him with a single deadly stroke.

Agon levitated up to the pavilion from next to the felled Denizen knight. The mages grabbed his hand and pulled him over onto the platform. "The casting may continue."

Viscus looked at his son with the greatest pride he ever felt. "It is so good that you can join us, my son."

The Archmages turned to look as an army poured in from their west flank. "This may, be it father." Agon said.

"This is not it." Delasy interrupted. The undead army is led by the Tyrant of the Damned and by somebody named Archduke. They destroyed the denizen's third wave and they are going to help us."

"Treant? The Tyrant of the Damned? How could this be?" Viscus asked.

"I don't trust this father." Agon said

"Neither do I. But what choice do we have. If we get out of this alive there will be many questions in need of answering. Let us resume our casting."

When Asfixius was within thirty feet of the pavilion he stopped killing soldiers for a moment and blasted the circle with his most powerful direct attack. The casting was interrupted again as Chamberlain Viscus dropped dead with green electricity crackling all over his corpse.

Justice and Alturek came forth from out of the crowd. Justice ran to the Princess's side. He noticed the prowess of the female warrior defending Corrine and yelled for her to attack the fiend. Citizens of Blakoepal, both the walking dead and the living clashed violently with the denizens in a battle that now could go either way. Alturek, Ashenath and the Blood Knight all engaged Asfixius as Corrine,

394

Elanor, Onyx, Delasy and Justice helped what was left of the Crown Guard defend the pavilion. Corrine felt lifted up by the presence of Justice despite the furious battle around her.

Now Attar and Minty were present, defending her and the spell circle. Then she noticed Agon above her in the pavilion standing over his dad and she was stricken again with the reality of the danger they were all still in. Her heart felt as though it skipped a beat from the sudden grief she felt for her uncle and more still for her cousin. She screamed and started launched lightning bolts faster and faster until she used up the magic of the staff.

Agon wept. "How will we complete the casting? My father was second only to the old man in arcane might.

As if in answer to him, the Tyrant teleported to the pavilion. He stood over the chamberlain's body as he appeared unexpectedly to the fright of the other casters. "Old man, it has been a while?" The Tyrant said.

"Not long enough I fear, Cadavranos." The old man responded.

"Shall we finish this spell?" The Tyrant asked raising his skeletal arms toward the two mages next to him.

The old man grasped the lich's boney hand and accidentally ripped the arm out of the lich's shoulder with a poof of dust. The old man held the arm, confused and barely able to see it. "Did I just rip your arm off lich?" Just then the arm cracked at the wrist and fell to the ground leaving the old man holding only the Tyrants dismembered skeletal hand. He promptly threw it down causing it to shatter.

"How embarrassing." The Tyrant said with a cackle. "This certainly will not due." The Lich grabbed the medallion around his neck which glowed red. Chamberlain Viscus's corpse traded places with the lich.

"Father?" Agon asked.

"No it's just me." The lich answered. "I needed a new body. It seems I really let the other one go." The look of death contradicted the animation of his body. The lich appeared like a grotesque version of the dead Chamberlain. The Chamberlain's body no longer had circulation. This caused the skin to seem loose and unnatural, forming lumps where pockets of blood coagulated under the skin.

Agon gritted his teeth in anger. "You will give that back when you are done with the spell lich."

"Of course, surely he doesn't mind if I borrow it for a short time? It is after all for the greater good, is it not?"

Agon threw himself into the casting. He felt the power of the circle nearly double. Certainly, the lich was much more powerful than his father had been.

Asfixius swung his massive sword striking the Blood Knights shield and knocking him ten feet back. With split second recovery, he swung again.

Alturek raised his sword to block. The force of Asfixius's swing caused for Alturek's own sword to be driven into his skull all the way down to his lips. Alturek fell backwards. He was never to rise again. Asfixius looked back at the force he had led to flank the pavilion. It was half the size of when they engaged. Elven archers now rained down arrows upon the rear of Asfixius's elite force, while elven swordsmen, knights and human monks charged with the advantage of surprise. The battle was in utter chaos. The forces of Blakoepal began to regroup, courage became confidence as the tide of battle rapidly turned. Enraged Asfixius made one more push forward only to meet resistance from Treant. Asfixius lunged with his sword impaling the knight and lifting him up off of his fiendish horse and dropping him upon the ground.

A Black Knight, Prince Orginus charged forward only to have his shield cut in half, leaving him with the bottom to protect himself. Orginus tried to press forward with his sword when the fiend punched with his off hand, causing a stone fist the size of a man to appear and strike the knight, who was rendered unconscious and sent a dozen feet back, crippling the guardsmen he crashed into with his heavy armor.

Asfixius swung his sword, this time at Ashenath who ran toward him. She ducked under his swing, rolling the rest of the way to him.

His swing clipped the Blood Knight in the head. The blow broke the Blood Knights helmet and caused the Princess's champion to issue a girlish scream.

Treant despite a great wound, stabbed his sword through the back of Asfixius at the moment the Blood Knight screamed. Treant looked over at the Blood Knight with surprise even as the fiend screamed and arched his back.

Ashenath called forth her weapon as she swung her arm. Transfusion appeared and severed the sword arm of Asfixius. The blood that was transferred to her made her feel a burst of strength and an explosion in blood lust. She drove her blade through the creature. Asfixius's blood was a narcotic to her and she wanted more. Asfixius laughed. His severed arm began to regrow while he used the other hand to crush Ashenath's skull. Holding her crushed head, the fiend spun around and thrashed Treant with the vampire's body. Treant landed in a heap severely wounded. Ashenath turned into a gas like mist and traveled to safety so that she could reform.

From the Opal came a bright blue light. The casting was complete. The archmages held hands as a beam of energy shot up into the air and out in a great wave that knocked everyone in the city to the ground. A deep blue radiance began to work its way up the fiend from its feet to its head. The fighting seized and the warriors of both sides watched as the fiend seemed to be erased from existence.

The Blood Knight removed her broken helm, it was immediately apparent that she was a Lady, and not a man. She had long red hair and a gash upon her head. She came to her feet and charged forward with her sword raised behind her. She swung with all her might and slashed the face of the fiend a moment before it vanished without a trace. Only two casters came to their feet, the Tyrant and Agon. All the others were dead having given up their life force to fuel the spell and save Agon. The Tyrant possessed no such life force and was therefore unable to share in its cost.

King Napsian was positioned at the Slumside wall and sensed the departure of his fiendish leader. "Order a full retreat to this section Belejez," He commanded.

The horns of retreat sounded. There was a great shout among the protectors of the Opal as the Denizens began their retreat.

"Drive the horde back into their pit! Corrine shouted, her scepter making her command audible to most of the City's defenders.

The Blood Knight stared at her and she stared back at the Blood Knight. "I have missed you dearly Baroness Avriel Ringheart, Champion of my crown." Corrine called to her. Avriel nodded her head in obeisance to her friend and liege.

Avriel looked over to the empty pavilion and stepped toward it as Treant stood and looked at her with anger. "Notice something missing traitor." His words cut her and she winced. Avriel stood in her armor, sword hanging in her hand and studied the pavilion for a moment. Then it dawned on her. It shocked her so much that she could barely breathe. Her vow of silence was satisfied by the defeat of Asfixius, so she spoke. "The Black Opal is missing. I don't understand."

Treant put his arms up to steady himself. "I saw you laid to rest. I don't understand." Treant collapsed.

Avriel considered if she should use her healing power and took a step toward him. Just then Valley rushed to his side. Her tears moistened his body. "Damn it Treant! You can't leave now! Not with your child growing inside me!" Valley's wailing carried over the battlefield intermingled with the cries of the wounded and the shouts of the victorious in a canopy of sounds that were in direct contradiction to the silence of the dead.

"He will not die," Imarra told her.

Justice looked at his sword covered in blood. He stuck it in the dirt and looked up at Corrine. Her hair was disheveled, her clothing bore burn marks and rips. Dirt and blood were smeared on her cloths and skin. Yet despite this as they stood amongst the carnage, the only thought that persisted in Justice's mind was how beautiful she was. "You have saved the city your majesty. You have done it."

She looked back at him as the sounds of the enemy fleeing and taking heavy losses in the process still carried through the air along with a frigid chill. She looked at Justice. She had sadness and relief crammed into a single heart. "Just call me Corrine today, ok Sweethearts." There smiles met, Justice grabbed her up, lifting her into the air in a great embrace. Then as he set her down in front of him, she kissed him, a kiss of true passion. For a long and incredible moment, they were not standing amidst a throng of corpses. For a fleeting minute the sound of warfare was silent. The sweet smell of Corrine's perfume somehow had survived the battle and was delivered to their noses by a cool breeze. They didn't even notice the cold white flakes of the season's second snow gently landing upon them and conspiring to cover the battlefield in a soft white blanket. The white roses of Corrine's bracelet changed to red.

It was this scene of blood and snow that the Opal had revealed to King Eratide on the day of Merriment, and a pavilion with no Black Opal, the city was now revealed to the world and hidden no longer.

THE END